The Lost

A Story of Christmas

By Wendy S. Scott

Published by Take Me Away Books, an imprint of Winged Publications

Editor: Cynthia Hickey
Book Design by Forget Me Not Romances

Fiction and Literature: Inspirational

ISBN: 978-1-952661-32-7

Disclaimer

While real locations are named in this book, the descriptions of places and people have been fictionalized to further the plot. No correlation or expectation of accuracy should be drawn from these fictionalized depictions and actual specific locations or people.

Dedication

For the two who most inspire me to pursue my dreams and to be myself:

To my mother Jacqui, or Rosie, as she'll be greeted in heaven by her mother:

She is the miracle of love and encouragement in my life who gives me wings to fly above the clouds, and confidence to stride intrepidly in my calling.

To Jesus, who has a wonderful, personal, and victorious plan for each of us:

His Triumph is our Hope, and His love is a personal journey He walks with each of us.

Psalms73

23Nevertheless I am continually with You; You hold me by my right hand.

24 You will guide me with Your counsel, And afterward receive me to glory.

25 Whom have I in heaven but You? There is none upon earth that I desire besides You.

26 My flesh and my heart fail; But God is the strength of my heart and my portion forever.

.

28 It is good for me to draw near to God; I have put my trust in the Lord GOD, That I may declare all Your works.

Prelude

"Come on. Come on!" His throat is dry from the crisp, night air, but he dare not stop and break his concentration.

All the way to the right, all the way around the perimeter, meticulously, frantically scrutinizing every possible feature in the darkness.

"This is ridiculous! Impossible!" He retraces the area back until he returns to the headlights again. No sign. No trace. Around the other direction he begins again.

When he finally reaches the far edge by the road, he collapses onto his knees. The flashlight tumbles from his hand and rolls away behind him. In front of him is darkness.

Heart pounding, mouth dry, he kneels in the wet snow. His hard breathing slows, as sadness and defeat effuse his soul. He starts to cry. Cry for his daughter. His body convulses with his hard, silent sobs. He inhales a great breath and wails.

"Oh God! Oh God! Please. Help me!"

He cries doubled over with his hands against the icy ground, letting the sobs flow until he is over-spent, and they gradually diminish.

In this moment, he feels peace wash over him. Deep inside, disputing all his anxiety, he hears a reassuring promise.

"It'll be all right."

He takes a deep, calm breath, and looks up.

"Thank you," he whispers.

In that instant, a red flash illuminates the silent, white landscape before him, holds, and then disappears.

Chapter 1: Father and Daughter

As his thoughts emerge from sleep, Bryce sifts through the sediments of memories and dreams, wondering at the source of deep sadness weighing on his soul. He opens his eyes to a dim hospital room and remembers.

In the solemn, blue morning he surveys his surroundings and finds his daughter's small face, enveloped in a white pillow, already watching for him to awaken.

"Daddy," she softly begins.

He smiles for her and reaches stiffly for his glasses beside the large chair where he fell asleep. He puts them on, stretches a bit, then sits up some and grins with satisfaction at his little girl.

"Morning. Yes, Pumpkin?"

Her brown eyes glint as they study him with a life-force that belies her frail presence.

"Daddy, it's Christmas Eve, and I want to go see the snow today." Her soft voice is steady and sure, like a secret truth. "You'll take me, won't you?"

His heart grows heavier, and the corners of his smile fall. His eyes deceive him in the low light, obscuring her features at times in shadow, adding confusion to these early morning thoughts.

"Oh Jasmine, I don't know . . . I don't think that's a good idea." His eyes locate the pink elastic strip still binding her left arm. "Not so soon after your procedure."

She lies silently, watching him wrestle with her request.

"I mean—" Slipping his fingers beneath his glasses, he rubs his eyes. "We'd have to check with the doctor."

Jasmine tilts her head slightly, listening for hope.

Scanning the room, Bryce sees the little decorated tree on the sink counter ("Daddy, I want a REAL one," she had entreated). Surprisingly, the hospital permitted it. The tree is surrounded by some of the many cards she received from school friends and family, now so far away.

He perches his glasses on his forehead and rubs his hands over his stubbly face with a Daddy groan. They smell like sanitizer. He would like a shower. . . She hasn't had a bath in months. Not a fun bath. She used to squeal, surrounded by floating toys, and slide around on her bottom, "I don't want to wash my hair! I want to play!"

She's grown so much in these last four years.

He stretches fully now, then leans forward to close the space between them.

"Honey, I don't even know where to go around here for snow." His eyes have adjusted to the dimness, and he sees his daughter's patient smile. Her thin, dark brown hair, now a few inches long, sprouts in various directions from her head—not quite long enough to style yet.

Jasmine's hand absently feels for something on her bed, then gathers a white stuffed animal into the crook of her arm. "I asked Miss Jacqui yesterday where *she* would go to see the snow, and she said she'd drive to Big Bear." Her soft voice details the mystery. "She said it's bea-*u*-tiful, Daddy. It's only three hours away, so we would be back before Mommy and Jake and Oscar fly in."

He looks at his watch, 6:02. Their flight gets in later at 4:00. That's a good 10 hours for them to drive to the snow round trip, with extra time to look around. The math won't help him escape it.

"Ahhhhh," he exhales, feeling himself surrender. "Let me talk to the nurse and check on all this, Pumpkin. You need anything?"

"Maybe a plain English muffin with jelly. And a coffee."

He stands up and stretches and groans again. "A coffee?"

"Yeah. For *you*," she giggles.

"For me?" Bryce steps to her bedside. "For me!" He reaches down and tenderly tickles her sides. She sinks into the bed giggling with muted delight. "How did you know I needed coffee? Huh?"

Her laugh tires into contented, shallow breaths. "Because I know you, Daddy."

"You do, huh?" He looks at the sparkle in his little girl's eyes and smiles. "You're right, Pumpkin. You do." He bends and kisses her forehead. She smells like stiff, disinfected sheets and unwashed baby's skin. He refills her water cup and tilts the straw-bend toward her, then makes sure the controls and her lip balm are in reach. "Okay. I'll be back in a bit."

Out in the sterile, partial light of the oncology floor, he hears quiet sounds and voices in other rooms. A soft, high-pitched whimper of a child is answered by the hushed, tender reassurance of a woman's voice, "I know, baby. I know. It's coming." A man walks groggily out of another room to the nurse standing a few feet away at a computer. She looks at his tired face as they talk solemnly, nodding, then she turns to stride purposefully away. As Bryce reaches the nurses' station, another nurse passes by into the first room carrying a vial in her purple-gloved hand. She is wearing scrubs with Toy Story characters and has bright purple laces on her white tennis shoes. She enters the room, and the woman soothes, "See baby? See? Here it is."

Bryce reaches the counter, and quietly waits for someone's attention. A middle-aged man looks up from the computer with a kind smile. "Good morning, Mr. Goodson. How is Jasmine doing today?"

The floor stirs around them as it emerges from another long night spent in dormant worry and fleeting rest into another day of managed hopes and challenges. Bryce looks back toward his daughter's room, puzzling through his thoughts, and then returns to the man's face—kind, patient, tired. "She's as cheerful as ever, Hector. How's *your* family? Do you have plans for tomorrow?"

Hector's eyes shine. "Yes, I plan to be here with you all—my second family. Our kids are grown and out of the house, so they'll come for dinner in the afternoon, when I get off work." The phone behind the counter chimes in muted tones. Another nurse answers the call. "And, of course, my beautiful wife, ever faithful, is going to cook tamales all day today." He grins with a gleam, "Yum."

"Sounds wonderful, Hector. My wife and her sister usually cook tamales for New Year's, but . . . you know," Bryce smiles, then shrugs.

"Well, Mr. Goodson, maybe I can sneak a few out of the pot for you tomorrow," Hector offers. "Where is Mrs. Goodson? Is she coming for Christmas?"

"Yes, actually. One of my sons had an event this week, so Felicia and the boys are flying in from Phoenix later today to celebrate Christmas and the New Year." The purple-laced nurse comes up to Hector and makes a brief comment. He nods and returns his eyes to Bryce. "Anyway, Jasmine misses them, of course, so it'll feel good to spend Christmas together."

"I am sure it will. Is there something that you or Jasmine needed this morning?" Hector presses, as parents and staff suddenly turn the quiet floor into a bustling scene.

"Yes, I'm sorry. Ummm . . . apparently yesterday, Jasmine talked to her day nurse, Jacqui, about possibly driving to the mountains to see the snow? I don't know if this is even possible, or a good idea, or what, but she seems determined to go today." He adds an uncertain chuckle. "I think she mentioned Big Bear? But I don't know if—"

Hector pulls up Jasmine's chart on the computer and is nodding as Bryce speaks. He then interrupts the trailing thought, "Let me just see if it says anything here. . ." He reads the notes to himself, and then continues, "Okay, it looks like Jacqui talked to Dr. Moreno about it yesterday, who said that since Jasmine's blood apheresis is over, and she tolerated that well, she should be fine to go. It's not until the second part of the trial, when we start the CAR T-cell infusion that we'll need to monitor her closely." He looks up from the screen, "If you go today, just pay attention to how tired she gets, and keep her hydrated and comfortable. She should be fine for the drive."

Bryce checks his watch again. 6:18. "I don't know . . ." He looks back at Jasmine's room. "I don't know." He pulls his palm firmly down his face and moans. "She is just so fragile still, after all the chemo she's been through, and then she got so sick with the bone marrow rejection … And now the blood apheresis really seemed to wipe her out. I mean, she's so weak . . . like what if . . . I guess I'm worried about her immunity. Hector, what do *you* think?"

Hector looks confidently at Bryce. "I know she's been through a lot, but it's Christmas. It's *her* Christmas. She knows what she can take." He leans closer, "Just ask yourself—would it make her happy?"

Bryce reflects on the question. Then he expels a long, satisfying breath, and peace smooths over his face.

"Yeah. Yeah, it would."

Hector smiles. "Okay then. Her night nurse, Adele, will go in to check Jasmine out before the shift change, and then how about I come in and help get her ready. Okay?"

"Yeah. Okay," Bryce nods. The tension in his chest eases. "Thanks. I'm gonna go grab some coffee."

Bryce navigates the hospital passages to the cafeteria through the now-familiar, self-contained world he inhabits apart from the outer world. He smiles and nods and exchanges hospital conversations with the other current residents and personnel—some he knows by name now, or by their stories. He leaves the cafeteria with his large coffee, a breakfast burrito, and Jasmine's dry English muffin, and pauses in the hallway of windows to view the city he doesn't know.

Outside is a mix of gray and white clouds, but on the far horizon, sun is breaking through blue skies. The aroma of coffee, warm in his hand, arouses his memories of home.

"God. Please help me."

He looks at his watch. 6:33. A bit early.

He pulls out his phone and calls his wife. It rings several times, and then her beautiful voice greets him. "Mi Amore. Is everything okay?"

The pressure in his chest relieves again. "Hi, Sweetheart. We're fine. I'm sorry to wake you."

"No, I was awake. I was thinking about everything to do today, and about coming out there, and . . . well, I just woke up *thinking*." Felicia's voice is calm, and quiet, and full of love. "I'm downstairs with some coffee, just spending time with God, you know?"

"I know. I can see you now, bundled up in your white, terrycloth robe. Your hands *wrapped* around a warm coffee mug. Your Bible open . . . Is that about right?" His heart warms and grows inside him.

"That's right, Amore. You think you know me, huh?" He can hear her smile.

"I think so. I think I do. Where's your sister?"

"Oh, she's still in bed. I'm trying not to wake her, but the smell of coffee will probably rouse her soon. Tyrell's at work, I guess."

Bryce holds the image of his wife in his mind, as they talk in the quiet morning. "Were the boys okay sleeping in Alex's old room?"

"Oh, yeah, they loved it." Felicia strains to talk quietly. "Jake, of course was playing it cool, but Oscar was just awestruck looking at all the trophies and awards and other sports stuff. Alex has always been like a hero to them, you know?"

"Yeah. That's good though. He's a good kid. So, are you guys all set for today?" Bryce watches the sky drift over the city as he sips his coffee with his wife.

"I think so, but honestly, it's hard to know. So far, our flight is listed on time, but the newsfeeds say the storm is affecting flights all over the country."

She seems to be checking again for updates, as her voice distances.

"Yeah, but that's all east of Phoenix, right?"

"It is. But I don't know. We'll see." Her voice returns, and he feels near to her again. "What about you two? How are *you* doing today?"

"We're good . . . but that's why I called." The little white plastic tab pulled back on his coffee lid nicks his nose when he drinks it. He tries to suppress it with one finger as he searches for his words. "Well. Jasmine woke up asking to drive out and see the snow today."

"What? Are you serious?" He can tell his wife has just covered her mouth. He can see her doing it. She will put her long, beautiful fingers up to her lips, touching them lightly, like keeping watch over her mouth, ready to stop secret thoughts from spilling out. She is so careful with words, with how they can bring both healing and pain. She always gives herself just a moment to think before she lets the first wave of fear, or anger, or criticism spew irretrievably out, and into hearts and minds.

"I know. I didn't think it was a good idea either . . . but she was determined. She had it all figured out. Apparently, she talked with her nurse yesterday about it, found out where to go, and then her nurse ran it by Dr. Moreno."

"And?"

"Well . . . evidently she said that it would be fine." Bryce explains what Hector told him.

"I don't know, Bryce. Is she strong enough?"

"Well . . . they all seem to think it would be good for her. It *would* make her happy—I mean, that's what we *want*, right?" The white, plastic tab eludes his control. "But I didn't want to tell her for sure until we talked about it."

"Hmmm … How far is it?"

"It's about three hours from LA to Big Bear. We'd have plenty of time to drive there, see some sites, and get back before you guys fly in."

"Oh, you must be tired after driving my parents around, and staying at the hospital for so long. Are you sure you're up for this?"

"Honestly, the more I think about getting us out of here for a while, the more I realize we need it." Bryce finally compresses the springy plastic tab into its slot in a minor triumph that again relieves some of his tension. "It just takes a little getting used to the idea. What do *you* think?"

"Well . . . I think you're right," Felicia sighs. "I have peace about it. And it is *Christmas Eve*."

"Would you rather we wait for you guys?"

"No Bryce, it was *her* idea to go today, even though we're coming." She encourages cheerfully, "'*Today* is the day that the Lord has made. We will rejoice and be glad in it.' Right?"

"Right. You're right Sweetheart."

"Okay, Amore. Call me when you're on the road and I'll talk to Jasmine, okay?"

"Okay. Give the boys a hug. Tell Tiana and Tyrell Merry Christmas for me."

"I will. Love you."

"I love you, too."

As Bryce approaches the room, he hears his daughter's soft voice quietly talking or singing, and he prepares a big smile for her as he enters.

"Daddy, are we going?"

She's already wearing her fuzzy, pink hat. "What do you *think*, Pumpkin?"

Eyes twinkling, she whispers, "I think we're going."

"I think you're right."

Jasmine talks in quiet wonder about the trip, and what she

hopes to see, as Bryce unpacks the dry English muffin, two packets of strawberry jam, and a plastic knife. She carefully peels back the seal on the jam and digs out the smallest smudge to spread on her English muffin.

"Do you think we'll see little birds hopping in the snow?" She takes a small, crunchy bite.

"I would think so." He sits back into his chair and unwraps his burrito. "Honey, does this smell bother you? I can eat it later."

"No. It's okay. Wouldn't that be cute? To see little birds hopping in the snow?"

"Uh-huh. Cute." He uncaps the hot sauce cup and pours some onto the end of the burrito, which spills off the folded tortilla onto his hand, and seeps into the cuff of his sweat-jacket. He tries to staunch it with a tissuey napkin, but it has soaked in.

"You have to bite it first, Daddy."

"Bite it."

"Yes. To give the sauce a place to go into."

"Oh, I see." He takes a theatrical bite of the burrito, and then pours a little sauce into the hole, where it stays. "Ingenious," he marvels. Jasmine spreads another dab of jam on her toast and takes a small bite.

"I think I'm going to save some of my English muffin for the drive, in case I get hungry. Maybe I can give some to the birds to eat. What do you think, Daddy?"

"Hmmm…" he considers as he chews. "I think they would really like that. I can see them hopping around picking up the crumbs you throw for them." He makes a little pecking motion with the fingers of his free hand.

She nods, pleased with his description.

"Daddy, doesn't the Bible say that God even *cares* for the little birds?"

Bryce takes another bite. "Umm hmm. He does."

After scooping another dab of jam, she pauses, and her eyes float for a moment toward the world outside the window.

"Not even *one* of them falls to the ground without Him noticing." Her eyes find Bryce again. "Right, Daddy?"

Her seriousness surprises him. His throat suddenly constricts, and his eyes moisten. "HMM…" He chews thoughtfully, composing himself. He takes a sip of coffee and clears his throat.

"That's right, Pumpkin. God loves *all* His little birds very much."

At this point, Hector comes in cheerily, with an armload of goodies. "Que pasa, Mija?"

"Hector!" she turns gleefully toward him. "My Daddy is driving me to see the snow!"

"That's what I heard, you lucky young lady. Adele says that you are in good shape and all set for the day, so I am here to get you ready for your drive." He sets his bundle down on the end of her bed.

Bryce pulls out his phone and checks the time. 7:13 "Hey Hector, I'm going to look up some info on Big Bear while you guys get ready. Is that okay?"

"Yes, of course, Mr. Goodson. You go ahead." Bryce takes another bite of his burrito and scrolls his phone, half listening as Hector and Jasmine talk.

"I brought two fresh blankets and two fresh pillows for you to take in the car. Sound good, Mija?"

"Yes. That sounds good, Mr. Hector," she nods, spritely.

He holds a plastic hospital bag open as he lists its contents. "Okay. We also have some bottles of water, and a packet of apple slices, a string cheese, a granola bar, and a packet of tissue. Do you want to take your lip balm?" he asks her.

"Yes, please."

"Okay, then we'll put that in here too, okay?" She nods again and retrieves it from her table, then aims, and drop-tosses it into the bag. "Good. Now what else do you want to take?"

"My lamb, of course" she teases, holding out a well-loved, plush white lamb. It has dangling, black-hooved limbs, and a cheerful smile, and is wearing a pink bow behind one black ear.

"Oh, your *lamb*. Yes, of course," Hector repeats reverently as he reaches for the toy.

Jasmine pulls it back into her arms with a smile—a motion that causes her to drop back into her pillow, where she is nearly lost. "No, that's okay. I'll take her."

"Okay, yes. *You* take her. What's her name?" he asks, moving to her closet to select clothes for the day.

"Her name is Lily." She is looking into Lily's familiar face and adjusts her bow.

"Well, Lily must be very special." Hector selects thick pink socks and motions for her to pull the covers back.

"She *is*. I got her for Easter when I was just a little girl," she recalls with quiet awe. He scrunches up one sock, inches it onto her tiny foot, and then begins the other.

"Oh, when you were a *little girl*. Now, you are such a big girl at nine, so you have had her a *long* time then." He gets out a pair of purple sweatpants, trimmed in pink piping, and helps her slide to the edge of her bed. "Here, Mija, let's put these on."

She leans on him to steady herself as he bends over to slide the pants onto her dangling legs. "Yes, I've had her a *very* long time. Since I was only five." She lays back and scoots the pants all the way up. Hector then brings over the matching sweatshirt, and they decide to just pull it over her nightgown, careful to straighten the sleeves and fabric. He helps put her slippers on, but sets aside her tennis shoes to take with them.

"Listen, you don't get your feet wet, okay?" He tells her seriously.

"Okay."

"Dad, you need to hear this too."

Bryce lifts his head from the screen. "I got it."

"You shouldn't walk in the snow, but if you get out, even for a few steps, put your sneakers on first," Hector adds.

"Okay," they both agree.

"Here, I am going to put some extra socks in your bag just in case. And you already have your hat."

"Got it," Jasmine nods, touching the hat on her head.

"Thank you, so much Hector." Bryce gets up to gather the things as Hector brings over the wheelchair for Jasmine.

"You can get this in and out of the back of your SUV, right?"

"Yes, I'm good."

"Alright. Jasmine's already had her medication for today, so you don't need to keep track of that."

"Perfect. Thank you again."

There is a light knock on the door, and a nurse, walks in, smiling brightly. "Hey, Sweetie!"

"Miss Jacqui, guess what? Daddy's taking me to the snow!"

Hector helps Jasmine climb into the wheelchair.

"That's what I hear! I am so glad it worked out!" Jacqui leans over and gives Jasmine a hug. "I'll be here when you get back, so have fun!"

Hector wheels her toward the door. "Hey Jacqui, I'm off shift now, so I'm just going to run them down and then take off, okay?"

"Sounds good. See you tonight."

Bryce collects the blankets and other things as they walk out, "Thanks Hector, you're such a great help and support for us. You *all* are."

"It's our pleasure. We love our families, Mr. Goodson," he smiles warmly.

"Well, *my* family calls me *Bryce*."

Jacqui follows them out of the room. "I hope you two have a great adventure."

"We will," Jasmine replies, then adds privately, "It'll be a *Christmas* adventure, huh, Daddy?"

"Yes, Pumpkin, it will," Bryce smiles. Then his lips tighten around the promise.

Chapter 2: Sisters

Felicia sets down her phone on the counter and picks up the coffee mug in both hands to take another sip. She pivots on her barstool toward the Christmas tree in the corner of the living room, dark in the dim winter morning. After a moment, she eases herself down from the stool, pads over and turns on the Christmas tree lights, shuffles back to the kitchen and pours herself more hot coffee, then returns to her stool. Setting her mug down on the bar, Felicia re-secures her robe, climbs back into her seat, and lifts her feet onto the stool beside her to admire the tree. She wraps her hands around the warm cup again and inhales the aroma.

"Ahhhh."

Her sister, Christiana, had set up a ceramic Nativity on the nearby cabinet, arranged on a pad of white fleece. When the tree lights are turned on, a little Bethlehem star illuminates over the scene. Felicia surveys the history of tree ornaments collected over the decades from family gift exchanges or shopping excursions. There is also a small military-themed frame hanging from a blue ribbon with a picture of their brother, Antonio, in his Army Ranger's uniform, along with a scattered assortment of homemade decorations created by a child. One is a flat, crooked little clay ornament shaped like a birthday cake, painted white, with green and red candles, and the word "Jesus" written on top in purple.

"That Alex . . ." Felicia sighs with a smirk and takes another sip.

A carpeted stair creaks, and in a moment Christiana enters the kitchen. Smiling, but a little groggy, she announces in a firm whisper, "I smell coffee."

"I'm sorry Tiana. I hope I didn't wake you."

Christiana opens the cupboard and pulls down a Christmas

mug—a dark blue scene with a sleigh and reindeer on the snow. "You didn't wake me, my nose did." She hastily pours coffee into the mug and then opens the refrigerator. "You know I have creamer in here."

"I know," Felicia replies tucking her legs back under the counter. "I drink mine black now, remember?"

Christiana pours the creamer into her mug and returns it to the fridge, shaking her head. "I don't even know you." She walks around and stands on the other side of the bar counter facing her sister. "Hmph. Black coffee," she chuckles and takes a sip.

"I *like* it," Felicia half-defends.

Christiana grins over her mug, observing her sister. She gestures toward the open Bible. "What are you reading?"

Felicia looks down at the page, then closes the book. "Ah . . . well, I have been trying to read through Isaiah, but lately I always end up at the Psalms. You know?"

"Yes, I know," Christiana contemplates. "I find myself in Psalms a lot these days. It's good for fear, it's good for sadness, it's good for frustration, *and* for all three at once."

Felicia studies her sister's face. "I'm sorry. With everything going on with Jasmine, I feel like I haven't really asked how *you* are doing. Is there something going on?"

Christiana searches for the words on the Christmas tree in the corner. Another swallow of coffee.

"Is it something to do with Alex?" Felicia offers.

Another thoughtful sip. "No . . . it's not Alex. He's doing really great, honestly. Really. I'm so proud of him starting college and everything."

Felicia waits, drawing in her sister's fallen expression. After a moment, she prods, "It's okay, Tiana. Try to say it."

Christiana shakes her head some, straightening her thoughts. "I don't know. I think it started earlier, but ever since Alex left for college this year, there has been this *thing* with Tyrell . . . I don't really know what it is . . . He's *different.*"

"Like in what way?"

"I don't know. He just seems like, *mad* about something, but he won't say what." Christiana turns and walks slowly to the coffee maker and adds to her cup. "You want more?" she holds out the pot.

"No, thanks. So, you asked him what was wrong?"

Christiana adds creamer and returns to her place. She leans against the counter, holding the mug to her chest in one hand. "Yeah, I asked him. . . but if I'm honest, I don't think it came out right. I mean, we were kind of arguing about something when he just took it to a new place out of *nowhere*. It really surprised me. I think I more like said, 'What is *wrong* with you!' than really *asking* him."

Christiana twirls the end of her long hair around one finger—something she does when she is worried, or thoughtful, or hopeful.

Felicia sees a teenage Christiana twirling her hair nervously over young Francisco coming to pick her up for the Prom. "He's too old for you Christiana," Papa had warned. "No, he's not!" she protested, already waiting by the door for him in her electric blue dress. "I will be *18* next month, so you can't stop me!" Papa got red, "I CAN stop you, Tiana! You are not 18 today!" But then Mama intervened, and shushed Papa, taking him aside. "You win today, but you lose much more when she graduates. And you won't change a thing." And so Tiana went, with Papa's admonishment to be a good, decent girl, and with Mama's tender warning, "Be wise, Mija."

Felicia zips the Bible case in front of her thoughtfully. "Well, what do you *think* it is?"

"That's just it." Christiana sets the mug down on the counter. "I *really* don't know. Something about *money*. Something about *Alex*." She gestures both hands toward herself. "Something about *me*." Her voice cracks a bit. "I think he maybe doesn't want *me* anymore."

"Oh Honey." Felicia slides off the stool and walks around the counter as her sister begins to weep. "I'm sorry." She hugs and rocks her. "You think it's *serious*?"

"I don't know . . ." Christiana wipes under her eyes with her fingers, and a sniff. "Thank you, Chia. I'm okay."

Felicia pats her shoulder and returns to the stool.

"It *feels* serious. It feels cold between us. But maybe it just seems more serious right now because Alex is out of the house, and it's just the two of us . . . and now it's Christmas . . . and *you're* going to be gone . . . and Tony is deployed again . . . and now Mama and Papa are away too? And with everything going on with your family and Jasmine . . ." She sniffs and shakes her head a little again. Then she laughs. "I'm just being a baby."

Felicia laughs, "No, you're not. No, you're not." The sisters look at each other and smile. "Tiana, I know you. You sense that something is going on, so there is."

"Oh, maybe not . . ." Christiana wipes her eyes again, and pulls a tissue out of her robe pocket to dab her nose.

"But listen to me. . ." Felicia looks intensely at her sister. "Listen to me. It *may* not be what you think."

"No?"

"You said it yourself, you *don't* know. Don't let the devil fill your head with ideas, and fear. *Pray*. *Believe* the best. *Open your heart* to your husband and find out." Felicia emphasizes with her finger. "Right?"

Christiana's shoulders relax some. She nods slowly re-listening to the words. "You're right."

"Of course. Come on. Tyrell *loves* you. He *does*. He's a *good* man."

"You're right. Yes. You're right." Christiana lifts her mug for a thoughtful sip, imagining already what she'll do. "You know, Alex is doing that Christmas outreach with his team tonight, so he's not driving back home until tomorrow morning." Her eyes wander to the gifts under the tree. "Tyrell should get home about 6:30 tonight. Maybe it's good that we're alone, you know? I mean, maybe we're supposed to have this night together so we can talk, without it starting as an argument first." She peers over her mug, planning as she sips her coffee.

"See? That sounds good." Felicia encourages.

"After I drop you off at the airport, I can make his favorite dinner, and set the table, and light some candles . . . I think this was meant to be!" Christiana lifts her mug to her sister.

"Perfect! I agree," and Felicia salutes her in return.

"Okay. Now *that's* figured out." Christiana nods satisfied. "What else shall we tackle? What would you like to do today before I take you to the airport?"

"You know, I am just so glad I got to see you. I can't imagine *not* seeing you at Christmas time. Especially right now. It worked out great for us to drive from Peoria and stay here last night."

"I was so glad you *asked*. I thought I wouldn't see you at all. I assumed you'd just drive yourselves down to the airport today, since it's not even an hour." Christiana swipes through the air to suggest, "it is nothing."

"Well, I really wanted to spend some time with you. I know the boys wanted to see you. *Plus*, it's cheaper to leave the car *here* for Bryce and the boys when they fly back. But *mostly*," Felicia's eyes flash a squinted smile, "we came because I just really needed to see my sister."

"Well, I am *sooo* glad you did." Christiana reaches over the counter and shakes her sister's forearm. "So, what should we do?"

Felicia picks up her phone. "Okay, it's about 7:15." She scrolls through screens.

Christiana pulls a hair tie from a side drawer and bundles her hair into a loose ponytail. "What time is your flight?"

Still scrolling. "Well . . . it's supposed to leave at 3:30 . . . but all the news feeds keep warning about flight delays because of the weather in the mid-west."

"So is *your* flight delayed?"

Felicia finds what she's looking for, reads it, then looks up. "Not yet." She sets her phone on the counter unconvinced.

"Well, maybe it won't be," Christiana shrugs.

"Yeah, maybe. They just make it sound like there could be a ripple effect." She picks up her phone absently again, but then sets it down next to her Bible. "I don't know. We'll just assume it'll leave on time."

"Okay. . . You have bags to check, so I should get you there by, what, 2:00?"

"That sounds about right."

"Okay. So what do you think, that's almost 7 hours . . ."

"Well . . ." Felicia begins. "I kind of wanted to make the boys breakfast. We've been so busy, and with Bryce and Jasmine gone in LA, we haven't had a very Christmasy time so far. We didn't even get a tree this year, so it's been kind of depressing, you know?"

"I know it has. Actually, I was thinking the *same* thing," Christiana grins, walking toward the refrigerator.

"You were?"

She opens the doors wide to review the contents. "Yes. I made sure we had enough eggs and bacon, just in case. I have some fresh salsa too, if you want an omelet and fried potatoes."

"Mmmmm," Felicia's eyes brighten.

"We can make pancakes or French toast for the boys." She closes the fridge with satisfaction and turns to her sister. "What do you think?"

"YES!" Felicia pops up from her stool. "Omelets for us, French toast for the boys!" She wraps her arm around her big sister and touches their temples together. "Thanks Tiana."

"*I'm* happy when *you're* happy," Christiana pats the hand resting on her shoulder.

They each roll up their sleeves and begin to tackle duties long ago assigned by years of breakfasting. One cuts potatoes and onions, and the other fries the bacon, activating that savory, bacony smell of family morning love.

"I was thinking," Christiana tends the bacon as it pops and sizzles. "I wanted to take the boys shopping for their Christmas presents. Do you think we could go to the mall and do that today?"

"Oh, what a great idea!" Felicia slices and chops.

"I just thought it would be a fun way to spend time together, and they'd probably enjoy picking out their own presents."

"That sounds perfect. Absolutely. And *I* would *love* that," Felicia flourishes the knife.

"Me too. We can eat at the mall before I take you to the airport. Good?"

"Good. Merry Christmas to us!"

"Yes, Merry Christmas to us," Christiana affirms.

Felicia walks over to the counter and retrieves her phone, knife still in hand, and scrolls it intently, knife waving. She returns to her cutting board and with a final touch to the screen, she sets the phone on the counter between them, and "O Holy Night" begins to play. She resumes chopping, and soon the two are nodding their heads and singing to the warm, majestic, rhythms of Christmas music, sharing stories and laughing as they work.

~

The combined aroma of fried bacon, onions, and potatoes wafts to the upper floor, and gradually arouses the boys out of their deepest dreams. Jacob is first aware. He lies quietly in his cousin's bed beside his younger brother, absorbing the environment. The familiar sounds of muted conversation, and music, and activity in the kitchen comfort his being. As his mind activates, he looks around Alex's room, memorialized with his many honors and athletic accomplishments. The walls display pictures of Alex at different events, wearing uniforms, or ribbons, many with Jacob's aunt and uncle. In the picture of his recent graduation, he is wearing a cap and gown with a golden cord draped around his neck. Each image is full of hope and joy, and humble triumph. Then, Jacob sees a picture on top of Alex's dresser, and the peace in his spirit ebbs away, twisting into a hard knot.

He is staring at the ceiling when Oscar stirs.

"I smell breakfast!" In a moment Oscar bolts upright and shakes his brother. "Common, Jake! I'll beat ya!" He scurries out of the covers, into his slippers, and races in a commotion down the stairs. Jacob takes a moment before hoisting back the double pile of covers and putting on his robe and slippers to follow him.

He stops at the framed picture on the dresser. It is his cousin Alex with his sister, Jasmine, on their family trip to Flagstaff four years ago. Jasmine is holding up a tiny little trout dangling from a fishing line. She looks like she is giggling.

Jacob picks up the frame and studies the image, holding his breath.

After a moment, he sets the frame back on the dresser. He lingers on it, then pinches his eyes closed and turns away. He pulls his phone from the charger and tucks it into his robe pocket before descending to join the others.

In the kitchen his brother is already fully engulfed in the scene. "Oh my gosh, Mamma! It smells so good! Merry Christmas Eve, Aunt Tiana!"

Christiana reaches down with one arm to hug the small, enthusiastic body wrapped around her waist. "Merry Christmas Eve, Oscar! Now go sit down and tell me how you want your eggs."

Oscar scampers quickly onto a barstool. "Scrambled!"

Felicia looks up from whipping her French toast mixture to greet the reserved Jacob. She smiles warmly, "Morning, Mijo."

Jacob walks dutifully to her and kisses her on the cheek. "Morning, Mom." He recedes before her arm can embrace him, and only brushes the back of his robe. He gives his aunt the same kiss. "Morning, Aunt Tiana."

"Good Morning, Jake. How would you like your eggs?" He turns and joins his brother at the counter.

"Uh, scrambled is good. Thanks." After a moment, Jacob takes his phone out of his robe pocket, and holds it sideways between his thumbs, playing a game.

The sisters exchange glances to say "You see?" and "I see."

Christiana cracks three eggs into a bowl and adds a splash of milk, then whisks before pouring them into the cast iron skillet with a crackle over the hot remnants of the fried bacon, onion, and potato grease. "Did you boys sleep okay in Alex's room?"

"Oh yeah, Aunt Tiana," Oscar effuses. "It's really cool in there."

Felicia sets out a new pan on the burner next to Christiana's, tosses a pat of butter in, and dips bread slices into her cinnamon-egg mixture. Laying a slice into the sizzling pan, she prods Jacob, engrossed in his game. "How about you Jake? Did you sleep okay?"

"Yeah, fine," he mumbles from behind the screen.

Felicia adds another slice to the pan and tends to them. "Jake, we're going to eat in a second, so you'll need to put that away."

Jake pauses his game and returns it to his robe pocket.

"Aunt Tiana," Oscar blurts, "is Alex coming home from college for Christmas?"

Christiana turns off the burner and retrieves plates from the cupboard. "Yes, he's coming, but he's doing something important with the team tonight, so he'll drive home tomorrow morning for Christmas." She scoops potatoes and eggs onto the first plate. "How many pieces of bacon do you want?"

"Two please," Oscar replies.

Christiana places two strips onto his plate and then hands it to Felicia to add the slice of French toast, who spreads a small pat of butter on it and cuts it diagonally to stack. "Here you go Oscar." He hops down and takes his plate. "Go sit at the table, we'll be right there. Jake, can you put the salsa and the syrup on the table? It's over here."

Jake quietly goes and takes them from the counter as Christiana scoops his eggs and potatoes onto his plate. "Jake, three bacon?"

"Yeah. Thanks" he replies setting the condiments out on the table. He returns for his plate from Felicia, now complete with two full slices of French toast.

"Hurry Mamma!" urges a small voice from the table.

"We're coming. Don't you eat yet!" Felicia laughs. She turns to Christiana, "Do you want to split this extra piece of French toast?"

"Yeah, why not? It's Christmas!" Christiana takes the omelet plates out of the oven where they were kept warm and completes them with potatoes and bacon. Felicia adds the French toast slices, then takes the grapefruit juice and fills the four glasses at the table. Christiana sets down the plates and turns to Oscar when they are all seated.

"Okay, you want to pray?"

Oscar jostles in his chair, "Yes!" He bows his head into his folded hands. "God, thank you for this awesome food, bless Aunt Tiana and her family, thank you for all your blessings. Bless our trip, and PLEASE heal Jasmine! AMEN!"

A quiet scoff emits from Jacob at this last request, and Felicia's eyes shoot open at him. He is staring at his plate. The sisters add an enthusiastic amen to Oscar's prayer, but Jacob is silent.

She lets the moment pass.

Jacob notices Felicia sadly watching him, and tries to shift the focus.

"So Aunt Tiana, what's Alex doing tonight with his team?"

"Oh my gosh, Mom! Aunt Tiana! This is so good!" Oscar blurts as he ravishes his food.

Christiana smiles, savoring a bite of omelet and salsa, "Thank you Oscar." Then to Jacob, "Well, the Wildcats like to get involved in Tempe's community, so Alex's football coaches asked for volunteers to hand out toys on Christmas Eve to kids in need. Alex really wanted to do it, so we thought he should just come home tomorrow morning rather than drive for two hours after the dinner."

"Wow, that's really cool," Oscar admires through a mouthful.

"Yeah, I can't wait to hear all about it," she continues. "He's always loved helping people."

"He's a special young man, Tiana," Felicia adds. "I'm sorry he won't be home for you tonight, but it's certainly for a good reason."

"Yes, it is," Christiana smiles, nodding, as she looks around the table. "Your boys are pretty special too."

"And Jasmine too!" amends Oscar cheerfully.

"Hey, Aunt Tiana," Jacob interrupts, "will Alex get to play in the Holiday Bowl next week?"

"It's possible, since it's the last game. Because he's a receiver, he says they might try him on special teams just to see how he does. But *next* year he is sure to get some game time."

"Is that what *he* says?" asks Felicia.

"Well . . . no. That's what *I* say," Christiana laughs. "Hey, a mother knows! Right, Chia?"

"That's true," Felicia nods. "No truer thing than that," she grins, and pokes Oscar in the ribs next to her.

He giggles and squirms a moment. "Moms don't know everything!"

At this provocation, she reaches over and tickles him more, making him laugh so much she worries he'll inhale his food "Pretty near! Especially when it comes to her kids!" She stops tickling so he can swallow. Felicia then turns toward her sister and announces like a game show host, "Hey Tiana, why don't you tell the boys what we're doing today before we go to the airport?"

"Well Felicia," Christiana parodies, "I'm glad you asked! Boys? How would you like an all-expense paid Christmas shopping spree at the mall?"

Oscar jolts straight in his seat with great excitement, "Really, Aunt Tiana?"

"Yep. That's my Christmas present to you. Anything you want (mother approved of course)" she directs at Felicia. "Up to $150 each. What do you think?" Her eyes connect with Jacob's.

"Thanks, Aunt Tiana, that's really nice of you."

"What about Jasmine's present?" Oscar worries.

Felicia rises to clear her plate, and Christiana does the same, leaning toward Oscar as she does. "Oh, don't you worry. I already have that covered, Mijo." She winks at him, and he smiles, reassured.

"Okay boys," Felicia directs, "let's clear the table. Then go get changed, pack your pajamas, and bring down your bags. I have to take a shower, but come right down when you're ready. Don't dawdle, okay?"

They all get up and clear the table. "Just put your plates into the sink," Christiana adds. "Bring everything over. You boys can play one of Alex's video games in the living room when you're ready. Jake, you know how to set that up?"

"Yeah. I got it," he replies. "Thanks." The boys clamor upstairs as the sisters put things away.

"Just leave the dishes," Christiana urges. "I'll do them when I get home."

Felicia scrapes the extra potatoes into a container. "Are you sure?"

"Yeah, I'll have plenty of time. I'll just put these few things away and wipe up. You go get ready."

"Okay. I'm going to take a quick shower and then call Bryce and Jasmine." Felicia puts the potatoes in the refrigerator. "Hey, did I tell you what they're doing today?"

Christiana wipes down the sticky syrup trail on the table. "What?"

"Jasmine asked Bryce to take her to the mountains to see the snow today before we get there."

"Are you serious?"

"Yeah. It's a little unnerving after all she's been through, but the doctor said it's okay."

Christiana rinses the sticky sponge at the sink, "So you're okay with it?"

Felicia smiles bravely, "I'm sure it'll be fine."

Christiana studies her face, "Okay then, good. By the way, did I tell *you* what my boss said?"

"What?"

"He thinks I have a good chance of getting that supervisor position. He said he'll *recommend* me."

"Oh, Tiana, are you serious?"

"Well, that's what he said. I think he means it."

Felicia hugs her sister. "Oh my gosh! That would be so amazing!"

"I know! Well, we'll see. It's not decided yet."

"Wait. Would that mean you could stop driving?"

Christiana grins triumphantly, "That's right. I might train drivers occasionally, but I'd be off the metro bus route."

Felicia squeezes her again, "Oh, wow! I am so excited! God, let it happen!"

"Thank you. We'll see." Christiana waives her on, "Okay, now go get ready."

"Yes. You can tell me more in the car." Felicia jogs up the stairs into the bathroom with a final squeal. "Yippee!"

She turns on the shower. "No more bus route," she muses, testing the water. "Thank you, Jesus."

Chapter 3: The Road Trip

Felicia combs her wet hair and is wrapping it into a towel when her phone vibrates. It is a text from Bryce: WE'RE ON THE ROAD, SO CALL WHEN YOU CAN.

She sits down on the bed and sets her heart. Then she decides to facetime them.

He answers the phone cheerfully and sets it in the holder, "Gooood morning from the Goodson family road trip!"

"Hi family! How's the adventure coming?"

Bryce recaps their progress. "Well, LA is a pretty busy city, even early on Christmas Eve, but after an hour and a half, it's more quiet out here away from the city, right Jasmine?"

A quiet voice strains through the ambient car noise "Much better."

"That's good. Hey Bryce, give the phone to Jasmine so I can see and hear her." Felicia is jostled some until Jasmine's soft, gentle voice is near. She appears fatigued.

"Hi Mamma."

"Hi Mija. How're you doing?"

After a pause, "I'm fine."

Felicia concentrates on decoding the clues to her daughter's condition. "Are you sure? You can go back if you're not feeling good."

Jasmine makes small, thoughtful, breath sounds before she responds, "No, I'm happy."

"Okay. . . But tell Daddy if you need anything. Alright?"

"I will Mamma."

"Well, I can't wait to wrap you in my arms tonight, Honey."

"Me too. I miss you, Mamma."

"*I* miss *you*. Have a good time in the snow. Can you give me back to Daddy?"

"Okay." There are more quiet breath sounds. "I love you."

"I love you, Mija." The the phone passes back to Bryce.

"Hi, Sweetheart."

"Bryce, don't let her get too tired." She urges

"I know," he glances at Jasmine in the rear-view mirror, then speaks quietly. "I think she's just saving her energy. She really wants this."

"Okay, Amore, but watch her."

"I will. So, what are *you* guys up to today before your flight?"

Felicia tells Bryce about the big breakfast and then Christiana's plans to go shopping with the boys.

"That's really nice of her. They'll enjoy that. But don't let her spend too much—I know things are tight for them."

"I won't. She just wants to do something special for the boys right now."

"Okay, but make sure they stick to the limit."

"I'll watch 'em good," Felicia laughs.

"Okay. Well, keep me updated on your flight, and I'll let you know how we're doing up here. It's what, about 9:00? And we're halfway to Big Bear, so I think the timing will work out."

"I know it will *all* work out," Felicia reassures with a confident smile.

"Ha! You're right, of course. Okay, I should go because it's illegal to drive and talk on the phone in California," Bryce laughs, and so they say goodbye.

Bryce hangs up and assesses Jasmine in the rear-view mirror. "How are you doing, Pumpkin?"

She's looking out the window a little sleepily and seems to think a moment before answering. His eyes shift between the freeway and the mirror several times, waiting. Then with a slow blink, Jasmine replies, still looking off into the distance. "My legs hurt."

"Oh. I'm sorry. What can we do to help?" His eyes again shift back and forth, waiting for her reply.

She's looking out her window, with her small hands folded into the blanket on her lap, and her little lamb cradled under her arm.

Then, almost as if it is a new thought, she begins meekly, "Daddy?"

"Yes, Jasmine?"

"I would like to get out of my car seat. It's hurting my legs." Bryce sits up straighter to look downward in the mirror at her thin, tender legs dangling from the edge of the seat.

"What—you mean, *while* we're driving? Or to stop and rest?" His heart quickens at the idea.

"While we're driving."

Horrified, he implores, "Pumpkin, you're still too small to sit without the car seat. And remember, we decided it's safer for you in the harness instead of a booster."

She is quiet as her eyes reach outward into the distant scene.

"Mommy would be angry if we let you ride without one. She trusts us to do the right thing."

Nothing.

As he watches for her response, he begins to see that her whole body, as he never noticed before, is entirely confined in the hard form of the car seat. Every aspect of her position is dictated by it—her arms, her posture, where she faces. She can't stretch, or relieve her leg pressure, or shift her weight. But still . . .

"Jasmine, it's dangerous. If we get into a car accident, you could get really hurt, or die."

Jasmine turns her eyes from the window with a blink and meets his in the mirror, holding them for a moment. Then, she blinks again and returns her focus to the beyond.

His heart dissolves in his chest, and his eyes return to the road, cast with dread. The two drive in silence. He looks at Jasmine again, as she patiently watches out the window. He looks back at the road. There is a road sign for the 18 Junction in a few miles. The city has receded, and towns have thinned the further east they travel. Ahead, some ways off, appear the mountains.

Breathe.

Think.

Breathe.

Then, a peace washes over him.

"Okay. How about we take the seat out when we get off the freeway? That's in about 12 miles." He smiles back at her through the mirror. His voice is calm. Real. Not talking to a child. "What do you think? Can you wait until then?"

Her eyes meet his, and she gives a child nod. "Okay, Daddy." She looks back out the window and squeezes her lamb closer to her body.

"Do you want anything?"

"No, thank you."

"Okay." He studies her for a moment. "Drink some of your water, Pumpkin."

She reaches for the bottle in her cup holder, uncaps it, and has three small sips, then returns it.

"Thank you."

Bryce pushes a CD into the stereo. "How about a little music?"

"Okay."

They have several CD mixes of Jasmine's favorite songs, since the SUV cannot connect to their smartphones. Getting a new stereo is on the list. The first song is Jasmine's favorite right now, "Pray," by CeCe Winans. The upbeat song begins.

"Good?" he asks. He sees her small, pink-fuzzy-hat-covered head nodding almost imperceptibly to the beat.

"Yeah. Not *too* loud," she cautions, and Bryce turns down the volume a few notches.

They both watch the road pass, absorbed in the music and in their own thoughts.

Together.

~

Twenty-five minutes later, the road climbs toward the mountain gateway to his daughter's Christmas wonderland. She is curled under the blankets leaning on a mound of pillows propped against the door. She peers out the window at the unrolling scene.

"Do you see the mountains coming?" he asks.

She searches ahead. "Yes," she replies with quiet wonder. "They have snow on them."

In the mirror, Bryce glimpses the empty car seat peeking above the 3rd row. His eyes wander to the shoulder strap of Jasmine's seatbelt, which is too high to cross beneath her chin, so he had to pass it behind her back.

He knows it is wrong. He knows it is right.

As they ascend the mountains, the forest grows around them. He concentrates on the narrow road ahead, now unable to look back at her safely.

After a few minutes the CD ends. "How're you doing, Pumpkin?"

A thoughtful breath. "Good," she exhales.

"Do you want more music?"

After a moment. "No. I like this."

They wind through the silent woods, as patches of snow gradually appear. With the gentle sway of the drive, Bryce feels the angst ease in his chest, and serenity fill the car. Almost joy. He inhales a long, free breath, and releases it.

Soon the snow covers the ground, and glistens in the sun-lit trees. He remembers how much Jasmine has always loved a drive in the mountains. She never got motion sick, like the boys did sometimes. She would smile, eyes gleaming out the window, savoring each turn. Felicia would ask, "You *like* driving in the mountains, don't you?" and Jasmine would exclaim, "Yes! It's fun! It's like a ride!" She seemed most content in motion.

Up ahead, Bryce notices a trickle of water flowing across the sun-dappled road. "Look over on the left. There's a little waterfall coming down the cliff." He points as they pass.

"Oooh, pretty."

The mountainside descends to the right as they climb increasingly further away from the long, open valley of civilization.

"Daddy, can we pull over and look at the view?"

Bryce considers the possible complications.

"Okay. Let me look for a safe place." A sign appears for a viewpoint, and he slows to take the turnout into a little parking lot overlooking the wide valley below. He pulls near to the end and parks, idling, so Jasmine can see the whole expanse. "How's that?"

"Good." She rolls down the window and leans her face into the cold air. She takes a steady breath, savoring the crisp, forest fragrance. "Mmmmm." She evaluates the scene, then asks, "Daddy, can we get out? I can't see over these bushes. And I want to touch the snow."

Bryce rubs his stubbly cheeks, assessing the terrain around the car. They are parked safely on blacktop, and there is a small bank of plowed snow around the edge before the landscape drops off.

"Yeah, we can get out. Let me put your shoes on. Okay?" He

turns off the car and goes around to open her door. She unbundles from the blankets and clicks off the seatbelt to put on her pink and purple princess jacket. Squatting at the door, Brice slips on her shoes and asks, "Do you want me to carry you?"

"No. Just hold my hand."

"Okay." He takes her small, warm hand, and helps her out of the car, steadying her careful steps on thin legs toward the open view. Once there, she reports "I'm okay Daddy. I just want to stand here for a minute." She looks up at him and smiles. "It's okay. It's good for me."

Bryce watches his frail daughter inhale deeply, and scan the long, sloping view, absorbing the wonder through all of her senses. Part of him is anxious for the security of the car, and part of him doesn't want to see the end of this moment.

"It's okay Daddy." She gently drops his hand, maybe sensing his unrest. He takes a step away and lets her stand alone. Her slim body balances with small movements as she surveys every glinting tree and jutting rock in the snow-dusted valley. In this quiet moment, the forest immerses their senses in the clean scent of snow and pine, the splashy trickle of water somewhere, and tiny bird-songs all around them. A sparrow flits into the bushes near Jasmine, and cheeps cheerfully before darting away. The two witness magnificence in silence.

After a few moments more, Jasmine inhales again deeply, and exhales her chilled breath through reddened lips. "Beautiful," she whispers.

Then she turns and looks up at Bryce. "Can you help me over to that snow?" She points to a pristine patch still in the shade a few feet away. "I want to touch it."

"Sure." He takes her hand, and they walk a few yards until her shoes are resting on the snow. Then she slowly squats down with some effort, and scoops up the fresh, white, powder in her red fingers. She stands again and examines the thin crusty surface captured in her palms.

"Look at it sparkle in the sun." She tilts her hands slightly to catch the light glinting on the crystals. "Daddy, I can see some of the snowflakes still." She examines her find, shutting one eye at times. "They're so pretty."

Bryce leans over to see, careful not to create a shadow on the subject. "You're right. They *are* beautiful. You remember, don't you? About snowflakes?"

She still studying them, she softly answers, "No two of them are alike. God made them each beautiful in their own special way. Even though they won't last. Right?"

A shadow casts over his face. "Yes. That's true."

"They are *all* beautiful. Each one," she nods emphatically.

He puts his hand on her soft hat. "Yes, they are Pumpkin." After a moment more. "Hey what do you want to do with that? It'll melt in the car."

Her hands are wet and red.

"I'm going to eat it," she giggles, and stuffs the fluffy mound into her mouth.

Bryce is surprised. "Oh wow . . . Gosh, Jasmine."

She giggles again.

He laughs at her unexpected gesture. "Is it good?"

Jasmine looks up at him with scrunched eyes, crunching and smiling as the snow collapses in her mouth. "Mmm Hmm," she nods.

Bryce chuckles at her elated grin. "Don't move!" He opens Jasmine's door and kneels on her seat to grab his phone from the console. He turns just in time to capture her with still wet, puffy, grinning cheeks. She laughs, and swallows the icy treat, then reaches toward Bryce, "Let me see it." They look at the picture together, her cold, wet hand on his, pulling it into her view. "Good one Dad. You can see the mountains too."

"Oh, Yeah. Should we take another one?"

"Yeah."

He bends over her, "Come here," and he scoops her up into his arms. They put their heads together and smile, and he takes a few wide photos with the whole vista behind them. They review them together. "How's that?"

"Perfect," she replies, satisfied.

"What do you think, Pumpkin. Ready?"

"Yeah."

At the car, Jasmine spies another waterfall across the road splashing down the cliff face, into a little gully, and trickling over the street. "Look Daddy. Can you take a picture of it?"

"Let me see." He sets her down and stands to take a picture, leaning against the passenger door. "It's too far. I'll go a little closer." He sees her blanket hanging out her door.

"I got it, Daddy." Jasmine sits, pulls the blanket inside, and shuts her door. Bryce steps nearer to the road, watching for cars, and zooms in on the waterfall to catch a shot of the clear splashes in the sunlight. He gets back into the car and shows her.

"Pretty," she approves.

"Okay, are you buckled up?"

Her jacket already off, Jasmine pulls the blankets up around her. "Yep."

"Are you comfortable enough? Do you want your shoes off?"

She resettles back into the corner of pillows. "They're off." Her energy has faded. Soon she sinks down again so her eyes are just above the window frame, with her legs curled under her, and her hands scrunched around the blankets at her chin.

"Alright then. Let's see what Big Bear has to offer. Shall we?" Bryce dramatically puts the SUV into gear and lurches forward as if he's driving a team of horses. "Hi-yah!"

They continue the winding drive in silence until several minutes later they reach a plateau where a sign reads, "Welcome to Big Bear." Bryce glances back at Jasmine, eyes sleepily vigilant. "We're here," he notes.

The forest recedes from the road, and cabins appear in groups as they drive into the town, busy with cars, and people, and Christmas decor. Large, festive swags span the street at intervals, country wreaths festoon the light poles and shop doors, and old-time Christmas scenes adorn store windows painted in holiday colors. There is a lake off to the left, and signs for the ski resorts off to the right. People in bright jackets and boots are walking to cars topped with ski racks. Cabins, and restaurants, and sport shops, and gas stations, and stores, and drive-throughs all bustle with people getting a late start on the slopes.

Bryce sees a coffee shop and turns in. They park at a small snowbank facing the road.

"I need to use the restroom. How about you, Pumpkin?"

Her little pink head nods. "Okay."

He goes around and opens her door to help put on her shoes.

"You need to drink more water, Jasmine, okay?"

She carefully drives her arm through the jacket sleeve. "Okay."

Bryce stands and looks at the several, slushy yards they will cross to the busy coffee shop. “How about I carry you this time?” She reaches up as he bends to scoop her into his arms again and carry her on his hip.

“Hey, remember when I used to carry you on my shoulders?” he chuckles.

“Yeah. I’m too big now,” she answers—perhaps sadly, or tired.

Once in the busy coffee shop, Bryce finds the bathrooms are single and unisex.

“Do you want me to come in with you?” He notes the handrails by the toilet for support.

“Just do the paper for me. I’ll be okay.”

Bryce lays down the toilet seat protector, then he stands outside the door, and after a few minutes, the toilet flushes. “I’m coming in,” he announces, and goes in to see if she needs help with her clothes or washing her hands. She washes, and he pulls a paper towel from the dispenser, then surrounds her hands with it playfully to pat them dry. “Do you want to stay in, or stand outside?”

“Stand outside,” and she opens the door to leave.

“Okay. I’ll be quick, but you have to guard the door for me, so no one comes in. Hold onto the handle, okay?”

“I will.”

When he comes out of the bathroom, the line at the counter is short. “Hey, do you want a hot cocoa? What says *Christmas* more than hot cocoa?”

She nods, “Yeah. No whipped cream.”

“Okay.” He directs her to sit at a nearby table and then orders their drinks. Waiting at the pick-up counter, he observes the café scene animated with chatting, moving, smiling tourists, half-bundled for their winter exploits. Then he sees Jasmine, sitting reservedly looking out the window, and wonders what has her attention. He peers through the painted glass, out past the parking lot, and across the street to where there are children sledding down a snowy hillside. Jasmine is watching the children climb the hill with inner tubes, and long red sleds, and yellow rubber rafts, and giant, plastic disks. Then, they come flying, gleefully down the snow in the bright sunlight, mouths open with laughter, vibrant color scurrying in every direction. They slide to a stop at a snowbank bordering the parking lot and then they pick up their sleds to walk back up the hill again.

Bryce gets the drinks and sits down at the table, placing Jasmine's hot chocolate beside her. After a moment, he peers out the window again. "It looks like they're having fun," he broaches sympathetically.

She lingers a moment on the scene, then closes her eyes, dropping her head a little. "Yeah."

His daughter's twinkle has dulled, and her patient demeanor is pinched into a tiny crease between her downcast brows. Bryce wants to zip her up into his jacket, close to his heart, and keep her safe there forever.

As he aches for his daughter's ache, a still, small, voice whispers to his spirit, "*I understand.*"

In a moment, overflowing love, great and pure, wells up in him and floods out the darkness. Bryce lifts Jasmine's little hand from the table, cradles it in his, and strokes the soft skin with his thumb. Her sad eyes lift to see a warm smile spreading across his face.

"Hey," he whispers. "Let's go find some birds and have a picnic. What do you say?"

She studies his eyes and tilts her head a little as the thought takes hold.

"Birds?" she echoes softly. "Yes, let's find some birds to feed, Daddy."

And in a twinkle, her peace has returned to her.

Chapter 4: Christmas Shopping

The once intrepid shopping party quickly become entangled in a department store lingerie section, the sisters prattling about how best to use their storewide 20% off coupon.

At this most insidious digression, Jacob plants his feet in the aisle, crosses his arms, and declares, "Mom!"

Felicia is busy at a sales rack. "What is it, Jake?"

Christiana evaluates a purple bra and panty set against her body.

"Mom!" Jacob elaborates, "We don't want to shop in this store. We don't want clothes, or underwear, or new sheets for our *own* Christmas present. We want to go out in the mall and look around."

Oscar sheepishly steps from his mother's side to the aisle beside Jacob, then mirrors his brother's stance.

Felicia chuckles. "So, this is a coup, is it?"

Jacob seems uncertain. "I think so."

The women laugh, realizing their transgression.

"Okay, Jacob." Felicia comes to the aisle, one arm slung with selections. "Leave your phone on so I can text and track you."

"I will."

"Here's the deal. You and your brother stay together." She scrutinizes each of them. "NEITHER one of you will leave a store without the other, Okay? And you DO NOT leave the mall. DO NOT talk to strangers AT ALL, only mall employees." She wags her finger seriously. "Got it?"

In excited unison, "Got it!"

Felicia takes Jacob's chin, still shorter than she by nearly three inches, and looks him fiercely in the eyes. "I am trusting you,

Jacob. *You* are thirteen, and *he's* only ten, so you're in charge, but don't bully him. Go places he wants to go and be patient. Work it out. Okay? Both of you?"

They both nod. "We will."

"Okay. You have about two hours to look around and pick out what you want. We'll meet no later than 12:30 and then go together to buy your choices. And don't waste your time with something you *know* I won't approve."

Oscar gives her a big hug and then tilts his face up for a kiss.

"You okay with this, Mijo?" she asks as she bends to him.

"Yeah, Mamma. We're gonna have fun."

~

At the end of negotiations, the boys leave behind the department store and enter, exhilarated with liberty, into the bustling Christmastime mall. They pass candle shops, baby boutiques, cookware barns, men's suits, watch and jewelry stores, bath and beauty. Passing the food court, Jacob remembers he has $5 and considers the treat he might have, but rather than share with Oscar, he decides against it. They descend the escalator to the ground floor and Jacob spots a knife and vape specialty store.

They walk in and peer through the glass cases at the array of knives. Some fold, some come with sheaths, some are multi-tools, some are for hunting, many with crafted wooden, or bejeweled, or metal hilts, and all with shiny, razor-sharp blades. Jacob pores over them.

After a few minutes, Oscar becomes uncomfortable, and advises, "Jake, Mom wouldn't let you get a knife."

"Dad said I can get one," Jacob retorts.

Oscar quietly persists, "Not like that."

A man sitting behind an open laptop in the corner of the shop dismounts his stool and comes to greet them in a booming voice. "Welcome to my store. How can I help you boys?"

Oscar replies, "We're just looking."

"No, actually," Jacob interjects, "I'd like to see that one right there." He points down at a large, gleaming, hunting knife fitted with a skull-embedded pewter hilt.

The man is burly, and has a gray, scruffy beard. He smiles kindly down at Jacob, puffing a thick, misty cloud from his enormous vape. The vapor is sweet smelling, like pipe tobacco, and it quickly dissipates. Oscar remembers his great-grandfather Jacob, his Dad's granddad, and misses him.

The owner leans over to see the knife, then looks at Jacob with sorrowful eyes. "I'm sorry son. You have to be 18 to buy a knife here." He points his vape at a sign posted on the counter. "And I can't take it out of the case for you," he continues, "because you're here without a parent."

Jacob turns embarrassed. "Okay," he stammers, "Well, my dad is going to buy me a knife, so we'll come back later."

The man nods thoughtfully, vape poised against his chin. "That's a good idea. You can pick it out together." Then he adds tenderly, "You know, in my experience, only *mean* boys pick out knives like that one." His eyes softly study Jacob. "You're not a *mean* boy, are you?"

Jacob's eyes wander to the floor. "No."

"I know. I can tell," the man punctuates with his vape. "You come here with your Dad, and you two pick out a good survival knife for when you go camping. Okay?"

Jacob meets the man's shining eyes, restored. "Okay. We will."

The two turn to leave. "Thank you," Oscar calls back.

"See you boys," chuckles the man.

~

After passing a few more stores, the boys find a hat shop, and go in to try some on. There is an impressive collection of cowboy hats that they tussle over, trying them and trading them, and jostling for the mirror. Most are too big for Oscar, but he thinks he looks handsome in them. They also venture to the fedoras, which Jacob thinks make him look slick.

Two doors down is a sunglass store, and Jacob suddenly becomes serious about finding a pair. He approaches the illuminated wall and begins trying on different looks. The glasses don't fit Oscar's face at all, so he loses interest and pulls a stool over to perch on.

"Why do you want sunglasses?" he asks.

Jacob evaluates himself in some rimless shades with a blue wire-top frame, and answers off-handedly, "I need them. Don't you see how much I squint in the sun?"

"No," Oscar replies, trying to recall.

"Well, I do."

A salesgirl comes over to Jacob. She is beautiful and about 16 or 17 years old. “Hi. Can I help you find a style?”

Enamored, Jacob breathlessly accepts her offer. “Sure.”

She brings over a selection, and he eagerly tries each of them, awaiting her comments. Sometimes she gives very specific critiques, “These frames are too large for your face,” or “these make you look sexy.” Other times she just says, “No” or “Yes.” His own opinion no longer seems to have bearing on which pair he likes.

They finally narrow down to two pairs.

“I don’t like those, Jake.” Oscar submits. “They’re too old for you.”

Jacob admires himself in the white-lighted mirror, switching between his two options. “Well, it’s not your decision, punk.”

“I’ll be right back,” the salesgirl explains. “That one pair has a smudge on it.” She goes over to the sales counter, looking through drawers, and is interrupted by another customer, who takes her to a different wall.

“How much are those anyway?” Oscar asks.

“I don’t know.” Jacob holds up one pair and reads the tag. “Oh my gosh. $150.” He then reads the other. “These are $230!”

“Holy cow, Jake! Do you want them THAT bad?”

Jacob gapes at the sunglasses like two hand grenades. “No, man. I thought they’d be maybe Fifty bucks!” he whispers. “I thought I’d have enough left for something else.”

“Well here she comes! What are you going to say?”

The salesgirl returns with a lens cloth. “Here, let me see those.” She takes the $230 pair out of Jacob’s hand and expertly cleans the lenses. “Now try that.”

“Thanks.” Jacob nervously tries them back on.

“What do you think?” She prods.

“Better,” he hedges.

“So, you think you want these, then?”

Jacob vacillates, “Ummm. . .” Then he puts on the other pair again, feigning to evaluate the two. Finally, he takes them off and timidly hands both pairs to her. “I-I can’t decide right now,” he chuckles. “I really like them both.”

She takes them, a little frustrated. “Well, I like the *first* pair better.”

Oscar, out of view, rolls his eyes. “You would.”

“What?” she dares, spinning toward him.

“Nothing,” he mumbles, and evaluates his feet resting on the dowel of the stool.

“Look,” Jacob stalls, “I just need to walk around the mall a little and think about it. I’ll come back and let you know.”

“Are you serious?” she chides him, hands full of the unbought glasses.

Oscar jumps down from the stool and carries it back to where he got it.

“Yeah, I’m sorry,” Jacob continues, now slowly backing toward the door. “You’ve been great. I mean, really great.”

“You’re serious,” she sternly repeats.

At reaching the threshold, Jacob adds, “I’ll be back to let you know.”

They hear her complain to her co-worker as they leave, “*Complete* waste of time.”

Once out in the mall, Jacob covers his face with his hands. “I can *never* go back into that store again!”

Oscar’s legs scurry to keep up with his brother. “Sure you can.”

“No I can’t, Oscar! I’m like on *video* and everything,” he emphasizes with sharp hand gestures as he strides away.

“*Sure* you can go back,” he breathlessly encourages. “Someday, you’ll *want* to buy sunglasses. *Then* you can show them.”

They reach the end of the mall and another department store. Jacob halts and faces his brother. “*Then*, I can show them? What does that mean?”

Oscar stops abruptly to avoid running into him. “What does it mean? I don’t know. Whatever . . . it is you’re *upset* about.” Oscar starts to laugh unexpectedly. He tries to hold it in, but can’t help himself. Then he asks, “What do you mean ‘they have me on video’? What does *that* mean?” He cannot contain his snorts of laughter.

Jacob reflects on the whole scene and starts to chuckle himself. “I don’t know what that means.”

Now Oscar is bent over in hilarity, earnestly trying to get his words out. “I mean, like they’d post a *warning* about you or something?"

Jacob thinks a moment, then shrugs his shoulders. "Maybe? It kind of made sense when I thought it." He imagines the staff having a big meeting and printing a still image of him to create a warning poster. He laughs, then shakes his head, "Whatever, man." He scruffs Oscar's hair, "Com'on, let's go up the escalator. I don't want to walk by that store on the way back. She might run out after me."

Oscar snickers, "She *would*, too. That would kind of scare me."

"It scares *me*," Jacob confesses. He checks his phone.

"Hey Oscar, we better get going. It's already 11:45 and we haven't found anything yet."

They step onto the escalator and Oscar grabs the rail beside his brother. "Yeah, but I'm having fun."

The boys enter the Sharper Image store to investigate the gadgets. They check out a multi-colored LED bouncing ball, a drone, a fancy kite . . . but as different things catch their eye, they drift on divergent paths. Jacob sits in a massage chair for ten minutes. Next, he examines the various blue-tooth speakers on display, testing each for sound quality. Then he notices the packs of multi-tool gadgets with a sign "great stocking stuffers," and wonders if this store has the same age restrictions on knives as the other one. His phone chimes, and when he looks, he sees it's already 12:17.

"Oh no!"

The text from his Mom reads, "HI KIDS. OUR FLIGHT IS DELAYED SO YOU HAVE ABOUT AN HOUR EXTRA."

"Good." Jacob sends a text in reply, then turns to tell Oscar, but can't see him anywhere. He hurries around the displays, scanning for him. Frantic, he goes to the front of the store and searches out the door to the left, to the right, and then across, but doesn't see him. He debates whether to venture out and look. Then he remembers his promise, "Neither of you leave the store without the other."

Jacob looks back into the store. "Oscar wouldn't leave." He begins a methodical search, calling unobtrusively for his brother. A nearby salesman asks if he needs help.

"Ahh," he hesitates. "Yeah. I'm looking for my little brother.

He should be in here somewhere."

"Sure, what's his name?"

"Oscar."

They split the large store and begin discreetly calling Oscar's name. When Jacob reaches the back, he finds Oscar and a little girl lying on their stomachs, facing off over a magnetic checkerboard.

"There you are!" Jacob declares. He catches the attention of the salesman, and points down, mouthing, "I found him." The salesman nods with a thumbs-up.

Oscar introduces his challenger. "This is Lindsey." He gestures toward Jacob, rising off one of his elbows, "This is my brother, Jake."

"Hey, Oscar, I couldn't find you. Try to stay where I can see you, okay?"

"I'm sorry."

Lindsey makes another move, legs extending behind her. She then waits, chin propped on her palms, wiggling her feet.

"Well, I was worried," Jacob scolds.

Oscar returns his attention to the board, then makes his move. "Why? You knew I wouldn't leave."

"Okay, wise guy. We should go." He lightly kicks Oscar's foot. "Did you pick out anything?"

"Yeah, but I still want to keep looking. How about you?" Lindsey makes another move, jumping several of Oscar's checkers.

"Yeah, I like some speakers, and a couple other things, but I don't know. Mom texted that we have an extra hour, so let's go."

"Okay." Oscar hops up to leave and Lindsey protests.

"How about our game?"

"You won." Oscar extends his hand to her. "Thanks for playing."

She shakes his hand. "Yeah, thanks."

He looks around the store. "Is that your dad?"

Lindsey gets up and puts the game on the shelf.

"Yeah. He's still shopping for my Mom."

Oscar turns to go, "Okay, see ya. Merry Christmas."

Lindsey gives a little wave, "Yeah, you, too!"

~

Out in the mall Oscar mourns, "I miss Jasmine."

"We'll see her in a few hours."

"I know." Oscar reflects a moment. "I mean . . . like how she *used* to be. . . We used to have fun together, didn't we?"

Jacob walks quietly, shoving his hands deep into his pockets. He intends to agree, but the moment passes.

They cross a bridge near the food court to finish the level, and on the corner is a Christian bookstore.

"Oh, let's go in there," Oscar urges.

Jacob stops at the store, "I'm not going in there."

"What? Why?" pleads Oscar.

"I'm not. There's nothing in there I want," Jacob waives dismissively. "This is a waste of time for me."

Oscar is hurt. "Well, *I* want to go in there, and you have to go with me. Mom said."

Jacob crosses his arms. "No, I don't. I just can't *leave* without you."

Oscar tugs on Jacob's wrist. "Aw, com'on! Just come in with me."

Jacob pulls his arm sharply away. "No! You go in if you want to *waste* our time. I'm staying out here."

Oscar looks at his brother's stony face and hangs his head as he walks to the entrance.

"And hurry up, will you?" Jacob charges him, then sits on the store's windowsill with his arms crossed.

After about ten minutes, Oscar comes out of the store. "Ready," he announces, and keeps walking down the corridor. Jacob pops up, surprised, and catches up to him. They next enter an electronics store, and Jacob scans the speakers, but doesn't see any he likes as much as the other store. They try some walkie talkies, but they don't have batteries. Jacob loses interest, and they leave.

The next store is Hallmark. Oscar stops Jacob. "I want to go in there."

Again, Jacob crosses his arms. "Well, I don't," he sasses, wagging his head.

"I'll be real fast," Oscar promises, and then bolts inside.

Without a perch to sit on this time, Jacob stands half facing the mall, half facing the store, tapping his foot. He counts his taps rapidly, as a haphazard timekeeping method, but finds himself repeating numbers or losing track as his mind drifts. He stops tapping his foot, then starts pacing in front of the store, hands in pockets, grumbling. When Jacob is about to charge in to retrieve him, Oscar comes out bright-eyed.

"Jake, do you have any money?" he asks breathlessly.

"What? Why?"

Still catching his breath from frenzied shopping, "I found this great Christmas card we should give to Mom and Dad. Us kids could all sign it!"

Jacob fingers the $5 bill in his pocket. "We don't need to get them a card," he dismisses.

"No, it'd be great!" Oscar persists. "Jasmine would *love* us to give them a card together! Com'on. Do you have any?"

Jacob shakes his head, turning away. "Naw, man, we . . ."

"I'll pay you back," pleads Oscar. "It's the last one, and it's *perfect!* I promise I'll pay you back."

Jacob drops his head in frustrated resignation.

"Great!" Oscar grabs his arm and pulls him into the store, over to the rack, where he snatches up the precious child-like card and presents it for Jacob's consideration. The front shows a midnight-blue starry sky, with a small nativity scene illuminated beneath. The words in white and gold across the top say, "God must have known you were the best parents He could give us."

"You like it?" beams Oscar. "I mean, it's perfect!" He starts to show Jacob the inside.

"No, that's fine man," Jacob waves him off. "We gotta get going. Just grab the envelope and check out." He hands the $5 bill to Oscar. "Hurry up. I'll see you outside."

Oscar soon pops outside, grinning with the tiny bag in hand. "Thanks, Jake!"

They go only a few stores further, when Oscar spots the See's Candy shop and walks brusquely to the entrance. "I'll be quick! I just want to check the prices," he calls over his shoulder.

Jacob deflates. "Com'on man! You're killing me!"

Oscar enters the white, meticulous storefront and then turns smiling to Jacob, beckoning him. "They have samples . . ." he taunts.

Jacob shuffles in to where Oscar is getting prices from the sales lady. He has a chocolate bonbon already in hand, and when Jacob joins him, the white-dressed lady sweetly offers him a sample. "Here you go Honey. Try a chocolate caramel."

Jacob takes it, moodily. "Thanks."

Oscar thanks the lady and checks the chocolate mini-Santa prices before they leave. Then he announces, "Okay, I'm done."

Jacob looks at him surprised. "You're done?"

Oscar shrugs amiably, "Yep. I found everything I want. I'm just following you now."

Jacob nods his head as they walk, "Cool."

They near the end of the mall again, and it appears there is little left to interest Jacob. He starts to think about some of the fun things he saw, like the speakers, and the drone, and maybe even the multi-tool. He kind of liked one of the hats they tried on, but he's still uncertain.

Just then his phone chimes. He looks at the text from his Mom: "HI BOYS! HOPE YOU'RE HAVING FUN! WE'RE IN THE FOODCOURT. WE SAW YOU WALK PAST US A LITTLE WHILE AGO. MEET US HERE BY 1:45. WANT ANYTHING TO EAT?"

"Do you want Mom to order any food?"

Oscar jumps in front of Jacob, "Yes! Tell her to get me a chick-fil-a kid's meal!"

Jacob texts back their order, and Felicia responds, "OKAY!"

"Man, I only have a half hour left," Jacob groans.

"Really?"

"Yeah, and I still don't know what I want."

As they approach the last store, Jacob's pace quickens excitedly.

"I can't believe it!" he exclaims, more to himself than to Oscar, who is scuttling double-time beside him. "Oh my gosh! What was I thinking? How could I forget!"

Jacob storms toward the entrance of a large skate shop, display windows filled with skater clothing and gear, and figures in motion, popping off tricks. Once inside, he rapturously scans all the clothing, shoes, and other gear. After a directionless moment, he heads straight for the back wall, where rows of skateboards are displayed on wire racks. He quickly zeros in on three or four of his choice favorites. He knows about the quality and features of each model, and rattles off questions to a passing clerk, arms full of shoeboxes. The young man looks like a skater, and soon abandons his boxes to engage the enthusiastic Jacob, who is favoring a particular board.

The guy interrupts Jacob, “Dude, hold on. Let me get you something from the back.” He retrieves the stack of shoeboxes and goes into the stockroom.

Jacob pivots to Oscar. “I can’t believe I almost forgot! Remember Mom said I could ride my board to school now? But then my old board got kind of jacked-up? Duh! I need a new board! And they have all the brands I like!”

The sales guy returns with another board in his hand. “Hey, this just came in. It’s the same model you want, but with upgraded trucks and wheels, *and* has this killer dragon graphic.”

Jacob takes the board reverently from him. “Man, this is awesome! *This* is the one I want.”

“Stand on it,” the sales guy suggests.

Jacob carefully sets the board on the floor, and steps onto it. He flexes his knees and feet, testing its agility, eyes wide with enchantment.

“That’s cool, Jake,” encourages Oscar.

Jacob picks up the board and inspects it with admiration. Then his eyes catch the price tag, and they sadden again.

“What’s wrong?” Oscar worries.

Discouraged, Jacob lowers the skateboard. “It’s $165 dollars.”

“It is? How much is the other one you like?”

Jacob picks up the castoff board and turns it over. “$130 dollars.”

“That’s good,” Oscar cheers some.

The sales guy seems to sympathize, “I guess $165 is too much?”

“Yeah,” Jacob mourns. “Especially with tax. I have a $150 limit.

“Well dude, that first board you picked out rocks!” The sales guy encourages him. “There’s, like no difference. And you can swap out for the upgraded trucks and wheels any time. If you buy them here, we’ll do it for free.”

Jacob pores over the dragon graphic, then evaluates the first board’s bright trademark logo. “Yeah. It’s a good board. That’ll be fine. I’ll take it.”

"Good choice, my man. I'll ring you up."

Jacob hands the board to the sales guy. "It's a present from my aunt, and she's coming back with me to buy it, so can you hold it for like an hour?"

"You bet." He takes the board. "It'll be at the register. What's your name?"

"Jake." Then Jacob looks at the dragon board and hands it to him as well. "Hey, can you hold this one too? Just in case."

The guy smiles and takes it. "Sure Jake. They'll both be up front with your name on 'em."

As they leave the store, Jacob hangs his head, hands in pockets, contemplating.

"You liked that first board a lot until you saw the other one. Aren't you happy?" prods Oscar. "You found what you wanted, right?"

He lifts his head some. "Yeah. I really *do* like that first board. I mean, it's exactly what I wanted." As they head toward the food court, he looks sideways at Oscar. "Yeah. I'm good."

"Good. Me too," chimes Oscar.

Chapter 5: Not One

Bryce and Jasmine drive through the Christmas-themed village bustling with people among the stores and cafes, or in transit to some winter adventure. The snowy mountain, traversed with ski runs and moving dots of color, ascends above the village on the right, dominating the skyline. Beyond the shops to the left, Big Bear Lake glints in the winter sun among woodlands dusted in powdery white.

"How's your cocoa?" Bryce watches Jasmine in the mirror take a tentative sip.

"Hot! But good."

"Good. Mine too." He gestures toward the lake. "Isn't that pretty?"

"Uh-huh." She is sitting quite upright, trying to catch every spectacle on each side of the car.

As the village recedes, the forest encroaches on the roadway again, and cabins appear nestled among the trees around the lake. Jasmine rolls down her window to taste the crisp air and leans out with her face into the wind. Beams of sunlight pierce through the tall, snowy pines and flash on the road around them like children playing and laughing in the sonorous blend of sounds gusting past the window.

A road appears on the left that leads directly to the lake.

Bryce slows and pulls into the center lane, then turns to Jasmine. "What do you think? Should we see what's down this way?"

She nods her pink head, looking down the lane. "Uh-huh."

The road leads behind a property full of rental cabins and ends with a large parking lot shared by the cabin and beach visitors. There are few cars in the lot, and no one is walking by the lake. Near the shoreline stands a small play structure crowned with the remnants of snow.

Bryce parks close as he can to the lake by a sidewalk that follows the shoreline along the trees. He sets the brake and turns to Jasmine. "How are you doing Pumpkin?" She appears ready for the next adventure.

"Good," she nods spiritedly.

"Good," he smiles. "Do you want to get out? Or shall we stay here and look at the view?"

"Get out," she affirms.

"Okay. How about we take the wheelchair down along that path? You can get all bundled up."

Jasmine nods. "Remember my English muffin for the birds."

"Yes, absolutely." Bryce gets out and slips on his winter jacket, then looks at his watch. 11:47. They'll have to leave Big Bear in about 45 minutes in order to pick up the family on time. He gets the wheelchair from the back and rolls it to her door. Already with her shoes and jacket on, Jasmine holds out a pillow to put on the seat before he helps her down into the wheelchair. He then takes one of the blankets to wrap over her legs.

"How's that?"

She nods. "Good."

Bryce grabs the bag holding the water, apple slices, and string cheese, and her leftover English muffin, and hangs it on the handle.

"You wanna take this?" He hands her the cup of cocoa from her door holder.

"Get your cocoa, Daddy. I can hold it too."

"Oh, thanks, Pumpkin." He opens the door and retrieves his cup from the center console, and hands it to her. "Maybe they'll keep your hands warm," he smiles.

Bryce rolls her down the walkway toward the beach, where the view expands across the glistening, dark, blue water to the shore on the other side. Tall evergreens enclose the lake, and in some shady places, the snow remains on the gray pebbles up to the waterside.

"It's beautiful," breathes Jasmine.

Bryce inhales deeply. “Yes, it is.” To their right a little ways is a picnic table on the edge of the beach near the trees. “Should we go over there and see if we can find some birds?”

Her pink head nods. “That looks perfect.”

Bryce rolls Jasmine along the pathway and parks her at the corner of the cement picnic table. He takes the goodies out of the bag and then flattens it for a serving plate. Bryce arranges the food for Jasmine, then takes his mocha cup and straddles the bench at the table. “Can you eat some of those apple slices?”

She nods, “Yeah.”

Bryce pulls open the string cheese wrapper and sets it on the bag. “Here, have a little bite and get some protein.”

“Okay,” she replies crunching a crispy apple slice.

The shade of the trees has preserved a pristine blanket of white beneath them. There is a mulberry bush nearby, alive with small chirping and stirring in its snow-dusted leaves. Jasmine turns toward Bryce wide-eyed, and whispers “Birds, Daddy.”

He opens his mouth and raises his eyebrows in wonder. “Wow,” He loudly whispers. “Just like you hoped for.”

Jasmine picks up the hard English muffin, breaks off a piece, and rolls it between her thumb and finger to crush it into crumbs. She tosses some onto the snow beneath the mulberry bush and watches for the colony flittering among the leaves to notice. The chirps seem to crescendo to a symphony in allegro.

“Are they sparrows, Daddy?”

Bryce watches the activity, waiting for the birds to notice the crumbs Jasmine has so lovingly cast for them—crumbs she has been planning to feed them since she first awoke, if not always.

“Yes, I think they *are* sparrows.” Growing strangely anxious, he begins to pray “God, let them take her crumbs.” Then, one of the puffy, round birds hops cheerfully to the snowy ground to investigate. It cheeps tentatively, and takes three tiny bird hops toward a crumb, tilts its head to one side, then to the other, looks up, then looks to the crumb and takes it, followed by another, gleeful, loud chirp. Then it hops quickly to another crumb, chirping and tilting its head, and snatches it up, emitting another satisfied proclamation. At this activity, the other birds begin to hop down to the snow and forage for other crumbs.

“They like it,” Jasmine delights, pinching off the toast and tossing crumbs at intervals. She intently watches the jubilant gathering peeping and hopping on the snow. “Aren’t they beautiful?”

Bryce, so concentrating on Jasmine’s experience, hasn’t processed the scene himself—these common sparrows, doing what they always do. Yet his daughter so thoroughly appreciates their sprightly, joyful nature, each with a unique, exuberant personality, puffing their little feathers, and conversing in a secret, twittering language.

“Yes. They are amazing,” he reflects with new admiration.

“And God knows *every* one of them. He doesn’t forget *even one sparrow*,” she expounds, casting her crumbs of love to the dainty creatures. “Not *one*.”

The two sit silently enjoying the scene. As the sun rises higher above the trees, it warms them in its light, and seems to intensify the birds’ exhilaration. They hop and flitter from the bush to the bright snow, back to the bush, and soon the commotion alerts other little birds, who fly in to join the sparrows. Some of the new birds have yellow chests, and some have pale red throats, each polite, and adding different cheeps or peeps or trilling notes to the festivity.

“Listen to them, Daddy,” Jasmine whispers reverently.

“I hear them. They’re delightful.”

Her face is bright with awe. “They’re so *happy*.”

They admire the tranquil performance, new birds flitting in, and others flitting out.

“Do you know what kind these other birds are?”

“Hmm. . . Finches maybe?”

“Finches,” Jasmine ponders. “They’re really pretty.”

Bryce considers investigating this on his phone, when it vibrates. It is a text from Felicia: JUST CHECKED THE FLIGHT AND IT’S DELAYED AT LEAST 1 ½ HOURS. YOU TWO HAVE PLEANTY OF TIME. HOW’S IT GOING?

“Is it Mommy?” Jasmine asks.

“Yeah. It looks like their flight will be delayed.” Bryce looks up from his phone through oscillating circles fogging his glasses from his warm face. “Do you want me to tell her anything?”

Jasmine tilts her head thinking, poised to break off more crumbs. “Yes,” she answers decisively. “Tell her it’s beautiful here."

"Okay. Hey," he holds out his phone, "Should we take another picture to send her?"

"Yes."

Bryce scoots down the bench toward Jasmine's wheelchair, then holds up the phone and takes a picture with the lake sparkling behind them. He extends the phone to Jasmine for approval.

"How's that?"

She puts her cold hand on his to see it. "Good."

He sends the message and picture.

"Hey Pumpkin, you're getting cold there. We should get going."

Jasmine tucks her free hand self-consciously under the blanket. "No, Daddy. Not yet," she urges. "I'm fine. It's just my hands. Please?"

He looks at her skeptically over the fog on his lenses. "Let me see." Then he reaches for her tiny hand and wraps it in both of his. He blows on her little fingers to warm them, rubs her hand playfully between his, and then kisses it gallantly.

"Okay, a little longer," he admonishes. "Hey--" Bryce opens the plastic bag and pulls out her extra pair of socks triumphantly. "Want to put these on your hands?"

"One hand," she agrees, and offers her left hand.

"Okay." Bryce slides on the sock. "But how about you try to eat a little more, and *I'll* keep feeding the birds."

Jasmine evaluates the English muffin remnants in her hand and surrenders it to him.

"Thank you. I'll do a good job, I promise," he reassures. Then in his best Yoda imitation, "You have taught me well."

She laughs softly, revealing a precious smile. "Daddy." She doesn't really know who Yoda is, but likes the funny voice.

"Okay. Now tuck your hand back in."

She bites another apple slice, then burrows her socked hand into the blanket and pulls it up to her chest. "Kay."

He throws a few crumbs. "How am I doing?

"Good," she nods. She takes a bite of her cheese.

Another bite of apple.

She lifts the blanket with both hands up to her chin, tucking her arms in.

Minutes pass as they watch the scene quietly.

"I feel like they take me to another place," Jasmine ponders.

Bryce is not sure what she means. He looks at her watching the birds.

"You had a good idea, Jasmine—to come up here."

He finishes scattering the crumbs, then retrieves her remaining quarter-slice from the morning. He detects a spot of strawberry jam.

"Here. Would you like to do the honors?" He offers her the remnant. She pulls the sock off her hand and takes it.

"Should I take a picture of the birds?"

She nods. "Yes."

He zooms in with his phone and decides to take a short video of the moment.

After a few more minutes of chirping jubilee, Jasmine casts the last of the crumbs in a fanfare. The birds gradually flutter away with final cheeps.

"Daddy."

"Yes?"

"Do you see that little pinecone over there?" She points in the snow near the bush.

"Yes."

"Can I have that?"

Bryce nods and gets up from the bench. "That is a great idea." He walks through the crunching snow and lifts the little closed pinecone from the ground, then brings it back to Jasmine for inspection.

"That's a good one. Do you like it?"

She turns it over in her fingers, examining every detail. "Yes. It's a good one."

"Here, I'll put it in my jacket pocket." She hands him the pinecone, and he tucks it safely away. "Okay. What do you say Pumpkin? All set?"

Jasmine nods and tucks her hands back under the blanket. Bryce gathers their trash and tosses it in the nearby receptacle. "Do you still want your cocoa?" he asks. She nods again, and he hands it to her, which she grasps with her sock-covered hand. "Okay. Let's get you warm then." He unlocks her wheelchair and turns her back toward the car. "Bye-bye birdies." He sings.

"Bye-bye," Jasmine faintly echoes.

"Thank you," he adds as they roll along the lakeside walk. He hears Jasmine repeat this in quiet tones.

At the car, he helps her get settled back in and buckled. He starts the car to get the heater going, then loads the wheelchair. Once in, he turns to face Jasmine. She has nestled her pillows into the corner again and is small in the seat. "I'll put your pinecone here." He sets it in one of the cup holders. She nods.

"Are you ready to head back?" Her head is resting against the doorframe, eyes turned wearily out the window. She still has her jacket on, now with both blankets drawn up to her chin.

"No," she breathes.

Bryce looks at his watch. 12:43. Now that the flight is delayed, they still have over an hour before they must leave, but she seems so tired. "Okay. . ." he hesitates "What would you like to do?"

Muffled by the blankets near her face, Jasmine offers a listless reply, "Drive around."

That sounds restful to Bryce. "Drive around." Perhaps even restorative. "You mean, like drive around the lake?" Her buried pink head nods slightly.

"Okay. That sounds good." Bryce drives back to the main road to continue their journey around the lake. There are few cars as they leisurely venture down the road away from the center of town. The majestic host of trees surrounding them creates a lulling interplay of light and shadow beneath the vaulted crisp, blue skies. Bryce locates a CD of light, classical music in the center console and inserts it into the stereo, turning the sound very low.

After several miles around the shadowy backside of the lake, the road narrows and enters a campground, where a tiny, unmanned khaki guardhouse is posted. A chain hangs across the entrance with a metal sign announcing, "CLOSED FOR WINTER."

"It looks like we can't go any further," Bryce concludes. "I don't think they maintain the road past here anyway." As he turns in front of the guardhouse, he looks over the campground. There are some small facilities, perhaps a store, and a café, and showers. Each camping spot is marked by a snow-covered picnic bench and fire ring. To the left, extending over the lake is a dock, also partially covered in snow.

Bryce turns to Jasmine, “It looks like fun here.” She is bundled up in the corner, looking out the window. “Okay, we’ll start heading back.” He finishes the U-turn and they follow the road back toward the village. In the rear-view mirror, he sees that Jasmine is in the same position, which now faces out toward the lake side. Only her eyes move, peacefully scanning the landscape.

After about a half an hour, they are back in the village again. Jasmine is now sitting up, with the blanket off her shoulders, surveying the scene out both sides of the car. A moment later, she points over Bryce’s shoulder out the left side. “Daddy, can we go in there for a few minutes?”

Bryce looks and sees the same little hillside across from the coffee shop that they had watched the sledders go down earlier. “You want me to pull into there?”

“Yeah. I want to watch them.”

“Okay.” Bryce agrees uncertainly, and turns into the parking lot, now less crowded, and parks facing the hillside. Their spot is sloped upward a little, so it is easier for Jasmine to see the hill. She unfastens her seatbelt and scoots to the center to watch.

After a moment. “I want to roll my window down,” she reports.

Bryce turns the car back on for the heater. “Go ahead.”

Jasmine rolls down her window to behold the bustling scene of colors and sledders, and laughter. She sips on her cocoa, moving her head from time to time to follow something. Bryce notices a lot of fathers with their children. He sees some mothers standing by the cars, or at the edge of the snow taking pictures. He looks back at Jasmine, eyes tracking the scene, and suddenly unbuckles his seatbelt.

“I’ll be right back.” He jumps out of the car, mounts the snowy ridge, and plods over to a father standing nearby at the end of the run. They talk for a moment, as Bryce gestures toward the car. The man looks over, then nods. Bryce returns and opens his door breathily. He pops his head around the seat to look at Jasmine, “Do you want to try it?”

Jasmine’s eyes widen with elation. “Yes!”

Bryce rolls up the window and turns off the car, then comes around to Jasmine’s door. He takes her into his arms and carries her carefully over the snow mound to where the other father is standing. By now, his son has joined him at the bottom of the hill, and they turn toward Bryce and Jasmine with welcoming smiles.

"Hi Derik, this is Jasmine," introduces Bryce.

"Hi Jasmine. This is my son, Marcus," replies the father.

"Hi Marcus," Jasmine waves timidly from her father's arms.

"Hi Jasmine. Nice to meet you," grins the boy of about 11.

Derik puts his hand on Marcus's head in approval and turns to Jasmine again. "Well, you ready for a little fun?" He is holding the edge of a bright red, plastic disk stuck upright in the snow. He leans it out, offering it to Bryce.

"Thanks! We'll be right back." Bryce grabs the edge of the disk in his free hand, and hoists Jasmine higher on his hip. Then he turns to hike up the packed snow along the edge, out of the path of descending sledders. As they climb, he hoists Jasmine a few times and struggles to grip the large disk while trudging up the hill. She clings to her father's neck, as he grunts and breathes heavily, emitting great puffs of steam, which fog his glasses and obstruct his vision.

"Are you okay, Daddy?"

He tries to see through the fog to the top of the hill, which seems hardly any closer. He hoists her up again, and grunts, "Yep."

Just then Bryce hears scampering feet draw up beside him. "Here, let me take that for you, Sir," sounds the chipper voice of young Marcus. He grabs the disk in both hands and walks beside them up the hill.

"Thank you, Marcus!" Bryce huffs.

"Happy to help! Hey Jasmine, you're going to like this run. It's fast, but not too bumpy."

After several more yards, Bryce pauses, breathing heavily, and pivots to walk to the center. "This looks like a good place."

Jasmine pulls on his neck like she's steering a horse. "No Daddy, higher."

Bryce looks down at Marcus and widens his eyes with comic effect. "'Higher,' she says," and he gestures for Marcus to lead the way.

"Higher it is," he replies.

Several more yards up the hill, Marcus stops and explains to Jasmine, "This is where I always go. It's the best place to start the run. I have a good spot too." He leads them across for several yards and stops.

"This is a good spot because you miss most of the ruts, and it glides really fast," Marcus reports.

Bryce, red-faced, nods with approval, "Sounds good." He turns to Jasmine, who is holding even tighter around his neck. "What do you think?"

She nods shyly. "Good."

Bryce sets her carefully on the snow and takes the disk from Marcus. "How will you get down? Walk?"

Marcus looks around and then appears to have solved his dilemma. "No. See that kid walking up with the red beanie?" he points back. "That's my buddy. I can get a ride from him." Bryce is amused by this solution, thinking how soon this young man will be getting rides in his buddy's car.

"Okay, Marcus. Thanks for your help." Bryce places the disk on the snow and carefully sits in it with his heels dug into the hillside to keep from sliding.

"Glad to do it. See you down there!" At this, he turns to meet his friend coming toward them.

"See you there," Jasmine adds, standing nervously by the disk. Bryce sees her evaluating the conveyance and the steepness of the slope, now more dramatic as they look down the hill.

"Are you ready?" He asks, holding his arms out to receive her. Her hands are clasped together beneath her chin, as she looks back and forth between her father and the hill. Then she nods her head fervently and outstretches her hands toward him.

"Okay, I'll help you. Just sit down here between my knees." He takes her hand and guides her around his foot, then half lifts her onto the disk. He wraps his left arm around her body as she clasps her hands up around each of his legs, gripping the fabric of his jeans.

"Okay. Ready?" She nods her head again and grips his legs even tighter. Bryce grabs the edge of the disk with his free hand. "Okay, here we go!" Then he lifts his heals from the snow and rests them on the edge of the disk, ready to dig them in again to steer or to slow their descent.

Immediately, they slip downward on the icy surface, picking up speed as they go. They jostle lightly over the contours, banking gently against small variations in the snowy terrain that redirect their path. Jasmine silently clutches her father's legs, pulling them closer to her so that he has less freedom to deploy them for control over their path. One looming mound approaches rapidly as they near the bottom, threatening to send them careening wildly. Bryce leans to the right in an effort to steer away, but to no avail. The haphazard duo slide up the side of the mound, which gently rotates them a half turn, causing them to traverse the remaining yards backwards, and come to a pillowy stop in the lower snow bank.

Bryce leans forward to see Jasmine's face, which is wide-eyed, open-mouthed, and exhilarated.

"Well?" he gives her a prodding squeeze.

A bewildered laugh of relief frees from her throat, as she, still clinging to one of Bryce's legs, smiles broadly in breathless awe. "Fun!"

Bryce is relieved. "Did you like it?"

Jasmine nods her head cautiously, still smiling with wide eyes. "Yeah."

Bryce looks up the hill, and seeing no danger, pulls his phone out of his jacket pocket, then spins the disk with his feet to include the backdrop of the hill. He hands the phone to Jasmine.

"Here, you want to take it?"

She takes the phone awkwardly in her chilled hands and maneuvers the image to frame their ecstatic grins with the whole bursting scene behind them.

"Good shot!" Bryce proclaims, quickly returning the phone to his pocket.

"We'll send that to Mommy too?" Jasmine asks, as Bryce prepares to stand.

He laughs a little, imagining Felicia's reaction. "We'll see."

Marcus comes running to them after the end of his run. "You guys went fast!"

Bryce sets Jasmine on her feet, mindful of the other sledders, and quickly gets up, disk in one hand, Jasmine's hand in the other, and guides her to a safer place out of the chute as she converses with young Marcus.

"Did we really go fast?" she asks. "It felt fast."

He walks excitedly beside them. "Oh yeah. You guys were flying!"

"Wow," marvels Jasmine.

They reach the place where Derik is standing, and Bryce holds out the disk to Marcus.

"You guys can go again if you want," the boy exhorts.

Bryce looks down at Jasmine, stimulated, but now worn, as she seems to evaluate the prospect of reliving the whole process.

"No, I don't think so," he begins, handing over the disk with a grateful smile. "We have to drive back to LA and pick up our family from the airport."

Bryce lifts Jasmine, small beside him, out of the snow and into his arms. She lays her head on the side of his neck, looking down at Marcus. Bryce then extends his free hand, "You have been such a great host, Marcus. Thank you for helping us so much!" Marcus earnestly shakes his hand.

"Yeah, thank you," Jasmine adds quietly. "I'll never forget you."

Marcus looks down at his feet, uneasily. Then he looks up at Jasmine with conviction. "I won't ever forget you, either, Jasmine."

Bryce turns to Derik and thanks him with a handshake as well, and then carries Jasmine back to their car, who waves shyly over Bryce's shoulder at the pair as they watch them go.

After settling in Jasmine, Bryce climbs in front, turns on the car, and checks his watch. 2:15. If the family gets in at about 5:30, it will be just about enough time to get back. He turns to Jasmine.

"Did you like that?"

She looks tired, but content. She nods emphatically. "That was the biggest hill I've ever been on."

He reaches between the seats and gives her leg a little shake. "I know! Exciting."

"Marcus was nice, wasn't he?" she adds, thoughtfully.

"He sure was. Hey, we gotta start heading back so I can pick up Mom and the boys at the airport when they get in. Did you see somewhere in town that you'd like to stop and grab a bite for the drive, and maybe go to the bathroom before we leave?"

"Taco Bell," she replies, clasping her little hands together.

Bryce makes a dramatic face, recalling that is her favorite fast food. "Ahhh, right. Taco Bell. Of course."

They drive away, waving good-bye to the little hill, and after several blocks, pull into the Taco Bell parking lot near the edge of town. They take turns using the restroom, and then they approach the quiet front counter. He scans the menu, holding her hand.

"What do you want Pumpkin?" He looks down for her reply, and she is leaning against him wearily, with her two middle fingers placed inside her mouth—something she has done since a baby to console her tired self. He hoists her again into his arms, and she leans her pink head on his neck, the fingers of her free hand searching up to play with his hair. He begins to sway with her, like he did when she was a toddler.

"What do you think?" he asks quietly, close to her ear.

She is looking in the direction of the young, uniformed man, attending the cash register. He smiles at her, expectantly. She pops the wet fingers out of her mouth and whispers to Bryce, not lifting her head, "Bean and cheese burrito," then re-inserts her red fingers.

Bryce speaks to the young man "Okay, a bean and cheese burrito, easy sauce—"

Jasmine pops out her fingers again to add, "No onions."

"Right, no onions on that." He asks her, "Do you want a soda?"

He feels her shake her head.

"No? Lemonade?"

She pops her fingers out. "Too sweet."

"Something else?"

"Tea."

"Okay, add a tea to that."

The young man presses the buttons, and asks "Would you like the kids' meal then? It comes with a churro for the same price."

"Yeah, sure. And then I'll have a deluxe combo burrito with a soda."

The young man reads back the order and the total, and Bryce shifts Jasmine to his other hip so he can retrieve his wallet and pay.

Bryce receives his receipt and cups to fill. "Thank you." He manages to get their drinks from the fountain one-handed, lids and all, just as the food is ready.

Back at the car, Bryce settles Jasmine in, distributes the food and drinks, throws out the cold cocoa cup, and takes a picture of Jasmine intrepidly holding up her burrito in the back seat, which he texts with a message to Felicia, "HEADING BACK NOW ☺." After these preparations, they set out on their journey back to the hospital, waving good-bye to Big Bear as they depart the village to descend the mountains. The day has been long already, but is still bright in the sky.

Bryce checks Jasmine in the mirror, who is leaning against her pillow-tower, taking small nibbles of her burrito, wrapper peeled back down over her hands. She dreamily views the silent forest passing by. They are quiet for many miles.

Bryce waits until the road is straighter to eat his burrito. As he unwraps it, he glances back at Jasmine again. She has set aside her rewrapped burrito, and is curled up into the corner, blankets pulled high, in deep sleep. His eye catches the corner of the unused child seat peaking over the last row, where he had relegated it earlier in their drive. He looks at her sleeping again and closes his eyes with uneasy resolve. Then he inserts a worship CD, intent on spending the long drive back to the hospital in peace.

Chapter 6: The Spirit of Christmas

Felicia and Christiana sit stretched-out at a 4-person table in the food court surrounded by piles of department store bags on the floor and seats beside them. They occasionally pick at the food remnants from their plates as they talk.

"Why don't you check again," urges Christiana.

Felicia lifts her phone from the table. "Good idea." She scrolls. "Yep. I knew it."

"Is your flight delayed?" Christiana absently forks another bite of lettuce.

"Yes." Felicia scrolls and expands screens. Finally, she sits back again, closing her eyes and shaking her head a little grimly. "It's been delayed about an hour and a half."

Christiana pokes her fork through salad scraps for missed morsels. "You were right. But that's not too bad, is it?"

"I know." She sets the phone aside. "It's just. . ." She searches the food court for the exact thought. "It's just that these past two weeks have been *so* hard. You know?"

"Yeah. I know." Christiana puts down the fork.

"It was hard enough to take Jasmine to LA for this clinical trial, but then to *leave* her there? You know?"

"I know, Chia." She reaches to her sister's hand and squeezes it.

"I mean, not to see my baby for *two weeks*—and her in the hospital?" Felicia's voice quavers.

"I know."

"It was easier when she was at the hospital *here* in Phoenix. No matter what, I never had to go a day without seeing her." She firmly wipes away moisture from under her eyes.

"Yes, of course it was." Christiana searches in her purse, then offers her a tissue peeking out from a little packet. "Here."

"Oh, thanks." Felicia pulls out the tissue and chuckles at her sudden outflow of emotions. "I just need to see her. You know?" She dabs under her eyes and nose.

"Yes, of course you do, Mija. You will. . ."

"I just don't know if I can take . . . waiting longer." At this, Felicia inhales sharply, and lifts her fingers to her lips. She leans a little closer to her sister.

"You know, I can set my heart on things to be expected." Then like a whispered secret that spills out, "It's the uncertainly . . . that's what I struggle with. That's what makes me . . ."

She sits up again shaking her head, and pinches her nose with the tissue. "It'll be fine. I know it will," she vows, inhaling deeply and dabbing her eyes a final time. She sets the scrunched tissue on her tray.

"Yes, it will." Christiana reassures. They smile at each other with their lifetime of knowing.

Then Felicia startles, picking up her phone, "Oh, I need to tell Bryce about the delay, so they don't hurry."

"So, they really drove out to the mountains today?"

"Mmmm Hmm," Felicia finishes the text. "Crazy, huh? He was *really* nervous to do it."

"Then, why did he?"

"It was Jasmine's idea."

"Really!"

"I know. I tell you, she's wise. And she knows how to handle Bryce."

"She *charms* him, huh?" Christiana pushes aside her tray and leans back.

"I don't know if it's that. It's more like she asks so *little*. She seems only to ask for what's really important to her. Then, no matter what it is, Bryce just feels like he should try to do it."

Felicia's phone chimes. She looks at it, then smiles and hands it to Christiana to see. "Look at this," she beams. It is the picture of Bryce and Jasmine grinning with the snowy mountain lake behind them.

"Cute. It looks really pretty there."

"I know. It does. I told Bryce to scout it out, and maybe we can all go up while we're there." She takes back the phone and starts texting. "I better tell the boys they have at least an extra hour."

Christiana looks over their plates and decides they have finished with their food. She leaves their drinks and takes the trays to the trash. She returns, hands on her hips. "So now that we have over an hour, did you want to shop some more, or wander around the mall?"

Felicia sips through the straw in her iced tea as she evaluates their packages. "Honestly, I think I'd rather stay here and just hang out. I mean, that was a great coupon you had, but I wore the wrong shoes, and I already spent too much."

"Me too. Plus, I'd rather just talk with you. I won't see you for a while."

"I agree."

"Okay, well, I'm going to the bathroom, and I have to be honest with you."

Felicia grins suspiciously, "What?"

"I don't know who I was fooling, but that *healthy* salad is not going to do it." Christiana grabs her purse and slings it defiantly onto her shoulder. She points at a food stand. "I'm getting those chili cheese fries. You can have some or not," and she strides off toward the ladies' room.

Felicia laughs, "Thanks, but I better not."

"That may be," Christiana calls behind her, "But you *will*."

Felicia sits, smiling to herself. "She's right. I probably will."

~

Sometime later, the two are absorbed in conversation as they meticulously swipe up drizzles of nacho cheese with crunchy French fry remnants. Felicia nods toward the mall. "Look. The boys." Jacob and Oscar are crossing the bridge toward them.

"Oh yeah. Jake looks serious."

"I know. He always does."

Christiana lifts a cheese dot with her finger. "Is that being a teenager, or something else?"

"*Definitely* being a teenager. But also, I think he's really struggling with Jasmine's illness—especially since we almost lost her, and then the Leukemia came back. It's made him, I don't know," Felicia's hand waives through word options. "Cynical."

"It'll help him to see her tonight."

"I hope so."

"How long will you be in LA?"

"I don't know really. The boys and Bryce come back with Mama and Papa next Friday, but I'll stay until the doctors release her. It depends on a lot of factors." Felicia dabs up crumbs and licks them from her finger, then sits back satisfied with the clean plate.

"So, you have to wait and see? You can't make any plans, then, can you?"

Felicia shakes her head, "No, not really." She sips her watery tea. "I mean, they have a tentative schedule, but it's a trial. They have to make assessments as they go."

"Wow. That's hard. But it's great that Jasmine has this opportunity."

"It really is. And the procedure has a high rate of remission. Dr. Slater's been wonderful. When Jasmine got so sick after we did the bone marrow transplant, right away he thought she'd qualify for the trial." Felicia's hand wanders down and touches her hip.

"Amazing. And the trial pays for it?"

"Most of it. We still have some expenses—a lot, actually. And our insurance will help with the hospital stay, but not other trial-related expenses."

"Well, that's good. That helps." Christiana rattles the straw in her empty drink and sets it down, disappointed.

"Yeah. It does. It's just hard trying to make life normal for the boys, and still have one of us with Jasmine all the time. Now, Bryce has to come back because the business is struggling."

"No kidding. I thought he has people to run the store."

"He does for the medical supplies, but he has only one other pharmacist working for him. Without Bryce, they can't keep up with all the prescriptions. He's worried about losing business permanently if he doesn't either come home and work or hire someone temporarily."

"Is he going to do that? Hire someone?"

"He's thought about it, but hiring another pharmacist is very expensive. By coming home, he can handle most of the prescriptions. That should get things on track."

"How about you? Was the office okay with taking time off

again?"

"Yes, they're great. And they love Jasmine. Besides, it's kind of the slow time for real estate, so they'll have enough agents. *We'll* miss the income, of course, but really, we're quite blessed. S*o many* families have it much worse than we do, you know? I don't see how they manage."

"I 'm sure you've met a lot of them."

"We have. It's heartbreaking."

Christiana picks up her cup and shakes it again, then sets it firmly down. "Have you heard from Mama at all?"

"Not since they went on the cruise a few days ago. Just the few updates on Facebook."

"Yeah, I saw those. Did you see her and Papa dancing in Ensenada?"

"I know! That was great! Who would have thought she could get him to do that?" Felicia wakes her phone to look at the Facebook page.

"Oh, I could see it coming. He has been so happy since he retired. He's like a whole new man."

"That's wonderful." She finds the jaunty photo of their parents dancing and holds it out. "Cute, huh?"

"Yeah," Christiana grins. "Was Jasmine glad to see them?"

"Oh yeah. Bryce said it really helped, since I'd left LA already."

"That was a good idea, wasn't it?"

"I know. When Mama told me they decided to take a Christmas cruise from LA to Mexico, I felt so relieved. They spent three days with Jasmine and Bryce before the ship sailed. It took some pressure off of Bryce, too."

"That was Papa's idea, you know."

"Really? No, I didn't know. How sweet."

"What about Bryce's folks. Are they going out to see Jasmine?"

"I don't think so. Candice came out here with her husband in the fall, but she doesn't like leaving Kansas City because she's taking care of her Mom, now."

"Oh, yeah. I remember. What about, Ken?

"Well, you know how down he's been ever since the divorce—he doesn't venture out much. But he and Jasmine spent some time together before we left for LA, and the boys and I went over yesterday to see him for a bit. He gave me her present to take with us. They'll probably talk tomorrow after she opens it."

"Are you going straight to the hotel tonight?"

"Yes. Hopefully Jasmine too, if we don't get in too late." Felicia checks her phone. "It's 1:15. I better let the boys know they have about a half hour, and they probably want something to eat." She texts them and soon gets a reply. "Okay, Chick-fil-a for Oscar, of course, and Texas Bar-B-Que for Jake. How did he know they had that here?"

"Remember when you guys came down over the summer and we went out to dinner? That's when Alex brought them here for a movie."

"That's right."

"Well, it was probably then. That's Alex's favorite."

"Ahh, that explains it," Felicia smirks.

"Did he order a brisket sandwich with a side of fried pickles and coleslaw?"

"He did. But with beans instead of coleslaw—he doesn't like coleslaw."

Felicia's phone dings. "It's Bryce. They're driving back to the hospital." She shows Christiana the picture of Jasmine holding up her burrito.

"What's she eating?"

"Probably a bean burrito."

"Can she eat that?"

Felicia looks at the image again and smiles. "Right now, she can eat anything she wants. But she doesn't eat much."

"Oh. I see. Well," Christiana stands, "guess what *I* want."

"What?"

"Coffee, and a giant *cookie*."

"Tiana! You can't be serious!"

"And you can't tell me you *don't* want one"

"Yes, on the coffee. I'll have *some* of the cookie."

"*Some*. Okay," Christiana smiles wryly.

~

A half hour later, the boys burst around the corner into the food court and see their meals ready for them. Jacob falls into his seat, "I'm starved!" Oscar stops and kisses Felicia on the cheek. "Thank you, Mamma."

As they both attack their food, Oscar attempts to describe their expedition with mouthfuls of chicken nuggets dipped in chick-fil-a sauce. He sips his drink and mumbles, "Mmm, lemonade," through a macerated crisscross fry.

"Slow down, there Mijo," laughs Christiana.

Felicia tries to talk to Jacob, whose eyes are on his food. "Did you both find something you want?"

Oscar nods excessively, dipping and stuffing his little mouth.

"Jacob?"

He aborts his next bite, "Yeah. I found a skateboard," then resumes.

"Okay," Felicia grimaces at his terse explanation. "And both of you are keeping it to $150? That means we have to think about tax, too."

"Yes." Answers Oscar.

"Yes. We *know*, Mom," Jacob quips.

Felicia assesses him for a moment, fingers resting on her lips. Then in a calm voice directs him. "Jacob, put down the food, please."

He sullenly sets down his sandwich.

"Can you wipe your face and hands?"

He complies, not meeting her gaze.

She rises from her seat. "Thank you. Please come with me."

He rises slowly and follows her toward the mall, where they stand and talk near the walkway. Oscar watches them as he eats, then looks at his aunt, who has not turned to watch them.

"Did you boys have fun shopping together?"

"Yeah. It was great. Thank you, Aunt Tiana." Oscar glances at the scene. Jacob is standing head downward before his Mom as she speaks. She reaches toward him and tugs lightly on the front of his shirt. He looks up at her, and nods.

"I'm glad you had fun," Christiana continues.

Oscar diverts his eyes back to his food as they return, and then adds solemnly, "It would have been great if Jasmine were here, too."

"I know, Mijo."

Oscar feels for the Christmas card bag tucked beneath his shirt in his waistband. Felicia returns to her seat. Jacob sits too. He takes a sip from his Dr. Pepper, then turns to Christiana. “Aunt Tiana, thank you so much for your gift. We’ve had a really good time shopping.”

Christiana glances at Felicia, then smiles at Jacob. “Well, you are so welcome. You boys mean a lot to me.”

When the boys have finished their meal, they all clean up their encampment, and collect their things to head into the mall.

“Where to first, boys?” asks Christiana.

Oscar picks up the pace anxiously. “All my stores are first. Jacob’s is the last store on this level.”

They first enter the Sharper Image, just across the bridge. “You guys can stay out here,” Oscar directs, taking Aunt Tiana’s free hand and leading her into the store. “We’ll be really quick.”

Oscar goes directly to a display and picks up a travel razor. “This is my first gift,” he declares.

Christiana looks at it, puzzled. “A razor?”

“Yeah! It’s a travel razor, and it works on both battery *and* electricity.”

“But, why do you—“

“It’s for my Dad. He always uses the plastic ones, but I thought he would like one of these.” Oscar’s eyes are bright and shiny.

Christiana admires the gift and then runs her hand over his soft hair. “Are you sure?”

“Yes. It’s what I want,” he exudes.

She touches his chin. “Good choice.”

They go up to the counter to pay, and as they leave, Oscar asks “Can you help me keep track, so I don’t go over?”

“Yes. I will,” she agrees.

As they exit, Felicia turns to them and excitedly prods, “Okay? What did you get?”

Oscar is reluctant to say, so Christiana injects, “I think he wants to show all his presents at once—later, right Oscar?”

“Yeah,” he nods relieved. “All at once.”

“Okay,” Felicia agrees. “Where to next?”

Oscar points “Okay, back across the bridge,” and the little caravan proceeds.

On the other side, they enter the Christian bookstore, leaving the two outside again. Oscar leads the way to the back, where the children's section is. He takes a DVD from the shelf, "We don't have this Christmas movie yet." Then, a few steps over, he takes a small royal blue, hooded-sweatshirt off the rack. He holds it up to himself for Aunt Tiana to see. It shows cheerful cartoon-like figures representing the nativity scene. Above the scene are the words in alternating red and green letters, "Happy Birthday King Jesus!"

Christiana takes it from his hand and studies it. Then, she smiles broadly at Oscar. "For Jasmine?"

He nods.

"That should be perfect."

They pay for the gifts and exit again, heading for the Hallmark store. Inside, Oscar shows her a beautiful, plumb-colored, leather album.

"A photo album," she ponders.

He points to the description on the front "Yeah, it's a scrapbooking kit. See, it has stickers and labels to put around the pictures."

"For your Mom?"

"Yeah. For her and Jasmine to work on together."

"Wow, that's a great idea, Oscar. Your mom has all those pictures on her phone. They can pick out some together and print them in LA. I like that!"

They pay for the gifts, then enter the last store on Oscar's list--See's Candy. Christiana asks, "Okay, what do you want to get here?"

Oscar goes to the pre-packaged chocolate boxes. "Can you help me pick out which box to get? You and Mom like the same things, right?"

"That's true," She replies suspiciously.

"So, tell me which box *you* like, so I'll know what kind *she* likes."

"Oh, I see. Well. . ." She looks at all the options. "Is it *only* for her?"

He thinks for a minute. "Ummm…she'll probably share."

"Okay, then." She looks over the selection and grabs a box from the shelf. "I like nuts and chews, and so does she. If you get this one, it has both milk and dark chocolate, in case she shares."

He takes it eagerly. "Thank you, Aunt Tiana!" When they go

up to pay, Oscar adds five small, milk-chocolate Santas. The white-dressed lady offers them each a sample, but Oscar confesses that he already received one earlier.

"Well, aren't you sweet," she remarks with southern-infused affection. "You definitely deserve a second one for that!"

He grins, looking at his aunt, and takes the bon-bon. "Thanks!"

They pay and as they are leaving the store, Christiana looks over the receipts and takes out her phone to add them. "Sees: $29.68, Razor: 25.43, album, uh, 28.62, let's see, sweatshirt and DVD, 30.20. Then she looks up at Oscar.

"You found some good deals, Oscar. That's $113.93. You said this is the last stop for you? It looks like you still have just over $35 left."

"$35? Good. There's something else I want, but we can get it on the way back after Jake gets his gift?"

"Okay," she nods. "Sounds good."

They exit, Oscar gripping his bags of treasure. He holds out the bonbon cup to his Mom, "Here Mom. Now we each had one."

Felicia smiles and receives it with delight. "Why thank you." She takes a delicate bite, "Mmmm."

Oscar turns to Jacob brightly, "Okay Jake. Now it's your turn!"

"Great!" Jacob remarks, then masking his impatience, "I'm glad you got everything you wanted."

The group follows Jacob briskly to the skate shop at the end of the mall. "They're holding it for me up front," he explains, turning at the entrance to discover how far the caravan has fallen behind him. He repeats this when they arrive, as they walk up to the counter.

"Hey man, you're back!" calls out the sales guy with another stack of shoeboxes in his arms. He sets them on a nearby bench and comes to the register. "I got this," he tells the other clerk.

"Yeah, this is my aunt. She's getting me the skateboard I picked out."

The sales guy, trying to help his young friend, pulls out both skateboards held for Jacob behind the counter. "Was it this one? Or this one?"

Jacob falters, "No man. I told you, I can only afford the $130 board. That other one is over my budget."

Christiana becomes uneasy, but asks anyway. "How much is

the other one?"

The sales guy turns the board over to look, "$165."

Sensing the ambush, Felicia steps in "Yes, sorry. He'll have to get the first one. That one's over the budget."

"No, it's not!" intervenes Oscar. He turns quietly to his aunt. "Use my money to pay for the rest."

She bends toward him, "Are you sure? That's about . . . uhh . . . $25 with tax. What about your other present?"

"No, *this* is what I want. I am buying *everyone* a gift."

Felicia interrupts, "What's going on, here?"

Christiana straightens up and smiles, directing her words at the sales guy. "Well, we're buying that dragon skateboard for Jake."

"No, that's too much," Felicia insists. Jacob is watching them, confused.

Christiana looks down at Oscar, and smiles. "It's *not* too expensive, because Oscar wants to spend the rest of his money helping Jacob get his skateboard," she announces with warm triumph.

"What?" Amazes Jacob. "You're what?"

"Dude!" injects the sales guy.

Felicia tries to come over and put her hand on Oscar's shoulder, but the packages on her arm buffet him. "Mijo! Are you sure?"

Oscar looks around at them all, a little frustrated. "Yeah," he replies with conviction. "That's what I want."

Jacob looks at his brother. His eyes redden. "Thanks, Oscar."

Oscar grins back. "Merry Christmas."

Jacob puts his arm around Oscar's shoulder. "Merry Christmas, little brother."

They ring up Jacob's board and before they leave, Christiana calculates the final tally on her phone. "Oscar, you still have $11.17 left."

"Perfect. There is something that I *really* wanted, and it was $10.50. Will that be enough?"

Christiana puts away her phone and hands him all his receipts. "Yes, it is. I think you'll even have some change," she smiles.

They walk back to the Sharper Image and all go in to see what Oscar had really picked out for himself. At the front gadget display he selects a palm-sized clear rubber ball with multi-colored LED lights that flash inside when it bounces.

He holds it up for them to see. "Isn't it cool?"

Felicia smiles, "It *is* cool."

"Look," he explains, pointing to the package, "it's guaranteed to last for *one year*. That means if I save the receipt, and it stops working, they have to give me another one!"

"Smart shopping, Oscar," commends Aunt Tiana.

Following the last purchase of the day, they depart the mall, talking and laughing.

At the car, they pack the new items in their luggage, but leave some with Christiana until they return. Christiana helps Oscar pack his gifts, but he puts the ball in his backpack, and holds out one other thing.

"Jacob, we need to leave your skateboard here," directs Felicia.

He quietly huffs. "Mom, I want to take it—Oscar gave it to me so . . ."

"No, we can't. It's too big, and you don't even have your helmet. Besides, it's off limits around the hospital, and we don't know LA enough to let you just skate around."

"Okay," he relents.

"Put it in the back, Jacob, and I'll take it in the house," Christiana reassures.

Jacob admires his dragon board one more time, still sealed in plastic to protect the graphics. He pulls out his phone and snaps a picture to show Bryce, then puts it in the back of the SUV. "Aunt Tiana? What's this bag of stuff?"

She pops her head out the driver window where she now sits, checking her phone. "What bag, Mijo?"

"This big garbage bag."

"Oh, my goodness," she flusters for a moment, then calls back, "That's Alex's old stuff. I need to donate it. See if you want any of it." She turns to Felicia, who is packing her suitcase on the passenger seat. "You know, he sorted through *everything* in his room before he left for college. I just haven't had the courage to let go of his old things yet."

Jacob looks through the items and finds the high school baseball cap Alex always wore with his initials written in sharpie inside. "I'll take his cap," he announces, and puts it on his head, then hops into the car.

Felicia puts her suitcase and other bags in back, then gets in the passenger seat.

"Any more updates on your flight?"

"I don't know," Felicia settles in. "I haven't checked since we left the food court. Let's just get there and we'll find out what's going on."

Oscar calls from the back of the SUV "Can someone help me put my suitcase back in?"

Felicia turns to Jacob, "Go help him, Jake."

Jacob grumbles something indistinctly about "grow up" and slowly gets out of the car.

Oscar hops into his booster seat and sets a package beside him, then buckles in.

Jacob returns and Felicia stops him "Look around the car, Mijo, and make sure we didn't leave anything. Okay?" He huffs again but is thorough in his duty.

"We're good," he announces and hops into the car again.

"Okay, here we go," Christiana confirms, as they leave the mall for the airport, the sisters talking all the way.

At the curb of the airport, they unload and double check all their luggage. The sisters hug, then Christiana envelops Jacob.

"Thank you, Aunt Tiana for the Christmas gift."

She gives him an extra squeeze. "You're welcome, Mijo."

When Oscar goes for his hug, he reveals the Christmas-wrapped See's candy from behind his back. "This is really for you, Aunt Tiana. Thanks for the nice Christmas."

Christiana takes the box with a knowing look, "I might have thought. Mijo! You shouldn't have done that."

"It's what I wanted," he smiles, and hugs her waist.

They all reluctantly separate, waving.

"Merry Christmas!"

"Have a good flight!"

"Give Alex and Tyrell our love!"

"Give Jasmine a hug for me! Tell Bryce we missed him!"

And on it went until a satisfied family, warm in their hearts, parted for the time.

Now Felicia's eyes turn toward the terminal entrance, and the still uncertain journey ahead.

Chapter 7: A Man's Heart Plans His Way (Proverbs 16:9)

The family rolls their bags to the check-in counter line, as Felicia, arms full with her carry-on bag, purse, and Oscar's booster seat, searches for their flight on the board. It's 4:00. She finds it and notes that another half-hour has been added to the delayed departure time. The airport is bustling.

"Okay boys, double-check your backpacks for things that should be in your suitcase—no toiletries, or anything heavy that we can just check."

Oscar opens his backpack and scoots the items around. He checks the front zippered pocket too. Felicia catches a glimpse of something shiny. "Oscar, what's that?"

He sheepishly pulls out a small pair of safety scissors.

"You can't take that on the plane."

"I'm sorry. I forgot they were in there."

"Okay, put that in your suitcase."

Oscar quickly lays down his suitcase, unzips the big zipper, tucks the scissors in with his toiletries, re-zips, and then hops up in time to move forward with the line.

"Jacob?" Felicia prods.

"I already checked Mom," he drones, intently focused on his phone.

They arrive at the counter and check their bags and the booster seat with an efficient ticket agent, who is focused on processing their boarding pass and tagging and weighing the bags.

"Excuse me, is there any further update on our flight?" Felicia wonders.

The man clacks in several entries concentrating on his screen to print out the baggage tags. "We only know what is posted on the board. You'll have to inquire at the gate." He prints the boarding passes and hands them to Felicia with a practiced smile. "Here are your boarding passes. You are at gate C7, and you're all set. Have a great flight. NEXT!"

Felicia and the boys plod with the crowd through security screening, then traverse the terminal, past newsstands, and coffee coves, and fast food fronts, and souvenir shops, to locate their gate. Jacob plops down in the nearest chair, dropping his backpack beside him, as if he had just endured the most exhausting journey. He takes out his phone, and re-occupies himself, as Felicia directs Oscar to leave a seat open between them.

"I'm going to put my carry-on here, so watch it. Jacob, please put your backpack out of the aisle."

Oscar puts his backpack on the seat with his Mom's bag, and then sits back. "Okay, Mom. I'll watch it."

"I'm just going up to that counter there and see what the situation is."

At the counter, Felicia overhears an agent discussing the flight with another woman, who is pleading, "But when will you know? I *must* get to LA tonight!"

"Miss, I am so sorry about the delay, but we just don't know any more at this time. Please, be patient. *Everyone* is hoping to get there tonight."

"But, I don't understand." The woman has a musical accent and emphasizes her words by touching a loose fist gently on the counter. "The storm is not here. It is *east* of here. Why can't we go *west* of here?" Her distress increases with every word.

Felicia looks up at the latest flight information, which now shows the departure time as simply, "DELAYED."

"Again, I am so sorry," agonizes the agent, eyeing the growing line behind Felicia. She explains to the whole crowd, "The storm has caused delays around the nation, so the plane that was expected to be *here* for your flight is out of position. We are doing everything we can, and we will notify you when we have a definitive update."

This answers most questions, and people step out of line for the time. The agent turns to the woman in front of her with warm eyes and attempts to reassure her. "Please be patient. We are doing our best."

"Thank you," replies the woman, and turns reluctantly to leave the counter. Felicia sees that she is young, perhaps early 20's, and is wearing a lovely orange head scarf. Felicia nods at her with a smile of shared sympathy, but the young woman's eyes are downward, and her thoughts are inward.

Felicia steps up to the counter. "I heard what you said, and only wonder if there are any flights available for later tonight."

The agent tiredly replies, "I'm sorry, I've checked. All our flights are fully booked. How many are you?"

"There's three of us." Then, Felicia adds, "We're going to see my little girl in the hospital for Christmas."

The agent's eyes soften. "Your little girl is in the hospital?"

Felicia leans forward, laying her hand on the counter, lessening the space between them. "Yes. She's getting an experimental treatment. My husband is with her, and my boys and I are flying out to join them over Christmas break."

The woman looks to her screen and starts clacking. "That must be so hard. What hospital is she at?"

Felicia tries to glimpse the screen. "She's at Children's Hospital LA."

"Oh, that's good. That's a good hospital." She continues clacking. "I used to live in LA."

After a quiet moment, eyes scanning and moving between screens, she shakes her head. One more screen, and then she offers regrets, "I'm sorry, I don't see anything available at this point."

Felicia saddens. "Okay. Thank you so much for checking, though."

"Can I see your boarding pass?" Felicia retrieves the tickets and puts them on the high counter. The agent looks at them and notes, "Well, this is good—you have an early boarding position, which could give you priority on any seats that might open on another flight."

"Oh, well, that's good," Felicia cheers some.

"An opening is possible, but honestly, it's not likely that we could seat all three of you."

"Okay, well I appreciate all you've done."

"My pleasure. If something opens, I'll let you know. In the meantime, sit tight. We may get your plane here yet," the agent smiles encouragingly.

Felicia steps away from the counter and sends a text to Christiana and Bryce. "FLIGHT DELAYED FOR UNDETERMINED TIME. WILL UPDATE YOU WHEN WE KNOW MORE. LOVE YOU!"

She walks back to the boys and finds Jacob playing a game on his phone, and Oscar looking around the terminal, observing people.

"Well, we may have to wait a while before we know," she announces with a sigh. Jacob has his ear buds in. "Jacob!"

Jacob doesn't look up. "I heard you."

Felicia's phone chimes. It's Bryce: "OK. KEEP ME UPDATED. JUST GOT GAS. STILL DRIVING. SHOULD BE BACK IN 45 OR SO. MISS YOU!

"Will we be able to go tonight, Mamma?" worries Oscar.

Felicia replies to Bryce, then faces him, "I don't know yet, Mijo. We'll have to wait and see. I am sure everything will turn out okay, though."

"Should I pray?" Oscar asks.

Felicia smiles at him. "That's a good idea."

Oscar holds out his hand for hers. Surprised by his urgency, Felicia fumbles to put away her phone, and crouches down to take it. Oscar looks at Jacob, occupied, and decides not to reach for his hand. He then bows his head in the midst of the terminal, charged with the commotion of humanity, and begins to pray. Felicia lowers her head.

"Dear God. Please help us get to Jasmine in time for Christmas. Help everyone get where they need to go and to see their families. Amen."

"Amen."

~

Christiana's phone chimes, and she juggles the items in her hand to retrieve it from her purse. It is Felicia.

"I'M SORRY. LET ME KNOW IF I CAN HELP," she replies and slips the phone back into her purse, perched in the seat of her shopping cart, then returns her attention to the three cans of beans before her. She pushes up her reading glasses to examine the labels.

"I wish I had time to make them myself."

She finally settles on "Original Authentic" and puts two cans in her cart.

At the end of the aisle, she passes the stacks of packaged tortillas. "Now *that* I do have time for," and she heads for the produce section. There she selects several ripe tomatoes, 2 large yellow onions, fresh jalapeño peppers, garlic, cilantro, limes, and romaine lettuce. She consults the list on her phone.

"Okay, fresh salsa, salad . . . Meat." She wheels to the butcher and selects a small skirt steak. A few feet further, she approaches the seafood counter. The aproned man behind the display smiles, "How can I help you?"

Christiana peers behind him to the empty lobster tank.

"Hi. You don't have any live lobsters, do you?"

"No, I'm sorry. We don't get much call for that around Christmas."

"Oh, well what do you have available?"

The man takes a few steps over and points into the case. "We do have these previously frozen tails."

Christiana looks at the gray, weeping tails, "Well, it was supposed to be a special dinner."

The man squints sympathetically, shaking his head, "I'm sorry, no. You might want to try the Fish Market down on—"

"They actually closed early." She assesses the frozen tails again. "No, that'll be fine. I'll take two, please."

"Okay." The man opens the case. "Like these two?"

She nods, "Yeah, that'll be fine. Thank you."

The man grabs the lobster tails with a plastic bag, and places them on the scale, then punches out the sticker. "So, do you boil them?" he asks, making conversation as he pulls a sheet of waxed butcher paper from the roll and wraps them.

"No, actually. Have you ever heard of Puerto Nuevo style lobster?"

He hands the package to Christiana. "I'm not sure I have."

"Well, it's a style of grilled lobster popular in Mexico, and you serve it with drawn butter, and pinto beans, and rice, and warm tortillas with fresh salsa. It's really delicious."

"That sounds amazing. I'll have to look up that recipe some time." The man rests his hands on the edge of the counter. "What do you usually drink with that?"

"Well, traditionally you serve a good Mexican beer, but I might get wine for tonight."

"White wine, you think?"

Christiana places the package in her cart. "That's a good question. My husband likes red wine, and we are also having carne asada steak with this, but I usually like white."

The man grins, "Maybe you should just stick with tradition. It's probably the best."

"Perhaps you're right," she agrees.

~

At home, Christiana unloads the groceries and all the packages from the day. She sets Jacob's new skateboard under the tree for his return, switches on the twinkle lights, and starts playing Christmas music over the speakers. She puts everything else away but sets out a new gift to wrap for Tyrell later.

Christiana first rinses and puts a pot of rice on, then she cleans the kitchen from the breakfast feast. Next, she washes the ingredients for salsa, and finely chops the firm tomatoes, the cilantro, the jalapeño, the garlic, and onion, the way her mother has always done it—on a wooden cutting board. "It adds flavor," she would say.

"JOY TO THE WORLD THE LORD IS COME," Christiana bellows exuberantly. She scrapes the salsa ingredients into a bowl and sets it in the refrigerator. Then she minces garlic, and slices onion, putting it in a bowl with fresh squeezed lime juice, olive oil, a few jalapeño slices, chili powder, cumin, Mexican oregano, and cilantro leaves, and stirs to blend it. She unwraps the skirt steak and slides it into a Ziploc bag, pours the marinade over the meat, squeezes out the air, and places it aside on the counter.

Next, she gets out her old wooden salad bowl, shiny from the light coat of oil, and sets the matching wooden utensils next to the garlic she has reserved, and the fresh block of parmesan. She notes that her jar of anchovies is still good, then rinses off the romaine leaves and sets them aside to drain.

She mixes the masa and is about to get out her tortilla press when her phone rings. It is Tyrell. She quickly mutes the music, noting the time. 5:30. Her heart quickens a beat as she answers.

"Hi! How's it going? . . ." She listens.

Now disappointed, "What do you mean you *have* to work?

Why can't they get someone else? . . ." Listening.

"Well, how late will you be? . . ."

Growing frustrated, "Tyrell, it's Christmas Eve . . ."

Indignant, "Well who am *I?* Tyrell, you have a family too. . . ."

Wounded, "But you're *always* the one to work late . . ."

Skeptical, "We don't need it *that* bad . . ." Listening.

Incensed, "I *mean* that it's Christmas Eve and your wife is alone, *that's* what I mean . . ."

"Of *course,* you have to go. . ." she renounces.

"Fine. Bye."

Christiana sets her phone down and surveys her kitchen full of plans. Her phone screen shows the merry icon of her waiting Christmas music, which she closes. She puts away the extra garlic, the wooden bowl and utensils, the block of parmesan, the cans of beans, and the bowl of masa. The rice is finished, and she shuts it off to steep in the pot. She puts the marinating steak in the refrigerator. The brown package of lobster tails sits on the shelf.

"That will go to waste."

She closes her eyes with the refrigerator door. "What a waste." The rest of the house is quiet and dark apart from the kitchen lights and the Christmas tree. She goes into the living room and turns on the lamp. Oscar's box of See's candy, wrapped in Christmas love, sits on the coffee table, next to the new gift she got for Tyrell.

"Ha!"

She sits on the couch, evaluating the two presents.

"Lord, help me."

~

Bryce pulls up to the entrance of the hospital, and parks in the 15-minute passenger zone. Jasmine's eyes flutter open, and she turns her head on the pillows to meet her father's eyes in the mirror.

"We're back, Pumpkin. How are you doing?"

She looks around, orienting in the darkness, and scrunches the blankets closer to her chin.

"Good," she groggily replies.

"Okay. Let's get you back upstairs, and then I'll park the car and bring the rest of the stuff up. Sound good?"

Jasmine nods.

"Okay, then. Let's put your jacket back on. It's pretty chilly."

Jasmine nods again and reluctantly uncovers herself to put her jacket on. Bryce goes to the back and pulls out the wheelchair, then brings it beside Jasmine's door and opens it. Jasmine slides her feet back into her slippers, and he helps her get into the wheelchair, taking one of the blankets to cover her lap. He locks the door, and wheels her into the hospital, through the vast lobby, past the gift shop, the smiling information desk, the comfortable furniture and colorful art inspirations, and into the elevator.

"Did you have fun?" Bryce asks.

After a moment, "It was beautiful, Daddy. Just how I imagined it."

"I enjoyed it, too. Very much."

Upstairs, Bryce rolls Jasmine off the elevator, "More than I thought I would, actually."

Jacqui is standing at the nurse's station and comes around the counter to meet them. "Well, that was a long day! You went on quite an adventure."

"We did!" replies Jasmine.

"Well, you'll have to tell me about it." Jacqui walks to the back of the wheelchair to take the handles. "How about I help her get settled, and give you a little break," she offers Bryce.

"That would be great. Thank you. I need to go re-park the car and get the rest of the stuff out." He bends to give Jasmine a kiss on her forehead, lifting her little hat some. "I'll be right back."

Bryce returns to the car, cleans out the trash into the nearby receptacle, opting to keep Jasmine's unfinished bean burrito, and drives the car into the parking structure. He gathers her shoes, her burrito, one water bottle, and the pinecone, and puts them in the plastic bag, carefully tucking the pinecone into one of her shoes. He decides to replace her car seat before he picks up the family, then he gathers the sprawling blanket and pillow pile into his arms, locks the car, and walks back to the hospital.

When he arrives at Jasmine's room, she is already tucked cozily into her bed, telling Jacqui about feeding the birds. Bryce sets the pile of bedding on the chair with the other blanket and unpacks the bag. Jacqui takes up the bedding, untangling the blankets from the pillows as Jasmine talks.

Bryce interrupts, "Jasmine picked out this little pinecone as her souvenir of the day." He pulls it out of the shoe and holds it up.

"Nice," nods Jacqui, folding the blankets and placing them on top of the couch.

"Where do you want your pinecone?" he asks.

"Right here," Jasmine points to her tray. "I want to look at it." Bryce sets it on the tray, then folds the bag to save for later. He takes off his jacket and drapes it over the back of a chair.

Jacqui puts the two pillows on the blankets and carries the stack to the door. "I'll take care of these and see what they have for your dinner."

"Where's Lily?" asks Jasmine.

Bryce stops and looks around the room nervously.

"Who?" asks Jacqui, paused at the door with her armload.

"Lily. My lamb. Where's my lamb?"

Jacqui returns and sets the blankets back down in the chair. "Oh Honey, I don't know." She starts carefully dismantling the pile. "I haven't seen your lamb." Bryce hasn't moved, hoping that Jacqui's reevaluation will produce Lily. His eyes scan under the chair, under the bed, by the door, on the bed, on the counter, in the trash. He tries to remember when he last saw it. It *had* to be on the way home. Even though he can imagine it, he can't be certain he saw it. He starts to visualize all the times in and out of the car. His heart sickens.

"Nope. It's not here," Jacqui nervously confirms. It's not in the bed with you?"

Jasmine pulls back the covers to reveal her slender, night-gowned body, alone. Jacqui looks at Bryce to gather the import of the situation. His eyes are fixed and wide.

"Mr. Goodson, why don't you go check the car again, and we'll do a good search around here, okay?" she coolly directs him. He nods, and retreats from the room, heart pounding, eyes scanning every floor, every surface, every nook, both possible, and impossible, for the little white lamb. He takes the same elevator, he asks at the information desk, his eyes cast far and wide as he exits the front of the building, pausing at the passenger loading, then crossing the lot to the parking structure. He tracks his way methodically back to the car, where he tears through it breathlessly, unfailingly. Unrequited.

He walks back to the hospital, now checking under cars and in trash cans, stopping again at the information desk, his desperation smearing the smiles from their faces, as they hurriedly jot his information and assure him they will stay vigilant. He approaches the room hoping for their success, and when he enters, Jacqui's quick expectant look tells him that the lamb is lost.

His heart aches, his face falls. He wills himself to Jasmine's bedside, eyes downward. He strokes the stubble on his face. His glasses begin to fog a little on the bottom.

"I'm sorry, Pumpkin. I looked everywhere. I don't know where Lily is."

Jasmine's eyes are wide, her mouth soft in astonishment. The room is still, holding its breath. Her eyes redden and moisten. She blinks a quiet tear.

Then with steady conviction, "Daddy. You *have* to go find Lily."

Bryce's mind staggers in disbelief. He stammers for the rebuttal. "Jasmine, I—I looked everywhere, I mean, maybe someone found her on the ground and will turn her in, but I looked *everywhere*."

"I don't mean look for her *here*," she persists.

His mind is reeling. "You mean at Big Bear?" *Absolutely not*, he thinks. Exhausted at the idea.

"Daddy, you *have* to find my lamb." Her reserved nature collapses in despair.

He runs his hand through his hair, imagining such a thing. He becomes firm, "Jasmine. No. I can't do that. We'll get you another lamb—just like her. I remember where we bought her, and we can—"

Eyes wild in fright, "Lily is not replaceable!" she insists, rebuking him just as firmly. "There *is* no other lamb like her. She's *my* lamb. She has *always* been with me. She has been with me through *everything*!" Her open hand thumps down on the bed beside her.

"Do you think that *one* lamb is just as good as *another*?" she challenges him, tears dropping from her eyes.

As good as another? *As good as another*? What is she saying? What is she thinking? He glances at Jacqui, who is a silent, trapped witness.

Bryce remembers Jasmine's challenge. "N—no Sweetheart. One is *not* the same as another," he pledges to her. "They are *all* unique. They are *each* special. They are *irreplaceable* to the ones who love them."

Her eyes hold his steadfastly in a promise. "Then find my lamb, Daddy. Find my lamb."

He stammers, anguished by the magnitude of its significance, and the impossibility of the task. "But—but it could be *anywhere*. All those *stops* we made . . ."

"No, Daddy. I *know*. It's gotta be at the *first* stop," she wipes her eyes with her fingertips, hopeful.

Bryce tries to recall. "Where we looked at the view? By that little waterfall?"

"Yes. Daddy, go there, and you'll find my lamb. I *know* you will."

She is smiling, little nose now pink—from the bright day, or from crying, he's not sure—nodding her little head encouragingly, now naked without the soft, pink hat she wore all day, her thin, short hair struggling to grow. He remembers her long, thick, wavy brown hair, like Felicia's, flowing around her shoulders.

His heart is heavy, envisioning that long drive, in the dark. Leaving Jasmine alone—for at least six hours. With her like *this*—her heart so intertwined with her lamb?

How can he *do* it?

How can he *refuse*?

He looks at Jacqui, who shrugs her shoulders apprehensively to say, "You could *try*."

Bryce takes his glasses off and runs his hand firmly down over his face. "Ahhhhh," he exhales."

"Thank you, Daddy!" Jasmine blurts, throwing her arms open to him.

He looks at her bright face and chuckles under his breath, *this is crazy*. "Okay, Pumpkin." He steps to her and bends to receive his hero's hug. "I'll try. Okay? I will do my *best*. And that's my only promise."

"I'm not worried," she beams. "You're not going alone."

"Ha," he blurts. "I'll need all the help I can get," and he turns to Jacqui, who anticipates his concerns.

"I'll take care of her here, and when my shift ends in about an hour, I can grab some dinner and come and visit with her until she goes to sleep." Jacqui turns to Jasmine, "How does that sound?"

"Great!"

Bryce grabs his jacket again, "But it's Christmas Eve, Jacqui, we can't ask you to do that."

"Oh, no it's fine," she waives. "My Mom is staying with her brother to celebrate Christmas, since I work again tomorrow. I would just go home to an empty house, and probably eat fast food, and watch "It's a Wonderful Life" again. You just go, and don't worry." She turns and winks at Jasmine, "We'll have some Christmas fun here."

"Okay, thanks." He checks his pockets for his phone and keys. "Hopefully, Felicia and the boys will fly in soon to take over, but I don't know for sure. You have my cell number at the nurses' desk, and it's on that little paper by her phone too, if you need to call to me." He bends and kisses Jasmine again, "Bye, Pumpkin."

"Bye, Daddy."

He goes to the door, hastily, "Thanks Jacqui."

"Happy to help, Mr. Goodson. Good luck!" she calls after him.

As he strides through the corridors, he takes out his cell and calls Felicia.

"Hi Bryce," she answers, a little dismayed. "Are you back at the hospital?"

He hesitates, "Ahhh, yeah. Any news on your flight?"

"Bryce, it doesn't look good. I have a feeling that they're about to cancel the flight, and then all these people will need to be rescheduled."

"Well, what do you want to do, Honey?" He crosses the parking lot to the structure, breathing loudly.

"What are you doing? You sound out of breath," she interrupts.

"I'll tell you in a minute. What do you think you should do?"

She hesitates. "Well, I don't think we can get a flight out tonight. We might be able to book one for some time tomorrow, but I don't know when. I would hate to fly in, who knows when, on Christmas day . . ."

"So, what are you thinking?"

"I don't know, Amore. . . What if we just *drove* there?"

"*Drive* here?" he echoes, full of angst. "I'd rather you didn't." Bryce reaches the car, climbs in, and starts it.

"I know, but we would be there in about five hours," Felicia lobbies. "It would be . . . like 11:00 when we got there."

Bryce leans his head against his arm on the steering wheel. "But Honey, we already talked about this when we made our plans. That's a long drive. There could be rain, or snow going either way. That car has been having problems, and now we'd be committing to driving *both* ways. It was supposed to be quick and simple."

"I know Bryce, but it's *not* 'quick and simple.'"

"But what about the flight we paid for? We can't get a refund on both ways. And I'm supposed to fly back with your parents, and you're supposed to keep the SUV. Now we'll have *both* cars to pay for parking, and then I'll have to drive all the way back again."

"But you *like* to drive," she reminds him.

"That's funny," he mumbles.

"What?"

"Nothing."

"Bryce, what's wrong?"

He sighs and collects his thoughts. "Look, Honey, I think that driving should be the *last* option. If we had originally planned it that way, I would have had the car serviced before I left, and I am not sure that the tires are good enough for both ways. I don't want you making that long drive, in the winter, at night, across a lot of open space. Maybe in the daytime, but not at night. Okay?"

"Okay, Bryce. We won't."

"Besides, by the time you get your luggage, wait for your sister, go back and re-pack the car, it'll be even later before you leave."

"I know. You're right. If we have to do it at all, which we probably won't, it will be tomorrow. Last resort."

"Good."

"Okay. Now what's going on there?"

Bryce sits up and takes a deep breath. "Okay, this is going to sound crazy."

"Bryce. What's wrong?"

"Okay. We lost Jasmine's lamb, Lily."

"Oh no."

"And . . . I'm going back to look for it."

"Back? Where?"

"Umm . . . To Big Bear."

"No Bryce, you can't. That's crazy."

"I know, but I *have* to. I promised."

"No Bryce. Jasmine should not have made you promise that."

"You didn't see her. She started crying . . ."

"She was *crying*?"

"Yeah. When I said we'd get her *another* lamb, she asked me if I thought that we could just replace her. That 'one lamb is just as good as another lamb.'"

"Oh Bryce, what does she mean?"

"What do you *think* she means?"

Felicia ponders the significance. "Oh, our poor Baby."

"Yeah, so you see? I *have* to go."

"But—how will you ever find it?"

"Well, she said she knew where to look. "

"Like she remembered something?"

"I don't know. Maybe. Or like she had a *strong feeling* it was there, for whatever reason."

"I just don't like the idea of you driving all the way out there again, you know?"

"I know. Me neither."

"She'll be alone a long time. Is she going to be okay? I hate to think of her sitting there all alone, worried about her lamb."

"You know, she was so relieved when I agreed to look. It was like I had already found her little lamb. She just seemed to let go."

"Really?"

"Yeah, and her nurse, Jacqui, said she'll sit with her—that they'll have some 'Christmas fun.'"

"But Bryce, she's a stranger. *I* should be there with her. This is not right. She'll just get disappointed again when you can't find it."

"Maybe, but for now, she seems fine. And besides, who knows. Maybe we'll have a Christmas miracle."

"Oh, I hope so."

"Okay, I gotta go. Keep me updated on the flight."

"I will. Love you"

"Love you."

Bryce places his phone where he can see it in the center console, then backs out to embark on his long, night's uncertain quest. Wearily, he puts the car into drive and leaves the hospital behind, venturing alone into the dark, unfamiliar, wilderness of a desolate Christmas Eve.

"Oh, God," he sighs.

Chapter 8: Aunt Tiana

Christiana gets up from the couch and goes into the kitchen. She heats some tea in her favorite Christmas mug and returns to sit in the center of the couch again. She rests her feet on the edge of the coffee table, leans back into the cushions, and cups the warm cup close to her chin. In the quiet house, her eyes wander over the lighted Christmas tree, and the little ceramic nativity. She takes a sip.

On the table at her feet sit a small, black, rectangular box, and the Christmas-wrapped pound of See's chocolates. After a moment, Christiana drops her feet to the ground and sits forward to retrieve the box of See's. She smiles wryly and unwraps the package, then opens the classic white box, removes the bubble-wrap liner, and surveys the assortment of bonbons. With a measure of glee, she selects the smooth, milk chocolate confection of her desire, leaving the lid propped open for her imminent return. She leans back into the cushions, feet up, resting her mug on her chest, and takes a first, rich, creamy bite. The sweet chocolate melts with consolation over her soul.

She sips her tea ceremonially after each small bite, and licks her fingers when the piece is finished, savoring the velvety sweetness. Then with delight, she sits up to assess more of the chocolate temptations, and selects another bonbon. She leans back again and releases a deep sigh. "Thank you, Little Oscar."

Her eyes wander back to the rectangular, black, gift box still on the table. She contemplates its fate, nibbling and sipping in repose. Finally, she licks her fingers and sits up to address the looming little box. She lifts it and opens the lid to examine the men's silver watch with cobalt blue accents sitting in a bed of red fabric. She removes the watch and evaluates the engraving on the back plate, sipping her tea. She reads, “All my love until the end of time.” She takes another sip.

“Ha!”

She replaces the watch, closes the lid, and sets it on the table. She takes another sip, studying it, like a body to be disposed of. Another sip.

“All my love . . .”

She reclines again, crossing her legs, fingers twirling her hair. Her eyes wander over the empty Christmas room. Another sip. They return to the little black box. Another cold sip.

She uncrosses her legs and sits forward, studying that box.

“Well,” she sets down her mug, “I can only do my part. The rest isn’t up to me.” She gets up, walks into the office and returns with a roll of wrapping paper, scissors, ribbon, and tape, and begins to measure out the love for her husband.

Fifteen minutes later, she sits back sipping her freshened tea and indulging in another treat as she evaluates the optimistic package on the table with the tag, “For My T.” She licks the residual chocolate from her fingers, pops up from the couch, and places the gift under the tree, then carries her mug to the counter, grabs her purse and keys, and heads out the door. “I need some real food, and I’m not doing another thing in that kitchen.”

~

The wet streets gleam with streaks of green and red lights after a light shower. As Christiana drives, her tires splosh rhythmically on the pavement. The downpour seems to have stopped for the time.

The line at the new In-N-Out is vastly longer than she expected. Cars come in from two directions, creating some uneasy Christmas tension, which everyone attempts to mitigate with orderly gestures, and shows of patience toward one another. As she debates whether to just back out and go somewhere else, two cars pull in quick succession behind her, complicating her escape.

While she awaits her turn to order, her phone chimes. It is a text from Alex, attached with a photo of himself wearing a dress shirt, tie, and a Santa hat, surrounded by several enthusiastic children: HAVING A BLAST WITH THE KIDDOS! LUV U!

Sunshine enters her heart. WONDERFUL! I’M SO PROUD

OF YOU MIJO! she quickly replies. Then she notices that Alex's text was sent to Tyrell also, clouding her thoughts again with questions. She begins to recall their strange argument many weeks ago.

It started when she noticed their credit card bill showed a $2,500 purchase that they hadn't discussed. Tyrell was leaving for the gym when she asked him what it was. He said a used jet ski and trailer. That it was a great deal, and it's something he's always wanted. Stunned, she asked him where it was, and he confessed that it was at his buddy's house until he could get the hitch installed on the SUV. She asked why he didn't tell her, and he said that he was going to. She couldn't understand how he could keep such a big secret from her, and she was hurt. But instead, she said:

"I don't understand why you spent all this money, when you know things are really tight right now."

Then he said, "Well, I'm in *debt* right now because of all the money we spend on YOUR son to go to that fancy college."

Shocked, she couldn't let the extraordinary accusation pass, and unleashed a confused tirade, "MY son? You're now saying MY son?"

His lips closed tight, he crossed his arms in defense. Bewildered at his silence, she bore deeper.

"Are you telling me that it didn't mean anything to you when you adopted him 15 years ago? When he took YOUR name? It means nothing that he hasn't known ANY other father but YOU? Certainly not Franco!"

She thought he would retract the weapon of his words, hearing the pain he had inflicted on her without warning.

He stammered and tried to retreat to the living room, her close behind, waiving the bill by her head as she spoke, but not because the bill meant anything anymore, but because she didn't have any idea what was happening. Finally, he turned from his retreat and faced her: "You don't understand!" He jutted his finger downward, preparing to incite indictments she had never heard raised.

"No, Tyrell, I don't understand." She opened her posture, she attempted to soften, but her energy was full of fear. "Please tell me."

He thrust his head away in disbelief, taking her tone as incredulity. "Hmph! You don't *want* to understand."

She took a step to close the gap, the bill still waiving with her hand gestures like a red cape. “I don’t *want* to understand? I don’t *want* to understand?”

He turned his eyes away. He blinked. Was it a tear? Was it angry restraint? Then he let loose, “What *am* I to you? I’m nothing! I am just some man who pays bills and does chores. *Who* am I to you really? You don’t even *respect* me!”

At this accusation, she turned around, took a few steps away, then turned back, full of disbelief, “I don’t know *what* you are talking about. *Where* is this coming from?”

He closed his mouth, he crossed his arms, he shook his head—longer than she expected—shaking an idea out, or away. Finally, “I can spend MY money *any* way I want. I get no respect—not from you, not from my job—I’m just some stand-in. A body, but I’m not really here, am I?”

At this she crossed her arms, the bill creasing into them. She opened her mouth, but no words offered themselves. She blinked, and started to feel the sting of tears, which she swallowed back. He stood waiting, arms slack.

Finally, she surrendered in quiet confusion, “I don’t know what you’re talking about. Fifteen years of marriage, and I don’t even know who you are.”

He didn’t respond. His jaw tightened in resolve.

She saw this and had a moment to decide. She was hurt. The pain seemed unjustified, and intentional, and the injustice arising in her overwhelmed all other perspectives. He made no attempt to heal or resolve the side-tracked dispute but stood silently. After a moment, “How dare you say that to me,” she coldly charged. Silence. Then, prodding him to respond, “It sounds to me like you want *out* of this.”

He didn’t confirm or deny. He crossed his arms again and turned his eyes away.

At his silence, she concluded the matter. “Well, you do what you need to, to feel like you have some *respect*.” Then she turned to walk away, and gestured a frivolous waive of her hand, the bill flapping like a white flag, “I don’t know where that came from. We’re having chicken and rice for dinner, if you feel like coming home for it.”

That was several weeks ago. They have been at a sterile truce since then, not willing to discuss it, and not openly acknowledging it might mean the start of the end for them.

~

An In-N-Out worker wearing raingear cheerfully approaches Christiana's car, with an electronic ordering tablet in hand. "Hi! What can I get for you today?"

Christiana orders a Double-Double with raw onions, French fries, and a chocolate shake. As she sits in line, inching forward occasionally, she notices a young man looking through a trashcan in the parking lot. He carefully pulls all the crumpled white paper bags out, and investigates the contents, if any. He sets each inspected bag on the ground and reaches for the next one. Occasionally he seems to find a few French fries, but little else.

She is startled by her phone ringing to life. It is Felicia.

She answers, "Hi! What's going on?"

Felicia sounds tense in her report, "Hi Tiana, I'm sorry, but I need a favor."

Christiana watches the young man carefully replace all the rolled up white paper bags back in the trashcan, leaving nothing on the ground to blow away. "Sure, what is it?"

"Ahh, well…" she begins uncertainly. "Okay. This is a big deal. I got booked onto a flight out tonight, but there are no seats for the boys."

"You're kidding." Christiana creeps forward and is now one car away from the payment window.

"I know it's a lot to ask, but I got the boys booked on a 6:30 flight tomorrow morning. I would wait, but there's something going on with Bryce and Jasmine, and she's alone right now. I just have to get out there."

"Is everything okay?" Christiana sees the young man go to another trash can. He is a little closer now and looks familiar.

"It's okay, but I don't want Jasmine alone right now. . . It's complicated. I can explain it later."

"Okay. So, you want me to pick up the boys, then?"

"Yes, please, would you? I am so sorry."

"No, it's okay. I have nothing going on. Are they ready now?" Christiana pulls up to pay and attempts to mouth her interaction with the polite cashier.

"Actually, my flight leaves in an hour. Can you meet them out front in about 45 minutes? I want to spend that time with them. Like about 7:20?" The cashier hands Christiana her receipt and thanks her, but the line has not moved forward yet to get the food.

"Yeah, I can do that. And then take them to the airport in the morning?"

"I'm sorry, do you mind?

"No, that's fine. *Any* way I can help."

"Okay. Have to go figure out their luggage. I'll talk to you in a bit, okay?"

"Okay."

"Thanks!!" Felicia hastily hangs up.

Christiana returns her phone to her purse, and watches the young man once again carefully replace the trash. He walks away toward another trashcan and crosses in front of the first car's headlights. She remembers where she saw him.

She was driving her route a few weeks ago, when he got onto the bus. He picked through the change in his hand, dropping in each coin until they were gone. It wasn't enough. He was embarrassed because he thought it cost less, and realized he was looking at the child's fare. He had a bulky, plastic garbage bag with him, and since she had already pulled away from the curb, he sadly suggested she just drop him off at the next stop. He looked like he had been walking around for a few days but seemed out of his element. She told him not to get off and handed him a pass for the whole day. He thanked her with a shy and grateful smile. She took the money out of her purse at the next stop and put it in the money counter. He seemed surprised.

"I thought you guys got those for free," he wondered.

"No," she explained, "We pay just like you do. I can't give away fares. But I am happy to help."

~

Finally, Christiana arrives at the drive-through window and receives her meal and shake. "Thank you." She pulls aside to put her straw in the shake and notices the young man examining what must be the last trashcan in the lot. A warm, light feeling fills her heart. She turns and pulls up near him.

"Hi!" she calls, setting her brake and stepping out of the car. "I remember you."

He looks up from his work, appearing more bedraggled, more

emaciated than he had before. He seems to be trying to recall her, when she adds, "I was your bus driver, I guess a few weeks ago?"

A big smile crosses his face, and he takes a humble step toward her. He starts to extend his hand but looks at it and thinks better. "Yes, I remember you! You were so nice to me. You really helped me out that day!"

"Well, I'm glad to hear." She notices he doesn't have the large garbage bag with him.

"Hey, where are your things?"

"Well," he begins, a little ashamed, "I fell asleep in the park—in the middle of the day too—and when I woke up, it was gone."

"Oh. I'm so sorry."

He shrugs.

"Can I ask—and it's not my business—but it doesn't seem like this is *your* kind of life. I mean, why are you out here?"

He looks around some, "It's not really my first choice."

"What happened, if you don't mind?"

He shrugs again. "No, I don't mind. After I graduated this year, I guess my step-dad got sick of having me around. See, I got a summer job, but I lost it, and when he found out, he just kicked me out. He said 'You're 18 now. Time to take care of yourself.'"

"Oh, I'm so sorry. What about your Mom?"

"Well . . . he won't let my Mom help me out, and he's in charge of the money anyway. I think she's a little scared of him."

"I see. I'm sorry. That's too bad."

"Anyway, when he kicked me out, I only had time to grab a garbage bag and throw some stuff in it, and that was it." He shrugs again, hands in his pockets, eyes downward.

Christiana evaluates the youth. "So, you've been on the street ever since?"

"Well, no actually. My friend's mom let me stay with them for a while. I think she was worried about me being out in the heat all summer."

"That was nice of her."

"Yeah, but they had a small place, and it got to be too much. I did get a job while I was there, but it took a long time before I actually started to work, and then longer before I was going to get paid. My friend's mom couldn't take me being there anymore, and so I had to leave. I guess because I had a job, she thought I'd figure it out. But my first paycheck was, like nothing, and it got hard to sleep outside and get to work and all that. It got complicated. Actually, I was trying to get to work that day on the bus when you helped me out. I think they just didn't like me showing up, not really clean, and I would hang around too long after my shift 'cause I had nowhere to go. They just decided to let me go."

"I'm sorry."

"Oh, that's okay. It was only part-time, and it wouldn't exactly pay for rent or anything. Anyway. I've been on the street probably a month now."

"What's your name?" She holds out her hand, "I'm Christiana."

"I'm Andrew. You can call me Drew—but not Andy." He shakes her hand.

"Well, Andrew. I have some dinner here. Double-Double and fries? How's that sound?"

His eyes widen, and his body animates in anticipation, "No, I can't take that from you, Ma'am."

She reaches into the car and pulls out the stuffed, white paper bag. "Christiana. And yes, you can." She hands him the bag, and then pops her head back in to retrieve the shake. "Do you like chocolate?"

He reaches eagerly for the cup, "I like everything right now! Thank you!"

Christiana's heart grows light and warm. She hears words she hadn't planned to say.

"You know, Andrew, there is a Father who loves you unconditionally. He doesn't care if you have a job. He doesn't care if you've messed up. He just wants to love you. Do you know who that is?"

He shrugs sheepishly. "God?"

"Yes. God loves you, and he's a wonderful Father. He has a good plan for your life, and He wants to help you with everything. It isn't a coincidence that I saw you here today—or that I saw you on my bus. God has a plan for you, and He wants you to know you can trust Him. Would you like to trust Him?"

"I would," he hesitates. "But I'm not very religious."

Christiana smiles. "I'm not very religious either. I just love Him because He loves me. You've heard of Jesus, right?"

"Yeah,"

"Well we celebrate Christmas because God loves us so much that he actually *left heaven* to come down and solve our biggest problem himself. He came to pay for our sins. He humbled himself and was born as a baby, grew up into a man, and then gave *His* life so that *we* would have life. So, we could live with Him forever. We would never be without Him. Does that sound like something you might want?"

"Sure. I would."

"Well, it's a free gift. You only have to believe that it's true. Do you think you can do that?"

"Sure. I mean, I know there's a God, I just didn't think He was that interested in me."

"Well now you know. You mean *everything* to Him. He gave *everything* to have you. You only have to tell Him you believe that Jesus did this for you. Even now you can tell him," she pats his shoulder and smiles.

"Okay." He surprises her, and bows his head, eyes closed. "God, I believe in Jesus. I need you to be my Father." He opens his eyes and looks at her, bright with a peaceful twinkle.

"There you go!" she laughs. "That's how you start your relationship with God. He will never leave you or turn His back on you. And He won't throw you out." Christiana smiles and gives him a big hug.

"Wow, thank you." His eyes are watering.

"Hold on, I have something for you." Christiana pops her head into her car again and releases the hatch. She goes to the back and retrieves Alex's donation bag. "See if there's anything in there you would like. It was my son's."

Andrew bends over and pushes through the bag. "There's a lot of good stuff in here. There's even a sports bag to carry it in. Are you sure?" He starts selecting out clothes and stuffing them into the high school duffle bag.

"Yes, take it all. He wanted to donate it anyway." Andrew pulls out a satin Denver Broncos jacket, thick and warm.

He holds it up to his slim, chilled body. "I think it will fit." He quickly slips it on and snaps up the front. "Oh, that's so much better. Thank you!"

"I'm so glad it fits. My son outgrew it last year. He plays

football, and he just really sprouted getting ready for college."

Andrew looks at the dark blue and orange jacket. "Broncos, huh?"

"Yeah. That's his team," she smiles fondly. "Just a minute." She gets into the car and sits down. After a moment she gets back out and stands facing him.

"You see that blue and yellow sign down the block there?"

He looks in that direction, "Yeah?"

"That's a good motel. I know the people who run it. Tell them I sent you, and you'll get a good deal. It should be about $50 a night."

"But—"

"Here's $125. That's all I have right now." She hands him the folded bills discreetly. "I want you to spend the next two nights there. Here is my phone number. Call me the day after Christmas, and I am going to take you down to the bus terminal to apply for a job. They need bus washers, and I think I can get you in. How's that sound?"

Andrew is speechless. His eyes fill with tears and he hugs her with all his strength. "Oh, Mamma Christiana! It's too much! It's more than I could ever hope for! You've saved me!"

She laughs. "No Mijo, God has saved you, I just get to help."

He hugs her again, tears flowing. "Thank you so much!"

"Okay, now do you want me to give you a ride down there?"

"No, I feel too excited! I need to walk there."

"Okay, but go *straight* there."

"I will. Don't worry! I'm going to eat this amazing meal, and then take a shower, and then sleep, sleep, sleep! If I can! And if this is a dream, I hope to never wake up."

"It's not a dream, Mijo. God loves you." She rubs the shoulder of the jacket fondly, beaming at his young joy.

"I believe it!" He lifts his face toward heaven and shouts with exuberance, "Thank you God!!"

Christiana opens the car door and sees the time, "I have to go right now, but listen,"

"I am listening!"

"When you get into your room, there will be a Bible in the bedside drawer. Start reading it. Look for the book of John."

"The book of John. Got it."

"Actually, your *name* is in there. See if you can find it."

"I will. Thank you SO much!"

"Merry Christmas." She hugs him again.

"Merry Christmas!"

She pats him on the shoulder, "Okay now, get going"

He smiles uncontrollably, "Yes, Mamma Christiana."

She gets in and restarts the car, "Actually, call me Tiana."

"Yes, Mamma Tiana. Right now." And he turns and obediently strides, tall and strong down the block. She watches him as he goes, then pulls out to go the other way. Waiting for the light to turn, she sees him bouncing along, getting smaller in her rear-view mirror, until he disappears under the blue and yellow sign.

"God bless him and keep him," she prays softly.

Her phone chimes with a text from Felicia: CHANGE OF PLANS. COME GET ALL 3 OF US. I'M GOING TOMORROW TOO. I'LL EXPLAIN. MEET YOU OUT FRONT IN 15 OR SO.

Christiana laughs. She hits reply: OKAY. ON MY WAY. As she approaches the onramp, she sees that traffic is stopped and appears to be backed up for miles. She looks at her traffic app, which alerts her to an accident, and recommends the longer way over surface streets around the accident.

"Hmm. . . every time it rains even a little." She texts again: I MIGHT BE DELAYED. THERE IS AN ACCIDENT. WILL LET YOU KNOW WHEN I AM CLOSE.

Felicia replies: OKAY!

Chapter 9: Hope Deferred

Felicia hangs up the phone and looks for the boys. When Bryce was explaining about losing Lily, she began to walk around the terminal, and is now dozens of yards away near a macaroon stand. She spots their gate, and then Jacob's head, still wearing Alex's cap, with white earbud wires trailing to his phone. Oscar, a seat away, is looking around at all the people. He turns his head and after a moment sees her. She waives, and he smiles, waiving back. She stops at the stand and buys a bag of 6 colorful macaroons, and a large bottle of water.

When Felicia returns with the treats, Oscar asks, "What's wrong, Mamma?"

Felicia looks at their gate counter for updates, then hands Jacob two macaroons. He eats the first in one bite.

Oscar receives his macaroons and asks again. "Mamma, what's wrong?"

Felicia sits down on the edge of the seat between them. "Well," she hesitates. "It looks like they lost Jasmine's Lamb on their drive to Big Bear today."

Jacob jolts upright in his seat, yanking the white cords from his ears, "What!"

"Unfortunately, your Dad looked everywhere, but can't find her."

Jacob stands, "You've gotta be kidding! Where'd they lose it?"

"Calm down, Jacob," Felicia urges, taking his arm, "Just sit down, okay?"

He resists her gentle pull, then sits. "What's he going to do?"

Felicia folds down the top of the macaroon bag and tucks it into her purse. "Well, Dad's going back to look for it."

"Won't that be hard?" Oscar worries.

She reaches over and rubs his back some, "It will take a long time to drive back, but Jasmine thinks she knows where they lost it."

"*How* long?" Jacob demands.

Felicia takes a steady breath. "About three hours."

Jacob slams his body back in his seat, slapping the chair arm with his palm, "Oh my GOSH!"

"Calm down, Jacob," Felicia warns him.

He shoots forward again, gesturing sharply, "That's six hours she'll be alone! And that's *if* he finds Lily. What if he doesn't?"

"I know, Jacob. I know."

He drops his head, shaking it, then firmly runs his hands through his hair. "I can't believe you guys lost her," he mumbles.

Felicia looks away from him, lips closed tight.

Oscar asks, "Should I pray?"

"Pray!" blurts Jacob. "We need to *get* there. I mean, Jasmine's *alone*. Without Lily!"

"Jacob!" Felicia covers her lips, then takes another deep breath. "Yes Oscar, please pray for Daddy and Jasmine." She takes Oscar's hand, and he bows his head. She takes Jacob's hand, refusing his stiffness.

"Dear God, help Daddy find Jasmine's lamb. Keep him safe. Give her someone to talk to. Help us to get there soon. Amen."

"Amen," Felicia echoes, peace easing over her.

Jacob retracts his hand. "We *have* to get there. Jasmine can't be alone on Christmas Eve."

"Okay, Jacob." Felicia stands. "I'll go find out our options." She smiles at Oscar, "Don't forget your macaroons."

"I won't. It'll be okay, Mamma. Don't worry."

Felicia looks down at him and strokes his hair, "Thank you, Oscar."

At the counter, there is an older couple trying to visit their grandchildren for Christmas. The airline agent scans her screen for information.

"I'm sorry, Mr. and Mrs. Chang, your plane taxied onto the runway in Denver, but the next storm-front has delayed their take-off. It's uncertain if they'll get clearance. We just have to wait to hear."

"What about openings on other flights tonight?"

The agent frowns sympathetically, "Everything else is still booked for tonight. Again, I'm sorry. Why don't you have a seat, and we'll let you know when we have more information."

The two walk away discussing their options, and Felicia approaches. "I heard what you said. I guess there isn't much to hope for tonight."

The agent smiles patiently. "I'm sorry Mrs.—"

"Goodson."

"Mrs. Goodson. The best hope for you and your family to fly to LAX tonight is if that flight can get out of Denver soon."

Felicia studies the area behind the counter as if the answer might be there, and no one has noticed it yet. "You did mention the slim possibility of a cancelled seat . . ."

"Yes, that's true, and there's nothing so far, but remember, even if there is a cancellation, it wouldn't likely be for *three* seats. Would you be willing to take *less* than three seats? I know you're anxious to get to your daughter."

Felicia looks back toward her boys, calculating. She turns to the agent, noting her nametag. "Grace?" she smiles, "I just realized. That is a perfect name for you today--you've been so patient with all of us."

"Thank you," she nods.

"You're right. I am anxious to get to my daughter. Something has come up and my husband had to leave her alone for several hours, so we're concerned about her being sick, and feeling alone on Christmas Eve. All this is to say, yes, I think if less than three seats become available, then I would take whatever there is."

Grace takes a slip of paper and writes down Felicia's name. "I will keep checking, and if something comes up, then I'll call you, okay?"

"Thank you so much. I really appreciate all your help."

Grace nods again, with a kind smile, "My pleasure."

Felicia returns to the boys. Jacob is slumped in his seat, cap down over his eyes, earbuds reinserted, focused on his phone. She sits between them. "Listen boys."

Jacob pulls out his earbuds.

"We're still waiting to hear about our flight, but I talked with the airline agent about another way to LA tonight. She said that if there's a cancellation on another flight, we could have the first option."

"Great," comments Jacob.

"BUT," she continues, "It is *not* likely that there would be *three* seats cancelled. There could be less. Maybe even just one. Now I don't want to leave anyone here, but I—"

"Yes, Mom," insists Jacob. "Take it! You *have* to get to LA tonight. Jasmine shouldn't be alone."

"Okay, Jake. What do you think Oscar?"

Oscar nods. "Yeah. Jasmine shouldn't be alone. You guys go if there's only two."

Jacob jumps in, "No, *you* and Mom go if there's only two."

"Actually," Oscar suggests, "How about only *you* go, Mom, and Jacob and I will stay *together*."

Felicia wraps her arms around them both and hugs them nearly out of their seats. "You boys are the best a Mom could hope for." She kisses each of them, Jacob scrunching his face in feigned protest as he resettles his cap.

Felicia's eyes and nose begin to moisten. "Okay," she sniffs. "I'm going to the bathroom for a minute. Anyone else need to?" The boys shake their heads. "Jacob, if the agent calls my name, tell her I'll be right back. Okay?"

He nods, "Okay." He puts only one of his earbuds in as she leaves.

A child slumped in his car seat across from them wakes up and starts to cry. He rubs his eyes as the mother tries to console him with food and embraces.

After Felicia goes to the bathroom, she takes a stroll around the terminal, circuiting down one side and up the other, thinking. Praying. Upon completion of each lap, she looks toward their gate to see if Jacob is standing at the counter. A peace gradually imbues her stride.

She arrives back at the gate to find Jacob as she left him. Oscar, however, is on the floor with the little boy of about three years old who had been crying. Oscar has his new ball out, and the flashing LED lights have captured the child's attention.

Felicia sits in Oscar's seat, entertained by their play. The mother looks at Felicia with a tired smile. "Yours?" she asks, referring to Oscar.

Felicia nods. "What's *your* son's name?" she asks the mother.

"Brandon." With her elbow on the armrest, she props up her chin in her palm. Every time she speaks, she must find the energy to tilt her head back and let the words out.

"Long day?" Felicia sympathizes.

"Ye-es," the woman leeks with emphasis.

"Are people waiting for you in LA?"

The woman resigns to the conversation and drops her hand from her chin. "Sort of. We're meeting my husband's parents in LA. But my husband has been stationed at Colorado Springs and is finally coming home. He's actually flying in on the plane we're waiting for. We're supposed to board and join him. Cute, huh?" She waives her hand dismissively.

"Wow, that's interesting."

"Frankly, I wish he would just come in and we'd stay here, but it's supposed to be this Christmas getaway at his parents' cabin for a week at Lake Arrowhead. Either way I'm fine. I just want him to get here."

"I can certainly understand that," Felicia agrees.

The woman returns to her resting position, eyes half-focused on her son. Sensing the conversation is over, Felicia watches Oscar roll the flashing ball back and forth with the toddler. She looks at Jacob to thank him for keeping an ear open, but he has replaced the other earbud and is intent on his game. She remembers the two macaroons tucked in her purse and pulls out the little paper bag, unrolling the top. She removes the bright green one, and rations it into three, tangy bites. The ball escapes the toddler, and Oscar hops up to retrieve it, then sits back down to resume the little game.

Felicia relishes the three small bites of the second macaroon and is sipping on water when an announcement comes over the loudspeaker. "Attention passengers on flight 279 to LAX: unfortunately, due to continued storms in Denver and elsewhere, we are unable to service your flight. Tonight's flight to LAX has been cancelled, and no other flights are available through this airline this evening. Your tickets will be honored at any other time, and we are adding a flight to LAX tomorrow to help accommodate displaced passengers. Please make your arrangements at the Southwest ticket counter downstairs where you check your bags. There will be numerous agents there to help you, or you may call the customer service number located on your ticket and make arrangements over the phone. Please pick up your checked luggage at the Southwest carousel listing flight 279. Again, we are sorry for the inconvenience."

The announcement repeats, as scores of fatigued non-travelers arise, and stretch, and gather their things. There is a general, but apathetic rumble of conversation, and in little groups people begin their egress, making calls, rolling out their carry-ons, shouldering their bags, moving in one direction like an impromptu parade. Some people surround the counter at the gate, but most are directed onward.

Grace catches Felicia's eye, and subtly gestures to her. Felicia sets her coat and carry-on back down and goes to the desk. Jacob takes his earbuds out, and trails behind her, followed by Oscar.

"I found a single seat cancellation to LAX at 7:50 tonight," Grace explains privately, conscious of the small line of desperate people speaking to the agent beside her. "There is a passenger stuck on another plane in Great Falls, Montana that will miss his connecting flight to LA. Are you still interested?"

"Take it Mom!" Jacob blurts, a bit too loudly.

"Shhhh," she cautions.

"Yeah, take it Mom," Oscar, small at the counter, quietly affirms.

"Are you guys sure?"

Grace urges her to hurry, "Another agent could take this."

"Do it, Mom," Jacob charges.

"Okay, yes, take it. Take it. Thank you," she accepts with relief.

Grace clacks on the keyboard for an intense moment. "Okay. I transferred your ticket to that flight. It will leave from gate C10, just at the end there." She prints the boarding pass and shows Felicia the specifics. "Since we are only now checking you in, you'll board last, but there will be a seat for you. I am trying to divert your luggage to that flight before it unloads. Your boys' luggage will be at the carousal with the rest of this flight."

Felicia takes the boarding pass and tucks it into her purse. "Thank you so much."

"I'm glad we could find a flight for you," Grace heartens.

"Now, to book my boys, do I need to go downstairs? Or should

I—"

"Oh, no. Let me see what I can find." She clacks again, scrolling through screens, then comes upon something. "Actually, it looks like we have some seats open tomorrow morning at 6:30, if you want to go early. Otherwise we can book you on the added flight in the afternoon."

"6:30?" protests Jacob.

"Hey," Felicia lightheartedly chides, "I thought you were anxious to see your sister."

"I know, I know. That's fine. Whatever."

"Oscar?"

"Yeah." He nods.

"That's the spirit," Felicia cheers. "Okay, book them for 6:30. Let's just hope Aunt Tiana also has the Christmas spirit that early in the morning."

As Grace changes their reservations, Felicia texts Christiana the new plan, and awaits her reply. She gradually becomes aware of the conversation between the other agent and the young woman standing beside her in a beautiful orange scarf. Felicia notices the agent shaking her head as they talk.

The young woman becomes very distraught again. "But I *must* get to LAX tonight! If I don't I will miss my plane to Pakistan tomorrow morning!"

The agent, overwhelmed by the grief suggests, "We might have an early flight that—"

"No. No!" the woman cries. "My Plane *leaves* at 6:00 am. I have to *check in* long before that. I *must* get there tonight!"

Trying to solve the woman's dilemma, the agent offers a suggestion, "Well, you could rent a car and drive to LA. You would get there in about 5 or so hours."

The woman, leaning on the desk, bends limply at the waist, "No! No! You don't understand," she cries in her musical accent. She touches her loose fist, clutching a tissue, against the top of the desk with each heavy word. "I *cannot* drive. I *do not* drive. I do not have a *driver's* license."

"Perhaps we can get you some help changing your other flight reservation."

She shakes her head in a kind of circle. "My father made that reservation. It would not be possible for me to change it. He is in

Pakistan, and I cannot get ahold of him right now. Please. Please!"

The agent looks through her screens one last time, and then prepares for the onslaught of distress. "I am so sorry. I have looked at every flight. We have no seats available for tonight. Your best chance is to see if there are any *other* airlines that have seats to LAX available tonight. But I don't have a way to do that *for* you. Perhaps the travel agent on the first floor can find you something."

The woman turns, "Thank you," slowly picks up her bag from a nearby seat and walks away from the counter.

Felicia watches the woman and is drawn to follow after her. "I'll be right back."

"No, Mom!" scolds Jacob.

Felicia walks quickly and catches up to the woman when she enters the restroom.

"Hi, I'm sorry to bother you. I heard you say you need to get to LA tonight. You sound very upset."

The woman turns to face Felicia, tears pouring from her eyes. "Oh! My Mother is dying at home in Pakistan. My father only this week told me how serious it was. He said he wanted me to finish my classes. Oh! I should never have come here! I should never have left my family!" She blows her nose with the already worn tissue, and Felicia steps quickly into a stall to get some toilet paper for her.

"Now my father tells me that she may die very soon, and to hurry home. I can't miss that flight tomorrow. I *must* see my mother! I *must* tell her how sorry I am, and how much I love her."

The woman starts crying loudly again, "I am sorry. This is not your problem."

Felicia's heart grows warm and light. "I think I can help you. Hurry. Come with me."

The woman looks at Felicia bewildered, but moves quickly to follow. They scurry across the terminal toward Grace, who has not left the counter yet.

"Grace, Grace," Felicia calls, still too far to explain. They arrive, a little out of breath. "Grace, can you switch my reservation tomorrow to—" She stops and looks at the young woman.

"Miriam," she fills in.

"Mom, no!" protests Jacob again.

'It's okay, Jacob," Felicia soothes.

"But what about Jasmine?"

"It's okay, Jacob."

Grace has already pulled up the flight reservations. "I can, but I should make sure there is still a seat on the morning flight for you so you can go with your boys." She clacks her familiar magic. "Yes, there is still one seat left—I'll hold that one, then go in and switch the other reservations." She turns to Miriam, "Can I have your boarding pass?" Miriam hastily places it on the counter. "I need yours as well, Mrs. Goodson." She clacks away at a furious pace, switching screens, and scrolling, and clicking. A few, painful minutes later, she hits print, and triumphantly hands each of them their new boarding passes.

"There you go ladies. A little joy in an otherwise long and difficult day."

"Thank you, Grace. You have been indomitable!"

"Well, that sounds like a compliment," she smiles. "Now if you'll excuse me, I have to move down to the other gate. See you in a few minutes, Miriam."

Felicia turns to Miriam and smiles comfortingly. "Better?"

Miriam beams at Felicia, speechless, clutching the boarding pass to her heart. Then she embraces Felicia firmly in her thin, strong arms. "I don't know how to thank you." She is crying again. She wipes her eyes, laughing.

"Why would you do such a thing for me? I am a stranger!" She dabs her nose with the bundle of toilet paper.

"Well," Felicia begins, then spreads her arms grandly. "It's Christmas. I did it in the spirit of Christmas."

The woman's face tightens, and she confesses in a low voice, "I am sorry. I do not celebrate Christmas."

Felicia's eyes hold her softly. "But *I* do." She touches the woman's forearm, smiling brightly, "And aren't you glad I do?"

Miriam's eyes grow wide, "Oh, yes. I am *very* glad that you do." She smiles, rocking her head, "*Very* glad that you do."

"Well," Felicia adds, "it gives me joy to be able help you, when you need it so much."

Miriam looks at Felicia fondly, "I don't know very much about your Christmas, but you make me very curious. You are so generous."

Felicia takes a thoughtful breath. "At Christmas, we celebrate when Jesus was born. You've heard of Jesus before?"

Miriam rocks her head, "Yes. In the Koran, he is called Isa. He is a great prophet."

"Yes, He is. But he is *more* than that. We believe that his mother, Mary, had never been with a man before he was born."

"Oh, yes," she grows excited, "*We* believe that too. She was a virgin."

Felicia grins, "See? You *do* know about Him. And since Mary was a virgin, we believe that Jesus's birth was a *miracle* from God."

"Yes," Miriam cheerfully agrees, "*We* believe that too."

"And that means that *God* was his Father. Jesus, or Isa, was God's *Son*. You see?"

Miriam looks confused for a moment, as she absorbs the concept. Then slowly, "I see what you mean. If no *man* was his Father, then *God* was His Father. . . I see."

"We believe that Jesus, Isa, was born so that he could grow up and then die in our place. He died to pay for our sins—do you know 'sins'?"

She rocks her head, "Yes, we have a word for that too."

"Good. Okay, so Jesus, Isa, died to pay for our sins, but then he rose from the dead again. He did this so that whoever believes in him would be able to go to heaven and live with God forever."

Miriam looks confused again. "You mean *all* you have to do is to *believe* this? And you can go to heaven?"

"Yes," Felicia reassures. "Just *believe* that Jesus, Isa, died to pay for your sins and that He rose to life again, and you can go to Heaven."

"For sure?" she puzzles.

"Yes, for sure. It's a promise."

Miriam contemplates the idea. Then she concludes, "*We* do not have this promise."

Felicia smiles broadly. "Well, now you know why we celebrate Jesus, Isa's, birth with joy and kindness. Because God first loved *us* so much that He gave the *best gift* of all--His Son—and the promise of *life*."

Miriam is deep in thought. "I will have to investigate this more. I have not heard these things."

Felicia begins to rummage through her purse, "Have you ever

read the New Testament? The book that has Jesus, Isa's words in it?" She pulls out a small book.

"No, I have not. We call it the Injil, but I have never seen one."

Felicia hands her the brown leather-bound book. "Here. I always carry one on the plane with me. I'd like you to have it."

Miriam puts up her hand. "No, I cannot take that. It is yours."

Felicia looks at it, then holds it out again, "I have my whole Bible in my suitcase. This is just the New Testament, the Injil." She smiles encouragingly. "Take it. I want you to have it."

Miriam studies the small book, then shyly accepts it. "Thank you." She smiles. "I will never forget you, ah—"

"Felicia."

"Felicia," she repeats warmly.

"And these are my sons, Jacob and Oscar."

"Very nice to meet you. Thank you so much."

"My pleasure." Felicia leans to hug the smaller young woman again. "And God bless you."

"God bless you, too," Miriam emphasizes.

"Well boys," Felicia turns to them, "We'd better get going—oh, I have to text Aunt Tiana too!" They walk back to their seats and gather their things. "Nice to meet you, Miriam."

"Thank you. Wonderful to meet you, Felicia," she replies, cheerfully waiving the small book and new boarding pass as she walks to the other gate.

Felicia texts an update to Christiana, and then one to Bryce. Christiana replies.

"I can't believe you did that Mom," Jacob comments, lifting his backpack onto his shoulder.

"Are you mad at me?"

He considers. "No-o."

"Because, honestly," she adds, "I never felt right about going without you boys in the first place. It's better that we go as a family." She smiles at both of them, and they each nod thoughtfully at this idea. They double check their seats and leave the gate.

"I think everything will turn out fine." Felicia encourages. "What do *you* think Jake?"

He hesitates, "No Mom. It was good what you did." He reflects more, then adds, "Yeah. It was good."

Oscar is quietly walking next to them as they head out of the terminal toward the baggage.

"Oscar?"

He nods, looking downward, hands tucked under his backpack straps. "It was good, Mamma."

"Besides, you *prayed* didn't you?" She reminds him.

"Yeah," he agrees. He lifts his face, grinning at his Mom walking beside him.

Felicia's phone chimes. It is a text from Christiana. She reads it, then replies.

"It looks like there's traffic from an accident, so we might have to wait a bit."

"What's new?" jokes Jacob.

"Very funny." Felicia puts her phone away. "Well, it'll give me time to figure out if my luggage stayed here or is on that plane to LA. And for us to call Jasmine and see how she's doing."

As they exit the terminal, "Everybody have everything? Last chance."

"Yeah, Mom," answers Jacob.

"Yeah, Mom," replies Oscar.

"Got your ball, Oscar?"

Oscar hesitates. After a few strides, he sheepishly replies, "No."

Felicia stops. "What? We have to go back—"Then she reads Oscar's face. "You gave it to that little boy didn't you?"

A guilty grin wriggles across his face. With knowing smiles, they all turn and resume walking. Felicia bumps her hip playfully against Oscar, and he stumbles a few steps away. He comes back and gently bumps Felicia's hip, which sends her bumping into Jacob, which he ventures to return.

Chapter 10: The Gift of Love

The cars stand on the freeway like penned cattle in the low evening glow. Some have their lights on; some have their engines running, as if this impatience will cause the herd to move forward again. The rest have resigned to the delay, brakes set, lights and engines off, awaiting the signal to rouse them again and continue their holiday journey. The far, rear fringe of the pack slowly unravels as police systematically direct vehicles to exit using the closed onramp.

The cars at the front of the pack, closest to the scene, nearly all have their lights on and engines idling. They are the most indignant, having missed by mere seconds the opportunity to escape the patrol car, now parked in front of them, when it weaved back and forth across the lanes, lights flashing, to create a traffic break. Although sympathetic concerning the horrible scene before them, these drivers cannot help but reflect on the preceding cars that had successfully navigated the crash site and are already at their merry destinations. Others, of course, are grateful they had not arrived too early to be engulfed in the dramatic incident.

The policeman who provided the traffic break stands by his patrol car, parked as a barrier across the middle lanes, and flanked by fiery flares on each side. The sporadic visits, or questions called out from the front line of cars has ceased for the time, though fresh demands for updates are likely pending.

"I am sorry folks," he had told the foremost group loudly, placating for their calm attention with his raised, open palms. "This is a serious accident and there are several injuries. The wreckage involves multiple vehicles across all four lanes. Please be patient, and we will clear a lane for you to pass through as soon as the victims have been transported, and we are able to tow one of the vehicles out of the way." That was 30 minutes earlier.

The officer has become lost in thought watching the steady activity of the accident scene, as work lights begin to illuminate the growing darkness. He looks up at the sky and holds out the palm of his hand to test for drops. Then he walks to the back of his patrol car and removes his raingear, folding it neatly, and places it into his trunk. He closes his trunk, and is readjusting his equipment belt and shirt, when he hears loud, persistent honking growing closer from the gridlocked cars. He turns and sees a car driving along the wall up the outside emergency lane, lights flashing frantically. The car gets within 50 yards, but encounters another car partially blocking the emergency lane, having drifted there at some point.

The car, now halted, persists in honking and flashing its lights, and the officer jogs over. The driver rolls down his window, anxious to speak to the officer, who stops him.

"Sir, you can't park in the emergency lane. We must keep this clear!"

The flustered man holds up one hand appeasingly, "I know. I am so sorry. But please! My wife has gone into pre-mature labor, and something is really wrong! Please can you help us?"

The officer bends to see into the passenger seat, where a pregnant woman has a gravely distressed look on her face, gripping the door handle, and cradling her abdomen. He approaches the car blocking the lane and directs surrounding cars so the driver can maneuver out of the way. He returns to the husband and charges him to follow up the emergency lane, then directs him to park adjacent to his patrol car. The officer calls dispatch and requests an ambulance for the woman. The husband parks the car and jumps out.

"Please, officer, we have to get her to the hospital, I think she's bleeding!"

The officer looks over the accident scene, and then tells the man to wait. He walks to one of the firefighters and then to another officer, and after a moment, returns.

"I'm sorry sir, they are still extracting one more victim, and we are awaiting tow trucks to come and remove the vehicles. There's a lot of emergency vehicles and debris, and we can't get you through yet. They understand the situation and are going to clear a path as fast as they can."

"Thank you!"

"In the meantime, I already requested another ambulance, which should arrive shortly."

"But please," urges the husband, "Can you come see what you can do? It's our first baby, and I don't know how to help her."

The officer thinks for a moment. "Sure, I'll come." He goes to his patrol car and removes his jacket, then opens the trunk and grabs the first aid kit. He calls out to the officer, who is attending the accident scene, "Park! Keep an eye out here. I'm going to check on the woman." Officer Park waves and takes position between the patrol car and the accident scene. The first officer closes the trunk and approaches the passenger side to talk to the woman through the window, which she seems unable to operate.

"Ma'am, I'm going to see how I can help you," he loudly explains. She nods, grimacing, as her head undulates to sharp waves of pain. The officer speaks into his shoulder mic, relating the situation to dispatch. They tell him to go to another channel. Once on the other channel, the dispatcher asks a series of questions, which lead the officer to carefully open the door, and calmly relay information between the woman and dispatcher. The dispatcher directs the two men to assist the woman to the back seat, where she can lay down and receive assistance. The husband and the officer coordinate, and help his wife gingerly into the back seat, where the husband gets in behind to support her back against him.

The officer goes to the other rear door with his first aid kit, preparing to relay information to the dispatcher. Hands shaking, he pulls on medical gloves and kneels one knee on the edge of the seat between the woman's feet.

"Ask her permission, then help her remove any pants or undergarments," the dispatcher coolly directs.

The officer looks at the woman, distressed, but concentrating intently. In the dim dome light, she appears to be about her late 30's. She is already nodding her assent to the officer's assistance.

"It's okay with you for me to remove your clothing?" he affirms. She releases a husky "Yes," then holds her breath again in pain. The officer carefully pulls off her sweatpants and underwear and sets them in the well of the floor. He immediately sees dark stains on his gloves, and reports to dispatch. "It looks like she's bleeding substantially."

The dispatcher comes back, "Ask her permission to examine for signs of the baby." The woman again is already nodding. "Yes!" forces from her throat. The officer fumbles for his flashlight and does not seem to understand how to retrieve it from his equipment belt. Finally, it releases, and he switches it on. He must stand outside the car and stoop to see between the woman's up-bent legs, flashlight trembling as he looks for signs of the baby. The woman groans in pain, and her husband talks soothingly to her, clasping one of her hands.

After a moment, the officer stands up and takes a breath. Then reports to the dispatcher, "I can't tell if the baby's coming, but I see a lot of blood." He hears the woman groan sharply again inside the car.

"Ask her for permission to feel for the baby," comes the dispatcher's methodical directions. "If she says yes, tell me if you can feel the head."

The officer, now perspiring in the chilled December night, kneels back down on the edge of the seat. "Ma'am, may I feel for the baby's head?"

The woman's eyes are tightly shut, and she manages to nod firmly several times, but only utters the hard sounds of holding her breath, and then releasing it, and then holding it again.

"Okay, Ma'am." The officer wipes his forearm across his wet brow, and then sets the still lit flashlight on the seat in front of him. Then he gently places one gloved hand on her bent knee, and tentatively feels for the baby's head with the other. After a moment, he withdraws his hand, and stands outside the car again. His heart is pounding. He inhales deeply several times to steady his breathing, then reports to dispatch.

"Dispatch, I don't think the head is coming out. It feels sharp—like an elbow or knee or maybe the heel of a foot? I don't know."

"Okay, Officer Jamison, tell the woman to *resist* pushing—*don't push*--and to try and control her breathing. The ambulance that was coming for the last accident victim is going to transport your pregnant woman first, and the second ambulance will transport the TA. They are coming southbound on the northbound lanes. Just remain calm and do nothing more until they get there."

The officer relays the information.

"See?" the husband reassures, "They'll be right here, Honey."

She nods and tries to smile. She is shivering.

"I have an emergency blanket, I'll be right back," announces Officer Jamison. He locates and replaces his flashlight on his equipment belt, and unrolls the gloves from his hands, tossing them onto the car floor, then he goes to the trunk of his patrol car. When he returns, the husband is comforting his wife and guiding her into steady breathing. Officer Jamison spreads the blanket over the woman, and her husband pulls it up to her chin. She concentrates on resisting another contraction until it releases.

The husband quietly looks at the officer, and asks in a calm voice, "Would you mind staying with us?"

The officer evaluates the situation. "Sure." He rolls down the window, closes the door, and leans in on the frame.

"Thanks. Did I hear your name is James?"

"Jamison, actually."

The man smiles, tiredly. "Officer Jamison. Okay. I ask because we're thinking about naming our son James." He laughs a little. "I just thought that was funny."

Officer Jamison smiles some, observing the now quiet woman.

"Well, Officer," the man continues, "Would you mind if I prayed?"

Officer Jamison glances around the dimly lit car. "Ahh… Sure. Go ahead."

The man closes his eyes. "Dear Lord, bless my wife and baby. I trust you with their lives. Bless Officer Jamison for his kindness. Amen."

A kind of peace fills the car. The man kisses the top of his wife's head, who smiles reservedly.

"Are you married?" he asks.

"Yes, I am."

"That's nice. Do you have any children?"

Officer Jamison sifts through possible answers. "Ahh . . . No. My wife and I have never been able to have any."

The man pauses in the dim stillness. "I'm sorry about that."

Jamison shakes his head. "Nah, don't worry about it."

"Well, I certainly understand what that's like." The man's voice is serene, reassuring. "We tried for *ten* years. I mean, we tried everything." He looks down at his quiet, grimacing wife."

"It actually got really stressful—like we started fighting, over *little* things. And then what was worse is when we *stopped* fighting. You know. That kind of *cold* silence that grows between you when there's nothing left to say." He shakes his head.

"Then one day I realized that I was losing my wife over it. So, I went to her, and told her, 'Let's forget all this. I love you and you love me. Let's just take the pressure off. If God wants us to be parents, then we'll be parents. It's up to him.' So, we prayed, and then let it go." He smiles, remembering. "Then we started having fun again like we used to. We went on dates, and, you know, just enjoyed each other."

Officer Jamison is quiet, waiting, but the man doesn't continue. "Is that when it happened?"

He laughs softly, "Yeah. It was an *accident*. Can you believe it? Completely unplanned."

Jamison considers these words a moment. "No kidding."

"Yeah. So, we've just decided to trust God with the whole thing. I mean, Sarah's 41 now, so it's a risky pregnancy. But honestly, it was God's idea. So, I gotta trust Him. You know?"

The Officer's radio squawks in his ear. "Officer Jamison, the ambulance is on scene, coming with a stretcher to your patrol car."

Officer Jamison steps from the car a few feet, sees the paramedics coming through the accident scene with the stretcher, and waives them over. They soon infiltrate the back seat through both doors, briskly evaluate the woman with a series of rapid assessments, then lift her onto the stretcher, and wheel her to the ambulance. The husband follows, offering love and encouragement to her. They load the woman and tell him to meet them at the hospital.

"You take good care of her!" he charges them.

"We will, sir," replies the one paramedic closing the door, adding "The baby's heartbeat is distressed, but strong. We'll see you there." The other paramedic, who is seated in the back of the ambulance leaning over his wife with a stethoscope, gives the husband a thumbs-up through the back window as they turn on lights and sirens to leave.

Officer Jamison sees that the tow trucks have arrived as well. He talks to the firefighters and the other officer, and then goes to report to the husband, who is watching the ambulance drive away. "They're going to clear that lane for you to get by. Just drive slowly and follow their direction."

The man is smiling hopefully, eyes wet, watching the ambulance disappear. "Thank you so much, Officer Jamison. Thank you! You don't know how much your care and concern has meant to me." He puts one hand gratefully on his shoulder and extends the other for an enthusiastic handshake.

"I mean, I love my son, and I want him. . ." he pauses with emotion. "But I NEED my wife. I don't know if you can understand that. She's my everything—she's my partner. No one knows me like her. No one loves me like her." He laughs, cries, and wipes his eyes. "Oh, what we've been through together—rain or shine. You know?" The man looks at the officer's face, expecting a response.

After a moment, Officer Jamison answers with a thoughtful nod, "I think I do."

Officer Park waives to Jamison. "Good to go," he calls.

Officer Jamison turns to the man, "It looks like they're ready for you. Just follow that officer." He follows the man back to his car, picks up his first aid kit from the ground, and closes it. The man climbs eagerly into the driver's seat. "You take care," adds Officer Jamison.

The man pulls forward, calling out the window with a waive, "God bless you! And Merry Christmas!"

Officer Jamison looks around the strange reality he had diverged from only fifteen minutes before. His mind and body fatigued from the adrenaline, he seems to have lost his bearings for the moment. Officer Park returns, silhouetted by the eerie glow of work lights, gridlocked car headlights, and sizzling-pink road flares.

"Jamison, you're still on the wrong channel. Switch over, they're calling you." Slow to process the instructions, he at last switches over his radio and calls dispatch. The dispatcher tells him to report when he's 10-8 and returning to the station.

Bewildered, he turns to Park, his field supervisor. "Why am I clear for EOS?"

Officer Park laughs and points to his shirt, "Come on man. You've got blood all over you. You can't work like that."

Officer Jamison looks down and sees the patchy stains, trying to recall if he has another shirt in his locker. Officer Park reads his eyes. "It's okay. You've done enough. We're about to open this lane. Help us direct these cars through, and then you're good to go. Go back to the station and write up a quick report, then head home."

Officer Park chuckles and slaps his back, then returns to the scene. Jamison reverberates from the contact. He looks down at his hands; they have lost their strength.

His radio squawks, and Officer Park signals for him to move the flares and begin directing the pack of cars through the single lane. Another officer comes with his flashlight, and as cars turn on their engines and lights again, the two methodically guide the motorists through the passageway and on to resume their Christmas affairs. Officer Jamison's equilibrium gradually restores through the routine work of directing traffic. Some tap their horns in thanks.

None of them certainly realize the smaller human drama that emerged right in front of them—one of many dozens, perhaps, playing out all around. Humbly. Privately.

~

The streets are serene as Officer Jamison drives back to the station. Waiting at a stop, he flips on his dome light and looks down at the stains on his shirt again, holding it out to see them. The light turns green and he shakes off his wandering thoughts, switches off the interior light, and proceeds forward. A moment later, he passes a lone figure walking on the dimly lit street. Officer Jamison drives nearly a block further before he decides to turn around. He pulls up slowly alongside the young man, pacing him a few steps before both come to a stop. Leaving his headlights on, he steps out of the patrol car and puts on his police jacket, covering the stains. He walks around the front of his car, passing through the lights, and approaches the bewildered, young man, eyes downturned. The boy pulls his hands out of his pockets and relaxes them by his side. He is ashamed and afraid.

Officer Jamison faces him sternly for a moment, studying him. Then he demands, "Hey. Where'd you get that jacket?"

The young man looks despondently down at the snapped-up jacket, pulling at the elastic waistband to evaluate it. He lets go but doesn't quite raise his eyes to meet the officer's.

"A woman gave it to me because I was cold."

Officer Jamison takes a small step back and crosses his arms, inspecting the shiny blue and orange jacket. "She did, huh?"

The young man gulps, and reluctantly meets his gaze. "Ahh. . . is there a problem, Officer?"

Officer Jamison's eyes settle on the bright orange patch with the initials ***AJ*** hand-sewn onto the upper left chest. A smile grows across his face, brightening his eyes. He shakes his head in amazement, then answers the young man.

"No. There's not a problem. No problem at all. It's just that—this is my son's jacket."

Chapter 11: But the Lord…

The quiet house erupts with life as the family piles in from the car, arms full of luggage and warm, white bags of In-N-Out burgers and fries. The home fills with the savory smell of melted cheese and onions and grilled beef and fresh-cut fries. They are laughing, and the door gets away from Christiana, keys still in the lock, and slams jangling against the half-wall behind it. The Christmas lights are still on from when she left to get herself a fast dinner, about two hours ago.

She pulls the keys out as Oscar and Jacob rush into the living room, rolling and dropping their luggage at the foot of the stairs, and then quickly turning to snatch the steamy white bags out of Christiana's hands.

"Oh my," says one sister.

"Are you hungry?" laughs the other.

The boys clamor to the table and start dividing the bounty, as Felicia deposits the cardboard carrier of shakes into the center to avoid the boys' piranha snaps. She sets her purse and carry-on bag in the living room, then helps her sister take out paper plates and napkins and joins the frenzied boys at the table. Oscar struggles to pinch catsup out of his mangled packets, while Jacob is three bites into his double-double.

Christiana removes the paper from her straw and inserts it with a dull "thwick" into her chocolate shake lid. "I have been wai-ting for this," she revels, and then draws up the thick, creamy-cold sweetness.

Felicia pauses over her unwrapped burger and looks around again, reevaluating her environment. "Oh, my goodness, where's Tyrell?"

Christiana licks up catsup with two French fries and inserts them in her mouth. "Mmm . . ." talking as she chews, "He had to work late." She doesn't meet her sister's eyes to avoid the discussion.

Mortified, Felicia apologizes. "Christiana, I completely forgot about . . ." pausing, now mindful of the boys, " . . .that you were going to make dinner tonight. I should never have called you to come get us."

Christiana savors the first delicious bite of her double-double since she envisioned it so long ago. She swallows and keeps the conversation light, "No, it's okay. Like I said, Tyrell had to work late anyway." She looks around the table and smiles encouragingly. "So, it's actually pretty cool that you guys came back."

Felicia takes a sullen nibble of her burger. After a moment, she reflects, "My goodness, I just talked all the way home about what happened at the airport, and about Bryce and Jasmine . . . I didn't give you a chance to tell me *anything*."

"No, don't worry about it," Christiana reassures, drawing from her shake. "Hmm, it's funny though,"

"What?"

"I was *at* In-N-Out to get *this* when you texted."

"You were? But you didn't—"

"It's a long story—that I'll tell you later. Okay?"

"Okay," Felicia agrees, not wanting to pry in front of the boys.

"No, it's a good story," she smiles, cheek bulging a little. "Everything's fine."

Felicia nods assured. "Okay." She tries her vanilla shake. "Mmm—Okay. *That's* good."

The table fills with small talk. Oscar tells Aunt Tiana about the little boy he met. Jacob finishes his meal and dramatically wads up the wrapper very small and places it in the center of the table. Then he slouches back into his chair, pulls his shake close for a long draw, and takes out his phone to continue his quest. He puts in one earbud, to be polite.

After several minutes, the ladies finish their meal and clear the table. Oscar is listening to their discussion, absently nibbling on the remnants of his fries.

Felicia throws out the white paper trash and spots the

Christmas mug on the counter. "Did you have tea?"

Christiana is wiping the salt and crumbs off the table, "Yeah, do you want some?"

Felicia rinses her hands in the sink, deliberating. "Actually, that sounds really cozy. Will you have some too?"

"Sure. It might help the food settle down." She rinses out her mug as Felicia gets another from the cupboard. "What would you like?"

"I *should* have peppermint . . ." Felicia confesses, "but Earl Grey would be tasty right now."

"Worried about the caffeine?"

"A little, but it'll probably wear off by the time I go to bed."

Oscar brings his paper plate over to the trash. "Aunt Tiana?"

"Yes, Oscar?"

"Well, since I'm here . . . I was wondering if I could maybe wrap the presents I bought today?"

Felicia and Christiana warmly exchange looks.

"Sure Oscar. I'll get some wrapping paper and ribbon out. Do you want to do it over at the coffee table for some privacy?"

Oscar appraises the living room, then nods.

Felicia heats their water, and Christiana retrieves the wrapping paper from the office, while Oscar takes his suitcase and rolls it mysteriously into the living room.

After setting things for Oscar, Christiana returns to the kitchen with the box of See's in her hand. "He's so cute, isn't he?"

Felicia notices that Jacob has both his earbuds in now, feet up on the next chair, concentrating. "Yeah, he's a good boy."

The microwave dings, and Christiana sets out the tea. "I have some things for you to wear tonight, if you need them."

"Thanks," Felicia drops in her teabag.

"I'm sorry they sent your bag to LA." Christiana opens the box of chocolates and offers them to Felicia, who delightedly surveys the options.

"That's okay. They said it will be waiting for me at the baggage claim office." She selects a rectangular dark chocolate and takes a micro-bite. "Mmm."

Christiana picks herself one and is about to offer some to Jacob when keys rattle in the door. She freezes, awaiting the revelation of the unexpected arrival. When the door swings open, a tall, clean-cut young man dramatically pokes his head around it, and peers into the kitchen wearing a magnificent grin.

"Surprise, Mamma!"

Christiana drops the box on the counter, "Mijo!!" and swiftly embraces the amused boy. "Come in!" Oh my gosh. Look at you! You look so handsome!"

Alex enters wearing a dress shirt, long, red tie, and neatly pressed slacks. After receiving extensive doorway hugs and admiration, his mom wraps her arm around his tall shoulders and escorts him into the room. She plants an adoring kiss on his cheek, "You are so handsome."

"Wow! I thought you guys were gone," Alex surveys his family.

Oscar soon emerges, scissors in hand, and comes to greet him shyly. "Hi Alex," he stands, smiling.

Alex bends down and gives his cousin a big hug. "Hi Oscar. You wrapping presents?"

Oscar grins bashfully, "Yeah."

Alex walks to Felicia, "Aunt Chia, good to see you." He hugs her warmly. Jacob watches his cousin intently and puts his phone and earbuds down on the table. Alex spots him in the corner.

"Jake, what's up man?" Alex goes around the table and extends his hand to Jacob. When he stands, Alex pulls him in firmly for a bro-hug, then steps back to look at him. "Man' you're getting big. Growing your hair out?"

Jacob smirks self-consciously, "Yeah."

"Looks good," Alex grins. "Like the hat."

Jacob blushes and tips down Alex's old hat, unable to come up with a slick reply.

Christiana, whose eyes are hungrily following her son, interjects, "Alex, what are you doing here? I thought you had that thing still?"

Alex goes and kisses his mom on the cheek, "I did. Man those kids were great." He leans back against the refrigerator, hands in his pockets. "I had a *great* time—and they let me help play Santa. It was really cool."

"I'm so glad, but—"

"Well, after me and the guys handed out the presents, and messed around with the kids for a while, they started calling everyone to the dining room to eat. The families sat together, and the kids were all talking about what they got, and, I don't know-- I just missed you guys."

"Aww… Mijo, you're so sweet."

"Anyway, my part was all done, so I decided to duck out. I just had to run back to the dorm and grab my stuff."

Christiana pats his arm. "I'm so glad you're here."

Alex looks around. "Hey, where's Dad?"

Christiana holds her smile fast to keep it from fading. "He had to work tonight, honey. We'll see him tomorrow."

Alex looks disappointed. "Oh, bummer. I wanted to show him the patch they put on our jerseys for the Holiday Bowl."

"I know, Mijo. You can show him tomorrow, okay?"

"Yeah, that's cool," Alex weakly smiles. "It's just that I have to leave early the day after tomorrow to catch the team bus, so this feels like a fast Christmas."

Then he breaks his solemn mood with a clap. "Hey! I smell burgers. Is there anything to eat? I didn't even stop for a *single* bite the whole drive--I just ate a protein bar on the way."

After some thought, Christiana excitedly recalls the carne asada marinating in the fridge. "How about some carne asada, rice, beans and tortillas?"

"Yes!" Alex claps his hands again, rubbing them. "How about it! That's what I'm talking about."

Christiana opens the refrigerator and starts getting out ingredients. "Give me about 20 minutes, and you'll have a feast."

"Great!" Alex turns to Jacob, "Hey Jake, wanna help me get my gear out of the car?"

Jacob jumps out of the chair, "Sure!" and follows his cousin outside.

The two walk a block before they get to Alex's car. "Somebody's having a party, huh?" Alex remarks at the streets full of parked cars.

"Yeah."

Alex opens the back door and pulls out his Wildcats travel bag, handing it to Jacob. "Can you take this for me?"

Jacob takes the duffle reverently, "Sure."

Alex closes the door and then pops his trunk.

"Got your helmet and pads in there?" Jacob hopes.

Alex pulls out a bulging garbage bag. "Nah, we leave all that at the locker room. They'll load it on the bus for us." He closes the trunk and starts waddling back to house, toting the awkward bag. He grins at Jacob, "*These* are Christmas presents."

"Oh. Cool." After a few steps, "Hey, do you think you'll get to play in the game?"

"No, probably not. It's a great team." Alex shifts the bag. "But I'm learning a lot. *Next* year, maybe."

Jacob chuckles, "Oh, yeah. For *sure*."

"No doubt my Mom will record it anyway—just in case."

"Yeah, no doubt."

They get back to the house, and Jacob follows Alex upstairs with his duffle bag. In his room, Alex sets the bag on the floor near his desk. "I haven't put the names and the bows on them yet. Just set the duffle on my bed."

Jacob sets the bag down and sits next to it on the bed. Alex sits in his desk chair and starts pulling out the presents one at a time.

"You actually *wrapped* them?" Jacob remarks.

Alex takes a sheet of card stock from one of his drawers and cuts out a little rectangle for his first gift. "Yeah, it was great. Some girl at our dorm had bought like four rolls of wrapping paper and a bag of bows, and she put her leftovers in the common room on our floor. I whipped these out this morning before my event—for free! Cool huh?" He carefully writes a name on the tag and folds it, then tapes it to the package.

"Yeah," murmurs Jacob, "I guess."

Alex reaches into the bag and feels around. "What? Don't you like Christmas?" He pulls out a bow, and holds it to the package, then sets it aside and reaches back into the bag. Looking sideways at Jacob, "Well?"

Jacob is sitting on the bed with his hands under his thighs, and when Alex looks at him, he shrugs his shoulders and looks away.

"Huh?" Alex finds another bow and peels off the back, eyeing Jacob for a response as he affixes it to the package.

"I guess," Jacob shrugs again.

Alex sets the first package aside and reaches in to pull out another. "You guess? Who *are* you?" he chuckles, then sets the next package on the desk and cuts out another rectangle. "Jake, you LOVE Christmas." He writes a name on the next tag and tapes it to the package. He takes the other bow and affixes it as well. Then he turns to face Jacob.

"Hey, what's going on, bud?"

Jacob looks down at his feet, and shrugs weakly. "Nothin'."

Alex studies his young cousin. "Nothin', huh?" He leans forward, elbows on his knees so he can meet Jacob's eyes. They start to water. "I don't think it's nothing, Jake." He reaches and shakes Jacob's knee gently, until Jacob looks up at him. When he finally lifts his eyes, a careless blink dislodges two tears. They streak down his stony face. He ignores them. His face reddens with effort, and he looks away.

Alex gently shakes his knee again to draw him back. "Hey, Jake. It's okay. It's okay." Jacob is facing the picture on his dresser. "Is it Jasmine?"

Jacob inhales sharply and buries his face in the crook of his elbow, now convulsing with silent sobs. Alex moves over to the bed beside him and wraps his arm around his shoulder. At first Jacob resists, but then he surrenders.

"Are you afraid?"

Jacob's hands cover his face, nodding fervently, now sobbing out loud. He tries a few times to say something, but swallowing sobs conflicts with his efforts to speak. Finally, he chokes out the words, "No--one will talk about it."

Alex squeezes his shoulder, "Talk about what?"

Jacob convulses harder, swallowing and choking on the words. Finally, he inhales deeply and the words come in a forced whisper.

"She's going to die."

Jacob abandons control, and cries freely, leaning into Alex's shoulder.

Alex wraps his other arm around him and cocoons him tightly, rocking him. "I'm so sorry, Jake. I'm so sorry."

Christmas music and the aroma of sizzling carne asada fill the house. Felicia stirs the beans, and turns down the flame, replacing the lid. She peeks into the living room at Oscar, who is busily writing among the wrapper scraps on the coffee table. The Christmas tree in the corner appears to crown his head with festive lights.

"Should I get out the salsa?"

Christiana turns the steak and tends to the onions. "Yeah, would you?"

Felicia opens the refrigerator door. "What's this?"

"What?" Christiana turns off the flame.

"This. In the butcher paper."

Christiana removes the steak onto a plate to rest and scrapes the bits and juices from the pan over it. She glances into the open fridge door, "Oh. That." She sets the pan into the sink and runs water over it.

"*That* was supposed to be a romantic dinner." She turns and leans her back against the sink, arms crossed.

Felicia takes out the salsa, closes the door, and frowns at her sister.

"What? It's lobster tails."

"Oh," Felicia saddens.

"I was going to grill them tonight."

Felicia sets the salsa on the counter. Then she brightens, and opens the fridge again, "So why waste it?" She grabs the package and sets it defiantly on the counter. "Let's broil them. It'll only take a few minutes, and Alex will love it."

Christiana looks at the disappointing bundle, then at her sister, hands on her hips. "You're right." She unwraps the package and starts preparing the tails.

The sound of a key in the front door startles them both. Christiana looks at the clock. 8:52. Tyrell enters, glancing around at everyone, and pensively closes the door behind him. Oscar is the first to greet him, "Uncle Tyrell!" as he runs over to him. Tyrell bends down to receive the eager hug.

"Well Oscar, I'm surprised to see *you* here," he marvels. "I thought you'd be in LA."

Oscar steps back from his hug and wraps his arms across his chest, tucking his hands under his armpits, and smiles, not sure what to do with himself.

"And we thought we wouldn't get to see *you*," he replies enthusiastically.

Tyrell looks down to him and puts a gentle hand on his shoulder. "Well, I'm so glad that you did, buddy." Then he looks at the women in the kitchen.

Christiana smiles uncertainly, "Hi Tyrell. We didn't think

you'd make it home tonight."

"Yeah, I got off early." He is reticent. "Hi Felicia. Good to see you."

Felicia walks to him and gives him a warm hug. "Good to see you too, Tyrell."

He turns to Christiana, "Hey, I'm gonna take my gear upstairs," he holds out the blue duffle.

Christiana nods, "Yeah, okay."

"Will you come up with me for a moment?"

Felicia steps back toward to stove, "I'll take care of this. Go ahead."

Christiana walks over. "Sure, Tyrell."

Tyrell adds, "It sure smells good in here, ladies."

The two ascend the stairs to "Hark the Herald Angels Sing."

Felicia checks her phone on the counter. Still no word from Bryce.

~

Upstairs, Tyrell closes the door behind them and sets his bag next to the chair he sits in every morning before work, putting on his socks and shoes, watching his wife sleep. He touches Christiana's elbow and guides her toward the foot of the bed.

"Here, sit down for a moment." He sits in the chair, opposite her. Leaning forward, elbows on the chair arms, he searches around the room for the words he needs to begin.

Christiana whispers to herself, "Oh dear God."

Finally, his eyes rest on her, and he begins solemnly.

"I met Andrew, tonight."

"Andrew?"

"Andrew." He repeats. "The young man that you helped today?"

"Oh, Andrew." Bewildered, "You *met* him? How?"

He licks his lips, thinking. "Christiana. Something happened to me tonight." He grabs the chair and scoots a foot closer to his wife.

"It made me realize what a fool I've been, and, and--" he tenderly takes her hand.

"Tyrell, what is it?" she anxiously evaluates his awkwardness.

He searches the floor, then looks into her face. "Baby, I love you so much. I—I—Just love you so much—"

Relieved, she drinks in the moment. "Oh Tyrell, I love *you*."

"And—I'm not going to let *nothing* get in the way of that love anymore. I don't want to lose you." He places her hand against his face, his eyes bright and wet.

She cradles his face in both hands, "Amore, I don't want to lose you either."

He looks down between his feet, shaking his head. "I guess I just started to think I wasn't a man because I couldn't have a son." He meets her eyes again. "I mean, all I ever wanted was to be a father—a *good* father. Not like *my* father—never around, always in jail. He didn't care about me."

Christiana wipes his moist face, listening, "I know."

He shakes his head adamantly before the words come again. "I mean, if it hadn't have been for my Mom, moving us out here, and away from the gangs—"

She kisses his damp cheek. "I know. I know."

"All I ever wanted to do was be the father *my* father wasn't . . . But then it didn't happen for us. And *I* was the reason why." He looks up at the ceiling, ashamed. "And, then I got so—*bitter*."

"Oh, Tyrell. It's okay," she kneels and wraps her arms around him.

"I thought, 'here I am raising another man's son. *Another* man's, and I can't have my *own*.'"

Sniffing and crying herself, "Baby, I'm only 37. If you want, we can get a loan for that hormone therapy, and try the in-vitro thing—if it's important to you, we can do it."

Tyrell shakes his head emphatically. He takes her hands and looks confidently into her eyes. "That's just it. That's what I *realized* tonight."

"What?"

He sniffs and smiles brightly. "I--I *am* a man. I am a *good* man."

She nods, fawning over him, "Yes, you *are* a good man."

"And I am a good *father*."

She laughs, crying at the relief. "Yes! Yes! You are a *good* father!"

He softly brushes the hair off her face, "Because of you, Christiana. Because of *you*."

Christiana succumbs to tears of joy.

Tyrell lifts her to her feet. "Baby, you *inspire* me to be a good man."

"Thank you, God," she quietly praises. "Thank you, God."

They kiss.

Tyrell admires his wife, nestled in his arms. "Yes. Thank you, God."

"Oh, Mi Amore." She strokes his cheek. They begin to sway to the distant song, "It Came upon a Midnight Clear."

"By the way. Andrew told me everything you did for him."

She pushes him back a step, "Wait. How did you meet him?"

"Well," Tyrell draws her back, "I see this guy walking down the street in *my son's* jacket—"

"You *saw* him? Where was he going?"

Tyrell laughs, "To get a pack of cigarettes. But he was on his way back to the motel."

"Oh, my. That boy. What'd you think?"

"He's a good kid." The couple sways in slow circles.

"Did you run a check on him?"

"What do you think?"

She laughs, "Tyrell, you'd look up the pastor if you thought—"

"I did, as a matter of fact. Good guy too," he smiles. Christiana slaps his chest playfully, and he twirls her away and back.

"Anyway, I *had* to check on him. *You* have invited him to Christmas dinner. . ."

She grins bashfully, "Oh yeah. I forgot."

"And *I*. . ." He spins her out again, and back, then dips her, ". . . I invited him to *stay* with us for a little while."

She stands upright. "You did?"

"I did. Is that okay?"

She reflects a moment. "Yeah. It is."

"At least until he gets a few paychecks." Tyrell adds. "It sounds like he's had a pretty raw deal."

Christiana embraces her husband again, kissing him on the cheek. "You are a *good* man, Tyrell Jamison."

"And I've decided something else."

"What?"

"I'm going to put in for the Juvenile Investigations Unit. I know you want me to get off patrol, and I think that's where I belong. I can do some good there."

She beams proudly, taking his face in her hands, "Oh, Tyrell.

You are a good *father* too."

"Thanks, Baby." He grins and kisses her loudly. "What do you think Alex will say about having a visitor? Maybe even staying in his room?"

"Well, you know Alex."

"Yeah. I think he'll be cool with it."

Christiana smiles broadly. "Well, let's go ask him and find out."

"He's here? I didn't see his car." Tyrell kisses his wife again. "What are we waiting for?"

Downstairs, they find him sitting at the table with a feast.

"Dad!" Alex gets up, throwing his napkin on the table, and strides to Tyrell, arms wide. They embrace, exchanging greetings, and hearty back pats.

"Merry Christmas, Dad."

"Merry Christmas. I've missed you Alex."

"Hey, come and eat this with me, it's too much!"

Tyrell looks gratefully at Felicia, and then at Christiana. "Are you sure?"

Christiana chuckles, "Yes! Please. It was meant for you anyway."

Tyrell pulls out the chair and sits down. "This looks so good." He sees Jacob, sitting in the corner, phone in hand. "Good to see you Jacob. Man, you've grown."

Jacob is eating a quesadilla Felicia made him. "Thanks Uncle Tyrell. I'm glad we got to see you."

Christiana hands Tyrell a plate with scoops of rice and beans already on it. He grabs a warm tortilla with butter, smears it with beans, selects some of the lobster meat, forks some carne asada strips, and tops his taco with salsa. "Oscar, come in here and keep us company," he calls.

"Okay!" Oscar has finished cleaning up his wrapping station and has repacked his presents. He wheels his suitcase aside, and grabs Jacob's new skateboard from under the tree.

"Look what Jake got from Aunt Tiana."

Christiana reheats her tea in the microwave and looks at her sister with a relieved smile.

Felicia mouths back, "Good."

Alex wipes his hands and reaches for the skateboard, "Let me see that, Oscar." Oscar takes it to him, and he turns it over, admiringly. "Whoa, Jake. That's a killer board you picked out."

Jacob smiles proudly, "Thanks."

Alex hands the board to Tyrell to examine, and then turns to his Mom. "Nice gift, Mom."

"I'm glad you approve." Christiana sets her tea on the counter by the barstools, overlooking the table. She opens the See's box and selects a milk chocolate bon bon, then offers one to Felicia, who selects dark chocolate, and stands by the microwave waiting for her tea to reheat.

Christiana sets the box in the middle of the table, and then takes the skateboard back out to the living room. "I'm not the only one who helped with that present," she hints.

Alex mumbles through a big, juicy, bite of his creation. "Who else helped?"

"Oh my, ladies," interrupts Tyrell, chewing another mouthful. "This is so good!"

Christiana comes back into the kitchen. "Who else helped?" she teases, touching under Oscar's chin as she passes him.

Jacob admits, "Oscar did. He used some of his Christmas money to help me buy it." He looks around the table, a little uncomfortably. Then he stops at Oscar and adds with more conviction. "Pretty cool, huh?"

Christiana settles on the barstool with her hot tea and piece of chocolate. "Oscar, sit down next to Jacob. You boys have some of the candy."

Oscar pulls out the chair next to Jacob. "I told you, Aunt Tiana."

"Told me what, Mijo?"

"That you'd share it with everyone," he grins, then leans across the table and scours the box for just the right choice. Everybody laughs.

"You were right. But how can I resist this family?"

"The best," Felicia agrees. Then she turns to her nephew, "So Alex, tell me. What's your major again?"

Alex, chewing fervently, catches Tyrell's eye, and grins, "Criminal Justice, of course."

"That's so interesting. What do you plan to do with that?" Felicia opens the microwave, removes her hot tea, and sits down on the barstool beside her sister.

"He can join the FBI with that!" Jacob interjects.

"Whoa! The FBI!" echoes Oscar.

Alex blushes, "Well, I have *a lot* of options . . . Definitely something in law enforcement." Alex scoops beans into his mouth, then suddenly exclaims, "Hey, Dad, I have to show you the cool patch they put on our jerseys for the Holiday Bowl."

"No kidding? Yeah, I want to see that. I sure wish we could go—"

Alex interrupts him, grinning broadly, "Next year, Dad. You guys will come then."

The room fills with affectionate chatter sharing stories and news since last all together. Felicia looks at her phone and sees that she has missed a text from Bryce at 8:47. "JUST OUTSIDE BIG BEAR. STARTING TO LOOK. WILL LET YOU KNOW."

In the din of happy voices, she envisions him searching in the cold, desperate, dark. Alone. Jasmine's hope weighing on him.

"Hey Mom, are you going to make cookies?" Alex petitions.

Christiana, caught up in the joy of watching her son and husband, and family enjoying each other, laughs a little, "Yes. Tomorrow, Mijo."

Alex rises from the table and puts his plate in the sink, and then sweeps around the counter to Christiana. "Tomorrow, Mamma?" He takes one hand and lifts her grandly from the barstool, then guides her like a ballroom dancer. "*Tomorrow*, my favorite cousins will be gone. Let's make them *now*, what do you say?"

Christiana blushes at the gesture, finding herself back in the kitchen beside her exhilarated, grown boy. "Now? You want to make them *now*?"

"Yes. Now," Alex encourages her, looking around at the faces following their little performance. "Don't we want to make cookies now?" he asks them, nodding enthusiastically. The others mirror him in agreement.

"See, Mamma? What do you say? We'll all pitch in, won't we?" Alex persists, supported by more eager nods and verbal assent. "Then they can take some to Jasmine and Uncle Bryce tomorrow, right?"

"Yes!" comes the emphatic chorus of male voices, Oscar particularly leaping up from his chair and clapping.

Christiana surveys the gleaming smiles of anticipation. The Christmas music begins a second cycle, and she glances at her sister, who is watching, smiling absently. Then in feigned defeat, "Well, why not? What kind do you want to make?"

The room erupts in triumph. "Yes!" cheers Alex. "Let's make your famous sugar cookies with frosting. You know, the Christmas trees, and snowmen, and angels—right?" he rallies the room for agreement.

"Let's do it," affirms Tyrell, meeting his wife's eyes with a quiet, broad smile.

As the joyous commotion begins, Felicia steps into the living room. She reads Bryce's text again, and replies. "PRAYING." She holds the phone to her chest, looks upward, and whispers, "Please God. Help him."

Chapter 12: . . . Directs his Steps

Nurse Jacqui enters the room with a coffee cup in each hand. She is wearing street clothes and has released her hair from its bun. She sets both cups on the swivel tray beside Jasmine's bed.

"Are you done with your pudding, sweetheart?" She takes the empty container and spoon and throws them into the trash by the door. "That's such a cute little tree your daddy found you." Jacqui returns to Jasmine, hands on hips.

"Can't I get you something else to eat? You hardly touched your dinner."

"No, thank you," Jasmine smiles softly. "Those mashed potatoes were really good, and I got full on them. And I have these crackers still from the chicken soup."

"Was that soup good?"

"Yeah, it was really good."

Jacqui removes the lid from her cup and inhales the aroma. "I always like peppermint mocha this time of year." The whipped cream has melted into the surface of the coffee, and a tentative sip leaves a thin line on her upper lip. "Mmm--I got there just in time before they closed, too. How's your tea? I told them not too hot."

Jasmine envelops the warm cup in her small hands and smells through the opening. "It smells good. I think it's still too hot."

"The guy that helped me said he didn't ever remember anyone ordering a child-size tea. I said, 'well, this child is pretty unique.'" She salutes Jasmine with her cup before attempting another sip. "I thought for sure you'd like hot chocolate instead."

Jasmine watches her companion tiredly sit down in the chair beside her. "I do like cocoa, but I had some today with Daddy. I sometimes drink peppermint tea with my Mommy."

"That's sweet." Jacqui crosses her legs and settles back in the chair. "So, your mom called while I was finishing my dinner, but I didn't hear what happened with their flight."

Jasmine's eyes wander to her cup. "They can't come until tomorrow morning." Then she looks up at Jacqui, "But they're coming really early, like 7:00. So that's good."

"I'm sorry about that. But that *is* pretty early. They'll be here before you know it," she cheers.

Jasmine smiles. "Yeah. It'll be okay."

"Did you tell your Mom about the Christmas carolers that came around?"

Jasmine scoots up in her bed, "Yeah! I told her they were nurses and doctors who go around singing after their shift on Christmas Eve, and that they sang The First Noel to us." Her eyes brighten. "That was awesome, wasn't it?"

"It was," Jacqui echoes, taking a sip from her coffee. "Where's the candy cane they gave you?"

Jasmine thinks for a moment, "Oh!" Then she feels around her blankets, "Here it is," and she lifts it triumphantly.

"Do you want me to open that for you? It might taste good with your tea," Jacqui giggles.

Jasmine holds out the wrapped candy toward her, "Yes, please." Jacqui stands and wrestles with the tight cellophane, finally tearing the nub at the end. She peels down the plastic a few inches and hands it back. "There you go."

"Thank you." Jasmine inserts striped treat into her mouth. "Yummy." She tries a sip of her mint tea. "It *does* taste good together."

Jacqui sits back down and looks at her watch, then takes another sip of her mocha. She kicks off her shoes, curls her legs up beside her on the big chair, and squints a cozy smile at Jasmine.

"Hey, you seem pretty chipper right now. It's after 8:00. I would have thought you'd be pretty tired after your long adventure." She sips her mocha again.

"I *was* tired. I slept all the way back." Jasmine envelops her candy cane thoughtfully with her lips. "Maybe that's why I'm not as tired now."

"Oh, I see."

"You look kind of dressed up. Are you going out?"

Jacqui looks down at her outfit and chuckles a little. "Oh, that. Well, one of the nurses on another floor told me to bring a change of clothes so I can go out with her and her friends after our shift tonight."

Jasmine takes a sip of her tea. "Do you still want to go?"

"No, Sweetie," Jacqui smiles broadly. "And actually, I never did want to go. See, they're a bit younger than me, and they have a lot more energy than I do. But, I brought the clothes anyway, just in case." She sets her cup down on the table beside her, and then picks up her purse from the floor. "I would much rather be with you." She opens her purse and retrieves a lip balm, uncaps it, applies it to her lips, caps it deftly, and returns it to her purse, then plops her purse back on the floor.

"You helped me get out of it, actually. I mean, I have to work again tomorrow, and I really can't stay out late having fun with them."

"Thank you, Miss Jacqui for staying with me. I know you're tired."

"It's *my* pleasure," she nods royally. "My house is quiet and empty tonight. What kind of Christmas Eve is that?" She picks up her cup again and holds it in her lap. "After tomorrow, I'll have several days off to relax and celebrate Christmas with my Mom, and uncle, and some cousins. It'll be nice."

"That's good." Jasmine licks her candy cane, then sips her tea.

"So, what would you like to do? Play a game? Watch something on TV?"

Jasmine smiles wryly. "Actually, we always read about Jesus in the Bible on Christmas Eve, but there's nobody here to read it to me." She sets down her candy cane, then stretches to pull open the drawer beside her bed. She can't reach the book inside and turns to Jacqui. "Could you read it to me?"

Jacqui's smile falls a bit. "Ahh--Sure, I can. If you don't mind me stumbling a bit here and there," she hedges. "The Bible is not really my thing, so I am not really familiar with it."

Jasmine eagerly tries to reach the book again, "That's ok, it *is* MY thing and I can explain it to you if you want."

Jacqui reluctantly uncurls her legs and sets her cup down to stand. She steps to the drawer and lifts out the purple-covered book, then hands it to Jasmine. "Here you go."

"Thanks!" Jasmine unzips the cover and flips pages until she finds the section she is looking for. She holds her finger there and then turns several pages back and forth until she finds another section and inserts a colorful bookmark. She holds out the Bible to show Jacqui the Book of Matthew, chapter 1. "See this first part here?" she points to some verses.

"Yes," Jacqui observes.

"You can skip that part. That's just some 'begat' verses. That's what my Daddy calls them. Start here. At verse 18," she points, "until the end of the chapter."

"Okay," Jacqui nods.

"Then flip to here," she opens to the bookmark in Luke, chapter 2, "and read this chapter. Okay?"

"Okay." Jacqui accepts the book.

"That's it!" Jasmine exclaims.

Jacqui sits with the book open on her lap, finger marking the starting point. She reaches for her cup. She takes a long sip. She sets it down, licks the cream from her lips, and curls her legs back up onto the chair. She sits back, resigned to her duty, finds her place, and after gathering her thoughts, begins to work her way through the words.

"This is how the birth of Jesus the Messiah came about." She looks up at Jasmine, now settled deep into her bed under the covers. Her face is alight with anticipation, eyes closed, listening.

"His mother Mary was pledged to be married to Joseph, but before they came together, she was found to be pregnant through the Holy Spirit." Jacqui finds her reading voice, and soon flows through the verses for her little audience.

" . . . an angel of the Lord appeared to him and said, 'Joseph son of David, do not be afraid to take Mary home as your wife, because what is conceived in her is from the Holy Spirit. She will give birth to a son, and you are to give him the name Jesus, because he will save his people from their sins. . .'"

She comes to the last lines of the chapter and reads them reverently, "And he gave him the name Jesus."

Jasmine pops open her eyes. "Is that the end of the chapter?"

Jacqui looks down to check. "Yes,"

"Good. Okay, now read that other chapter, please." She closes her eyes again.

"Oh. Okay." Jacqui flips to the bookmark and finds the next starting place. She begins again, stammering through the first unfamiliar words, then finds her pace.

"So, Joseph also went up from the town of Nazareth in Galilee to Judea, to Bethlehem . . ." She continues reading and soon finds herself reciting words she has heard before.

"And she gave birth to her firstborn, a son. She wrapped him in swaddling cloths and placed him in a manger, because there was no room for them in the inn." The page shows a color illustration of a stable with Mary and Joseph, and the baby in a manger of straw.

"And there were shepherds living out in the fields nearby, keeping watch over their flocks at night. An angel of the Lord appeared to them, and the glory of the Lord shone around them, and they were terrified." Jacqui turns the page and sees another illustration, showing angels bright in the night sky over a field of shepherds and lambs.

"But the angel said to them, 'Do not be afraid. I bring you good news of great joy that will be for all the people. Today in the town of David a Savior has been born to you; he is Christ the Lord.'"

She reads on, ". . . Suddenly a great company of the heavenly host appeared with the angel, praising God and saying 'Glory to God in the highest, and on earth peace to men on whom his favor rests.' When the angels had left them and gone into heaven, the shepherds said to one another—"

Jasmine softly interrupts the recital, but Jacqui doesn't quite hear her words.

She stops reading and looks up. "What Sweetheart?"

Jasmine's eyes are closed; her face is serene. "I've seen an angel," she repeats, quietly. "They're *beautiful*."

Jacqui looks blankly at Jasmine, uncertain how to respond. Then she closes the book on her finger, "Wow, that's amazing," and picks up her mocha. She shakes it distractedly before taking a last sip, and then sets the empty cup back down.

"I know you don't believe me." Jasmine opens her heavy eyes. A smile curls brightly on her face, "but you'll find out some day that it's true."

Jacqui replaces the bookmark, closes the Bible, and sets it aside on the nearby table. "I--" She lifts the empty cup again and shakes it, then sets it back down. “I didn’t say I don’t believe you.” She folds her hands in her lap.

Jasmine scoots upright again.

Jacqui avoids her eye contact. “It’s just, so remarkable.”

Jasmine’s hand searches over the bedding for something, then stops and returns to her. She absently rolls down the top of the blanket in her small hands and holds the bundle as she details her encounter.

“The *first* time I saw one was when I had chemo right after I was diagnosed and got a bad infection and was *really* sick. An Angel came to comfort me and make me stronger.” Jasmine’s head sways with wonder as she recalls the episode.

“The *second* time I saw an angel was when they gave me the bone marrow transplant. I got very sick with GVH disease and I got weaker and weaker until I went deep inside myself. Then an angel took my hand and lifted me out, and I floated away with him.” Jasmine lets go of the rolled blanket with her right hand and lifts it upward as if someone is gently taking it. Then it returns softly to her lap.

“It was so wonderful,” she marvels. “All I felt was love, love, love. Like no one has ever felt on earth. A love that fills you and makes you alive.” Her eyes are upward, in her memory, above the room.

“Then the angel brought me to a bright, beautiful place full of light, and there were bright beautiful flowers and colors.” Her eyes descend briefly to Jacqui, “Colors like you don’t see here.” They float upward again.

“Then Jesus came. And he said my name.” She closes her eyes and her arms fold gently around herself. “And he put His arms around me, and just loved me. It was so wonderful.”

She opens her eyes directly into Jacqui’s, her voice reverent, and instructive. “Just like in the Bible, I saw His ‘glory’ around Him. The light and the singing. . . It’s just . . . magnificent.” She closes her eyes again.

“And Jesus looked into me and smiled with such peace. There is so much peace with Him that you can’t imagine. It’s like nothing anywhere is wrong.”

Jasmine consoles herself, swaying her arm-wrapped body, remembering. “I said ‘Oh Jesus, I love you.’ And he said ‘My little lamb, it's not your time yet, but soon. Can you go back for a little while?' I said, 'I want to stay with you, Jesus.' And he said, 'Very soon, when your work is finished, you will come live with me.'"

She stops swaying, and opens her eyes to Jacqui, joy emitting from her face. After a moment, it fades some.

"And then the Angel brought me back to this broken world."

Jacqui's eyes linger wide with the vision.

After a quiet moment, Jasmine continues. "The *third* time I saw the angel, was when my parents had to tell me that the bone marrow didn't work, but that we were going to try a new treatment at another hospital. The angel stood behind Mommy and Daddy with his wings spread wide, protecting them. He told me the new procedure would not work, but that I should let them try." She lifts her hands in a small gesture, and then sets them on the bed. "So here I am."

The child's face is full of joy.

Jacqui is silent.

After a moment, Jasmine's eyes fasten with hers. "You are one of my assignments, Miss Jacqui. You are special, and Jesus loves you so much. You have a purpose in your life, and it is better than you could imagine."

Stripped of pretense, Jacqui listens, daunted.

Jasmine studies her companion.

"Your baby is in heaven," she reveals.

Jacqui's face grows cool and hardens. She stammers, "I have *never* had a baby." She bends and picks up her purse to leave.

Jasmine persists. "A long time ago, when you were in high school, you thought you were going to have a baby. The boy and you decided to get married. But you were not happy. You were too young. You thought it was a bad mistake. But then you found out you *weren't* going to have a baby, and so everything went back to normal."

Jacqui's face clouds with confusion, then wonder, and she slowly sets her purse back down. "But—"

"You were glad because you were so young. The boy went away, and you never saw each other again. But this was sad because you loved each other. And now you're still not married."

Astonished, Jacqui reflects, "The right guy just never came."

"But you had a dream one night, years later. In it, you were alone in a hospital room. Then they laid a baby girl on you, and you knew you had just had her. You looked at her small body and kissed her damp head. You could smell her newness. You held her, and in that moment, you felt a mother's love."

As the girl retells the dream, Jacqui sits forward on her chair. "It was so real. But then I woke up, and I didn't have her. I didn't know what to think. I had never confirmed if I was pregnant and always wondered." Her eyes search far away. "But the dream—I could still smell her."

Jasmine leans forward, hands on her bed. "It was true, Miss Jacqui. Jesus wants you to know that you *do* have a daughter, and she is waiting for you in heaven." She pats the bed softly with one hand. "Tell me her name. I know you named her, even though you didn't think she was real."

Jacqui is now crying, deeply. She pulls a tissue from her purse and wipes her eyes and nose methodically before she answers.

"Her. Name is Rose. After my Grandmother. But how do you know all of this?"

Jasmine sits back and smiles. "Rose. That's pretty." Then she looks at Jacqui tenderly.

"I'm going to die soon. I won't ever leave this hospital." She beams, euphoric. "But that's okay. I *want* to go home, when Jesus is done. God lives in my heart, so He sends the Angel sometimes to comfort me in this hard place."

Her hands turn upward on her lap to explain. "The Bible says that 'The angel of the LORD encamps all around those who fear Him and delivers them.' So now Jesus tells me everything He wants me to know for His special purpose."

A spirit of joy, filling the room, emanates through Jacqui's being.

"He has a special purpose for you, Miss Jacqui, if you only believe."

Footsteps come toward the room, and nurse Lani pops her head through the door with a big smile. "Ahh, Jacqui! You have too much fun! Keep my patient awake!" She laughs and waves her hand at them. "I joking. Hey, you need something, Miss Jasmine?"

Jasmine smiles cheerfully. "No Miss Lani. Thank you."

"Okay," she backs away from the room. "I check back later," and she strides away in her soft, squeaky shoes.

Jasmine looks again at Jacqui, who holds a quiet, elated smile. She dabs her eyes, then sets her hands down in her lap, and looks at them thoughtfully. She looks up, again.

"Thank you, Jasmine. For sharing that with me."

Jasmine grins. "You believe, don't you?"

"Ha," Jacqui chuckles, and dabs her eyes again, turning away, toward the dark window. Then she turns back to Jasmine and nods, "Yes. I do."

"Good. You can keep my Bible."

Jacqui locates the child's purple-covered Bible on the table beside her—the one she had set aside. "No, I can't take your Bible. What—"

"You have to. I want you to remember me," Jasmine insists.

Jacqui studies the book. Then she lifts it, zips the cover closed, and sets it in her lap. She lays her hands on it, and humbly returns Jasmine's smile.

"Okay. Now let's make a deal," Jasmine proposes.

"Okay. What deal?"

"After I die, *you* tell my family what I said about heaven. They can't hear it now. They aren't ready. But they'll need to hear it then."

Jacqui ponders the weight of the assignment. She begins to cry again a little, quietly. She wipes her nose and looks into Jasmine's joyous face. "Yes. Yes, of course. I will tell them." Then she tilts her head, puzzled. "Wait. What's the deal?"

Jasmine grins. "When I get to heaven, I'll tell your little Rose how much you love her and miss her."

Jacqui rises from her chair and engulfs the girl in tears and embraces. Soon, she is gently rocking Jasmine, humming some child's tune.

When she is finished, she gives Jasmine another squeeze.

"Miss Jacqui?"

"Yes, Sweetheart?"

"Can we pray for my Daddy? He needs help."

"Yes, of course." She holds Jasmine's hands. "Can *you* do it?"

"Yeah." Jasmine pinches her eyes closed, "Jesus, help my Daddy. He needs you. Send an angel to be with him, and to help him with his assignment. Amen."

"Amen."

~

As Bryce navigates the curvy mountain road, the headlights scarcely illuminate the coming landscape, painfully retarding his progress. His lights sweep vaguely between the steep rock-face rising to his left, and the dark, snowy forest dropping away on his right, with the white flashing lane markers as his maddening guide.

He had gotten lost looking for the gas station where they stopped on the way back. It took three errant exits and one disoriented sidetrack to find the same one. As he expected, but hoped otherwise, Jasmine's lamb was not there. His heart has been pounding since.

Now back in the mountains, everything looks so different and unfamiliar from their day trip. At every curve he expects to see the sign for the little viewpoint where they had stopped, but it seems much further than before. Torturously further.

He is fatigued and achy, and his legs are stiff and numb. His eyes are dry, and he hardly dares to blink and moisten them. He can't even look down to see how fast he is going. He is trapped eternally in the same, agonizing position, repeating the same, small movements that he began the day with. Accelerate, press the brakes, turn to the right, accelerate, press the brakes, turn to the left, eyes fixed in one line of sight. Over and over and over and over. Right. Left. Right. Left. His mind starts to wander.

"There!" In a flash, he spots the viewpoint sign. He slows and scans for the turn-out. The black pavement expands to the right and he navigates into the parking lot. Once his headlights illuminate the area, he recognizes the large paved viewpoint they had parked in so long ago.

Bryce drives toward the edge of the blacktop, tires popping on small gravel, and aims his headlights toward his search area. He pulls out his phone and texts an update to Felicia.

"Hmm. After 9:00 already." He rolls down his window part way before he gets out of the car—his habit ever since one of the kids accidentally locked the doors with the engine running, and he couldn't get back in.

Bryce opens the hatch and looks through his cargo for the flashlight. The rear of the car is poorly lit, and he riffles through, feeling and taking out things, but not locating the flashlight. He goes to the passenger side door to check the glove box, but it is locked. “Dang!”

He huffs back to the driver’s side and opens it, unlocking all the doors. He climbs in, riffles through the glove box, and still doesn’t find it. Then he opens the arm rest of the center console and feels around until he finds it. “Finally!” He snaps down the arm rest and clicks on the flashlight. It is still bright. “Thank you!” he exclaims, a little facetiously.

He closes the driver door and walks around the area, searching for the little lamb. He soon learns to keep out of his own headlights as he looks, but struggles to clearly view the scene. The black pavement is still covered with white patches, causing him to investigate each one for the little white lamb. The turn-out now seems monumentally larger than earlier that day, and he decides to implement a grid pattern.

“Why couldn’t the lamb be pink or purple?” Bryce searches for it with a frantic mind as he methodically walks back and forth. His heart pounds in his neck, and his mouth dries as he hyperventilates the cold air. His wasted breath illuminates a white shadow in the headlight beam, fogging his glasses momentarily with each exhale before fading.

“Come on. Come on.” He systematically traverses the entire blacktop. Foot by foot he investigates. He crouches down, and shines the flashlight under the car, carefully, impatiently scanning every white mound. He walks behind the car, nearer the road, pacing out a grid in the dark with his flashlight from the edge of the road, back to his car.

“Come on. Come on!” His throat is dry, but he dare not stop for water and break his concentration, or lose his place on the grid. After inspecting the entire blacktop, he arrives at the car again, and opens the driver door. He grabs the last bottle from the drink holder and gulps the water until it is gone. He tosses the bottle in the back and takes off his jacket. He returns to the edge of the blacktop near the bushes and begins to carefully examine the snow-covered ground, the shadows, and the shrubbery.

“Come on. Come on.” He tries to envision what he will do next if the lamb is not here—how he will have to do this same, frantic process at every stop where they opened Jasmine’s door. “No! Come on!”

He now scans off the edge of the blacktop outside of the

headlights to the right of the car. He points his flashlight hopefully, disappointingly at every possible shape. He pauses over red winter berries wondering if Lily's bow was red or pink. He examines dark splotches for her dangling hooves. All the way to the right, all the way around the perimeter, meticulously, frantically scrutinizing every possible feature.

"This is ridiculous! Impossible." He retraces the area back until he reaches the headlights again. Then he methodically searches the snow around the bushes to the left of the headlights—painstakingly, every shape, every anomaly, every possible set of lamb eyes, every white mound nose, exhaustingly, beyond his physical ability to endure. When he reaches the far left edge by the road, he collapses onto his knees. The flashlight tumbles from his hand and rolls a short way, pointing its beam behind him. In front of him is darkness.

"She said it was here. She was certain of it," he quietly protests. Heart pounding, mouth dry again and no water left, he kneels in the wet snow. His hard breathing slows, as sadness and defeat effuse his soul. He starts to cry. Cry for the lost lamb. Cry for his daughter. His body convulses with his hard, silent sobs. He inhales a great breath and wails.

"Oh God! Oh God! Please. Help me!"

He cries doubled over with his hands against the icy ground, letting the sobs flow until he is over-spent, and they gradually diminish. After a moment, he straightens, wipes his face with his sleeve, and puts his hands on his thighs, preparing himself to rise--willing himself to the next stop to begin again. As he crouches there, away from the running car, the pounding in his ears from his own heart and other sounds gradually fade. In the quiet stillness, he hears the trickle of water splashing nearby.

He turns his face to tune-in the happy sound from hours ago, when he and Jasmine took their picture and discovered the little roadside waterfall. He can't see it now, but he can in his mind.

In this moment, he feels peace wash over him. Deep inside, disputing all his angst, he hears a reassuring promise.

"It'll be all right."

He takes a deep, calm breath, and looks up.

"Thank you," he whispers.

In that instant, a red flash illuminates the silent, white landscape before him, holds, and then disappears.

Chapter 13: All We Like Sheep Have Gone Astray (Isaiah 53:6)

She puts the breakfast dishes in the dishwasher, wipes down the counter, and then turns to inspect the kitchen, hands on hips. Digital sounds emitting from the living room fill the house with screeches, shots, crashes, and explosions. She looks at her watch. 11:45.

"Man, he is so late."

Sirens now wail over her thoughts. "Justin!" she calls. "What did I tell you? Turn that down, Baby. You're giving me a headache."

"Yes, Mommy," comes the small voice, and the volume decreases.

"Thank you, Baby," she calls back. "Now I can think," she tells herself. She lifts her phone from the counter and makes a call. It rings once. Twice. "I don't know why he got him that game anyway," she adds. Three times. "Stealing cars is not a game for a 10-year-old." Four times.

VOICEMAIL: "This is Travis. Leave a message. Or don't." BEEP.

"UUghh. Okay, Travis." She whispers loudly. "You are over an hour late. You *need* to give me a call."

She hangs up firmly and sets her phone down. She crosses her arms—thinking. Her son sits on the floor in front of the TV, tilting his head and contorting his whole body to steer the image on the screen. She chuckles and smiles. Beyond him is the twinkling Christmas tree full of ornaments from their past. She refused to put *some* up this year—like the ones Travis had brought home from the different countries where he was deployed, or those marking their years together.

Her eyes target the small, Christmas-framed photo of the two of them, which hangs in the center of the tree. He is in his navy dress uniform, and she is wearing that dark orange mock sweater he loved on her. They had gone on a harbor cruise, and there was a photographer taking pictures. Travis loved the photo and bought it in three sizes. It was their first year of marriage—before she became pregnant. Before he was deployed as a corpsman to the Middle East.

Justin loves the picture and won't let her leave it off the tree. After two years, he still hopes.

Fuming, she picks up the phone again, and calls. It rings once. Twice. Three times. Four times. She hangs up. She calls again. Once. Twice. Three times. Four times. She hangs up. She calls again. Once. Twice. Three times. Four times. She hangs up. She calls again. Once. Twice. Three times.

"Wha!" comes the heavy, exacerbated voice on the other end.

"Travis! Where have you been? You're an hour late!" she scolds in a forced whisper

There is a pause, then a slow voice. "Keisha?"

"Yes, it's Keisha. Who do you think it is?"

Another pause, and some rustling, fumbling sounds. "Aahhh. . . Oh. Hey Baby. What's going on?"

Keisha strides briskly to the back of the house, and steps through the sliding glass door out to the small yard. The little black and white terrier jumps from her bed in the sun and trots over wagging her tail. Keisha sits on the step and pets the dog, who keeps licking her hand.

"What's going on? Are you kidding me Travis?"

"Whhaaat?" comes his groggy, thick reply. "Wha' dis it? Wha's going on?"

She pulls the phone away from her ear and shakes her head, then returns it again. "Travis! You're drunk! I can't believe you're drunk!"

He lets out a long, loud exhale that blasts into the speaker of the phone. Then the slow, slurred reply, "Wha? . . . No—no I'm not . . . It's jus—"

"I can't believe it!" The dog dances around her, wagging her tail, licking whatever exposed skin she can reach. Keisha pushes her away several times trying to concentrate. "You *know* you are supposed to pick up Justin for Christmas Eve. We agreed you could have that tradition, as long as you *don't* drink!"

Another blast of breath comes through the phone. "Wait, I know Baby. I'm coming. I'm on my way—"

"Oh no you don't." Keisha attempts to occupy the dog with one hand, as she jumps and tries to climb onto her lap. Finally, Keisha slides open the door behind her and scoots the dog into the house, then shuts it again.

"Travis, you said you got help. You said you have been sober for two months."

A sad groan emits from the other side, and crescendos into the slow, thick, pitiful words, "Ooohh, I know Keisha. I did. I got help. But the trouble is, you know the VA, they—they—they are all messed up. They—they couldn't get me an appointment, and then my—my anxiety meds ran out, and they—they wouldn't refill them unless I—"

Keisha rests her head on her knees, listening until her impatience interrupts him. "Look Travis. I *know*. I *get* it. But you HAVE to figure something out, okay? You gotta get whatever help you need. Just do it, Okay? Your son needs you. You gotta pull yourself together."

She hears sobbing on the other end. "I know, Baby. You're right. I'm sorry."

"That's fine, but we don't need you to be *sorry*. You gotta find a way to *live* again. For your son's sake. Okay?"

"Yeah. Yeah. Keisha, I'm gonna do it. I will. I'm gonna do it."

Keisha rests her forehead on the palm of her hand, listening to old promises. "Okay. Travis, I gotta go."

"Oh. Yeah. Okay. Ahh . . . Merry Christmas. Tell Justin I said Merry Christmas."

"Okay. Bye." She hangs up, crosses her arms over her knees, and lays her head on them. After a moment, she hears scratching on the glass door and turns to find the dog stroking her little white paw down the glass. Keisha slides the door open a crack, and the wiry dog bounds out, dancing again around her legs.

Keisha sets her feet on the bottom step to level her lap. "Come on Daisy," she calls, patting her thigh. The dog springs onto her lap and licks her nose affectionately, then wobbles on her master's legs, turning around to receive caresses on her back.

"I didn't ask for *you* either," she scolds teasingly, scruffing Daisy's head. She sits for a time petting the dog, thinking. After several minutes, she picks up her phone again and makes another call. The phone rings and then there is an answer.

"Hi, Mr. McKinney? This is Keisha Parsons. I made our usual reservations for tonight under Travis Parsons. Do you still have that? . . . Yes, three nights. . . Yes. Well, I just wanted to let you know that *I'm* coming instead, not Travis, okay? . . . Fine, yes, thank you. . . Perfect. How's the weather? . . . Oh, that's good. Well, we're getting a bit of a late start, but we should be there around 5:30, if that's okay. . . Fine. . . Yes, we'll see you then. Goodbye."

Keisha hangs up, and the dog jumps off her lap, turning to look at her human, tail wagging. Keisha grabs her little snout friskily. "I guess that means you too."

She takes a deep breath, sighs, then hoists herself up to make the announcement. She slides open the door, and the little dog scampers into the house springing and trotting around. Keisha stands beside the TV until Justin pauses the game. He is sitting cross-legged, and after he sees her expression, he sadly sets the controls away from him.

"He's not coming, is he?" He quietly hangs his head.

"I'm sorry, Baby." She takes a few steps, then sits down cross-legged beside him against the couch. She puts her arm around him and gives him a squeeze. "Your daddy loves you, Justin. But he is just struggling so much, you know? He's sad about the things he saw in the war, and that shows how he really is a good man." She looks down to him. "But he's still figuring out how to deal with all of it. You understand that?"

Justin's hands dangle loosely in his lap. He nods his head, looking at them. He lifts one hand and brushes his cheek.

Keisha wraps her other arm around him, and he turns and clasps his arms around her waist, burying his head in her chest. "I want Daddy to get better."

She rocks him. "I know, Baby. Me too." She kisses his head and cradles him for a moment.

Then she holds him out and looks in his eyes.

"But for now. . ." she begins, playfully shaking him with each word, "we have a tradition to uphold!" She stands up dramatically and points one finger high in the air, "The Parsons Family retreat!" This gesture sends Daisy springing around the room.

Justin's eyes widen, "We're still going?"

"It's a tradition, isn't it?" Keisha sasses, hands on hips.

Justin thrusts his fist into the air, "Yes!" Then he jumps to his feet and runs around the room waving his arms wildly over his head, the frenzied dog on his heals as he chants, "We're still going! We're still going! We're still going!" Then he stops. "And Daisy too?"

"Yes, Daisy too."

The celebration continues, "Yea!!!! Yea!!!!"

Keisha laughs, then holds out her hands to settle him down. "Okay, Buster, come here. Now listen." The boy returns to his mom, breathlessly. "I have some packing to do, and I need *your* help."

"But I packed all my stuff already."

"I know. You did a good job. But now I have to pack *my* things, and there's other things we need to take for Christmas."

"Like the tree?"

"No, not the tree. They have a tree for us, but if you want, you can grab 10 of your favorite ornaments—"

"And the Christmas presents? Want me to—" "HA! Sneeky. Don't you touch those presents. I'll take care of those."

"What about the stockings?"

"Yes, take our stockings. But I also need you to get Daisy's food, her treats, and her dish, and her leash, her inside bed, her sweater, and those little bags—"

"Her poop bags?"

"Yes, those."

"Okay, got it."

"Alright, then. I'll get the rest."

~

About an hour and a half later Keisha stands beside the car assessing all the things to be loaded. "This was a lot easier with the SUV." After some wrangling, she manages to get their bags, the dog's things, and most of the Christmas stuff in the trunk. But some of the Christmas presents are too big, and she puts them in a garbage bag on the floor of the front seat. Their winter jackets also come in the car, and Justin brings his little backpack of things to play with on the three-hour drive from San Diego.

Justin opens the back door and Daisy leaps in first. Then he tosses his backpack on the seat beside him, and climbs into his booster seat, snapping in the seatbelt. Keisha does a final check of the house, and then gets in the driver's seat. She turns around and greets her eager passenger, legs dangling, expectant grin.

"Ready?"

"Ready!"

They first stop at a gas station, and Keisha checks the tire pressure and fills the tank. Next, they stop at a drive-through to grab lunch before getting on the long road ahead.

Keisha looks back in the rear-view mirror as she pulls out her chicken sandwich and unwraps it. "Got everything, Baby?"

Justin is digging through the Happy Meal box and flips a floppy French fry into his mouth. "Mmm, I don't see any catsup."

Keisha hands him her bag, "Check in here." He rustles around and finds two packets.

"I found them." He hands the bag up to Keisha.

"Good. Anything else?"

He thinks for a moment. "Ummm . . . Music!"

"Oh, music. Okay." She turns on the radio and looks back in the mirror. "What kind of music are you in the mood for, Mister?"

"Ahhh. . . Christmas music!" he punctuates with a French fry.

Keisha laughs. "Yes, of course. *Christmas* music." She presses the scan button. "Let's see what we can find." After several tries, "Oh Come All Ye Faithful," tunes in.

"How's that?"

Justin bites his cheeseburger. "Mmm… Good." He gives a thumb's up.

"Good." Keisha turns up the volume, and they begin their journey eating and singing loudly--especially to "Up on the Housetop"—sound effects and all.

After about 2 ½ hours, they begin to ascend the mountains. Soon the reception fails, so she turns off the radio. Daisy, who initially hopped back and forth between the seats begging for snacks, has finally settled on the pile of coats next to Justin and is asleep.

"Sorry we can't get any more music." She checks Justin in the mirror.

He is looking out the window. "That's okay. I think we heard all the songs anyway."

The road starts to wind as the white forest grows up around them. She looks at him again. He is staring afar off.

"Need anything, Baby?"

A thoughtful pause, then quietly. "No. I'm good."

The shadows have grown dark across the road as dusk approaches. The clock on the dash reads 5:10.

She checks him again. "Are you sad? About Daddy?"

He rests his chin on his hand, elbow propped against the window frame. "Yeah. A little."

As the curves sharpen, she concentrates on the road ahead. One of the tires seems to slip, and Keisha notices that water trickling down the mountain occasionally trails across the road. She grips the wheel attentively and lifts her foot some off the gas.

"I know, Baby. I'm sad too." She switches on her headlights in the low glow of evening.

"I miss him."

"I know you do. I miss him too."

Quiet.

"Mommy, doesn't he love me?"

She glances in the mirror and meets his gaze. "Yes, Baby. He loves you so much. Don't you doubt that. He just needs help."

He turns his face back toward the window.

"Are we going to church tonight, like we used to?"

She ponders this question for a moment. "Tonight?"

"Yeah. It's Christmas Eve. We always used to go on Christmas Eve to that church up there."

"You remember that? We haven't done that for . . . three years."

"Yeah. . . I remember."

Keisha's heart beats a little faster. "Well, Baby . . . That depends on what time we get there, I guess."

"What time does it start?"

She glances at the clock again. "It used to start at 7:00."

"What time will we get there?"

"Ummm . . . a little before 6:00, but—"

"That sounds like enough time. Doesn't it?"

She hesitates, "But we have to check in, and unpack the car. . ."

"Oh."

The forest passes.

He is quiet.

She is quiet.

"We'll see how it goes, Okay?"

He is quiet.

"Okay."

They sway in silence up the winding, frosty mountain road.

"Mommy?"

"Hmmm, Baby?"

"Don't you believe in God anymore?"

She inhales a sharp, short breath.

His eyes look for hers in the mirror. "I mean. It just seems like we really need Him now. Don't we?"

"Justin. . ." She shakes her head. "I . . . It's just—"

The front tire slips on another icy stream and begins to slide.

Keisha grips the wheel and tries to straighten it, but the car glides off the road, brushes the guardrail, jostles through bramble down a steep, rocky slope, broadsides a tree, then slams to a stop against an outcrop of boulders.

Keisha's ears ring as she opens her eyes to the startling scene. She can scarcely hear until the disorienting din subsides. In the icy blue light, she sees a pillowy white form draped in front of her. She touches it and realizes the airbags have deployed. She feels her face and finds it swollen and numb; her eyes are puffy and gritty. There is pressure across her chest from the taut seat belt bearing her full weight. In the waning light, she can see through the windshield some boulders and trees holding the car on the steep hillside.

"Justin! Justin!" She calls. He does not answer. She tries to find him in the rear view mirror, but can't. She turns her body to look over her shoulder, and a sharp pain sears her hip. Pushing through it, she grasps the seat beside her for leverage to look into the back seat. She sees him, head dangling forward, body slumped against his seat belt. There appears to be a smear on the window beside him.

"Justin! Justin, Baby! Justin!" There is no response. She fights the pain, and stretches for his hand, but it lies awkwardly on the seat next to him, out of her reach.

She honks the horn to wake him up, but it makes no sound. She yanks on the handle to open her door, but it is wedged, and she has no leverage.

"Justin! Justin! Wake up!"

She searches for something heavy or sharp to break her window, but this movement causes pain to shoot from her right hip, sharply down her leg, all the way to her foot.

"Ah!"

In the waning light, she pushes aside the airbag to investigate and discovers her leg wedged and misshapen under the dashboard. It must have been locked against the brake pedal when they went over the edge. She tries gently to dislodge it, and the sharp pain infuses her body with hot blackness. Nausea rolls upon her and she nearly faints. She forces herself to breathe steadily and regain her composure.

She presses her left foot against the floor to relieve the weight from her right leg, reducing the pain to a dull throb. Her mind begins to focus again.

Her phone—where is her phone? Everything on the seat beside her, her purse, everything in the center console, her drink, her charger, the loose change, was all flung out of place. Had her phone been in her purse, or in the console? She reaches up and switches on the interior light. It works, but does not illuminate the floor. Beneath the other deflated airbag, she sees the sack of Christmas presents spread over the passenger floor space, but she can't reach the bag to move it and search for the phone. Even if she could, she has nothing to grab the phone with.

"Seri! Call 911!"

She listens. She hears nothing. If she *knew* where it was, she could see if the phone responds, or if a call goes through. She looks at her feet, between the pedals to see if the phone had been launched there. She searches the dashboard, in case it flew forward, but sees nothing.

She concludes that her purse must have landed in the passenger seat floor well, but can't see it through all the obstructions. She feels around the sides of her seat and finds nothing. Then she reaches back to the space between her son and her. She discovers a jacket and pulls it toward her. She reaches up to the rear-view mirror and adjusts it until she can partially see her son.

"Justin! Justin!"

She is silent for a moment, listening. She hears the sound of his soft breathing.

He is wearing his favorite US Navy hoodie, with the little hood flopped onto the top of his drooped head. She evaluates his position in order to drape the jacket over him. She wads it together, and slings it over her shoulder, holding onto one sleeve, and it unfurls toward him. It misses and falls to his feet. She gathers it up and tries again. After a few more times, it lands a little folded on his back.

She rests for a moment, then reaches back in the space between them again. She finds the strap of his backpack and stretches until she can just barely grasp it between her first and second fingers. She draws it closer until she can gain a firm grip. Finally, she pulls it to herself and searches through the compartments for something helpful. She finds a water bottle, and uncaps it for a rationed, desperate sip. She returns it to the bag. Further investigation only yields puzzle books, pencils, erasers, a granola bar, and some miscellaneous, but seemingly useless items.

She lifts the passenger airbag and tries to move the sack of presents with one of the pencils to look for her phone. Once again, she cannot get enough leverage on the plastic surface to move the heavy bag, or even puncture it. Exhausted, she rests and thinks.

She zips up the backpack, and gently swings it behind her, bumping it against her son's leg.

"Justin! Justin!"

She tries again, harder. He doesn't respond.

She begins to shiver. She sets aside the backpack, and rests. The pain floods higher and dulls her wits. She feels behind her seat again and touches something warm. Daisy. She can only stroke the small patch of slick fur, but can't get ahold of the little dog or tell if she is breathing. She finds the sleeve of the other jacket resting on the dog and stretches until her first two fingers can lightly grip the nylon fabric. She patiently draws it closer, until she can grasp it, with agonizing relief. It is her son's jacket. She wraps it around the front of her shoulders, under the seatbelt, and slips her arms into the sleeves as best she can.

She rests and thinks. Her left leg grows weak supporting the weight of her whole body in position, outstretched for footing on some prominence in the floor-well. If she relaxes it at all, her weight shifts excruciatingly against her mangled right leg, trapped in the crumpled compartment. She grips the steering wheel and pushes with her arms to shift some weight off her leg, but it is strenuous, and she must relent. There is blood on her hand, but she is not sure from where. Her mouth thickens with dryness.

Trembling, Keisha, unzips the backpack and sips the water. She replaces it, scans the car again, then switches off the interior light and the one remaining headlight to preserve the battery. She now sits in almost complete darkness. She hears the steady, shallow breaths of her son. There is no other sound except the occasional creak of the cooling engine, or quiet tap of some specimen of nature falling around the car. She detects the faint smell of gas, and perhaps some other car fluid. The quiet is calming.

"I have to think. Think!" She grabs the steering wheel and tries to gingerly adjust the pressure off her legs again. She finds she can gain relief by shifting her body weight against the steering wheel with her arms crossed in front of her, tucked in against it. She rests her head against the top of the wheel, as the intense pain subsides.

"Okay. Think! What have I missed?" She tries to process through the available items, remember where her phone likely was, envision how to get to her purse, how to wake Justin, how to get help. . . Around her thoughts go, deliberating over all these questions and possibilities and solutions . . .

Remarkably, her body grows numb, and at some point, which she has no sense of, Keisha succumbs to sleep.

~

Keisha awakes abruptly. This shock causes her to flex her left leg, sending electric jolts of pain from her right leg through her body. The darkness is disorienting, and her confines frightening. Her heart strikes sharply in her chest from the sudden pain and panic, and she grips the steering wheel in agony. Slowly, breathing heavily, she regains her awareness of the situation, and braces her aching left leg to relieve her right. As her breathing steadies, her mind races again and she tries to recall if she had discovered any possible solutions.

"Justin, Justin," she calls reflexively again, with little verve. As she listens, she realizes what has awakened her. His breathing has changed and is now harsh and raspy. It sounds guttural and staccato as if from some blockage or swelling. The struggle intensifies, and his breathing becomes sporadic. Then, the sounds stop.

Adrenaline surges through her.

"Justin! Justin! Baby wake up!" She pulls the small jacket sleeve off her arm, grabs the backpack beside her, and swings it back at him. It only bumps his leg and falls away. She grabs it again and this time flings it at his body. It thuds against his shoulder but fails to revive him.

"Oh God! Oh God help me!" she shouts. "God, don't let him die!" She stretches for him with all she has. She tries to turn in the seat and reach for him, but her trapped, excruciating leg holds her fast.

"No God! You have to help him! God Please! Please God, Please God! Help him!"

She reaches back stretching against her confines time and again. Her left foot, fighting for leverage, finds the brake pedal haphazardly and she thrusts against it, extending her very furthest to reach him, but only brushes the top of his thigh. Her foot slides off the pedal with shocking pain to her right leg, stealing her breath.

Adrenaline now waning, she fades again, shackled to her seat, sobbing exhausted and hopeless.

"Oh-ho God," she quietly pleads. "God, no." She weeps into her cold, numb hands.

Then she stops. "What is that?"

She holds her breath. She hears it again. A voice in the quiet distance, calling.

"Hello?"

Chapter 14: To Seek and to Save that which is Lost (Luke 19:10)

Bryce's heart quickens, infusing his body with weightless energy. He leaps to his feet and takes several strides up the road where he sees a damaged guard rail, and a faint scar in the snow descending the slope into the darkness. He grabs the flashlight from the blacktop and tucks it in his back pocket, then runs back toward the SUV, as he breathlessly dials 911. He jumps into the driver's seat, hastily reverses the car, then speeds forward across the blacktop several yards to the wound in the landscape, where he aims his lights and activates his hazards.

"911. Where is your emergency?"

Panting, mouth dry, "Hello. I'm eastbound on the 18 a few miles outside of Big Bear, and there's a car here that's gone off the road. I think there are still people trapped in it."

"Okay, sir. Did you see the accident happen?"

Bryce sets the brake and leaps out, jogging to the guard rail. There is a gap in the railing after the turnout, which leaves several yards of roadway unprotected. He stares down into the darkness, unable to discern any shapes, as his headlights only pass over the road.

"No, I didn't see it. I don't know when it happened. But I saw a flash of light—like a taillight or brake light. Someone is down there, and there's damage here, like a car went over the road."

"Okay sir. Where exactly are you?"

Bryce starts down the steep, snow-powdered bank, clambering through the trail of destruction.

"I'm at that view-point, where you can pull out. It's right there. I have my lights and flashers on. Please hurry."

"Sir, I already have fire rescue and paramedics dispatched. Tell me what you can see."

He slips a little, and lands on his rear. "I'm going to look now, but I need to put you in my pocket to free my hands. Hold on."

"No, sir, don't go down there."

Bryce tucks his phone in his shirt pocket and continues feeling his way down the scar in the snowy hillside. Winded, he calls out "Hello?" He grabs onto nearby branches to keep his balance on the slick ground. He slips again, sliding into some rocks. He gets up, pushes his glasses back up on his nose and picks his way in the dark through the prickly underbrush. He calls again.

"Hello?" Suddenly he hears muffled cries and muted thumps.

"Yes! Yes! Help! Help us!" Then a little light comes on, illuminating the location of the car, 15 more yards or so.

"I see you!" he calls again, and then remembers the flashlight in his back pocket. He shines it and finds the back of the car. "I'm coming!" he calls.

He slips and falls again, sliding and stopping himself with his foot against the back-passenger tire. He tramps to the passenger side and shines the light across the front seat into Keisha's swollen, desperate visage.

"My son! Get My son!" she waives at him frantically. Bryce yanks on the passenger door handle, but then sees the dented scar and missing paint along both doors. They won't budge. Bryce pulls out his phone to report the two victims, but the line is dead. There is no signal.

"Hurry!" Keisha pleads. "He stopped breathing!"

Bryce replaces his phone and climbs around the back of the car. He slips, crashing his knee into a rock. He scrambles to the other side and pulls at the back-door handle. It won't open.

"Is it locked?" he yells.

Keisha frantically fumbles for the controls on her door. They hear the click "Oh, thank God," she calls. "Hurry, please!"

Bryce yanks open the back door and dives in across the seat. He releases the boy's seatbelt and swiftly pulls his limp body toward him.

"I got him!" Bryce grunts.

"Oh, thank you God!" Keisha's voice quavers breathlessly. "Please, just take care of him."

"I got him," Bryce grunts again and hoists the boy's arms around his shoulders. "I called 911. They're on their way," he strains, starting up the slope carrying the boy on his back.

"Oh, thank you!" she calls. "Don't worry about me. Take care of him!"

Bryce crawls up the rough terrain holding the boy's wrists over his shoulders with one hand and climbing his way in the dark with the other. After an arduous trek, exhausting the last of his adrenaline, he finally arrives at the top of the road. There he lays the boy down on the blacktop in front of the car lights and tilts his small head back. Bryce pants, catching his breath for a moment, then quickly bends near and listens for breathing. He then pinches the boy's nose and gives him two short breaths. He listens again, and then begins giving him chest compressions.

"ONE, TWO, THREE, FOUR, FIVE, SIX, SEVEN, Come on Jesus! TEN, ELEVEN, TWELVE, THIRTEEN, FOURTEEN—"

Suddenly the boy convulses once, and begins to cough, and then a soft groan. Bryce stops compressions and listens for breathing. He hears the steady sounds continue for several breaths. He notices some moisture following the contours of the boy's face from his right temple, but can't see the injury in the dim light. Bryce puts his hand on the boy's chest and gently shakes him.

"Hey there," he quietly calls. "Hey buddy." The boy doesn't respond. Bryce listens again, and hears the breathing continue.

"Thank you, God," Bryce whispers. He decides not to carry the boy to his car, in case of a spinal injury. He uses the boy's hood to tilt his head and maintain the airway, then goes to the SUV for his jacket, and spreads it over him. He rubs the small hands one at a time in his to warm them. Then he hears the loud downshift of fire engines approaching, and soon the flashing lights descend the hill and turn with majestic grandeur into the lot.

Bryce stands and waives. "There's a boy here!" The yellow-jacketed crew comes jogging over. Two paramedics bring equipment and encircle the boy, taking vitals and assessing him.

Bryce points down the embankment scar, "There's a woman trapped in the driver's seat. I think she's pretty hurt."

"Okay, we got it," says one, slinging a length of rope onto his shoulder and unloading more equipment. The rescue team converges at the top of the road and assess their approach before they harness up.

One of the paramedics asks Bryce about the condition of the boy as they intubate him.

"Uhh, he was unconscious in the back of the car, and he wasn't breathing. I gave him CPR, and he started breathing on his own." Bryce hears the other paramedic call over the radio for Lifeflight to meet the ambulance at some other location.

The two then load him onto a stretcher and secure him. "That's great work, sir. What's your name?" They roll the stretcher into the back of the ambulance.

Suddenly, Bryce is cold. "Ahh, Bryce. My name's Bryce."

"This yours?" One of the paramedics hands him his jacket from off of the boy and jumps into the back. "Well, you did good Bryce. You probably saved his life." The other paramedic closes the doors and gets in the driver's seat. The ambulance pulls out, lights and sirens, and heads down the mountain.

As Bryce watches them leave, another firefighter approaches him. "Sir, can you move your SUV back into the lot there, we need to get some equipment over here."

"Oh, yeah, sure." Bryce gets into his car and backs it up and parks it, idling. He leaves his lights on to help illuminate the area. He puts on his jacket and leans against the front of his car, between the headlights. As soon as the first ambulance pulls away, a second ambulance arrives.

One of those paramedics walks over to the crew at the top of the road, but the other comes to Bryce and stands with him a moment. "How's it going?"

"Ahh, good," Bryce answers.

"Are you the one who called it in?" He asks.

"Yeah. I called it in."

The guy points at Bryce's jeans. "Looks like you went down there too. Did you?"

Bryce looks down at his scuffed-up jeans, splotched with dirt and wet from the snow. "Yeah. I went down."

"So, you brought that boy up, then."

"Yeah, I did."

The paramedic gives him a pat on the arm. "Nice job."

"Thanks."

"Hey, are you hurt at all? Maybe you got some scratches on

your legs and hands?"

Bryce looks at his hands in the headlight beam. There are scratches and mud on them. "Nah, I think I'm fine."

"Need anything then? How about some water?"

Bryce swallows dryly. "Oh yeah. That would be great."

The other paramedic walks toward them from the scene.

"Hakim, can you grab a water?" The other paramedic stops at the ambulance, gets a water bottle from the back, and brings it over, handing it to Bryce.

Bryce cracks open the cap, "Thanks." He guzzles most of the water. He puts the cap back on and tucks it in his jacket pocket. "Thanks. Hey, how's it going over there?"

Hakim answers, "They're taking the equipment down there now to get her out. It'll be a little while. How'd she seem when you were down there?"

Bryce thinks a moment. "I don't know. I think she was hurt—trapped certainly. I didn't ask. She just wanted me to get her son out." Bryce starts to shiver as soreness, cold, and fatigue overtake him.

"Okay. That's good." He turns to the other paramedic. "Massy, we need to get the backboard ready to rope down, so let's get all the gear set."

The two start to leave. "Hey, can I ask?" Bryce interjects.

The first paramedic turns to Bryce, "Yeah?"

Bryce shrugs his shoulders a little. "Well, do you think you need me to stick around?"

Massy looks uncertainly at the other paramedic, then turns back to him. "Well, did you see the accident happen?"

"No, I didn't see it happen. I told 911 I didn't see it."

"Oh. Well then, you probably don't need to stick around," he concludes.

"Okay, thanks." Bryce tucks his hands into his jacket pockets against the cold. "You see, my daughter is in the hospital in LA, and I really have to get back to her."

"Well, I certainly understand that." Massy holds out his hand to shake Bryce's, "What's your name?"

"Bryce." He shakes it.

"Okay, Bryce, let me run it by our supervisor." He walks to one of the other firefighters, and his partner returns to the ambulance. As they talk in the flashing, lighted scene, another set of flashing lights descends the road, silently illuminating the mountainside, and then pulls in behind the main fire truck. It is the sheriff's department, and a deputy gets out of the vehicle and walks over to the Firefighter in command of the incident. After a moment's conversation, Massy and the deputy walk back to Bryce.

"Hey Bryce, this is Deputy Inoye. He's gonna get your name and let you go on your way. You take care now."

"Thanks, I appreciate it." He watches Massy join Hakim at their ambulance to pull out a backboard and other equipment.

The Deputy gets a pen and a notepad from his breast pocket and addresses Bryce. "Hi sir. I understand that you did *not* witness the accident?"

Bryce pulls his arms close to his body. "No. I didn't see it happen. I just noticed a red light flash on the hillside and figured it out."

The deputy is writing in the SUV headlights. "Okay, then. I just need your name and contact info in case we have any follow-up questions, and then you can go."

Bryce gives him the information.

"Okay, sir. Thanks for your help. You have a nice evening now," the deputy nods.

"Okay, thanks."

~

Bryce pulls the bottle from his jacket pocket and swallows the rest of the water. He climbs into his car, and tiredly puts it into gear. The dash clock reads 9:43. He pauses at the road, then pulls out, turning right to continue his long quest. His heavy body hunches over the wheel as he slowly drives toward Big Bear. When he arrives, he first stops at the Taco Bell and parks in the darkened lot. The blacktop is sloped, and there is little snow left to hide the missing lamb. He walks into the vacant restaurant, not noticing the sign.

"Sorry, we're closed sir," calls the young man from the counter.

"Oh, okay," complies Bryce. "It's just that I was here several hours ago with my little girl, and I wondered if anyone turned in a little stuffed white lamb. It's very important to her."

The cashier shakes his head, "I haven't gotten anything."

Bryce takes another uncertain step forward. "I'm sorry, but can you just look? It would have been hours ago. I drove all the way back from LA to check."

A voice comes from the back, "You drove back from LA?"

"I'm sorry, yeah. So, can you just check around please?"

The manager comes to the front, "Yeah, of course." He looks through a box, and then checks another shelf behind the counter. Bryce hears the sound of food containers being scraped and stacked in the kitchen.

The manager disappears into the back, then finally returns shaking his head. "I'm sorry. It's not here. And we just cleaned the bathrooms, so it's not in there either."

"Okay, thanks." Bryce starts to leave. "Hey, I know I'm asking a lot, but do you suppose I could use your bathroom? It's been a long drive" he chuckles listlessly, "A long day, actually."

The manager nods. "Yeah, sure."

Bryce goes to the restroom and when he is done, he washes his sore, dirty hands, wipes his stubbly face, then cleans his glasses, which have mud and smudges on them. He sees the worn-out face of a man he doesn't know. He dries his hands, then carefully cleans out the sink of dirt and water and leaves the bright restroom. The dining room lights are now off.

"Thanks guys," Bryce waives over his shoulder as he leaves.

The cashier calls to him "Hey wait a minute. Here, my manager wanted to give this to you." He slides a white bag and a large, empty cup toward Bryce.

"Really?" Bewildered, he walks back and looks in the bag. There are two burritos. "Oh, that's so amazing. Thank you," he laughs tiredly. Then he calls toward the back "Thank you!"

The cashier grins, "No problem. You can fill that cup, if you want."

"Yes! Thank you so much!"

"You bet. Merry Christmas."

"Ha! Oh man. Merry Christmas," Bryce chuckles, accepting the gift. He fills the cup with Mountain Dew and snaps on the lid, "I gotta stay awake."

The young man follows Bryce to the door and locks it after a last "thank you." Bryce exits, climbs into his SUV, and guzzles some soda. Then he peels the first burrito wrapper and in three voracious bites, nearly finishes the entire thing. He wraps the rest and returns it to the bag, takes another large draw on his drink, and lets out a big sigh. He starts the car as the remaining store lights flicker off and pulls out of the lot toward his next destination—the little cafe.

There, he slowly navigates the dark parking lot, illuminating it with his headlights, and getting out to investigate when he needs to, but finds nothing. He takes another swig of his drink, then pulls out toward the lakeside beach. He drives slowly on the dark, quiet, street until he recognizes the turn, then follows the desolate road flanked by the parking lot and forest to their original parking spot. He shines his headlights on the lot, but then finally, tiredly, climbs out with his flashlight, as there are many more mysterious white mounds than the cafe parking lot.

Body stiff, he wills himself to sweep the area with his flashlight. He kicks the different snow shapes, and follows a loose grid pattern again, straining through tired eyes and fog on his glasses. Finally, he straightens himself, arching his back with a groan. He sees the moon rising in the east and turns west to face the lake. The walkway that he and Jasmine took earlier glows in the moonlight, leading to the lake. There is a trashcan along the path, and he wonders if someone found the lamb and tossed it in there. He goes to it, but it is empty.

Moonshine reflects on the lake. "Jasmine would like to see this," he sighs. "I wish she could." He begins to retrace their steps up the path, pointing his light and searching around. Soon, he stands on the beach near the water's edge. The moonlight stretches across the dark, mirrored water. He turns off the flashlight, tucks it into his back pocket, and sits down on the edge of a cement fire pit, facing the silent lake. It's so beautiful. So peaceful. So, shimmering in the midst of the dark.

His mind wanders over the day, visualizing each moment, and recalling the sequence of stops. His heart, pinches at the thought of the little lamb—lost forever. He begins to shiver—overspent in body and soul.

Bryce sighs, "But that boy. He's safe." He shakes his head quietly, reflecting on the events.

He looks up at the black sky, speckled with stars, and a passing cloud that glows in silver light. "God, you saved that boy."

Then his eyes stretch out over the dark lake, searching. "But Jasmine's lamb. Lost." He glances around again, expecting to discover the desecrated little body.

He tucks his hands in his jacket pockets and looks up. "Poor Jasmine . . . Lost."

His body trembles. His breathing tightens in the cold, black air. It constrains his throat. Quiet weeping swells within and overflows his soul. He relents, allowing it to live outside of him, and possess him with sadness. Now he cries easily, without passion or strength.

In his spirit he hears a tender whisper.

"Bryce. Let go."

After several moments, he lowers weakly onto his knees, hands open in his lap.

"God, thank you for the boy. I know that was you. His life is precious."

He sniffs, with heavy breaths fogging his glasses. ". . . And Lord, I don't understand what you're doing with my little girl . . . But God . . . I choose to trust you with her care. I release her to you. . . She's yours. I know you love her."

He wraps his arms around his chest and holds them tightly. He rocks there for a joyful moment, and then spreads his hands toward the sky. "She's yours."

In that moment of surrender, he hears a still, gentle voice deep within.

"I know your pain, my son."

His being lifts and fills with warmth and peace.

He stands, inhales deeply, and slowly releases it, then takes a last long look at the dark, shining lake, and leaves, humming softly, "What Child is this?"

In the car, Bryce takes out his phone and texts Felicia: SORRY SO LATE. DIDN'T FIND THE LAMB. HAVE INTERESTING STORY THOUGH FOR YOU TOMORROW. HEADING BACK NOW. MISS YOU.

He waits a moment, but there is no reply. He turns on the car. 11:21. He leaves the lot and follows the road back to the main street, back through town, back down the mountain, back to LA, and back to his little girl. He carries a weightlessness inside that he is too fatigued to sort out.

Three hours, one stop for gas, restroom, and coffee, and one cold burrito later, Bryce pulls up to the hospital parking garage and sets the brake on his long journey. 2:42. His body brings him to the dim, quiet floor, and to his daughter's room, where he locates the remaining water bottle from their trip and guzzles over half of it. Then he quietly grabs a pillow and blanket from the closet, kicks off his dirty shoes, and settles himself into the couch. He sets his alarm for 6:20, plugs his phone into the charger, and puts it on the table beside him. Closing his eyes, he finally capitulates to exhaustion.

Jasmine stirs. "Daddy?" she whispers. "Did you find my lamb?"

Bryce's eyes widen in the dark. "Uhh. . . No . . . I'm sorry Pumpkin. I looked everywhere."

She is silent, and perhaps has drifted off. Then in a soft, playful tone she teases, "No Daddy. I think you *did* find my lamb." And she serenely drifts back to sleep.

Chapter 15: Let Your Light so Shine (Matthew 5:16)

A loud, annoying sound persists beside him, arousing Bryce from his deep sleep. He bolts up, locates and silences the alarm, and scours his mind to identify the reason for this disturbance. He sits poised to scramble to his feet as soon as he receives clarification.

"Merry Christmas, Daddy," comes the cheerful greeting from Jasmine's bed.

"Oh." Bryce hoists his heavy feet off the couch to the floor. He cradles his tired face in his hands for a moment, then rubs them invigoratingly all over his skin. He puts on his glasses and snaps a festive smile on his lips. "Merry Christmas, Pumpkin," he sings groggily, arising and stepping to his daughter's bed. He looks into her bright eyes, and repeats, "Merry Christmas," as he bends down to receive her embrace. "Ah," he gives her an extra squeeze, "I love you, Pumpkin."

"I love you too, Daddy," she giggles.

He straightens with a wry grin, "How about I go get Mommy and the boys?"

"Yes!" Jasmine nods.

"Okay!" He grabs his bag from behind the couch and pulls out fresh pants, socks, and a shirt, and changes in the bathroom. He washes his face, brushes his teeth, and then returns to put his disheveled shoes back on. He takes the phone from the table and sees Felicia's text from half an hour before: READY OR NOT, HERE WE COME!

He slides the phone into his pocket, grabs his keys and wallet, and bends to kiss Jasmine a on her head.

"Okay, Pumpkin. After I get the family, we're going to drop their stuff off at the hotel, but we'll be back to get you in a bit."

"Okay, Daddy," she grins.

He's at the door and adds, "Oh, maybe see if your nurse can help you dress after you eat?"

"Okay," she nods gleefully, hands clasped together.

Bryce steps out of the room and sees Hector at the nurses' station. "Merry Christmas, Hector. Hey, I'm running to get the family from the airport and then over to the hotel. We should be back in a couple of hours or so to get Jasmine. Maybe her nurse can get her dressed in a little bit? If not, that's fine too."

Hector has a fatigued smile, "Oh sure, Mr.—Bryce. We can do that. You had a late-night adventure, huh?"

"Ah, you could say that," Bryce chuckles as he backs toward the exit.

"Sounds interesting. Merry Christmas."

~

Bryce gets a text as he approaches the airport: WE'VE LANDED. NEED TO GET OUR LUGGAGE.

OK, he replies and scans the airport signs for direction. He circles the terminal three times until he sees his little, tired family emerge. When he pulls over, he leaps out to hug and greet each of them with joy and relief, and they all break into chatter as they load the car. Once seated, Felicia pulls a large plastic container out of her carry-on and removes the lid. "Want a cookie?"

Bryce thrills over the white-frosted delectables, "Yes!" He snatches one and savors a mouth-watering bite. "Delicious," he mumbles.

"*We* made them, Daddy!" Oscar proclaims.

"You did?"

"Yeah," the boy bristles in his booster seat. "With Aunt Tiana, and Uncle Tyrell, and Alex. We all did it together!"

Bryce looks back at his boys. "I think you made good use of the extra time together."

Oscar squirms. "Yeah. It was fun!"

"Did you have fun, Jacob?"

Jacob shrugs. "Yeah. It was pretty cool."

The family recounts yesterday's events to Bryce, first shopping, and then the flight problems, and then being surprised by

Alex, and how he's going to the Holiday Bowl game. Felicia is helping Bryce navigate with her phone.

"Bryce, I want to stop and get some groceries on the way to the hotel."

"Groceries?"

"Turn right up here at the light. Yeah. They gave us a special discount on the suite because Jasmine is staying long-term at Children's Hospital, so our room comes with a kitchenette. Turn left at the next light. I want to get some food so we don't have to eat out all the time."

Oscar interjects, "Can we make Christmas breakfast? I'm so hungry!"

Felicia grins at Bryce. "Yes, of course. We can do that."

The family divides duties in the store to gather the fruits and snacks and other essentials for the next several days. It was Bryce who located the freshly baked, breakfast pastries with icing, and brought them for approval. They were accepted. Oscar brought two cartons of orange juice. Jacob submitted Tater Tots and asked for deli meat. Felicia grabbed the yogurts, but also the pudding cups. Finally, after checking the list twice or more, with some addendums, the family loaded the bounty into the SUV wherever it would fit, then found their way to the hotel. After several meandering trips back and forth from the car, all the luggage and groceries were at last in the room.

Jacob deposits the last bag on the table, slumps into one of the living room chairs, and takes out his phone to sign into the wi-fi. Oscar helps his mom unload the groceries and put them away.

"Hey Honey," broaches Bryce, "would you mind if I took a quick shower?"

Felicia scrutinizes her ragged husband, "Yes, Amore, I think you should."

Bryce goes into the spacious, limestone-tiled bathroom and turns on the shower. He gingerly undresses, noting the smudges of dirt, along with scratches, bruises, and abrasions on various parts of his body. He scoffs at the miniature complimentary razor, but takes it into the shower anyway.

"Ahhhh." The warm, soothing spray rejuvenates his body. He washes his hair and body, moving slower and slower until he stops, facing the exhilarating stream. After several minutes, he breaks inertia and lathers his face to shave.

Bryce emerges from the bathroom, pink and redressed, toweling his hair with some vigor.

"This is a cool room, isn't it Dad?" Oscar bounds toward him, grabbing his hand. "Come see." He takes him across the living room to the other room. "See? There's two beds and a bathroom in here, too."

Bryce looks around, nodding. "Nice."

Back in the living area, Felicia delegates the luggage.

"Oscar, you and Jacob take your bags into your room."

"I got these." Bryce takes her bags into the master and returns, thoughtfully. "Hey Felicia, where's Jasmine going to sleep?"

"I'm sleeping on the couch," inserts Jacob. "While she's here."

"Thanks Jake. Are you sure?"

Jacob shrugs, "Yeah, sure. I like the couch."

The family drives to the hospital and parks in 20-minute passenger loading so they don't have to carry things all the way to the structure. They walk toward the entrance, where a news van is parked out front, and pass a two-person crew on the sidewalk as the female reporter is explaining, "However, sources indicate that. . ."

In the hospital elevator, Felicia grips Bryce's arm, "Oooh, I can't wait to see my baby!" She wipes a finger under her eye and beams at Bryce. When they arrive at Jasmine's room, Felicia pops her head through the open door. "Merry Christmas, Mija!"

Jasmine is sitting on the edge of her bed getting help from Jacqui with her shoe. She outstretches her arms. "Mamma!"

"I'll be right back," Jacqui quietly announces.

Felicia sets her purse on the floor and lifts Jasmine from the bed. She holds her in her arms, hugging and swaying and kissing tenderly around the child's beaming face.

"Hello, beautiful. I have *missed* you so much."

Jasmine nuzzles into Felicia's neck. "I've missed *you*, Mamma."

After another moment, Felicia sets Jasmine back on the bed, sweeps off her little pink hat, and plants a final, loud kiss, "Mmmwa!" on her forehead. She wipes her moist eyes again with a chuckle and turns to the boys. "I think somebody else wants to say hi, too."

Oscar is waiting with an eager grin and gives Jasmine a big hug. "Merry Christmas!"

Jacob comes over beside Jasmine and wraps his arm around her small body. She clasps her arms around his waist and locks them together.

"Merry Christmas, Little Sis." He squeezes her to himself, and she holds onto him tightly.

"Merry Christmas, Big Brother." They look at each other and give a final squeeze. Then Jacob finds the wheelchair in the corner and pulls it to the end of the bed where he sits in it, hands in his hoodie pouch, and occupies himself rolling it back and forth. Oscar kicks his shoes off, climbs onto the bed, and lies on his stomach next to Jasmine, chin propped on his palms.

Bryce surveys his family with satisfaction as they excitedly exchange adventures. After a few minutes, he claps his hands once, interrupting their chatter. "Well! We're all here! Come on, let's go. We have a Christmas to celebrate!"

Felicia retrieves her purse from the floor. "Yes! What do we need? What's the plan?"

"Okay," Bryce evaluates the room. "Jake, can you get the Christmas tree?"

"Sure."

"Alright, then Felicia, you make sure Jasmine has the clothes and things she needs in her bag."

"Okay."

"And I'll get my stuff together, and Oscar,"

"Yes!"

"You keep your sister entertained."

"Okay!" Oscar flips his legs around and slides his socked feet to the floor. He finds Jasmine's other shoe and crouches to help her put it on. Then he takes the brush from the end table, scampers back onto the bed behind Jasmine, extends his legs around her, and soothingly brushes her thin hair. Jasmine closes her eyes at his soft touch.

Bryce comes out of the bathroom with his toiletries, and puts them in his bag, as well as the wadded-up clothes from yesterday. Felicia walks around the room picking up lotion and lip balm and Jasmine's slippers and other things to put in her bag. Jacob waits in the wheelchair occupied with his phone.

Jacqui walks in with a prescription bottle and hands it to Felicia as she packs.

"Hi. Here's Jasmine's maintenance dosage for the next few days."

"Thank you," Felicia smiles, and puts it in her purse.

Jacqui quietly asks to talk to Bryce, who sets down his bag and follows her out the door. After a moment, Felicia also goes out.

" . . . but somehow they found out, and now they want to talk to you," Jacqui explains.

"Bryce, what's going on?"

Mystified, Bryce hesitates to explain.

"Does your wife know?" asks Jacqui.

Bryce looks at Felicia sheepishly, "Ahh. . . no. I, ahh . . . didn't get a chance to, um, explain it yet."

Felicia takes his sleeve. "Bryce. What is it? What happened?"

Bryce pulls off his glasses and wipes his hand down his face, then replaces them. "Ahh . . . Okay. So, did you see my text from last night, saying that I had an interesting story to tell you?"

"Yeah?"

"Okay . . . Well, while I was in Big Bear last night looking for Jasmine's lamb,,,"

"Yes?"

"Well, I discovered this car that had slid off the road and down the hill."

"What?" Felicia raises her fingers to her lips. "Are you serious?"

"Yeah. It was crazy."

"Oh, my goodness, Bryce. What happened?"

"So, I called 911, and I went down there to see if they were okay."

"You went down?"

"Yeah. And there was this boy in the car, and he had stopped breathing, so I got him out, and ahh . . . gave him CPR."

"Are you serious? Is he okay?"

"I don't know." Bryce turns to Jacqui, "I mean, he started breathing, but—"

"No, he's okay. You *saved* his life!" Jacqui explains. "He had some brain swelling, but they got that down last night. He's recovering now."

"Oh, thank God! Oh Bryce, I can't believe it! That's amazing!" Felicia hugs him, bewildered.

Bryce looks at Jacqui. "But I don't understand how the media found out."

She checks her watch, "Actually, the morning news is just ending. Let's see if we can catch anything on it." They reenter Jasmine's room and Jacqui turns on the TV. She checks the channel for the news crew out front. The anchorman is talking, with an image of Keisha on the screen behind him.

"Once again, our top story this morning is being called a Christmas miracle. Last night, a woman and her son were driving through the mountains to Big Bear when they hit a patch of ice and slid off the road, down the steep embankment. Apparently, they were trapped there for several hours, undetected, until a passing stranger happened to notice the flash of their brake light, *in the dark*, and decided to investigate. He called 911, then *remarkably* climbed down the embankment and rescued the boy, just when he had stopped breathing. The man then gave him CPR and saved the boy's life. Our reporter, Maizie McCrery was on the scene at the San Bernardino hospital when, his mother, Keisha Parsons arrived."

The video clip plays showing a battered Keisha on a stretcher outside the emergency entrance, appealing to the camera.

"Please, help me find the man that saved my son. They said his name is Bruce, or Bryce, and that his little girl is at a hospital in LA. Please, I want to thank him!" As she is wheeled into the hospital, the camera pans out to the reporter.

"Well there you have it—a mother's grateful plea."

Jasmine's hospital room erupts with astonishment.

"Daddy! Was that you?"

"Oh my gosh, you're a hero!"

"Dad! That's amazing!"

The anchorman resumes the report. "We now have Maizie McCrery live with an update. Maizie, what have you found out?"

"Thanks Eli. Well, as you already know, reports tell us that the boy is recovering nicely, though he and his mother were taken to different hospitals. Keisha Parsons had severe breaks in her right leg, and some smaller injuries, but she underwent surgery on that leg last night, and she is *also* recovering today. We reached out to the Sheriff's department, but they are not commenting on the hero's identity until he gives his consent. They may try to contact him today, but since it's Christmas, they would rather that he come forward."

"Okay, Maizie, so where are you now?"

"Well, Eli, we received a tip from a parent that the hero might be *here* at this hospital. We are hoping that whoever he is, he hears this report and contacts us so that Keisha can thank him, personally. I'm Maizie McCrery reporting from Children's Hospital Los Angeles. Eli, back to you."

"Thanks, Maizie. Amazing story of heroics, and a little Christmas miracle."

Jacqui mutes the TV and turns to the family. "This isn't the only station carrying this story now. It's just the one who broke it."

Bryce is baffled. "But how did they even find out about it?"

"Who knows? Reporters listen to police and fire scanners. Sometimes they have contacts or get tips directly from first responder agencies. Either way, you need to decide if you want to talk to them or not. I don't think you can keep this a secret."

"Oh my gosh." Bryce, suddenly fatigued again, turns to assess his family.

Jacob urges, "Do it Dad! You have to."

"Yeah, do it, Dad," echoes Oscar gleefully. "It's so awesome. My Dad's a hero!"

Bryce holds his hand up, "I'm not a hero, Oscar, I just . . ." He turns to his wife for help. "Felicia?"

She smiles broadly, a twinkle of ardor in her eyes, "Oh, Mi Amore." She takes his face in her hands and kisses him softly on the lips. Then she scrunches her face with pleasure and hooks her arm through his, standing close to him. She turns to Jasmine. "I think we let Jasmine decide what to do."

Jasmine puts her finger under her chin, like she is pondering the question. Then she smiles, "Of *course* we should tell them. When we leave, you can go tell that reporter. She'd like that."

"Okay," Felicia nods at the verdict.

"Okay," nods Bryce.

Jacqui looks at Bryce. "Don't worry about the press on our end. We're not allowed to disclose any information, so you are in complete control of what you reveal."

"Oh my gosh," Bryce astounds. "This is crazy."

Jacqui winks at Jasmine, "I guess that wasn't a wasted trip after all, was it?"

Jasmine winks back, "Of *course*, it wasn't."

"Alright troops, lets grab everything," martials Bryce. They all take up their responsibilities to depart. Jacqui helps Jasmine into the wheelchair, which Jacob has just vacated.

"Jacqui," adds Felicia, "We plan to have Jasmine with us at the hotel a few days, as long as it's okay with the trial. We'll be in touch, but call us if you or the doctors have any questions or concerns."

"Will do. You all enjoy."

Bryce hands Oscar his bag and takes the handles of the wheelchair. "Thanks so much, Jacqui for keeping Jasmine company last night."

"Yes, thank you Jacqui," embellishes Felicia. "You have been a saint."

Jasmine takes Jacqui's hand and pulls her close to kiss her on the cheek. "Thank you, Miss Jacqui."

Jacqui positions the pink hat smartly on Jasmine's head and then touches her nose. "Thank *you*, Jasmine." Their eyes connect. "*So* much."

"I hope you have a Merry Christmas, Jacqui," Felicia adds.

"It already is. Merry Christmas to you all."

The family departs, nervous as they descend to the lobby and walk out the front door. There, they see the original news reporter, and now two other news crews. Bryce takes a deep breath as they approach her. Watching the interview later that night, they all thought how funny it was to see Jacob holding the little Christmas tree the whole time—like a silly Christmas play.

"Are you Maizie?" Bryce asks her.

"Yes. I am."

"Hi," he begins bashfully. "Well, I'm Bryce. I understand that you're looking for me?"

Maizie's eyes grow big. She smiles in genuine surprise and grabs his arm. "You're Bryce! Oh, my goodness gracious!" She has a thin southern accent, imperceptible in her report. "Wow. Bryce. What an honor to meet you!" She extends her hand, "Yes, Maizie McCrerey. Thank you so much for coming over to me. We have been *looking* for *you*!"

Maizie's cameraman alerts her that the other two crews are coming over.

"Listen Bryce," she confides, "I know this won't matter much to you, but I'm the one who broke this story last night, and I've had little sleep trying to develop it—would you mind giving *me* an exclusive interview?"

"Exclusive?" Bryce asks puzzled.

"Yeah, well, they'll *eventually* get the interview, but, we'll get it first. Is that okay with you?"

Bryce shrugs, looking at his family. Felicia nods.

"Sure," he replies. "It doesn't matter to me."

She turns and waives off the other reporters, "Sorry folks. It's an exclusive." They drop their shoulders and stop. "Is that him?" one calls out.

"I'll let you know in a minute," Maizie calls back, then turns to the family smirking. "I don't even want them getting *that* info out before *I* do." Maizie untangles the microphone cord some and then addresses Bryce. "Okay, so if it's okay with you, we're going to interview you. We're not live now, so we don't have to worry about how long it is, or if you say something in a way you don't like—we'll just edit it before we broadcast the mid-morning news. Okay with you?"

"Sure," Bryce timidly agrees.

"Okay, so we're going to start rolling now, and I'll just ask you some questions— "

Bryce interrupts. "Before we start, I want to know. How did you even find out about this?"

Maizie smiles wryly. "Well, that's a little miracle itself. I was on-call as the field reporter last night because the regular reporters get the holidays off. So, it's my opportunity to do something really special. Anyway, Chuck and I had just wrapped up a report for the 11:00 news on a violent convenience store robbery which seems to be part of a series that started in LA. It was a real downer, I thought, for Christmas Eve. Anyway, we were all the way out there in San Bernardino to cover it, and I wasn't interested in just wrapping up for the night. So, we got a bite to eat and I started calling some contacts. One at the Sheriff's department knew about the accident in Big Bear and told me that a civilian had rescued a boy. The victims were being transported to a hospital in San Bernardino, so . . . I turned on the scanner, and pretty soon I heard the paramedics communicating about their ETA to the hospital. We drove over there, and a few minutes later, the ambulance pulls up. We asked the driver if it was one of the people who had been rescued in Big Bear, and he said it was. I thought we could interview the paramedics when they came back out, but when they rolled her off the ambulance, she saw us and made them stop. She asked if she could make a public plea for the man that rescued them. I said 'Sure!' and we rolled video on her, right there going into the hospital. When the paramedics came back out, we got some details about what had happened. They said that all the way to the hospital she was asking them about you, and what they knew, but all they knew was that your name was Bruce or Bryce and that you had a daughter at a hospital in LA. So that's what we went with this morning."

"Huh!" Bryce wonders.

"Look," Maizie adds, "That woman is so grateful. You saved her son. She desperately wants to thank you."

Bryce is thinking, absorbing it all.

"This is a good thing," Maizie reassures.

The family all pats him.

"Dad, that's great,"

"Bryce, I'm so proud."

Maizie holds up her mic. "Okay. Ready?"

Bryce nods and exhales. "Sure."

Maizie positions herself. "Okay Chuck, roll."

"Rolling," confirms Chuck.

"Maizie McCrery reporting from outside Children's Hospital LA. Ever since we heard of the heroic rescue of the little boy and his mom Keisha Parsons in Big Bear last night, we have been searching for this mysterious Christmas Miracle man on behalf of the grateful mother, and now, thankfully, we've found him. Bryce, do you mind giving us your full name?"

"Ah, sure. Bryce Goodson. This is my wife Felicia, my boys Jake and Oscar, and our daughter Jasmine."

"Thank you. Okay, Bryce, can you please tell us what happened last night in Big Bear, and how you came to be in such a remote place so late at night?"

"Ah, well, actually, I was up there looking for my daughter's toy lamb."

Maizie looks down at Jasmine, "And is this your daughter?"

"Yes,"

"Sweetie, can you tell us your name again?" She holds the mic out to Jasmine.

Jasmine waives a little, "Hi, I'm Jasmine."

"And you lost your toy lamb in Big Bear?"

"Yeah. Daddy took me to the mountains yesterday to see the snow and feed the birds for Christmas. We lost my little lamb."

Maizie turns to Bryce, so that's why you were up there? You went all the way *back* to find her lamb? At night?"

"Yeah. Well, we didn't realize it was missing until we got back to the hospital. Jasmine was really upset, and she was convinced she knew where it was. So, I drove back last night to look for it. I had actually just finished searching at this viewpoint, when I stopped to catch my breath. That's when I saw the red flash."

"You saw a red flash?"

"Yeah. It was totally dark everywhere, and then I saw this red light flash up the hillside for just a moment, and then it was gone. The only thing it could be was from a car, but there weren't any around. I went to the edge and there were signs that a car had gone off the road, but it was too dark to see it down there. So, I called 911 and then I went down the slope to see what I could find out."

"You went down there? In the dark?"

"Yeah, well I had a flashlight. Anyway, I was calling out and then I heard someone calling back for help. When I found the car, the woman yelled for me to get her son out of the back seat—that he had stopped breathing. All the doors were stuck, but I finally got him out, and took him back up the hill. He wasn't breathing, so I gave him CPR, and then pretty quick, he started breathing again. Anyway, after that, the cavalry showed up and took over. So, they're both okay, then?"

Maizie smiles broadly, "Yes, they're both going to be fine, thanks to you Mr. Goodson—"

"Bryce."

"Well, Bryce, that's quite a remarkable story. Anything you want to say to Mrs. Parsons? She'd like to thank you in person."

"Oh, honestly, it was my honor to be there and to be able to help out. I want to wish her a Merry Christmas, and maybe after the holiday, and a little rest, we can talk."

"That sounds just right," Maizie affirms, then turns to Jasmine, "What do you think of your Daddy, Jasmine?"

Jasmine looks up at her Dad admiringly. "He did good. I told him to go find my lost lamb, and he did."

Maizie looks astonished. "You're right. He *did* find a lost little lamb, didn't he? I bet you didn't expect something like *that*, did you?"

"Yes, I did," Jasmine confidently replies.

Still amazed, "You did?"

"Yes. God told me something special was going to happen." She explains thoughtfully. "I knew it was important for my Daddy to go back and look. I wasn't sure why, but I knew it was very important."

"You're saying, God told you?" The reporter is captivated by Jasmine's revelation.

"Yes. God talks to us all the time. We just have to listen. People are *very* important to Him, and He's always telling us things, like 'smile at her," or 'help him,' or 'talk to her,' or 'do this nice thing' or a hundred *other* things. He *wants* us to help people. Yesterday God told a boy named Marcus to let me try his sled. He was so nice—it made me feel loved."

Jasmine smiles back at Bryce. "That's all we have to do every day. Just trust God and be a hero to someone. *Everyone* matters to God."

Astonished, Maizie returns the mic to herself. "Everyone matters to God," she echoes. "Well, bless your heart. What more can we add to that?"

She faces the camera. "Trust God and be a hero. That sounds like a perfect Christmas message to me. What do you think, Goodson family?"

Everyone nods and pats Jasmine encouragingly.

"Does anyone have anything to add?"

Jacob leans forward, pushing the Christmas tree into Oscar's back, "I do."

"Okay, young man." Maizie holds out the mic to him.

"If you're in Big Bear, keep an eye out for my sister's lamb. It's very special."

Maizie turns to the camera again. “Well, you heard him. Hopefully, there will be another Christmas miracle for this courageous, wise little girl. Thank you Goodson family so much for sharing your story. We wish Keisha Parsons and her son a speedy recovery, and with thankful hearts, a Merry Christmas to you all. This is Maizie McCreary reporting from Children’s Hospital, Los Angeles.”

Chapter 16: A Christmas Celebration

Felicia turns off the burner and covers the pan of melty-cheesy, green-chili scrambled eggs. She warms the pastries in the microwave for 30 seconds and carries the plate of bacon to the small dinette, while Oscar sets out the silverware, and then takes the glasses and the orange juice carton to the table as well.

Bryce steps back and evaluates the little Christmas tree, now twinkling on the corner of the coffee table. It is perched over an arrangement of small presents he had unloaded from Felicia's suitcase.

"What do you think?" he asks the room.

"Good, Dad," approves Oscar spritely. "Oh, wait," he adds, and scurries into his room. Soon he returns, pleased expression, with three additional packages to place under the tree.

Bryce watches his son ducking under the small branches, positioning the gifts expertly.

"Whatcha got there, buddy?'

"It's a surprise." Oscar pulls back one of the packages, which is soft and shapeless, and examines it disappointedly.

"Oh."

"What is it, Oscar?" Felicia asks from the kitchenette.

He looks at the package, and then brings it to Bryce for inspection, "There's a tear in the wrapping paper."

Bryce takes the gift and assesses the damage. "Hmm . . . I see."

"Daddy, is there any tape to fix it?"

Bryce glances around the hotel room for a possible solution. "I don't think so, buddy." He reevaluates the problem. "You know, the hole isn't very big. Maybe we could use the bow to cover it."

Oscar gingerly takes the package and ponders the suggestion.

Then he looks up brightly, “Yeah. I think that would work. Can you help me, Daddy?”

“Sure,” and they proceed to extricate the bow and relocate it to the new position, sealing and concealing the blemish.

Oscar holds out the package and declares, “That did it,” then replaces it under the tree.

“Okay everyone, breakfast is ready,” announces Felicia.

Jacob and Jasmine are squeezed comfily into the large armchair, each with one white earbud inserted into an ear. They are handing Jacob’s phone back and forth, playing a game. Jacob takes the phone and hits pause. Jasmine pulls the earbud out of her ear and hands it to him.

“I like that game, Jake.”

He sets the phone on the end table and gets up, then holds out his hand to help Jasmine out of the pit of the chair. “I thought you would.”

The family finds seats at the table while Felicia scoops eggs and Tater Tots out of the pans, onto the plates, and distributes them. After each consumer has received a plate filled according to their predilections, Felicia sits at the table and nods, holding a hand toward her husband.

“Bryce?”

Bryce smiles. “Yes, of course.” He takes her hand, who takes Oscar’s, who takes Jacob’s, who takes Jasmine’s, who takes her Daddy’s.

“Lord, we have so many things to be grateful for. We can’t list them all to you right now. We thank you for our family, we thank you for this special time together, we thank you for the things we’ve seen you do, and we thank you for your Son. Amen.”

“Amen,” affirm all.

Bryce takes a pastry and passes the plate around. Jacob pours his orange juice, then helps the smaller ones with theirs. The amazing tale of Bryce’s heroic adventures is raised again, and many questions are asked, details demanded and retold. The table overflows with laughter and joy, filling happy hearts and stomachs with Christmas gladness.

After the final, savory morsel has been stuffed, and the table is cleared, the clan gathers onto the couch and chairs around the little Christmas tree for the ceremony of gifts. Felicia disappears into the bedroom for a few minutes while the family teases each other and chats excitedly. She returns with three filled stockings hanging from her fingers, each with a child's name on it, which elicits elation from the siblings. Felicia searches for a suitable place to hang them, but when it becomes apparent that this ritual is not feasible, she distributes each to the owner, and sits beside Bryce on the couch.

"Thanks, Mom," rings the chorus. They delve into their stockings of small treasures, excavating with delight various chocolates, and candy canes, and sour candies, and gum, and packets of malt balls, as well as Oscar's Santas, which he had turned over for safe-keeping.

"I'm impressed," Bryce confesses, holding his wife's hand. "You brought all this?"

Felicia confides slyly, "No, just their stockings. Remember when I went back into the store to use the restroom?"

"Ahhh . . ." Bryce admires, "Very clever."

Felicia hands him one of the chocolate Santas.

"For me?"

"*These* are from Oscar," she brags.

Once everyone is enjoying a treat, Oscar becomes anxious and asks if he can pass his gifts out first. With everyone's consent, he hops up and selects one, then takes it to Jasmine, selects another one, then hands it to Bryce, and selects the last one, then hands it to Felicia.

"Oh, my."

He returns to his chair, passing Jacob. "And you have yours, Jake."

"No kidding?" Bryce wonders. "Jake, what did he get for you?"

"Ahhh . . . he helped me pay for a skateboard I picked out. Aunt Tiana bought it. It's at her house."

"Wow! That's great, Oscar. Jake, did you get a picture of it?"

"Yeah."

"Okay! I want to see that later."

Felicia looks at Oscar. "Mijo, who do you want to go first?"

"Ahh . . . "Oscar looks around seriously, "Daddy."

"Me? Okay." Bryce tears off the paper and pulls out a box. "What is it?" he amazes, reading the outside.

"It's an electric travel razor!" Oscar delights.

"What?" Bryce tugs open the box and extricates the razor, admiring it. "No Kidding!" He locates a little plastic tab and pulls it out, then tries the switch. To everyone's surprise, the razor begins to hum.

"Wow, Buddy!"

Oscar bristles in his seat, "It's rechargeable!"

Eyes wide, Bryce holds the razor to his face, and it begins to grazzel over his errant whiskers. "That's great, Oscar! What a perfect gift!" He shuts off the razor and gets up to hug his son. "Thanks Buddy!

Oscar, looking pleased, announces, "Okay, Jasmine next."

Jasmine, who has receded deep into the big chair with Jacob, pops a candy cane out of her mouth, "Me next?"

She tries to scooch up some, while amused Jacob merely watches, snickering at her predicament. Finally, she spreads her arms across Jacob and the arm of the chair and swims out of the crevasse. This struggle launches the package from her lap, onto the floor, where Jacob retrieves it, after composing himself somewhat.

"Here you go."

"Thank you," she huffs with feigned irritation.

Oscar notes that the newly relocated bow had survived the turmoil, and still conceals the marred wrapper.

Jasmine returns the candy cane to her mouth, and begins to carefully deconstruct the package, mindful of the love that wrapped it. It soon reveals the royal blue hoodie, folded to showcase the front artwork. She holds up the sweatshirt, captivated by the little scene of nativity characters. She smiles with a twinkle at Oscar.

"Oh, *thank* you, Oscar."

Oscar animates with joy.

Felicia anxiously prods, "What is it? Show us."

Jasmine turns it around, then announces, "HAPPY BIRTHDAY KING JESUS!"

"Oh, Mijo, that's so cute!"

Jasmine scoots to the edge of her seat and slips the sweatshirt over her head. Jacob helps her tug the fabric over her body, then flips the hood off her head. She looks down, admiring it.

"I love it, Oscar." Oscar launches from his seat to give her a hug. "Merry Christmas!"

"Thank you, Oscar," she effervesces.

He points to the wrinkled wrapper, now on the floor. "There's something else."

Jacob hands it to Jasmine, and she pulls out the animated Christmas DVD.

"Ooh," she croons.

"We can play it tonight, can't we Daddy?" Oscar contends.

Bryce eyes the TV, "I think there's a DVD player. We'll check later, Buddy."

"Okay." Oscar looks at Felicia. "You next Mommy."

Felicia enlivens, "Oh, now my turn." She locates the tape on one end of the package and begins to meticulously peel it back. "Okay, let's see. . ."

"Just tear it, Mom," coaxes Jacob.

Felicia hurries the process, and soon lifts the album from the wrapper. "How pretty, Oscar!"

Oscar leaves his seat again and stands by his mother. "It's one of those scrapbook albums." He opens the cover and slowly turns the stiff pages. "See?" He turns to the back section. "There's all these stickers and labels to decorate your pictures with memories."

Felicia examines all the accessories of colorful images, and words, and embellishments that can be applied throughout the album. "Mijo, this is beautiful."

"Yeah, and I thought that you and Jasmine could print some of our favorite photos from your phone, and you guys could make it together while you're here."

Felicia looks at Bryce, then back at her son.

"Couldn't you?" Oscar entreats.

Felicia takes his little face in her hands, "Oscar, this is a *perfect* gift. What a wonderful idea!" She kisses him noisily on the lips. "Thank you. I can't wait to work on it." She turns to Jasmine. "What do you think?"

Jasmine is nodding emphatically. "That's a fun idea, Oscar."

Felicia takes her phone from the coffee table, "In fact, let's capture a few memories right now. Everyone hold up your gifts from Oscar." She takes grinning pictures of everyone. Oscar takes the picture of her.

She sets the phone in the middle of the table. "Okay, now

anyone can take a picture today."

Felicia looks as if she is about to assess the other gifts, when Oscar interjects.

"We have one more thing." He pulls out the Christmas card addressed to Mommy and Daddy and hands it to Felicia. "It's from us kids," he announces, grinning at the others.

"A card?" Felicia marvels.

"Wow, kids," Bryce adds. They open the envelope and observe the little Christmas scene together. Bryce reads, "God must have known you were the best parents He could give us."

They open the card and Felicia reads the inside, "Even when we're all grown up, we'll still need your love."

Bryce reads the little scripture inside the cover "We love Him because He first loved us. 1 John 4:19." He looks at the children. "Aww . . . You all signed it." His eyes are glimmering.

Felicia tears up, "Oh, you kids are the best."

They get up and kiss or hug each child. "You all are sneaky!"

"We signed it while you guys were busy this morning."

Felicia peruses the card adoringly again, then clasps it to her heart. "I love it. I'm going to keep it forever," she pledges.

She opens the card and sets it upright on the table, so it can be seen. She beams at her children one last time, "That is so special," and turns her attention to the little tree. "Okay. Now, it's *our* turn." She picks out the first gift to hand to each family member, and little by little, all of the gifts are distributed, unwrapped, admired, recorded for history, and in many cases, immediately freed from their packaging.

At the end, Felicia is trying on the beautiful freshwater pearl and coral jewelry set Bryce had bought while her parents were in town, spending time with Jasmine. "Those little beads between the pearls are real gold," he explains, as she eagerly fastens on the necklace.

"I love them!" She runs her fingers over the double string of jewels.

Bryce investigates the package on his new car stereo. "It says it has Bluetooth, so I don't even have to plug it in to play music."

"Yes," Felicia explains, "but it has the USB port to charge your phone."

"Man, I wish we could have it for driving around here, and for your drive home," he muses. Felicia is trying to clasp the matching bracelet and turns to him for help. "You can. I paid for the installation, and they have stores here in LA. We'll just run it down there."

"Fantastic!"

The kids are all testing their aim on each other shooting the foam dart guns they received, including several extra rounds of ammunition. The boys don't spare Jasmine their attacks, firing at her in the chair from various coverts throughout the room, but both boys converge to collect and restock her ammunition when she runs out. Her gun and darts are pink, Oscar's gun and darts are dark orange, and Jacob's gun and darts are blue. The ground rules they immediately established are that no one can use another's gun, or another's ammunition, even if it is easier to access during a barrage, and particularly not against the owner of said ammunition.

After a while, Jasmine tiredly declares again, "I'm out," and sets her dart gun on the table beside her next to her candy cane. She curls up into the chair, with one hand tucked into her hoodie pouch, and the fingers of her other inserted into her mouth. Felicia sets the jewelry box and the wrapping paper on the coffee table, then goes into the kids' room and returns with a pillow and throw-blanket.

She sets them on the couch, then goes to Jasmine. "Mija. Want to get cozy?"

Jasmine nods, and Felicia bends over and collects her to bring back to the couch. Jasmine curls up against the pillow on her mom's lap, and Felicia drapes the blanket over her.

Bryce gets up, "Hey boys, help me clean up a bit, will ya?"

They retrieve all the darts and return them to designated holding areas, then pick up all the wrapping paper and unwanted packaging and stuff them into spare shopping bags. After the presents have been taken to the proper rooms, Jacob plops down in his chair and takes out his phone.

Oscar asks, "Are we going out again?"

Felicia and Bryce exchange questioning looks.

"No, Buddy," Bryce concludes. "I think we're all pretty tired."

"Good." He trots into the bedroom and returns a few minutes later in his socks and pajamas and picks up his new puzzle book and pencil. He climbs onto the couch next to Jasmine's curled up legs and lifts the end of the blanket over his lap. He lays his hand lightly on her shin and fiddles with the blanket in his fingers when he is not writing in his book.

"Bryce, what do you want to do for dinner? Room service?" asks Felicia.

Bryce walks to the window and opens the curtains. "I don't know," he ponders. He looks out over the sky. The darkening blue horizon is streaked with a thin, deep orange glow. The lights of the city are coming on and twinkle in the twilight. Bryce sighs deeply, still fatigued, but content.

"Hey, it looks like there's a taco shop on the corner that's open. Does that sound good?"

Felicia hesitates, "Tacos for Christmas dinner?"

Bryce turns around. "No? Okay. What sounds good? Room service? Sandwiches?"

"I don't know . . ." Felicia appears pained by the exhausting decision.

"I could go see if the restaurant downstairs is open, and if the menu looks good . . ."

"Maybe . . ." She looks around at the others. "What do you guys want?"

Oscar announces, "I'm not that hungry. A taco and beans sound good."

"I could eat a carne asada burrito," adds Jacob, intent on his screen.

Bryce turns to Felicia, "What are you hungry for? I can stop at two places."

She thinks a moment, then concludes, "Honestly, if they have pozole, that would be amazing."

"Sounds good to me," affirms Bryce. He looks at Jasmine, "Pumpkin, is there something there you think you'd like?"

Felicia is stroking her daughter's hair and face. "Mmmm . . . Maybe chips and guacamole?" she softly replies, eyes closed.

"Okay. I'll add a quesadilla everyone can nibble on." Bryce looks up the taco shop and calls to place their order. Then he stuffs his feet into his soiled shoes, grabs his wallet and room key, and kisses Felicia. "I'll be right back."

After he leaves, Felicia picks up her phone and scrolls through missed posts and alerts, and sends Christmas wishes to many, including her parents. She's a little too tired to explain the story of Bryce's heroics, and the matter of the lost lamb. "Tomorrow, after some rest."

Shortly, Bryce returns and divides the food, placing shared items in the center of the coffee table. After they pray, he de-lids the container of hot soup, and carefully hands it to Felicia, who spoons the spicy broth gingerly into her mouth over the sleeping head of her daughter.

The boys scoot their legs under the coffee table to eat, and Bryce sits on the edge of the couch on the other side of his wife, only now realizing that this is his third Mexican meal in a row. He rationalizes that fish tacos are completely different than the four burritos he had yesterday. He squeezes the lime and pours hot sauce over the fried fish, turns on the TV and starts flipping through channels. It's 6:00, and the evening news is on.

"Once again, the top story today is the Christmas miracle." The anchor recaps the harrowing events of the previous night, and the details of Bryce's heroic actions. The report now includes footage of the scene and the wreck, still entangled on the mountainside.

"Sheriff's report that the father of the boy will come tomorrow when crews hoist the wreckage so he can retrieve the personal belongings of Keisha and her son, and more importantly, the Christmas gifts still sitting in the car."

They next replay the video of Keisha's plea for the man who saved them, with a voiceover report. "This was Mrs. Parsons's heartfelt appeal for the hero that saved her and her son. Earlier today, Maizie McCrery tracked down the mystery man and father of three at the Children's Hospital Los Angeles, where she interviewed him and his remarkable little girl. Here is that interview now."

They next play what appears to be Bryce and Jasmine's entire interview, including Jacob's admonition to look for Jasmine's lamb. The family erupts in cheers as the clip plays. They compliment each other, as well as laugh some at Jacob holding the tree so seriously, which he takes good-naturedly.

The piece concludes by echoing Jasmine's Christmas message, and urging viewers to watch all the clips and interviews on their website by clicking on the hotbutton, "The Christmas Miracle," or by going to the Facebook page, where they can "like it," and post messages and comments.

Seeing this newscast renews excited chatter about the events through the rest of dinner. Jasmine had sat up when the broadcast came on, and now Oscar shuffles over on his knees to give her a little hug.

"That was so good, what you said, Jasmine." He pats her shoulder. "God really used you."

She beams tiredly, hair disarrayed some. "He did, huh? Thanks Oscar." She leans back into her mother's arms, as they all return to eating and talking. Soon, Bryce gets up to throw out the trash and save leftovers in the fridge. The boys arise without being asked, and help. Once the mess is clean, Bryce stands in the kitchen, wondering.

"Did you get us any coffee, Honey?"

"Coffee? Yeah, but do you want a whole pot?"

"No, just a cup. I'm pooped and it's only 6:30. Besides, I want some for the cookies."

She gestures toward their room, "Well, they have that mini-coffee maker on the counter outside our bathroom, and you can make just a cup."

He pivots that way, "Ah, perfect. Do you want some?"

"No Amore, but can you just make hot water for me? I have some tea."

"Okay." Bryce heads toward the room, "When I come out, we'll watch that Christmas movie Oscar got."

Jacob thoughtfully lowers his phone. "Hey Jasmine, I'll set up the new iPad Aunt Tiana got you on the wi-fi, and we can download that game we were playing. That way it'll be bigger."

Jasmine plucks her fingers out of her mouth. "Okay."

Felicia interjects, "I'll charge it tonight, but I need to fix the settings before you do all that. Okay, Mijo?"

"Yeah, okay."

Bryce comes out in his sweats and a T-shirt with socked feet. He sets his coffee on the table "Where's your tea?"

"No, just set that on the counter. I'll get it and go change too." She rubs Jasmine's shoulder, "Sorry, Mija, I need to get up."

Jasmine sits up to let Felicia out, and Oscar slides in to take her place. Jasmine squinches a smile at him, then resettles on the pillow, and he starts to tickle her back.

Bryce unwraps the movie and inserts it into the DVD player. He locates the controls, and after several unsuccessful attempts, finally reads the little sign posted beside the TV and soon the movie's top menu appears on the screen.

Felicia returns, hair down in her white robe and hotel slippers. She takes her steeping tea from the counter, brings over the container of cookies, and sets them on the coffee table. "Kids, do you want any milk?"

"I do," requests Oscar, "just a little."

"I guess I will too," adds Jacob.

"Jasmine? Anything?"

"No."

"Okay. Try to drink your water, though."

As Felicia pours the milk, Jacob pivots his large chair around to face the TV, and Bryce turns off the overhead light, then settles into end of the couch with his coffee and the remotes. Felicia passes out the milk and attempts to squeeze in next to Bryce.

"Are you comfortable Jasmine?" she asks, bending a little toward her.

"Hmm yes," she lazily replies, satisfied with Oscar's tickling service.

"Okay, then everybody, schooch down a smidge. I want to sit next to Daddy."

The two children squirm down toward the other end, and Felicia snuggles in the crook of Bryce's arm, draped over the back of the couch. He grins at her.

"Nice," she coos.

Jacob stretches over the back of his chair and takes two cookies. Bryce picks up the container and offers it to those on the couch, who each take one, except Jasmine.

"Do you want a bite of my cookie, Jasmine?" asks Felicia.

After a moment a soft reply. "A small one."

The movie begins. Felicia breaks off a bite and hands it to her, which she tastes, but holds onto the rest for when she's ready.

After a prelude, the animation begins, narrated by Luke's Gospel.

"Mommy. Miss Jacqui read this to me last night," Jasmine quietly explains. "Wasn't that nice?"

Bryce pauses the movie, "Did she? That's great Pumpkin."

"Yeah. She's really special."

Bryce restarts the movie. As the narrator reads, the animation depicts a distant panoramic view of a white-stoned village, gradually drawing closer until it centers on the majestic Temple of God.

"Mommy," Jasmine whispers.

"Yes?"

"Can I have a sip of your tea when it cools?"

"Sure, Mija."

The narrator continues the account as the scene depicts Zachariah's encounter with the angel Gabriel.

"Mommy?" Jasmine whispers.

"Yes, Jasmine?"

She pauses thoughtfully.

"This is my favorite Christmas ever."

Chapter 17: Beauty for Ashes (Isaiah 61:3)

Keisha evaluates the glowing button beside her in the darkened room. Slivers of light piercing between the slats of the closed blinds faintly illuminate the shapes of furniture and walls. She blinks several times. She lifts her left hand and finds the cumbrance of an IV in her arm. Tentatively, she feels her face, finding it swollen and somewhat foreign. The door of her room is closed, shutting out light, muffling voices and activity. Her eyes return to the glowing button, and with uncertain daring, she presses it.

After a few moments, the door opens quietly, and a nurse enters her room.

"Hi, Mrs. Parsons. How are you doing?"

"Uh . . . fine, I think."

"Would you like this door open? Or would you like it closed a little longer?"

"Oh. Yes, open please."

The nurse props open the door, switches on a light, and then comes to Keisha's bedside.

"I'm your nurse, Brenda. It's good to see you awake." Brenda slides a pulse oximeter onto Keisha's finger and notes the reading.

"You might remember, but you came in with several severe breaks in your right leg, and doctors performed surgery last night to reconstruct the bones. Would you like to see?"

"Uh. Yes. Okay."

Brenda gently pulls back the covers to reveal Keisha's leg, encased in plaster with a ring of metal rods inserted around her thigh.

"Oh. My goodness."

"I know--it's unsettling to see. I just need to check your circulation." Brenda gently pinches Keisha's big toe. "Good." She carefully replaces the covers. "But your surgery went well." Brenda informs Keisha on some of the specifics concerning her care and limitations at this point.

"The doctor will come by later to answer any more questions you might have."

"Okay. Thank you."

"How comfortable are you? How would you rate your pain on a scale of 1-10?"

Keisha evaluates her traumatized body, then replies, "Maybe a 4?" Her lips and tongue are thick with dryness.

Brenda looks at the whiteboard near the door. "You'll get your next medication in 30 minutes, so hopefully we can take the edge off that some. Are you feeling nauseous at all?"

Keisha tries to wet her lips. "No, I don't think so."

"Okay. Well, I'm going to bring you some ice chips to start with, and if that's fine, then you can have water. We'll see how that goes before we bring your lunch. Sound good?"

"Yes, thank you."

"Would you like your blinds open?"

"Oh, yes please."

Brenda opens the blinds to reveal a cloudy day. "There you go. I'll just get your ice chips."

Keisha stops her at the door. "I'm sorry, but when can I see my son?"

"Your son?"

Anxiety crawls across Keisha's face. "Yes, Justin. We were in the accident together." She clutches her blankets. "I don't know where he is now."

Brenda looks at her for a moment before she smiles. "How about I find that out right now. Okay?"

"Oh, yes. Thank you. Thank you."

Brenda leaves and a moment later a young woman enters with Keisha's ice chips.

"Hi, Mrs. Parsons. Can you give these a try?"

Keisha spoons a few chips into her dry, warm mouth. "Mmm. Thank you." She tips up the cup and crunches on several more.

The woman pours her some water and inserts a straw. "I think you are good to go. I'm going to have your lunch sent up, and you can give it a try. Any requests?"

"Coffee, please." Keisha tentatively sips on her straw.

"Okay. I'll make sure coffee comes with that. Give us a ring if you need anything," she smiles, then leaves.

Keisha looks uneasily around the room. None of her things are visible. People pass, but don't enter. She hears laughing somewhere in the hall. A woman walks past her door with a present in her hand. A man is wearing green scrubs imprinted with red and white candy canes. Her fingers wander over her swollen cheeks, and brows, and light abrasions. She tries to settle her fidgeting hands on her stomach. She takes another sip of water. Her eyes wander out the window. She watches a small group of white seagulls, wings outstretched, lifting and gliding with gusts of wind, exchanging places, and then diving. Several drift downward and come to rest in the parking lot. They take her tumultuous thoughts with them.

After several minutes, there is a quiet tapping on her door where a man in uniform poises with a tray. "Mrs. Parsons?" he asks cheerfully.

"Yes."

"I have some lunch for you." He comes in and sets the tray on her swivel table and repositions it over her lap. "Do you know how to sit up?"

"Uhh—" "Here let me show you." He comes over and points out the features of her bedside controls.

"Thank you."

"This cup has your medication, so take that after a bite or two of food. Do you need anything else?"

Keisha looks at her tray. "I don't think so."

"Okay then," he heads to the door, then pauses. "You just let us know. Merry Christmas!"

"Oh, yes. Merry Christmas."

Keisha surveys the tray of macaroni salad, a cup of chicken soup and cracker packets, an egg salad sandwich, a small bowl of fruit, and a pudding cup, along with her cup of coffee. She takes a small bite of the macaroni salad. Someone passes the door, and she looks up. It is not Brenda. She takes another bite of the salad.

Someone else passes. She fumbles to open the cracker packet, finally releasing a spray of crumbs with her clumsy fingers. She sops one cracker in the soup and eats it. Someone passes. She sops the other cracker, then takes a bite of the egg salad. Someone stops at her door, then turns away.

Keisha takes a deep, breath and forces the air slowly through her nose. She tosses the medication from its little cup into her mouth, sips her water, and pushes the tray aside. She removes the lid from her coffee and stirs in a packet each of creamer and sugar, then reclines some in her bed. She watches the little white flock ascend again from the parking lot, lifting on the up-drafts as she sips her coffee.

After many long minutes, Keisha sets the remains of her cold coffee on the tray and swivels the table aside. She looks at the door. "Where is she?" She evaluates the call button again. A tapping on the door startles her.

"Oh, I'm sorry." It is Brenda.

"No, it's okay. Have you found out anything about my son?"

"Yes, I have." Brenda walks in with a piece of paper in her hand. "Your son was flown to a different hospital because he was unconscious, and they have a pediatric neurosurgeon on-call there. He arrived with some swelling around his brain, but they determined that he did not have a skull fracture. They started him on a medication called Mannitol, which actually reduced the swelling so that he did not need a more invasive procedure. The charge nurse remarked that it was really amazing, considering he had been unconscious for several hours. They thought that the cold temperatures helped keep the swelling down."

Keisha begins to breathe again. "So, is he okay?"

"Yes. He's recovering nicely, and they just need to monitor him a few more days."

"Oh, that's wonderful. Thank you, God."

"Yes, absolutely," Brenda grins. "I know it's hard to be apart on Christmas day, but I have the phone number for the other hospital and his room number written down, so you can at least call him." She sets the information on her table. "They said he's sleeping again right now, but that his father is with him. You can call the nurse's station in a while and see if he's awake. I also gave them your information here, and you should get an update from his doctor."

"So, his *father* is there?"

Brenda halts at her incredulous tone.

"*Travis*? Travis is at the hospital?"

"Uhh, apparently."

Keisha's eyes shift to the window. "How? How did he know?"

Brenda shows discomfort. "I'm sorry if that's a problem. The staff always tries to contact family if they can. They likely got his number from your phone. *Is* there a problem . . .?"

Keisha softens. "No. That's fine. I was just surprised."

"Are you sure?"

"Yes. No, it's good. I'm glad." She scans the room. "Is my phone here?"

"I should think so." Brenda opens the closet. "Would it be in your purse?" She brings it over to her.

"Oh, I'm so glad they thought to look for it." Keisha searches the pockets and finds her phone. "Oh, thank God, it's here." She tries to wake it, but the battery is dead.

"Do you have a charger?" asks Brenda.

Keisha flits her hands. "In the car, of course."

"Well, I'm sure we can scare one up for you to borrow." She points to Keisha's end table. "In the meantime, you can use that phone to call the other hospital, or whoever you need to."

"Thank you, Brenda. I really appreciate everything."

"My pleasure. Your doctor will come in an hour or so to see how you're doing. But—" Brenda puts her hands on her hips teasingly. "We thought you should know that you've caused quite a stir today."

"*I* have?"

She grins. "Yes, you have, missy. Everybody is talking about 'The Christmas Miracle,' all because of you!"

"I don't understand."

"Do you remember last night, when you arrived at the emergency bay, you saw a reporter there and called her over?"

Keisha reflects for a moment. "Oh, yes, I do."

"Well, starting first thing this morning, the news has been playing that video of you trying to find out who the *hero* is. They got the whole story, and now they are calling it 'The Christmas Miracle!'"

Keisha's thoughts drift again to that voice in the dark. "Hello?" She muses with awe, "It *was* a miracle."

"That's not all."

"No?"

"No," Brenda adds with glee. "They *found* the man this morning."

"They did?"

"Yes. It was on the afternoon news. They *found* him. They interviewed him too. It's pretty good, from what I hear. The news station has been calling and checking on you today, and said they'll help connect you two after Christmas."

Keisha's countenance brightens. "That's wonderful!"

"You should know," Brenda adds encouragingly. "A lot of people are saying this is just what we need at Christmas time. Good news and a little miracle."

The harrowing events flash through Keisha's mind again, and the moment when the stranger's face appeared. "I'm glad."

"Anyway, it looks like you're still working on that food, but I'll come back to check on you." She points to the TV with a grin. "It's about 4:00. You might want to see if the news is on again and catch that interview."

"Oh, thank you."

Brenda leaves Keisha to her thoughts, which wander out the window again to the seagulls, gliding in the blustery wind. After a moment, she inhales deeply, and slowly releases it again.

"It's going to be alright," she whispers. She swivels the table back over her lap and resumes nibbling on her lunch, then turns on the TV and searches until she finds the news broadcast. Soon, an image of Keisha, disheveled and lying on the stretcher, appears queued behind the anchorwoman as she introduces the story.

"A local news story from earlier today, dubbed 'The Christmas Miracle,' has gone viral. This woman and her ten-year-old son were driving from San Diego to Big Bear yesterday evening for Christmas, when suddenly, their car slid on some ice and went off the road. Authorities say the two remained trapped and injured in their car on the steep hillside for several, freezing hours that night. Then, the unthinkable happened—the boy, who was unconscious, suddenly stopped breathing. But as it would happen, at that very moment, a man passing the area caught sight of their taillights and bravely investigated. First responders explain that the car was well-hidden on the steep embankment, but somehow the man climbed down in the dark, navigating rocks and bushes, and arrived just in time to rescue the boy. He pulled him out of the wreck, carried him up the hill, and gave him CPR—all after calling 911. However, he didn't stick around for any thanks, so this grateful mother made a heartfelt plea to find him on her way into the emergency room late last night."

Next, the video of Keisha plays. Then the anchorwoman returns and another video is queued behind her head, this time showing a man—the face Keisha saw in the darkness.

"Well, Maizie McCrery tracked down that man this morning, and here is the surprising interview that he and his own daughter gave."

They play the video of Bryce describing the extraordinary events that aligned to rescue Keisha and Justin.

"Incredible," Keisha whispers.

Then, Jasmine begins to speak from her wheelchair.

"I told him to go find my lost lamb, and he did," she explains. "God told me something special was going to happen."

"How did she know?" Keisha wonders.

"God talks to us all the time. We just have to listen," Jasmine continues, as the reporter seems to recede from the interview. She finally turns to the camera, astonished, and sums up the little girl's remarkable insights.

"Well, bless your heart. What more can we add to that? Trust God and be a hero," she professes. "That sounds like a perfect Christmas message to me."

"Amen," Keisha quietly affirms.

She turns off the TV and gradually becomes lost in these thoughts, watching the avian acrobatics.

Soon, her doctor arrives to explain her injuries and the surgery, as well as her prognosis. He departs after answering her questions, pledging to return tomorrow. As he leaves, Brenda appears with a phone charger.

"One of the nurses had this, so hopefully your phone will recharge before he leaves at 7:00." She plugs the charger into the socket nearest Keisha and hands the end to her. "There you go."

"Thank you, *very* much." Keisha accepts the cord and inserts it into her phone with a *bleep*. “By the way, I *did* find the story on the news. Everything was even *more* amazing than I already knew it was.”

“That’s what I *heard*. I only saw part of it since I’m at work, but it’s all on YouTube now, so I’m going to watch the whole thing when I get home.”

“Yes. Well, it’s . . . inspirational,” Keisha marvels.

“I’ll check it out,” Brenda smiles, taking the lunch tray as she goes.

Keisha turns the TV back on and soon finds the story again on another station, but with fewer details. She watches it one more time on the same station at the top of the hour. She flips through the channels, but nothing captivates her interest. She turns the TV off and sits quietly, watching the evening encroach on her seagulls.

“Wow. Thank you.”

She picks up the note paper with the information for Justin’s hospital. She lifts the phone over to her table and dials.

The line rings. “Yes, can I please have the 3rd floor nurses’ station?”

She is transferred. A nurse picks up the line moments later.

“Hi. My name is Keisha Parsons. My son, Justin is there in room 312. Is it possible to know if he’s awake?”

The nurse puts her on hold, then she returns.

“Oh, he is? Yes, *please*, thank you.” Keisha endures two rings before she hears the voice of her son.

“Mommy?” he answers excitedly.

Keisha animates at his voice. “Justin, Baby! Are you okay?”

“Yeah, Mom!” comes his cheerful reply. “My head hurts some, but I’m okay!”

“O, Baby, I am so happy to hear your voice. You sound a little—”

“They put a *tube* down my throat,” Justin reports with zeal. “When I woke up, I couldn’t talk, but then they pulled it out! Isn’t that cool?”

“Oh my.”

“Now, I have a tube coming out of my hand, and like,” Justin pauses, as if evaluating the wound, “*seven* stitches on my head.”

“You have *stitches*, baby?”

“No, Mom. It’s okay. It’s not that many. But they said that I *almost* had to have my *head* drilled! The medication they gave me worked, though, so I only got stitches."

"Oh Justin." Keisha tries to sound upbeat. "Well, I'm glad it's only a *few stitches*."

"I made Dad take a picture of them when they changed my bandage. It's really cool looking."

Keisha becomes nervous. "Is Travis there with you?"

"No, he and his friend just left. He's going to see you. He said he'll be back later and bring some pizza for us for dinner."

"Pizza?" she scoffs.

"No Mom, he *asked* if it was okay. They said that I can't eat anything *before* 7:00, but if I'm still doing good *after* 7:00, then I can eat whatever I want. And I'm *starved*."

"Okay," she replies uncertainly.

"Mom, are you okay? Will I be able to see you soon?"

"I'm okay, Baby. They had to fix my leg. It was broken pretty badly."

"How broken?"

She hesitates, then mirrors his own upbeat attitude. "Oh, well it's broken in *three* places, cool huh?"

"Gosh, Mom."

"Yeah, I broke my ankle, my thigh, and the round part of my hip joint."

"Wow!"

"Wait until you see it. There are these metal rods sticking out of my thigh, like I'm part machine."

"Really?" he amazes, a little frightened. "Does it hurt?"

"Yeah, it hurts some, but it's going to get better every day. Right?"

"Right." He hesitates, "How about Daisy? Is she okay?"

Keisha recalls the soft, warm touch of the motionless dog. "Baby, I'm not sure. I told them about her, but it was really crazy down there. We'll try to find out, okay?"

"Okay." His voice is forlorn. "I hope she's safe and that someone found her for us."

"Me too." She encourages him. "But everything is going to turn out okay. Right Baby?"

Justin cheers some, "Yeah, Mom." He pauses. "Can I ask you something?"

"Yes, of course."

"Well, what happened? No one here really knows except that we got in an accident."

"Hmmm . . . Okay," Keisha gathers her thoughts. "You remember that we were driving on that curvy road?"

"Yeah."

"Well, I think we drove over some ice, and the car just slid right off the road, and down a steep hill, with bushes and rocks and trees, and then we crashed into some big boulders."

"I don't remember."

"I know. I think you hit your head and were knocked unconscious."

He is quiet for a moment. "Then what happened? How did we get out?"

Keisha inhales deeply. "Baby," she begins, "that is the most amazing part."

"Really?" he asks, fascinated. "Tell me."

Just then Travis appears at her door, hands in pockets, head downward. Another familiar man stands behind him, who connects with Felicia's eyes. He smiles and gestures toward Travis, then gives her a thumb's up.

"What Baby?"

Travis nods at Keisha and slides quietly into the room, then comes and kisses her on the forehead. He smells like mint and seems sober. He steps away and sits in the chair by her bed, then gestures for her to ignore him and keep talking. The other man waives at Keisha, then signals for Travis to text him, and leaves.

"Will you tell me? What happened? How did we get out?" Justin repeats, getting anxious.

"I'm sorry, Baby. Your daddy just walked in." Travis lays his hand over his heart, and furrows his eyebrows in sorrow. Then he again gestures for Keisha to just keep talking.

She sighs peacefully. "Of course, I'll tell you. It's an amazing story."

Keisha then details every tense and harrowing event of the night, dramatizing the account with exciting commentary. She describes when he stopped breathing, and her frantic attempts to wake him, then her desperate prayer.

"And *then* . . ." she melodramatizes.

"What!" Justin implores.

"Just when there was no hope . . ." her eyes fasten on Travis, sitting rapt on the edge of his seat as if he were uncertain of the outcome. Then she smiles inadvertently, perhaps sparked by their familiarity. Travis tilts his head curiously at this signal.

"Tell me, Mom!" explodes Justin, giggling.

"Just then," she grins wryly, "I heard a voice. Far away. 'Hello?' it said. And I started yelling 'Here, Here! Help us!' And then, *there he was*. My answered prayer."

Keisha describes the thrilling rescue and the remaining events as she knew them. When she comes to the dramatic end, Justin's built-up tension releases an astonished gasp.

"That's amazing!"

Travis also unwinds, as her gripping report culminates.

"But wait!" Keisha adds, prolonging the performance. Travis sits forward again.

Keisha next recounts the events concerning the news crew at her hospital, the news reports on their "Christmas Miracle," and finally the astonishing interview of their heroic rescuer and his daughter.

When Justin hears these last details, he asks his mother to repeat several aspects, and answer specific questions about Bryce, and Jasmine, and the inspiring things she said.

As Travis listens intently, he shakes his head in bewilderment. At one point he lifts his hands and covers his face. Then he softly begins to cry, head bowed deeply.

"She said, 'Trust God and be a hero'?" Justin prods his mother ardently. "She *said* that?"

Keisha is distracted by the broken vision of Travis, rocking himself quietly in the chair.

"Yeah, Baby. That's what she said. 'Trust God and be a hero.'"

After a moment, Travis looks up at Keisha, and meets her eyes with resolve. He firmly wipes the tears from his face with his palms, and nods thoughtfully to himself. He sets his jaw, effectively banishing the pitiful addict, and as Keisha watches, the resolute man she once married reemerges, unfettered.

She is captivated by this transformation. Something stands up inside her.

"What do you think now, Mommy?"

She wonders if she missed something. "What do I think now?" she echoes.

"About God. Do you believe in God now, Mommy?" Justin gently prods.

"Do I believe in God now?" she repeats, disoriented. Travis rises from his seat, tall, strong. He takes two calm, determined strides to Keisha's bedside, nodding peaceably at her. Then reaches to her hand, fiddling with the blankets, and covers it with his.

Keisha blooms a smile.

"Yes, Justin. I believe." Travis grins and squeezes her hand with familiarity. Her smile brightens, and she shakes her head at him—half scold, half tease.

"I believe with all my heart."

"Merry Christmas, Mommy."

She settles her eye into her husband's gaze. "Oh, Baby, it *is* a Merry Christmas."

Chapter 18: To Everything there is a Season (Ecclesiastes 3:1)

Bryce lies on the bed listening to the indistinct laughter and conversation coming from the other room. He inhales deeply, holding it, expanding his lungs, then slowly releases it with satisfaction. He stretches out his arms and legs, feeling the cool place in the bed beside him with his hand. He smiles. After several moments, he unplugs his phone from the charger, finds his glasses on the end table, and puts them on to look at the screen.

"Wow." 10:15. He glances disbelievingly toward the window, but the blackout shades are drawn. He scrolls through the texts and messages left while his phone was on silent. He decides to tend to them later.

Another thoughtful stretch, and Bryce rolls out of bed. He inserts his feet into the hotel slippers that Felicia set beside him. "Hmm . . . nice." He walks to the window and pulls aside the shade, expecting bright daylight, but the sky is overcast and blustery. He finds the hotel robe Felicia laid out on the nearby chair and slips into it. "Not bad."

Out in the living area, all the colorful foam ammunition has been expelled and scattered like confetti. Weapons now aside, Oscar is in the kitchenette helping his Mom set the table. Jacob and Jasmine are scrunched together in their chair again, this time with Jasmine's iPad held between them. Jacob's blankets and pillow and some candy wrappers are strewn about the couch.

"Hi Daddy!" greets Oscar and hugs him after putting napkins and silverware on the table.

"Morning Buddy." Bryce puts his arms around Felicia, removing the scrambled eggs from the cooktop. "And good morning to you."

She turns her face to be kissed. "Good morning, Bryce," she grins. "Sleep well?"

He laughs a little. "Yeah, I guess I did." He picks a Tater Tot from the other pan and pops it into his mouth. Felicia swats him, "You go sit down." He scoots out of the kitchen and clears a few darts and Felicia's Bible from the table.

"Good morning, you two."

Jasmine looks up from the screen, evidently quite absorbed. "Good morning, Daddy." She is still wearing her royal blue Christmas hoodie and holds out her free arm to collect a squeeze around her father's neck.

"Thank you, Pumpkin." Bryce eyes his eldest son. "Jake? How'd you sleep?"

Jake has taken control of the iPad for the moment and is typing on it. "Mmm . . . good."

"Daddy, look." Jasmine points to the iPad. "Look at all the nice things people are saying on Facebook."

Bryce looks over their shoulders and sees the busy Facebook page of the local news station.

"What's all this?"

Felicia sets yogurts on the table. "I logged them onto my Facebook account so they could follow the hashtag that someone started about her interview."

"What *hashtag*?"

"Okay, come on everyone. Breakfast is all ready," Felicia announces. "Put the iPad down for now and come eat." Jacob and Jasmine climb out of the chair and come to the table. Oscar is already seated.

Felicia reaches her hand to Jasmine and Oscar as the family follows her lead. "Jasmine, do you want to pray?"

Jasmine nods and clears her throat in quiet reverence. "Dear Jesus. You are so amazing. We love you so much. Thank you for our family. Thank you for our food. Thank you for being so good to us. We give today to you."

"Amen," all echo.

As everyone begins to eat, Bryce asks again. "What were you saying about a hashtag?"

Jasmine opens a yogurt and sets it on her plate next to a small scoop of eggs. "Mommy let us go to the website—the one from the news? And we found all these nice things people are posting about what we said on TV, right Jake?"

"Yeah," Jacob affirms through Tater Tots and eggs. "There was a link to their Facebook page with all the posts, so Mom let us log onto her Facebook account and follow them."

"Yeah," Jasmine adds excitedly. "It's called #TrustGodBeAHero. Daddy, they like what I said about God. Can you believe it?"

Bryce is stunned. He looks at Felicia.

"It's true. People are commenting on what she said about trusting God and doing something nice for someone, and some of them are sharing stories about the nice things she has inspired *them* to do."

"Really?" He takes Jasmine's hand and squeezes it. "Wow, Pumpkin. Look what you started!" He looks around at the family, amazed. "Wow. What to do you think, Oscar?"

"It's really good," he squirms, smiling at Jasmine.

"It really is something," Felicia echoes, nodding with approbation.

Jacob nudges Jasmine, "Good job, Sis."

"Good job, Jesus!" Jasmine beams. She digs a spoon into her yogurt triumphantly.

After the family enjoys their meal together, the children gather on the couch around the iPad, with the little Christmas tree twinkling on the coffee table. Bryce and Felicia clean up from breakfast in the kitchenette, though Bryce slows their task with smooches and cuddles. When they finish, they sit at the table together—Bryce with a coffee refill, Felicia with tea—and watch the kids engrossed in their quest.

Bryce wonders if it's safe for them to see all the posts.

"Well, I talked to Jake about it. We agreed *not* to post anything, and to only follow the hashtag and posts directly connected with the station's webpages. He's in charge of making sure everything is clean."

"You sure?"

"I'm sure," Felicia grins. "I trust him. He's very protective of her."

The prolific responses keep the siblings actively engaged in conference.

"Jake, read that one to Mom and Dad," Oscar urges.

"This one?"

"Yeah."

Jacob finds the place and begins to recite, "I JUST GAVE A GIRL A RIDE HOME WHO WAS WAITING IN THE SNOW AT A BUS STOP. GOD TOLD ME TO HELP HER. NEVER DID THAT BEFORE. JASMINE WAS RIGHT!"

Bryce is stunned. "That's really great. But I don't understand. What snow? Where was that?"

"I don't know," Jacob explains. "But these posts are not just from around here. I mean, the YouTube video of our interview has blown up. There's already . . . " he switches screens, "over 200,000 views! Isn't that crazy?"

"Wow, Jake. How's that possible?"

"People have been sending the video link to each other since yesterday. There's thousands of followers already, and they're all posting this kind of stuff."

"Wow!" Bryce repeats.

"Mija, that's wonderful. And Jake, thank you for finding all of that. And for keeping a watchful eye over what everyone reads."

"Yeah, Mom. I know. I'm on it."

"What's that hashtag called again?" Bryce asks. "Trust God . . ."

"#TrustGodBeAHero." Jacob reiterates, "Just like what Jasmine said."

Bryce types the words into his phone. "Amazing, you guys."

"You too, Dad," adds Oscar. *You* were the hero!"

"Ha!" chuckles Bryce. "Not on purpose. That's just how it worked out."

"That's the point, Bryce."

Jasmine laughs. "Yeah Daddy, that's the point. It was scary, and you didn't *have* to do *anything*. But something inside told you to do it. That was God, and you *did* it."

"You're right Pumpkin." Bryce raps the table with his verdict. "If we trust God, He'll help us do things that really matter, big or small."

The kids return to their investigation, and Bryce refills his coffee and sits in one of the chairs, to check on his phone messages. Felicia sits on the couch and pulls out her phone.

"Hey, Mija. Do you want to help me pick out some of your favorite photos? I'm going out to get some things and I thought I'd print them for the album."

Over the next half hour they select dozens of photos dating back several years, and put them in a folder for Felicia to print. Felicia then gets up to get ready.

"Bryce, any requests? I'm picking up some groceries and other things."

Bryce looks up from his phone. "No. You know what I like," he smiles.

"Alright. I'm taking a quick shower and then I'll go."

"Okay. Actually, you're not going to a Walmart or Target are you?"

"Probably, so I can print the pictures."

"Hey, can you see if they have any tennies? My shoes are wrecked."

"Yes, I'll look." Felicia gets ready, and after a while, she leaves.

Bryce reads through his many Christmas texts. One text from his mom in Kansas reads: REMEMBER MY FRIEND JUNIE IN ARIZONA? SHE SENT ME THIS VIDEO ASKING IF IT'S YOU. WHAT HAPPENED?" The YouTube link to their interview is attached.

He will find as the day wears on, and over the coming days, there will be many more of these questions—including from dozens of people he had lost touch with. For now, he decides to send a group text outlining the events to his closest family and friends, along with the link his mom sent to him. Bryce works nearly a half hour on composing this text, while the children continue to follow updates, and periodically read various posts to Bryce.

At some point, Oscar gets up from the couch and finds his way onto Bryce's lap. He settles in, legs curled up, leaning against his chest. Bryce finishes amending his group text, then sends it.

"Hi Buddy. What's going on?" he asks, setting his phone aside.

"Just saying hi," Oscar quietly replies.

"Aww. Thanks." Bryce gives him a little squeeze and kisses the top of his head. "Man, you're getting big. How's it going over there?"

Oscar is watching the two siblings on the couch together. "Daddy, it's just so amazing. Isn't God doing something amazing?"

Bryce looks at his two children, tracking the ripples of a Christmas Miracle.

"Yeah. You're right, Oscar. He is."

Bryce's phone vibrates with a text from Felicia.

"Hey kids, Mom wants to know if we want spaghetti or chicken for dinner."

"Spaghetti!" they answer in unison.

"Spaghetti it is." Bryce attempts to reply with Oscar resting on is left arm, but it's hard to reach. "Sorry, buddy. I need my arm."

Oscar gets up and picks up his gun, then wanders through the living space picking up his foam ammunition. He loads his gun and takes shots at various targets in the room, and when he is out again, he asks "Daddy, can I have a cookie?"

"Sure," replies Bryce, fielding more messages.

Oscar retrieves a cookie from the kitchen and takes a bite.

"Oscar, listen to this one," Jasmine calls to him. "Jake, read that one."

Oscar walks behind the couch and looks over their shoulders, nibbling on his cookie as Jake reads the post.

"MY SON HEARD ABOUT HOW JASMINE FELT LOVED WHEN A BOY SHARED HIS SLED, SO TODAY WHEN HE SAW A SAD LITTLE GIRL PLAYING ALONE AT THE PARK, HE LEFT HIS FRIENDS AND ASKED HER TO PLAY. SHE WAS SO HAPPY. LATER WHEN I TOLD HIM HOW PROUD I WAS, HE SAID "GOD WANTED HER TO FEEL SPECIAL, LIKE JASMINE."

"Oscar," exudes Jasmine, "That's something *you* would do!"

Oscar blushes. "I don't know."

"It's true, dude," Jacob teases. "You gave away your *new ball* to that kid in the airport."

Bryce looks up from his screen. "What happened?"

"Yeah, there was this kid crying in the airport while we were waiting," explains Jacob, incredulously. "Pretty soon, Oscar is on the floor playing with him with the new ball that he got from Aunt Tiana. And then when we went to leave, Oscar *gave* it to him. Can you believe it?"

"Wow, Oscar," Bryce grins proudly at his son. "That's a very nice thing to do. We'll have to get you another one of those."

Jasmine turns around and smiles at Oscar. "See?" She reaches up and wiggles his hand playfully.

"Okay Oscar," Jacob challenges. "If you're so nice, get me a cookie."

Oscar walks away from the couch to get the container.

"Jacob . . ." corrects Bryce.

"I mean, would you *please* get me a cookie?"

Oscar opens the cookie container and places it on the coffee table.

Bryce takes a cookie, and a new text pops up from Maizie at the news station: HI BRYCE. I HAVE 2 MESSAGES AND A QUESTION FOR YOU. FIRST, THE WOMAN YOU RESCUED, KEISHA, WOULD LIKE TO HEAR FROM YOU SO SHE CAN THANK YOU. HERE IS HER CELL NUMBER: (number given). SECOND, A MAN NAMED DERIK CALLED SAYING YOU MET HIM AND HIS SON SLEDDING IN BIG BEAR. HE WOULD LIKE YOU TO CALL HIM. HERE'S HIS NUMBER: (the number). THIRD, IF SOMEONE CALLS ABOUT JASMINE'S LAMB, SHOULD WE JUST GIVE THEM YOUR NUMBER? LET ME KNOW! THANKS, MAIZIE.

Bryce replies his thanks and gives permission to provide his number to anyone who thinks they have found Jasmine's lamb. Then he wonders if Derik had found the lamb, and perhaps that's why he's calling. He gets up and goes into the bedroom to call. After a few rings a man answers the phone.

"Derik?"

"Yes?" Replies the man.

"Hi, this is Bryce. You told the news station you wanted me to call?"

The man chuckles, then harshly whispers to someone, "It's Bryce."

"Hey, Bryce. I am so glad you called!" Derik speaks loudly over background noise. "Man, we heard about your crazy adventure after leaving us the other day!"

"Yeah, I know. Can you believe it? How'd you hear about it?"

"Well, it's kind of all over town up here." Wind gusts into the phone over Derik's words. "My wife and Marcus and I went into town for breakfast this morning and saw this flyer posted on the door with a picture of your family. It said, IF YOU FIND THIS LITTLE GIRL'S STUFFED LAMB IN BIG BEAR, CONTACT THIS NEWS STATION. It also said to check out the story on the webpage. Marcus recognized Jasmine and wanted to look up the story. So, we did!"

"Wow, it's so amazing how the story has gotten around."

"That's what I hear." The background wind suddenly quiets, and so does Derik's voice. "You know, Marcus was so honored that Jasmine mentioned him in the interview. We all got to talking as a family, and . . . well. I don't know. We just felt like . . . Well, we know that your family is going through a tough time. I got the impression you're here for treatment for Jasmine . . . " He trails off, suggesting Bryce might affirm this idea.

"Uh . . . Yes, Jasmine's is getting treatment in LA, and her Mom and brothers just flew in from Arizona for Christmas together."

"Well, I don't know if this would help or not, but I know it can kind of get stressful with all that going on . . . Anyway. We'd like to offer to bring your boys up to Big Bear for a little winter sport excursion. Just for a couple days."

Bryce hesitates, "Go up there, huh?"

"Yeah," Derik eagerly explains. "Look, I know you might have plans . . . it's just that--well, my sister and her family kind of went through something like this, and I know how hard it can be on the other kids sometimes to hang around the hospital." He pauses. "It's just . . . I don't know. Really, God just put it on our hearts to offer, and we hope you consider it."

"Wow," Bryce contemplates. "I . . . I mean, that's a great offer. . . I certainly think the boys would like to do something like that . . ."

Derik adds, "We would take them skiing, or snowboarding, or just sledding if they want. It's all our treat."

"Oh, well . . . We couldn't ask that!"

"No. We'd *really* like to."

"Wow. That's amazing. Thank you, Derik." He ponders for a moment. "I think that if we took you up on that, we could certainly pitch-in on the cost. But it's a great offer. I guess I just need to talk it over with my wife, and the family."

"Yes, please do that. So, just letting you know that we're coming down *tomorrow* near LA so my wife can return to work, but Marcus and I are driving back to our cabin the next morning for a few more days of fun. So, we can pick your boys up in the morning on the 28th, and then we're coming *back* from Big Bear on the 30th."

"Okay, Derik. That sounds really great. We'll talk it over and I'll let you know."

"Good. Just let me know by, say 10:00 tomorrow night. Okay?

"Okay. Thank you so much. I will."

They hang up, and Bryce sits for a moment lost in many thoughts. He decides it is a good time to return Keisha's call. After several rings, a woman answers.

"Hello?"

"Hi. Is this Keisha?"

"Yes, this is Keisha."

"Hi." He clears his throat. "Ah, this is Bryce Goodson. The station gave me your number and said you wanted me to call?"

"Oh my goodness, Bryce! Thank you so much for calling!" Keisha's voice animates with breathless excitement.

"Oh, well. . . I'm happy to."

"Oh, you have no idea how much you've done for me and my family. I just had to thank you!"

Bryce stands and begins to pace around the room. "Well, *trust* me, it has really been my honor." He chuckles a little. "I don't know if you realize all the excitement the two of us have caused because of this, but—"

"I know!" Keisha exclaims. "Who could imagine all this would happen. I saw the interview of you and your family, and I have to tell you, that is one remarkable little girl you have Mr. Goodson."

"Please, call me Bryce."

"Bryce. Yes, well, she has made a real impression on my whole family. And I've been following the post they started—TrustGodBeAHero. Have you seen those? They are remarkable!"

"Yes, actually, my kids found them."

"Oh, my. It's so inspirational. And I tell you, I believe she's right. All of it. She's absolutely right," Keisha effuses.

"Yeah. She's pretty amazing," Bryce muses. "She has *me*

convinced that God had it all planned."

"I know. I *see* that now," Keisha muses. "I mean, how else could you explain everything?"

Bryce lets the question hang, as his mind replays the heart-pounding sequence of events that night—a red flash in the quiet dark, a boy motionless in the cold, a moon-streaked lake and his surrender.

"You can't really," he professes. "At least I can't—without God."

"Neither can I. You know. Just before we slid off that road, my son asked me if I still believed in God. We've had some rough times in our family. It seems like you've had some too." Keisha saddens. "Well, I wasn't sure what I was going to say to him. I mean, *they* can tell, you know?"

Bryce snickers softly, "Yeah. They can."

"But I tell you, when Justin stopped breathing, I had *no* trouble, *no* pride, *no* other hope, but to call out to God for his life," Keisha's voice quavers ardently.

"I certainly understand that."

"And *just* at that moment. *Exactly* after that prayer. In *direct* response to my cry . . . I heard your voice. 'Hello?' I'll never forget the sound of your voice. It will echo in my mind until my last day. And then, *there* you were." Keisha pauses before she goes on.

"So, *no* one *ever* again can change it . . . no devil in my ear . . . and *whatever* else happens—I *know*. I *know*. You understand?"

"Yes," Bryce ponders. "I think I do."

"I *know*," she repeats, her voice cracking.

"Yes," Bryce affirms. "I understand."

Keisha clears her throat. "Well . . ." she adds lightly. "I didn't intend to say all of that."

Bryce pauses quietly. "I'm glad you did, Keisha." He takes a deep breath, releasing it as he speaks. "I think I needed to hear that."

She is quiet. "Okay. I'm glad." After another pause. "You know, Bryce. I realize this is a lot to ask, but I had hoped to meet you somehow. My husband and I *both* want to thank you. He's driven up to Big Bear today because they are pulling up our car and he's getting our dog and our things—and the *Christmas* presents . . ."

"Oh, wow. Yeah, some Christmas, huh?"

"Actually," she laughs. "It's *actually* the *best Christmas* I've had in . . . probably four years. Maybe *ever*. They even found our little *dog* wandering around up on that lookout point! I thought she died in the accident!"

"Huh. I'm glad they found her."

"This whole thing has done a lot to change our outlook—to help us all appreciate what truly matters." Her voice fills with amazement. Honestly, it's given me *great hope*. That means a lot."

"I'm glad. It's certainly been eye-opening."

"Again, Bryce, I don't know how to thank you."

"Well . . . You're very welcome. It's done a lot for my family too."

Keisha sighs deeply. "So, I know you have a lot going on, but I really would like a chance to thank you in person. I know my husband would, and so would my son. They are trying to transfer him to my hospital tomorrow while they keep him under observation. I don't know if you can find a way to drive here, but I'll be stuck in this hospital a while before they can move me closer to home. I'd love to meet you before then, but if not, then I understand."

Bryce stops pacing. "Well, Keisha, let my wife and I see what things look like. I'd like to see you and your son again too, so if I can figure it out, I will. Okay?"

"Thank you, Bryce. I appreciate it."

The two exchange warm goodbyes.

Bryce goes to the window and ruminates over the gloomy day. He is restless. He changes out of his sweats, and shoves his feet into his battered tennis shoes, not bothering to untie the dirty, debris-snarled laces. As he grabs his wallet and hotel key, the front door opens with greetings from Felicia.

He helps her in with the bags. "Is there any more in the car?"

"No that's it. Your shoes are in here, if you want to try them."

"Thank you!" Bryce takes the bag, flicks off the old shoes, and tries the new ones on, deftly tying them. He stands and flexes, taking test steps. "These are perfect, Honey. Thank you." He gives her a kiss, then helps her unload the groceries.

"You're welcome." She looks over at the kids. "I see their taking a break from the social media, huh?"

Jake is sitting in the comfortable chair playing on his phone feet up on the coffee table. Oscar is on the couch looking through his puzzle book, and Jasmine is lying on her side next to him, with her head resting on the pillow in his lap. She has a throw-blanket over her, and is sleepily watching the Christmas DVD again, her two middle fingers resting in her mouth.

"Oh, I guess so," he wonders. "I was on the phone. Jake must have set it up for her."

Felicia turns to Jasmine, "You doing okay, Mija?"

Jasmine nods languidly. "Mmm, hmm."

"Well," Bryce broaches, "I was thinking about taking a little walk—stretch my legs a little. Would that be okay?"

"Sure, Bryce. Don't you want a sandwich or something?"

Bryce pats his stomach. "No, I'm still full. Thanks though." He kisses Felicia. "I won't be very long."

"Okay. Don't get lost," she teases.

"Funny."

As he heads to the door, Oscar carefully squirms out from under Jasmine's pillow.

"Daddy, can I come with you?"

"Uhh . . . Well. . . Sure, buddy. Jake, wanna come?"

"No."

"Okay then, Oscar. Hurry up and change."

They exit the hotel and head down the street as Oscar excitedly talks about all the things that have happened, asking all kinds of curious questions, and the conversation becomes quite lively. The surrounding blocks consist of strip malls and other businesses, but Bryce wants to look for a body of water, or a little park to walk by, which they never find. They do locate a gourmet ice cream shop and decide to sneak a scoop. In the center of the small strip mall is a fountain surrounded by several flower beds, so they sit there and eat their ice cream.

When they are done, Bryce calls up to Felicia to get their ice cream orders and adds in new servings for Oscar and himself as well. They return to the room to find Felicia sitting on the couch watching the news with Jasmine's head lying on her lap, eyes closed.

"I'm getting up to make dinner, Mija," she says softly in Jasmine's ear and then slides out. Oscar comes and sits with her, taking up his puzzle book again. Jacob looks up from his phone, earbuds in, and shakes his head slightly.

Bryce quietly puts away the ice cream, sensing Felicia's concern.

"What's going on?" he whispers.

"I don't know," she says seriously. "I sat down to show her the pictures and see if she wanted to maybe put some in the book, but she just wanted to rest. So, I sat with her and checked my messages. Her head is a little warm and clammy, and she gets the shivers sometimes. Maybe we should take her back to the hospital."

"Did you ask her how she feels?"

"I did. She said she's fine. I just let her sleep, but I want to know what you think."

Bryce looks over at Jasmine, curled up against Oscar's lap. He's tickling her back again, and she seems to be asleep.

"Well, sometimes she just needs to recharge her batteries. Maybe let's make dinner and give her time to rest. Then when she wakes up, we'll see how she's doing."

"Okay."

~

Later, the aroma of meat and garlic spaghetti sauce permeates the suite. Felicia calls the boys as Bryce finishes setting the table with silverware, salad, and hot bread. Oscar whispers to Jasmine, then slides out, leaving her on the couch.

Bryce crouches beside her, eyes now fluttering open.

"Hey Pumpkin?" He smooths some of her hairs from her forehead, feeling her clammy skin. "Do you want a little scoop of spaghetti and some salad?"

Jasmine shakes her head.

"No?" Bryce gently lays his hand on her back. "You're not feeling good, huh?"

She shakes her head again. Bryce looks up at Felicia, who is watching uneasily as she measures noodles onto a plate. Bryce rubs her back.

"Maybe we should go back to the hospital," he suggests. "I think that's a good idea."

Jasmine shakes her head again, then quietly adds, “I want to stay here. With everybody.”

Bryce looks at Felicia again and shakes his head. Oscar’s eyes are wide. Jacob stares down at his food, his forehead propped in his hand. Felicia shrugs somewhat to say, “What do you think we should do?”

Bryce bends toward Jasmine again. “Okay, Pumpkin. Do you think you could have a little sip of your protein shake if I bring it over?”

She nods a little. Felicia gets the bottle out of the refrigerator, inserts a straw, and brings it to Bryce.

“Here you go, Pumpkin. Try a little sip.” Jasmine lifts herself on one arm and takes a sip of the shake. She nods, and then eases herself back down. Bryce sets it on the coffee table by her.

“Try to have some more when you can, okay? And some water too.” He stands and joins his family. The chair where Jasmine sits at the table remains vacant, leaving a line of sight open for her family to see her.

Felicia nods at her husband and reaches out her hand to him.

“Okay.” They all take hands, and Bryce offers a prayer expressing humble thanks, hope, and trust in God.

After the family has finished the food and dishes, eaten their ice cream, and watched “It’s a Wonderful Life,” on-demand, they prepare for bed. Felicia whispers in Jasmine’s ear, “Do you want to stay in Oscar’s room, or with us tonight, Mija?”

There is a quiet pause. “You, Mamma.” Felicia signals Bryce, and they exchange sorrowful looks. He delicately scoops Jasmine from her mother’s lap and carries her into their bedroom.

The boys gloomily collect their things, kiss their mom, and shuffle into their room. Felicia clears the coffee table of trash, straightens the couch cushions, and turns off the TV to a darkened room. Out the window appears the twinkling flow of lights from a city she doesn’t know. She walks over and scans the glimmering horizon. Above are gray clouds, illuminated by the yellow-orange glow of the city. She places her hand on the cold window seeking some familiar vision for solace.

After a moment searching the sky, she steps back and sighs.

“I still trust you.”

She turns from the window, shuts off the Christmas tree lights, and walks through the dark shadows into the next room.

Chapter 19: A Time for every Purpose under Heaven (Ecclesiastes 3:1)

In the dim morning light, Felicia tucks Jasmine's shoes into the bottom of the duffle bag at the end of the unmade bed. She rolls up her small jacket and other garments, and places them on top of the shoes, then searches the room for needed things. The bathroom door creaks open revealing Bryce standing in the steam-filled room with a towel around his neck rubbing his hair dry. He stops and looks toward the bedroom doorway.

Felicia turns and sees Jacob looming behind her, staring at the motionless form of his sister bundled in the middle of the bed. He gapes at his mother, packing the bag, as if he might complain. The expression could be disgust—or fear.

"I'm sorry, Mijo," she whispers. "I tried not to wake you."

Jacob's arms are stiff beside him, with fists. Bryce walks quietly to his son.

"We need to get Jasmine back to the hospital, buddy. You and Oscar are going to stay here for now."

Jacob's eyes shift skeptically to his father.

"You can have cereal and hang out awhile before you get ready," Bryce continues, "And I'll be back in a bit to get you, okay?"

Jacob's lips close tightly as he listens. He looks at Jasmine again, then turns sharply and leaves. "I thought this was supposed to make her better," he chides, scarcely restraining his voice.

~

Bryce opens the door of the back seat to collect Jasmine from Felicia's care. She nestles against him, swaddled in a throw-blanket, and lays her face against his shoulder.

"I'll be right up," Felicia announces, getting in the driver's seat to park the car.

Up at the hospital room, the bed and staff are ready, waiting for them. He gently lays her warm body on the mattress, and tugs down the wrinkles of her royal blue Christmas sweatshirt before tucking her in the covers. The charge nurse, Emmie, comes in and brings Bryce out of the room to talk, while her nurse, Dante, begins taking vitals and assessing Jasmine. He removes Jasmine's sweatshirt and starts an IV.

Several minutes later, Felicia arrives and kisses her on the forehead, "I'm here, Mija." Felicia pulls the chair close to the bed and sits, laying a hand on her leg. She begins to hum softly.

After several minutes, Bryce enters the room.

"Okay, Dr. Moreno is coming in at 3:00, but she's ordered some tests before she gets here." He stands beside his wife, hand on her shoulder, as they keep watch over their daughter. After a moment, he smooths the thin hair from Jasmine's forehead and studies her face. Then he bends and kisses her clammy cheek.

"I love you, Pumpkin." He stands and watches her a moment more, then steps back to the couch and sits, a few feet from his wife.

They endure perpetual minutes in troubled silence.

Finally, Bryce gets up and walks to the window.

"I wonder of your parents are having fun," he ponders, looking out over the hospital buildings.

Felicia's hand rests gently on Jasmine's leg. "It sounds like it. My Mom emailed me a few pictures with details. She says they've met some nice people, but they're a little anxious to get back, too."

"When does their ship get back?" He sits on the couch again.

"On New Year's Day—about noon, I think."

"Oh." He stands again and takes off his sweat-jacket, and sits again, crossing his legs.

After a few moments,

"Hey, Bryce?"

"Yeah?"

"Why don't you go get us some coffee, would you mind?"

He stands. "Yeah, you want coffee?"

"If you don't mind. We didn't get any this morning."

"Yeah, sure. Sounds good." He checks his pockets. "Anything

else?"

"Ahh . . . maybe like a breakfast burrito? Or something like that?"

"Okay, good idea. Text me if you think of anything else, okay? I'll be right back."

"Thanks, Mi Amore."

Felicia lets out a little sigh, then scoots her chair closer to the head of the bed. She leans near, taking up Jasmine's hand, and hums softly, sometimes quietly singing, "You make me happy, when skies are gray. . ."

~

Bryce's phone rings as he reenters the room, hands full. He sets down the coffee carrier and the burritos and leaves to take the call in the corridor. He answers the phone walking away from the rooms to the windowed hall that overlooks the parking lot.

"Hello?"

"Hi, I'm sorry. Is this Bryce?" asks a man with a drawl.

"Yes, this is Bryce."

"Hi. I'm sorry to bother you, but the news station gave me your number." The kind, gruff voice hesitates as he explains his quest. "I heard that you're looking for your little girl's toy lamb. That she lost it in Big Bear?"

"Oh. Yes. We think we lost it up there somewhere, but we're not sure where. Do you know anything about it?"

"Uhh. . . well . . . first of all, I just last night realized that anyone was looking for it. You see, they have posters here all over town. I guess everybody here knows about what you did, and about your little girl being sick and all . . ."

Bryce's heart knocks quickly. "Did you find it?"

"Ahh. . ." the man clears his throat roughly. "Well, I own the rental cabins down there near the lake, and I was out checking my property Christmas Eve, oh say around . . . 4:30 or so. And then I spotted something over in the parking lot at the lake, so I walked around over there and saw—well I think it was your missing lamb, there."

Bryce's eyes widen. He starts running his fingers through his hair. "Are you kidding? Do you have it?"

"Yeah, well . . ." the man's voice turns cautionary. "I *did* pick it up. It was getting kind of dark out there, so I brought it back to the office to take a look at it. And well . . . to be honest, it didn't look so good. I mean, I think it was run over, maybe. It was dirty and wet and had like black marks on its fur. It was torn up some, too, from maybe the tire going over it, I'm sorry to say."

Bryce starts pacing. "Well, what did you do with it?"

"Ah, well, honestly? I couldn't imagine that any child would want to see their little toy like that, so I decided to throw it out."

Bryce stops. "You threw it out? Oh no!"

"Well, now hold on a minute. When I went into town yesterday and saw the poster, I came straight back, and I went and I dug it out of the dumpster. So, it's not pretty, and I don't see how your little girl would still want it, but I have it. I have it right here."

Bryce exhales. "Oh, thank God. You have it."

"Yes, Sir. I do. Can you come up here? Or would you like me to send it to you?"

Bryce starts pacing again. "Okay, let me think." He imagines presenting the little disfigured lamb to Jasmine.

"Wherever you want, I can send it, don't you worry," urges the man.

Bryce stops pacing and props his glasses on his forehead, then draws his hand firmly down his face. He forgot to use his new razor this morning.

"Let me think," he repeats, replacing his glasses. "Okay, I got it. I'm going to give you an address, if you can send it there as soon as possible. I'll pay you back for the shipping cost."

"No, Sir. You don't need to pay, it's my pleasure. I've got it. Okay, so what's the name on the address?"

"Okay, it's Christiana Jamison," Bryce then spells the name and gives the man Christiana's address.

"Okay, I got it," he confirms, after repeating all the information.

"Thank you so much. You don't know what this means to us," Bryce pledges.

"No, it's nothing. I'm happy to help."

"Oh, what's your name, by the way?"

"Mike, Mike King—King's Cabins," the man replies heartily.

"Thanks, Mike. Merry Christmas to you and your family." And the two hang up.

When Bryce returns to the room, Felicia has already eaten half of her burrito and set it aside. She is sitting back, talking to Jasmine as she sips her coffee. Jasmine's eyes turn toward him.

"Hi Pumpkin! How you doing, bright eyes?"

"Good." She replies softly, blinking with a tired smile. He kisses her forehead again. She is still a little clammy.

"You seem better, huh?" he asks, hands on his hips.

Felicia sips her coffee calmly, then answers for Jasmine. "They think she got pretty dehydrated, and that really made her tired. The IV seems to be helping."

"That's great," he smiles and reaches for his burrito on the table.

"So, they drew some blood for a CBC," continues Felicia, "and now we're waiting for them to come take her for a CT scan."

Bryce rolls down the wrapper on his burrito, "A CT, huh? Okay," he nods positively, and takes a bite. He is about to sit down when Felicia's and Bryce's phones both vibrate. Felicia looks at the message.

"It's Jacob again," she reports. "He wants to know when you're going back to pick them up."

"They're ready? He wants me to get them?"

"Yes," she explains emphatically. "And I told him that Jasmine was doing better, so they want to come right now."

"Okay." He rewraps his burrito and grabs his coffee. "Love you Pumpkin." He gives his wife a kiss, "And you, too. Be right back."

"Love you," the girls reply.

~

Bryce parks the car and runs up to the room to get the boys. "Hi, guys. Did you get enough to eat?" He walks past them to his bathroom and comes out again, razor buzzing over his cheeks. The boys' reply is mixed.

"How about a breakfast burrito? We can get one in the hospital or drive through that taco stand."

"Drive-through," answers Jacob.

Several minutes later, the boys come striding into Jasmine's room eating the remnants of their burritos and carrying their day's entertainment.

"Hi Jasmine," cheers Oscar walking to her bedside. "We brought your iPad."

The boys surround her bed, as she daintily sips some juice and nibbles on a dry English muffin with jam. Oscar abandons his burrito and climbs onto the bed with Jasmine.

"Want to hear some riddles?" he proposes, opening his new puzzle book.

"Sure," she agrees. While the siblings enjoy each other, Bryce takes Felicia into the hall to explain the call about Jasmine's lamb, and how he decided to have it sent to Tiana.

"I thought maybe she could get it cleaned and fixed up some before Jasmine sees it."

"That's a good idea. I'll tell her it's coming."

"I mean, Jasmine shouldn't see it like that, don't you think? With what she said, and how she feels about it? And--and all that."

She evaluates his insinuation. "You're right. We won't tell her about it until we hear from Tiana."

"Okay." He turns to the room.

"Hey, Bryce." She takes his hand. "I was thinking about that woman that you saved."

"Yeah?"

"Well, you said she wanted to meet you and thank you in person, right?"

"Yeah?"

"Well, I think you should do it. You should go meet her."

Bryce is surprised. "I—I didn't say I *would* go."

She looks into his face and tugs his hand a little. "Yes, but I *want* you to go."

"You *want* me to go? Why?"

She wraps her arms around his neck, thoughtfully. "Well, I want you to go because it would mean a lot to her. And because we're just waiting around here right now. Plus, it's a good time to go . . ." Felicia lists determinedly.

"But—"

"And I want you to go because you need a *break*. *We* are here now."

"But I don't need a break—I"

"*Listen* to me. You *do*. And you might not get another one."

He studies her "I win" expression, and laughs.

"Okay. I'll call her and see if it's a good time to come. I think it's over an hour away, though."

Felicia smiles peacefully. “That’s perfect.” She looks at the time on her phone. “It’s 10:15 now. Dr. Moreno isn’t even coming in until 3:00, but she still has to look at the test results. You’ll get there by 12:00 and can stay until 1:30 and still get back in time. Besides, Dr. Moreno will wait for you.”

Bryce looks around the corridor uncertainly.

“I’ll text you if something comes up before that, okay?”

He takes a deep breath, and slowly exhales. “Are you sure?”

“Absolutely.”

~

Bryce makes arrangements with Keisha and takes a peaceful drive to the San Bernardino hospital. He arrives to find Travis, Keisha’s ex-husband, waiting out front.

“Bryce?” he asks, extending his hand?

“Yes, I’m Bryce.”

“I’m Travis, Keisha’s . . . ah, husband. Justin’s dad.” They shake hands. “I thought I recognized you—my son has made me watch that interview of your family about ten times!” he laughs.

“Oh, wow. No kidding!”

As the two walk to the elevator, Travis explains that he wanted to thank Bryce in person, before he saw Keisha.

“I mean, man, what *you* did—” Travis rests his palm against his own chest. “What *God* did—I gotta tell you. It *completely* changed my life.”

“Oh. Well--that’s great.” They enter the elevator.

“I don’t know what Keisha told you about me, but honestly, I have been a mess,” Travis confesses. “Hey, have you ever been in the service?” he asks, grasping Bryce’s arm.

“No, never have.” When they leave the elevator, Travis stops again and faces him.

“Well, I was a medic for the navy, and I got sent to the Middle East.” He puts his palm on his chest again. “Since then, I can hardly talk about the things I saw and experienced there—things you can’t un-see.” The man’s eyebrows pinch together as he shakes his head.

“I’m sorry,” Bryce encourages him. “I can’t even imagine.”

“Well, I admit it. When I came back, I was not the same man. And I couldn’t cope. I lost all faith, and I started drinking—really bad . . . I drove away my wife.” Travis looks away, shaking his head sadly again.

Bryce waits.

"All that changed the night you saved my wife and boy." His eyes animate. "You know, I really blew it Christmas Eve. I was supposed to pick up Justin for some father-son time. But instead, I got drunk. That's why Keisha took him to Big Bear herself. She was *so* mad. And I realized I really blew it, so I called my sponsor—he's ex-military too. He came over and stayed with me that night while I slept it off, so I wouldn't keep drinking. In the morning, I listened to the message the hospital left me, and I *had* to get up there to see my family. But my buddy didn't think I could drive yet, so he drove me up in my own car." Travis shakes his head again, disbelievingly. "He's a good guy. His sister lives in Riverside, and she came and picked him up for Christmas dinner and all."

Travis looks straight into Bryce's eyes. "When we got here, *first*, I went and saw my boy, and *then* I saw my wife, and if *that* wasn't enough to straighten me out," he wags his finger with conviction, "I heard what your little girl said in that interview: 'Trust God and be a Hero.' And that did it!" Travis claps his hands together suddenly, waking both of the men with a jolt.

"Wow!" Bryce startles.

"*That's* what I forgot," continues Travis. "Your little girl was *right*," he swipes his finger through the air emphatically. "I forgot to trust God. That devil almost got me. He almost stole *everything* from me. But, if I trust God, *He'll* make me the man I'm supposed to be for my family. No doubt. No *doubt*," he repeats with resolve.

Bryce is awed by the joyous vitality exuding from the man before him.

"Wow!" he repeats.

" 'Wow,' is right Bryce. That's *it* for me." Travis places his palm on his chest again and lays his other on Bryce's shoulder. "I'm not touching another drop. I'm sold out. I'm sold out, and I can trust the One who bought me," he nods decisively.

Bryce chuckles, "That's great, man!"

Travis relaxes his posture. "I know that's a lot to take in," he smiles broadly, "but I just felt like you needed to hear that. You needed to know what all God has done with you and your family. And that's just with *my* little family." He winks and nudges

Bryce's arm affectionately.

"Thank you," Bryce nods deeply. He offers his hand and they firmly shake. "Thank you."

The two men continue toward the room, conversing, and enter as new-found friends. Keisha's bruised face lights up when she sees Bryce. Her son is at the hospital too and has been wheeled into his mother's room for the visit. When Bryce enters, Justin beams, full of life, seeking a hug from his rescuer. Joy and excited chatter quickly fill the room, and for a time, the present stresses melt into laughter and smiles, and astonishing hope.

When Bryce arrives back at the hospital parking structure, his phone vibrates with a text from Felicia: DR. MORENO CAME BY THE ROOM TO ASSESS JASMINE AND WILL BE READY TO TALK WHEN YOU ARRIVE.

His stomach hollows. PARKING NOW, he replies.

At the room, some of the lights are turned off, and the boys are quietly sitting on the couch, Jacob with his phone and Oscar with his puzzle book. Jasmine is a small mound curled up in the bed. Felicia whispers, "We'll be back in a few minutes," and takes Bryce into the corridor. "We're going to Dr. Moreno's office."

Bryce is unsettled. "What's going on?"

"I don't know, Bryce. Jasmine was really enjoying the boys. They didn't get too wound up, or anything. Jake was reading her some social media posts, and we even responded to some questions that people had about Jasmine's illness. They keep asking, and they really want to pray for her. Oscar got all excited about people praying, so I briefly explained her situation. Anyway, she seemed to enjoy listening and being a part of it, but then she got quieter and quieter."

They round the corner and stand outside Dr. Moreno's office. "Anyway, the staff came and took her for the CT scan about 2 hours ago. I thought that after she came back and rested some, she'd feel better, but it's just like last night. She's clammy and weak. So, we're just letting her rest."

Felicia knocks lightly on the closed door. "Come in," calls Dr. Moreno. The doctor is looking at her computer screen. "Have a seat," she warmly directs.

"I'm sorry to say that Jasmine's leukemic cell count has rapidly multiplied since we last checked, and the CT scan reveals that the blasts are collecting around her chest and lungs. Her liver and spleen are swollen and, of course, she is experiencing a lot of joint and bone pain again. We also see some minor bruising starting to appear. We'll do the bone marrow biopsy to confirm, but it is clear that she is undergoing an aggressive relapse."

Bryce and Keisha look at each other with trepidation. Bryce hesitantly asks, "Okay, so what's the prognosis?"

"Well, as you know, we collected the T-cells from Jasmine's blood, which have been integrated into CAR T-cells, and now the expansion process is nearly complete for infusion back into her bloodstream." Dr. Moreno removes her reading glasses and leans closer, folding her arms on the desk. "However, in order for the CAR T-cells to effectively fight her Leukemia, she must have a low disease burden. We were hoping that her relapse would progress slowly, but it has not, so it looks like she will need a high dose of chemotherapy as part of her conditioning regimen before the CAR T-cell infusion."

"Another *high* dose?" Bryce whimpers.

"Unfortunately, yes." She looks back and forth between the parents. "We know she has not always tolerated the high doses well.

"No, she gets so sick," Felicia reasons.

"I know. And since her disease is refractory, we know the chemo won't be entirely effective. However, the cancer is returning quite fast, and it would overwhelm the CAR T-cells. We need to start giving her high doses tonight, after we get the biopsy. This will significantly reduce the disease burden and give the CAR T-cells a better chance to expand and persist to fight her cancer. It's really her only option to defeat it."

After a quiet moment, Felicia asks, "When would she get the T-cell infusion, then?"

Dr. Moreno puts on her reading glasses and studies her desk calendar. "Well, we originally had her scheduled for the 5th, but the CAR T-cell count should reach our target by the 31st. We'll just need to speed up some of the conditioning regimen." She looks at the couple confidently over her glasses. "I think we should do it then and get Jasmine some help fighting this right away."

Felicia and Bryce glance at each other in sad resignation. Bryce squeezes his wife's hand again.

“Okay, Doctor. Thank you.”

Bryce and Felicia leave Dr. Moreno’s office, gravely discussing the developments. They become certain that the boys could not endure watching Jasmine go through another round of high-dosage chemotherapy.

“What should we do, Bryce?” urges Felicia. “It’s enough for *us* to be here without them sitting around watching her get so sick again.”

Bryce remembers the offer that Derik made to take the boys to Big Bear for a few days and tells Felicia about it.

“What do you think Bryce? Do you trust him?”

Bryce reflects for a moment, “Yeah, I think he’s a good guy. But how do you feel about the boys not being here a few days?”

Felicia touches her fingers to her lips, eyes seeing things in her mind. “Well, I think that they should *not* be here for this. You know?” She reaches down and takes Bryce’s hand for reassurance. “It will be easier on all of us, and they can get away and have some fun. Don’t you think?”

“Yeah, I think so.” He squeezes her hand. “Let’s tell the boys, and then I’ll call him.”

They walk back to the room and find Jacob and Oscar both silently watching Jasmine in the low light. The couple exchange affirming looks.

“Hey, boys,” whispers Bryce, “Come out here for a minute.” The boys listlessly slide off the couch and walk to the corridor, where Bryce explains the offer.

“You guys remember that nice boy and his dad that Jasmine and I told you about? The one who let us use their sled?”

They don’t answer, they just look at him, waiting.

“Well, his dad wants to take you guys to their cabin in Big Bear tomorrow for two nights. You guys can ski, or snowboard, or go sledding . . . What do you think?”

They don’t speak for a moment, glancing between Bryce and Felicia’s waiting faces.

“But what about Jasmine?” Oscar worries.

“Jasmine *got* to go to Big Bear,” Felicia reassures. “We’ll be around here a few days taking care of her, and you guys will get pretty bored while she rests.”

Oscar is uncertain and looks at Jacob for direction. He seems uncertain too.

"Look," encourages Bryce, "*We* wanted to take you to do those things, and this way you get to go and have some fun. It's okay. Go. Enjoy. You'll be back in two days, and maybe by then, Jasmine will be feeling better. Okay?"

Jacob squints some, deliberating, then shrugs. "Sure."

"You want to go?" verifies Oscar.

Jacob turns to Oscar, "Sure," he hits his shoulder lightly. "It'll be fun. We'll be back soon. I want to try snowboarding and see if it really is like skateboarding."

"Okay," Oscar agrees, cheering some. "Okay, we'll go."

When Bryce calls and confirms the plans, Derik asks to speak with the boys and introduce himself. He gets them excited with all the *guy* adventures the four of them will have, and soon the boys are eagerly talking about their trip. At 5:00, they hug their Mom goodbye, and kiss sleeping Jasmine so Bryce can drive them back to the hotel. He drops them off to get packed then returns to the hospital with dinner, and some clothes and things for Felicia to stay overnight. The boys don't get far in their task, sidetracked in messing around and shooting each other with their dart guns.

When Bryce arrives at the hospital, they gently stir Jasmine awake.

"Mija, wake up baby." Felicia masks her trembling voice with a sing-song tone.

Jasmine wills her left eye open a slit, and groans softly.

"Hi, Pumpkin," urges Bryce, smoothing the hair from her forehead. "Hi Pumpkin," he repeats as her eye closes, then rolls languidly under the lid, and strains to stickily part again. "Honey, we need to talk to you, okay?" he persists.

Felicia jiggles the small arm lightly, "Jasmine? Can you listen, Mija?"

Jasmine turns her head off of the pillow some, and she focuses one eye on her mother, "Uh-huh," she affirms breathily, then pinches her eye closed again in a grimace.

"Jasmine, Honey, you're getting sick again, so the doctor needs to take another bone marrow biopsy, Okay Pumpkin?" Bryce explains, stroking her hair. "And then they need to start you on chemo again, Okay? To reduce the cancer. Do you understand?"

Jasmine nods, eyes closed, and writhes some.

"We're sorry, Sweetie," Felicia strokes the little warm hand. "Should we pray? You want us to pray first?"

Jasmine nods again, eyes tight shut, lips dry and pale.

"Okay," Felicia continues, "God, bless Jasmine. Take away her pain. Be with her right now. Please make her feel better."

Two nurses enter with a biopsy kit.

"Amen," adds Bryce.

As they prepare for the procedure, Bryce gives a final kiss to Jasmine and his wife.

"Text me, okay?"

Bryce arrives at the hotel and sits in the car collecting his thoughts before going up. When he enters the room, he playfully hounds the boys back to packing for the trip. They wonder if they should bring their guns to play with, but Bryce suggests that Marcus might not have a dart gun, and that no one would probably want to use the pink one.

"Besides, that's Jasmine's, and we promised," Oscar reminds everyone.

As the boys pack, Bryce empties his pockets, sets his phone on the kitchenette counter and tidies up from the morning. He wakes his phone frequently to check it. When he is done, he wipes his hands and puts a cup of leftover coffee in the microwave to reheat.

Finally, a text: STARTING CHEMO NOW. NEXT ROUND TOMORROW. ANOTHER THE NEXT DAY. A BREAK ON THE 30TH. THANKS FOR THE SALAD. KEEP PRAYING.

Bryce replies: I WILL. CALL IF YOU NEED ME.

He sighs deeply. "I should be there."

Oscar comes out and sees Bryce staring at his phone.

"Daddy?"

"Hi Buddy." Bryce sets his phone aside. "Hungry?"

The men order pizza, kick off their shoes, and put their socked feet on the coffee table as they watch guy movies on-demand. They eat more Christmas cookies and ice cream, and finally drag themselves to bed at midnight, anticipating tomorrow's excursion, and the snowy exploits that await.

Bryce doesn't fall sleep for two more hours.

Chapter 20: He Has Made Everything Beautiful In Its Time (Ecclesiastes 3:11)

As the door quietly widens, a band of light expands into the dark room. The nurse pads in and changes Jasmine's IV bag. She steps out again, and a moment later returns with a syringe that she injects into the bag's port. She delicately lifts Jasmine's hand and attaches a pulse oximeter to her finger for several seconds, then tucks her hand back under the covers. The nurse then erases and replaces the time and readings on the whiteboard, and partially closes the door as she leaves. Jasmine moans and moves some. From the bedside chair, Felicia watches her daughter now resting after an unsettled night. The bedding sits re-folded on the end of the couch, but Felicia is still in her nightclothes. After a moment, her eyes return to the book opened on her lap, which she illuminates with the light on her phone.

Hours later, Felicia has changed and sits bedside humming when Bryce slips into the room, dim from the gloomy day. He sets a tray of coffees and burritos on the table and exchanges concerned looks with his wife. He kisses her on the lips, closing his eyes in the moment, then sits on the couch to eat.

Over the next two days, Bryce and Felicia take turns staying with Jasmine overnight. They update most of the family except for Jacob and Oscar, who have been sending texts and pictures of their adventures. By the afternoon of the 30th, the couple is discussing what to say to the boys when they return, who may feel like they were tricked into going when they understand how sick she is. They decide to be honest, but not detailed about the concerning developments.

Later that afternoon, Felicia goes down the corridor into the hall of windows to have a long phone conversation with Christiana. After listening supportively for some time, Tiana offers some good news.

"I got Jasmine's lamb in the mail today," she announces.

"You did?" Felicia becomes anxious.

"Yeah, and I looked it over. Honestly, I think I can fix it up nicely. It won't be perfect, but I think I can get it pretty clean, and the tear in the fabric is on the seam, so I should be able to sew that just fine."

"You think so? Oh, Tiana. That would be wonderful. Thank you!"

"Absolutely. I'm going to start on it tonight, okay? I'll let you know how it's going tomorrow."

"Thank you so much. That's such a relief, you know?" Felicia brightens.

After the two hang up, Felicia returns to the room and sees Bryce holding a cup for Jasmine, who is sitting up some, sipping tentatively from the straw.

"Hi, Mija!" she effuses, nearing the bed. "Look at you! Drinking some water?" She gives Jasmine an exuberant, not entirely silent kiss on the forehead, then stands back, smiling hopefully.

"Can you take another sip, Pumpkin?" encourages Bryce. Jasmine nods, then takes the straw into her dry lips again and sips on the water. "That's great." He sets the cup on her tray and swivels it within her reach, then uncaps her lip balm, and offers it to her. Jasmine weakly accepts it and applies it to her lips. She slides her lips together and holds the tube to Bryce.

Bryce smiles and recaps it. "They're bringing some apple slices and some other snacks for her until dinner."

Felicia ardently surveys her daughter's face. "That's good, huh Mija? Feeling a little better?"

Jasmine nods. Then she carefully touches the top of her head with her open hand. "Can I have my hat?"

"Sure." Felicia gets the pink hat from the closet and hands it to her daughter with a sympathetic smile, who grins wearily and pulls it onto her head.

By the time the boys arrive at the hospital after 4:00, Jasmine has energized some. Bryce goes down to meet them and Derik in the drop-off zone, and the two boys talk excitedly all the way up to the room. Bryce has to interrupt them before going in and explain that Jasmine had some chemo to get ready for the T-cell infusion tomorrow, and that the boys can't touch her or her things right now. They worriedly listen and nod in compliance.

As they enter with trepidation, they see Jasmine sitting up with the tray of small snacks in front of her, nibbling on her toast and jam. She is watching a cartoon on TV without the sound on.

When the boys walk in, she cheerily inquires, "Wasn't it beautiful up there?"

Oscar's face brightens, and he comes near her bed, hardly restraining himself from climbing onto it with her.

"It was!" he affirms. "Jake took some pictures on his phone. We'll show them to you."

Bryce sets their bags down in the corner. "Boys, come wash your hands before you touch anything. Jake, give me your phone first." Jake pulls his phone out of his coat pocket and hands it to Bryce. Both boys remove their jackets and thoroughly wash their hands, jostling elbows at the sink. Bryce sanitizes the phone with an alcohol wipe and hands it back to Jacob, and soon the brothers are sharing their pictures and telling Jasmine stories about the trip.

"Oh, check this out," remembers Jacob, scrolling through his photos. "Look at this one." He hands his phone to Jasmine.

"That's me and Marcus!" she marvels. The picture shows Jasmine on Bryce's hip, looking down at Marcus with the sled in his hand. She can't tell who is talking.

"Yeah, Derik texted it to me," Jacob explains. "He said he took it just after you went down the hill. Oh, and Marcus wanted me to make sure I said 'Hi,' to you."

"He's nice," Jasmine reflects.

"He is. They're *both* nice." Oscar adds.

~

The family enjoys each other for another hour, but then Bryce senses that Jasmine needs a break, and the boys need to eat.

"We'll come back tomorrow before her infusion," he reassures urging the boys to say goodbye and grab their things.

As they leave, Oscar returns to Jasmine's bed, fighting the urge to touch her. "You get good rest, okay?"

"I will," Jasmine smiles tiredly back.

The boys return the next morning after methodically showering and putting on clean clothes. When they enter, Felicia is lying on the bed next to Jasmine, who is propped up and alert. They are adding the pictures to the album Oscar had given them and decorating each page with stickers and fun labels from the scrapbook kit. The boys dutifully wash their hands again, then go to the bed to receive Jasmine's tour of the memories selected for the album. The first picture shows the three of them right after Jasmine was born, and Oscar was just over a year old. The rest of the photos are of various holidays and camping trips and projects around the house—silly pictures, bath pictures, and special days together.

"We're not done yet," Jasmine announces.

"These look so good. You're doing a good job," Oscar admires.

Jacob flips back through some of the pages, thoughtfully evaluating the fun embellishments. "Yeah. These are all good pictures." He looks at Jasmine. "These are *good* memories."

Felicia observes the seriousness of Jacob and smiles softly. "Can I show your Dad?" She takes the album and climbs out of the bed. "Remember, you boys don't touch her or get on the bed."

Jacob squints skeptically at Felicia, who had just been in it, but doesn't comment. "Can we look at the Facebook posts on Jasmine's iPad?"

"Sure," Bryce replies, and locates the iPad to sanitize it with alcohol wipes before handing it to Jacob. He stands on Jasmine's left side of the bed, holding out the iPad to her to see the different posts he discovers. Oscar scurries over to Jasmine's right side, and pulls the extra chair over, turns it backwards, then climbs in and leans over the back so he can get close without touching anything.

"Wow, Jasmine. Check it out!" Jacob exclaims, handing her the iPad. "Look! Your interview on Youtube has 750,000 views now!"

Jasmine looks at the number count in disbelief. "Oh my gosh, that's so awesome."

"That's amazing, Jasmine!" Oscar squirms, leaning further to see.

Jacob takes the iPad and logs onto his mother's Facebook account to follow the #TrustGodBeAHero thread. "Wow, there's a *lot* more posts since we checked last."

Jacqui comes to the door in her street clothes and knocks lightly. "Hi folks, can I come in?"

Jasmine sees Jacqui and radiates. "Jacqui! I've missed you!"

Jacqui walks shyly into the room and over to Jasmine. "Hi, sweetie. I've missed you too! I had the week off, figuring you were going to be at the hotel, but I hear you are getting your T-cell infusion today!" Jacqui carefully restrains herself from embracing the child.

"That's right," Jasmine quietly affirms. "They're doing it a little early, though."

"I know, Honey. But I'm going to pray for you, and God will know just what to do, alright?"

"Yes, He will," Jasmine smiles.

"Hey, guess what I did Sunday?"

Jasmine's grin broadens, "You went to church!"

"Now how did you know that?" she teases.

"I'm so glad. Did you like it?"

Jacqui nods, "I really did. A co-worker has asked me before, so I went with her to church. My Mom went too," she adds with a wink.

"That's wonderful," Jasmine beams. They share a private look between them.

"Well, I just came in to drop off some paperwork due before the New Year, but I wanted to pop in and tell you I'm thinking about you today, and that I'll be back at work tomorrow. How's that sound?"

"Good." Jasmine nods emphatically. "Then you can tell me about your vacation."

"Okay. We'll talk," Jacqui affirms. She looks around the room at the family and smiles at Felicia. "12:30 today, right?"

Felicia nods, "Yes, her infusion is in less than two hours."

"Okay." Then she turns to Bryce, "Can I talk to you for a second?" she asks cheerfully, gesturing toward the corridor.

"Sure," he replies and follows her to the door. "Be right back."

"Now, you boys be good, okay?" Jacqui teasingly warns as she leaves. "Don't wear her out and keep your germs to yourselves."

"Yes, Ma'am."

Jacqui leads Bryce to the nurses' station, where another nurse, Angela, is working on the computer.

"I was talking to Angela, and she said that the father in 321A is going to take his son and daughter to Disneyland tonight for New Year's Eve and give them a break from the hospital. You've probably met him, Nat Delacruz?"

Bryce concentrates for a moment. "Oh, yeah. He's got a little girl here too."

"Well," Jacqui continues, "he heard that Jasmine is getting her T-cell infusion today and knows that she's going to need a lot of rest. He offered to take the boys with him. He thinks it would be good for his kids and for yours. He wanted us to run it by you before he tells them."

Bryce considers the generous offer a moment. "Ahh . . . I should talk to Felicia. Do you know when he's leaving?"

"He says he's not in a hurry, since they are open late," Angela explains. "He wants to stay for the fireworks, if that's okay—to kind of celebrate the New Year. He can wait until Jasmine starts her infusion if you want."

Bryce nods, thinking it through. "Actually, that would probably be great. Let me talk to Felicia, and then I'll go over to their room. 32. . .?"

"It's 321A."

"Okay, thanks you two."

"You bet," replies Angela.

"We hope it works out," Jacqui adds, and Bryce returns to the room.

After discussing the offer with Felicia, they decide to accept. When they tell the boys, who have never been to Disneyland, their eyes immediately widen with excitement. But then concerns arise about leaving out Jasmine.

"We can't go without you," Oscar plaintively confesses.

"Yeah," Jacob agrees. "I want to hang out here for New Year's Eve. We can all go together when Jasmine is feeling better."

Jasmine gets a sour look on her face. "You guys are crazy. You *have* to go to Disneyland for me and take pictures because I can't." She turns and looks at Bryce and Felicia shaking her head a little. "I can't," she repeats. They nod sympathetically. Felicia's eyebrows pinch together, and her fingers rise to her lips.

"Besides," Jasmine continues, "I am going to need a break from you guys. I love you, but . . ." Her hand lifts some, and then falls open on the top of the blankets.

There is an absorbing silence in the room for a moment. Then Bryce adds awkwardly, "That's right, boys. The doctor says she will need a quiet rest after the infusion, so really, this is the best for everyone today. I say go for it." He turns nodding again toward Felicia, who catches it and nods toward the boys until everyone, but Jasmine, is nodding almost hypnotically in agreement.

Oscar studies his parents, and then observes Jasmine's stalwart expression. "Okay," he relents. "I'll go."

"Yeah," Jacob concedes. "It'll be great." He tells Jasmine, "We'll do the recon on all the best rides and take pictures and then tell you all about it when we get back."

"Tomorrow, probably. In the morning," adds Bryce.

"Yeah, in the morning," Jacob confirms.

"And remember, " Felicia interjects, "Papa and Nana come back from their cruise tomorrow, so we'll get to hear all their adventures too."

The room fills with happy responses in anticipation. Bryce then excuses himself to make arrangements with Nat and to give him money for the park. When Bryce returns, he announces that they are all set to leave when Jasmine starts her infusion, and that Nat will take the boys back to the hotel after the park. The adults then discuss some further details and determine that Felicia will go back to the hotel to stay with the boys for the night.

The siblings again become absorbed in their investigation of how far and wide Jasmine's words have inspired people to trust in God and do good things. As time passes, everyone grows more anxious with the prospect of Jasmine's life-giving infusion drawing closer.

Bryce goes down to the car for the jackets and when he returns, the room is full of nervous energy.

"Tell Dad about that guy and that gang," Oscar blurts.

Jacob scrolls on the screen, "Okay, yeah. So, this guy posted that he was walking home from work last night, and that he saw some gang members messing with this other kid. I guess it is a rough neighborhood. Anyway, he said that usually everyone minds their business because you don't get involved with gang members, and he wasn't sure what was going on anyway. But then he heard them hitting and threatening him and he remembered what Jasmine said about trusting God and being a hero. He said he just felt all this courage come up, and he started walking back to them yelling, 'Hey, leave that kid alone!' and he couldn't believe it. They just ran away. He made sure the kid was okay, and then told him why he did it. The kid started crying, he was so grateful."

Bryce glances at Felicia, appreciatively. "Wow guys. That's so amazing."

Jasmine smiles with her bright eyes, "Daddy, God *is* amazing."

Bryce chuckles, "Yes, Pumpkin, you're right. He is amazing."

"Daddy," Oscar interjects, "There's so many stories that people are telling about being brave or doing the right thing." He wriggles against the back of the chair he's leaning on. "It's like Christmas is still going!"

"You're right Buddy, it is!"

"That's true!" adds Felicia.

"It is?" Jasmine wonders.

"Yes!" Felicia repeats with great conviction. "It's *just* like Christmas is still going!"

Jasmine turns to see Jacob. "Do *you* think so?" she implores.

Jacob is caught off-guard and his eyes break away. Then they return to her. "Sure. I think so."

Jasmine grins, her eyes scrunching with joy. "Good! Because I LOVE CHRISTMAS!" She wraps her arms tight around herself at this exclamation, and the room erupts with laughter.

"Give me my hoodie!" she playfully demands, again outstretching her arms. "I want to wear my Christmas hoodie because it is still CHRISTMAS!"

Bryce obediently marches to the closet and withdraws the hoodie with reverential pomp, as the others respond in continued cheers of hilarity and celebration. He parades around the room in a pageantry of honor, then presents the majestic cloak to her highness, in bemused dignity, before carefully donning her in the royal blue vestment, protecting her ready port in the process.

This reverie discharges the underlying tension temporarily and summons a spirit of hope. The family spends the remaining time discussing the different encouraging posts that the children discover and talking about the many good things that people are saying and doing.

As time approaches, anxiousness builds again. At about 12:10, Jacob irritably observes, “All these people keep asking how Jasmine is. What am I supposed to do?”

“We should tell them about the infusion,” Oscar implores. “Then they’ll pray for her!”

Felicia contemplates a response, watching Jacob’s stern face.

“I think that’s a good idea, Oscar,” she concludes, turning to Bryce for confirmation.

“Yes, I agree. Jasmine?”

Jasmine slowly nods, then announces, “Yes. Praying is good.”

“Well, I don’t know what to say,” Jacob blusters, lifting the iPad futilely.

“Would you like me to write something?” Felicia offers.

Jacob holds out the iPad and Felicia spends a few minutes composing the response. She thoughtfully types, considers, and revises the post as the family waits in silence, then announces, “How does this sound?” She holds out the iPad to better see it.

OUR FAMILY IS SO ENCOURAGED TO READ ALL YOUR INSPIRATIONAL POSTS IN RESPONSE TO JASMINE’S MESSAGE. SHE THANKS YOU SO MUCH FOR YOUR SINCERE PRAYERS AND KIND THOUGHTS. AS MANY OF YOU KNOW, SHE IS BATTLING LEUKEMIA AND WILL RECEIVE AN EXPERIMANTAL TREATMENT TODAY THAT WE HOPE WILL HELP HER IN HER FIGHT. PLEASE PRAY FOR HEALING AND SUCCESS. BLESSINGS, THE GOODSONS.

When Felicia finishes, she looks up at the family. “How’s that?”

The men nod, observing each other, agreeing, “Yeah, that’s good.”

Jasmine hesitates, and then adds brightly, “Tell them thank you for the best Christmas ever, and Merry Christmas.”

“Yes, that’s very nice,” Felicia approves, and begins typing again, quietly reciting some of the words as she goes. “Okay. There!” she announces with satisfaction. “It’s posted.”

“Mommy,” Oscar quietly intrudes. “It’s almost 12:30.”

Everyone's eyes turn to the clock on the wall, and a sudden nervousness seizes them.

"Yes, it is," Felicia calmly affirms, then produces an encouraging smile.

Oscar entreats, "Can we pray before they do it?"

"Oh, yes. Of course!"

Oscar hops up from his chair and fervently washes his hands.

"Hey spaz," Jacob chides, "What are you doing?"

Oscar squirts more liquid soap on his hands, rubbing them together again under the running water. "We're going to pray for Jasmine, and we have to hold hands."

Jacob rolls his eyes with a sigh.

"You're right, Mijo," Felicia assents, and goes to the sink to join him.

"I can't argue with that," concedes Bryce, and soon the three are drying their hands and walking readily toward the bed.

Jacob is standing to the side, arms crossed self-consciously. "I'll just hold Mom's hand," he pouts," and watches as the others chose a position. Oscar eagerly takes Jasmine's right hand, and Bryce urges Felicia to take her left hand. Bryce takes Oscar's hand, and the two parents entreat Jacob to step in and accept theirs, at the corner of the bed, which he relents to do with clammy palms.

The little circle bows their heads, eyes closed, as Felicia begins the prayer.

"Lord, thank you for the doctors and this hospital. Bless them with wisdom. Thank you for our little Jasmine. Fill her with peace, and healing. Bless our family with hope and joy." She ends these words with a catch in her voice, and squeezes Jacob's hand. His breathing quickens, his throat constricts, and he clears it quietly, swallowing a few times, then squeezes Bryce's hand abruptly.

Bryce clears his throat. "God, take care of our little girl. Watch over the infusion and cause it to succeed. Be with her every moment . . ." His voice quavers, and trails off, then he squeezes Oscar's hand.

"Jesus, you are so awesome! You can do anything you want to! We love Jasmine so much, so please take good care of her for us. Thank you for all the people praying, and for all the great things that are happening because of what Daddy did and what Jasmine said. Amen."

They are about to release hands when they hear the unexpected voice of Jasmine adding her quiet, earnest prayer.

"Tell Jesus thank you for the best Christmas ever. Please take care of my family. Please show them I am safe in your care."

Just before Jasmine's prayer, Jacob is startled by the sound of someone walking in the corridor, thinking they are coming in, and he looks up. Instead, he sees Jasmine—head up, eyes open—looking toward the foot of the bed as if she is speaking directly to someone, standing there beside him. A strange warmth floods him.

The nurse enters to prepare Jasmine for the procedure, followed by Dr. Moreno, who enthusiastically shakes everyone's hands, and turns to Jasmine with a warm, confident smile.

"Are you ready, Jasmine? This won't hurt at all, but it'll make you pretty tired the rest of the day. Okay?" Dr. Moreno nods encouragingly.

"I'm ready," Jasmine replies, meeting her eyes with resolve.

Another nurse enters with an IV bag filled with a pale, pinkish-yellow fluid.

"Here they are! Millions of your CAR T-cells," Dr. Moreno exudes as the first nurse secures Jasmine's sleeve above her port. "Jasmine, what an adorable sweatshirt! I love it." Doctor Moreno tugs down the fabric to see the image better.

The family, still standing around from their prayer, draws closer as the nurse attaches the line into Jasmine's port.

"Okay, ready?" Dr. Moreno repeats.

Jasmine nods with a nervous smile.

"Okay, go ahead," the doctor nods.

Everyone holds their breath as the CAR T-cells are released.

The family watches Jasmine closely.

Finally, "Everybody stop staring!" she scolds.

They laugh some of the tension away.

"You're right, Mija."

Nate appears in the doorway with a boy and girl behind him. The girl waves to Jasmine.

"You boys ready to go?" he asks into the pensive room.

"Yeah, time for you guys to get going," Bryce urges. "Jasmine needs to rest now."

"Good idea," Dr. Moreno adds. "It'll be easier for us to have the room quiet and cleared the rest of the night while we monitor the infusion.

"You guys have fun for me at Disneyland!" Jasmine encourages them.

Jacob picks up his jacket and trudges to the door. "We will," he musters.

Oscar gets his jacket and hugs his mom and dad.

"We love you Jasmine," he pledges with a small, strong voice that reverberates with hope long after he departs the room.

Hours later, Bryce is awakened in the dark. He lies disoriented on the couch trying to discern the cause. Then he hears a faraway pop, followed by a crackling sizzle.

"Daddy," comes Jasmine's quiet voice. "Are those fireworks?"

He evaluates the next low boom, and then a faraway CRACK CRACK. He turns groggily to his daughter, propping himself up on his elbow.

"Yeah, Pumpkin. I think it's midnight. Do you think you can get back to sleep?"

She listens to the festivity a moment.

"Daddy, I want to see the fireworks. Take me to the windows. Please?"

Bryce sits up on the couch, vigorously rubs his face, and puts on his glasses. "Aren't you tired?"

Jasmine's eyes glint in the low light. "I've been sleeping. I want to see."

Bryce stands and stretches with a grunt, and then turns to look out the window. He doesn't see them anywhere on the horizon.

"They must be on the other side."

Jasmine folds back her covers, still wearing her Christmas hoodie, and scoots to the edge of her bed. "Hurry, Daddy."

Bryce relents, and brings the wheelchair over and helps her in. He puts a folded blanket from the closet on her lap, and wheels her silently into the dim corridor. As they pass their puzzled nurse, Bryce whispers, "We're going to see the fireworks."

She smiles and nods. "Sounds fun."

"Do they always do this on New Year's Eve?"

"I think it's from a concert."

"Oh."

At the windows, they see the fireworks are not far away. The colors glitter and flash in the dim hallway, lighting the walls behind them.

After a moment Jasmine wonders, "Do you think these are the ones Jake and Oscar are watching at Disneyland?"

"No, theirs were earlier," he whispers. "They're already back at the hotel."

"Oh."

"But you know, they could be watching from there."

Jasmine follows as a rocket ascends into the sky and explodes into a bright chrysanthemum bloom, then sizzles into squirmy trails.

"That would be nice."

The two watch the celebration decorate the sky with brilliance.

"It's the New Year, now isn't it, Daddy?" Jasmine ponders.

"Yes, Pumpkin. It is." He looks at her in the flashing light and adds jovially, "Happy New Year."

Her eyes are fastened on the dazzling display.

"Hmmm . . ."

The finale begins, and dozens of diverse rockets fire in a heart-pounding three-minute spectacle. Bryce watches his daughter, her eyes sparkling.

"You know. . ." she quietly observes among the frenetic booms and pops, "The colors in heaven are even *more* beautiful." Her voice is far away and full of wonder. And then, almost to herself,

"You can't really imagine how beautiful it is."

Chapter 21: Also, He has Put Eternity in their Hearts (Ecclesiastes 3:11)

Jacob's eyes suddenly open. They pierce through the ceiling tiles, searching outward toward a fading memory. His heart is pounding, and his chest and abdomen are tight, as if he had been crying in his sleep. He swipes his eyes, and there are no tears. The burden rises in him again, though he can't fully identify it. It gets closer and is about to materialize in his mind when he sits up abruptly, pivots on the edge of the bed, and plants his feet on the floor. In the dim light, he sees his brother, sleeping deeply with the blankets peeled back and tangled in his sprawling legs.

Jacob picks up his phone and releases it from the charging cord. 6:12. He swipes absently between screens, then sets it face-down back on the table. He surveys the room and the two piles of clothes stacked askew in their respective suitcases. There are white towels strewn on the tile floor near the sink outside the bathroom, as well as stray orange and blue foam ammunition scattered throughout the room. He picks up his phone again. 6:13. He returns it to the table. He lifts his bare feet and rests them on the edge of the box spring, elbows on his knees, and runs the top of his head down through his hands over and over. He stops and cradles his face. Then he rubs his eyes firmly and shakes his head violently, the way boys clear fluid from their ears. His eyes fall on the sleeping Oscar again.

After studying him for several moments, Jacob expels a thunderous sneeze.

The innocent Oscar stirs, but remains just beneath the surface of sleep.

Jacob expels another sneeze, full reverberation.

Oscar arouses some, and then stretches listlessly as Jacob wipes the spray of spit from his chin with the bottom of his T-shirt.

"Oh, you're awake too, huh?" Jacob quips.

Oscar lifts his head and squints at Jacob confusedly. Then drops his head back on his pillow and rubs his eyes. "What's wrong? Couldn't you sleep?" he wonders, trying to grow alert.

"Nah, I slept fine."

Oscar listlessly rolls onto his side to face Jacob in a first-stage attempt to arouse himself. "What time is it?"

Jacob shrugs. "I don't know." He picks up his phone and looks at it. "Like, 6:20."

Oscar forces his little body up and sits cross-legged on the bed, placing his pillow on his lap. He yawns, "That's early," and his head hangs slightly from gravity. He sleepily looks up at his brother, eyes twinkling, "Hey, that was fun yesterday, wasn't it?"

Jacob leans back on his hands. "Yeah, it was pretty cool."

"Mr. Delacruz was really nice—and he didn't get all cranky when we messed around."

"True."

"I think Abby likes you," Oscar teases.

"Nah."

"But she *is* pretty," Oscar persists.

"Yeah, she's okay."

"I think Harley was pretty fun," Oscar continues, now dangling his legs off the bed.

"Yeah, but he got all whinny on that one ride, the Matterhorn."

"Hey, what was your favorite ride?" Oscar prods livening up some.

"Oh, no contest—Space Mountain. I wish we could have gone twice."

"Yeah, I liked that one a lot." Oscar pauses thoughtfully. "Mine was the Pirates of the Caribbean."

"Mmm . . . Yeah, that was a pretty good one, too. Not the best, though."

"Those fireworks were awesome, though, right?"

"Definitely," Jacob approves.

"I mean, we were like right under them! They were all booming, and crackling, and the sparks were even floating down like they could catch something on fire!"

"Yeah, it was pretty impressive."

"Hey! It's New Year's Day!"

"Yeah. So?"

"Well, Papa and Nana are coming back today!"

"True."

"We get to tell them all about Big Bear and Disneyland, and then hear about their cruise . . ."

"Yep."

"I can't wait to see them!" Oscar amps up a moment then remembers. "I wonder how Jasmine's doing."

Jacob sits up, acting a little bored with the conversation. "Yeah, I don't know. Mom probably knows." He plants his feet on the floor again and gets up. "Anyway, I'm hungry. I'm getting some cereal," and he heads toward the living area.

"Yeah, Mom probably knows." Oscar replaces his pillow, straightens his blankets some, and trails after his brother.

~

After breakfast and showers, Felicia arrives at the hospital with the boys. They enter the room, and Bryce gets up and greets them with an exuberant smile.

"Hello Family! Happy New Year!"

"Happy New Year," they each reply. Oscar goes to his Dad and hugs him around the waist.

"Jake. Come on, Buddy, how about a New Year's hug?" Bryce prods. Jacob gives his father an obligatory side hug, then stands along the wall by Jasmine's bed. Felicia embraces Bryce with a loud kiss, "Happy New Year, Mi Amore."

Jasmine is taking in the family scene with serene pleasure. She has a nasal cannula for oxygen resting under her nose.

Jacob is watching her intently.

Felicia sets her purse by the couch and bends to kiss Jasmine. She hears a slight rasp in her breathing, which seems to be the cause of Jacob's alarm.

"Hello Mija," she croons, leaving a faint lipstick smudge on her clammy forehead. "Happy New Year!" She pulls out a tissue and wipes the smudge smartly from its place.

"Happy New Year, Mamma," Jasmine grins, then erupts in a brief cough.

Felicia's face sours exaggeratedly, "I heard that you snuck out to watch the fireworks last night at *midnight*, is that right?"

Jasmine nods enthusiastically a few times. "They were beautiful," she replies softly.

Felicia steps to the sink and washes her hands. "Jake, why don't you show Jasmine those great pictures you took and tell her about your Disneyland adventure."

The boys follow Felicia's example and go to the sink to wash their hands.

"Here, Jake," Bryce suggests, "give me your phone again." Bryce opens an alcohol swab and cleans it.

~

Soon the boys are back by Jasmine's side, sharing stories and showing pictures, and explaining in detail their favorite rides and things about the day. Bryce and Felicia step out of the room to talk.

"Anything new about her fever and congestion?" Felicia prods anxiously.

"Dr. Moreno is getting updates on all her vitals and she'll be in shortly." Bryce explains. "We talked a little while ago, and she said that most CAR T-cell patients experience some immunotherapy toxicity—such as fever, congestion, blood pressure drop. She said it's her body's reaction to the infusion. They just need to monitor her for a rapid escalation, which could be symptoms of a dangerous syndrome."

"What would that mean?"

"We'll see. I think that they have medication to counter it, but we're not at a place to talk about that yet. For now, she wants to see how Jasmine's body adjusts. I mean the CAR T-cells are fighting the cancer, so there's a lot going on in her. Jacqui's been checking on her about every hour and charting any changes, and they are managing her symptoms for now."

"Okay." Felicia lays her hand on his chest. "Bryce, I don't know if Jake can handle the stress of sitting around watching her get sick again. You know?"

"I know," He laces his fingers between hers. "Your parents are coming in, so maybe they can help distract him some."

Felicia looks at Bryce's watch. "Okay. It's 10:40. They are scheduled to dock at 12:30."

The two discuss what time Bryce will go get them and bring them back to the hospital.

Felicia embraces him again. "Thank you for doing that. You're so kind." She lays her head on his shoulder and rests in his arms a moment.

"Mmm. My pleasure." They kiss and re-enter the room.

Oscar looks up from his backward chair by Jasmine's bed. "Gosh! You have to see how many people are praying for Jasmine!" Leaning over the back of the chair, he has control of the iPad, and holds it up triumphantly.

"How many posts are there, Jake?"

Jacob sits on the couch playing a game on his phone. He doesn't look up. "Like 2,000."

"Can you believe it?" Oscar bristles with delight. "2,000 people are praying for Jasmine!"

"Wow, buddy. That's awesome," Bryce encourages.

"Do you want to hear some of the posts?"

Felicia sits on the couch next to Jacob, who retracts his outstretched leg from the seat to make room. "Yes, of course, Mijo!" She reaches down to her purse and pulls out her phone. "Let me just send a message to Nana first."

Oscar continues exploring the posts and hands the iPad back and forth with Jasmine a few times.

"Honey," Bryce begins, "I'm going to grab a coffee and then see if Nat's here to thank him for yesterday. You all good?"

"Yes, tell him thank you for me too," she replies, typing on her phone.

"Want anything? Coffee?"

"No. I've had enough. Thank you"

" 'Kay." He kisses her distracted cheek. "Be back in a few. You guys want anything?"

Oscar looks up hopefully, "Sour Gummy Worms?"

"Ahh, sour. . . Okay, I'll see if they have them."

"They have them," Oscar clarifies.

"Jake?"

"Starburst."

"Okay . . . Jasmine?"

Jasmine inhales to answer, which triggers a jagged, phlegm-filled coughing bout. Everyone looks up from their preoccupations and grows increasingly anxious for it to stop. Jasmine shakes her head several times to communicate her answer, and finally regains control. She takes a smooth, shallow breath, and whispers, "No."

Jacob's eyes return to his screen. He draws his feet up onto the edge of the seat and slouches down behind his knees.

"You okay, Pumpkin?" entreats Bryce.

Jasmine nods.

"Okay, then. I'll be back in a few minutes." Bryce and Felicia exchange uncertain smiles as he leaves.

When he returns about 30 minutes later, he pops his head in. "I have some visitors with me who want to say hi." Two faces appear in the doorway, waiving politely.

"Hey Jasmine, it's Abby and Harley!" Oscar waives at them and then dismounts his chair to go to the door.

"Hi, Jasmine," they both call to her with empathetic smiles.

"Hi," she waives back.

Jacob has set his phone aside but remains rooted in the couch.

Bryce pulls a pack of mints from a paper bag and rolls down the top again. "Here, Buddy," he urges Jacob. "Go say hi." He holds out the bag of candy until Jacob reluctantly arises. He plods across the room and takes it from his father. "Why don't you guys go out to the walkway where the windows are."

The children agree and go out. A moment later, Oscar returns. "Can I take the iPad to show them some of the posts?"

Bryce looks to Felicia.

"Sure," she nods.

Bryce sits in Jacob's place and takes out his phone. He looks up at Felicia thoughtfully.

"You know, Nat confessed that he was the one who called the news station and told them it was probably me."

Felicia glances up from her phone, "He was?" What did he say?"

Bryce chuckles some. "He felt bad, but," he shakes his head in disbelief, "I said that it turned out pretty good."

"I think so," Felicia agrees, and glances over at Jasmine, who has slid down in her bed and pulled the covers to her chin.

"How you doing, Mija?"

Jasmine settles her head into her pillow. "Fine," she quietly exhales. "Just resting my eyes."

"Is everybody wearing you out?" Felicia suspects.

Eyes closed, Jasmine feels around her bed for something, then stops and tucks her arm beneath the covers.

"No," she airily responds, "I like everybody here." She drifts into sleep for a while and the parents occupy themselves quietly on their phones.

A while later, Bryce looks at his watch.

"Well," he announces, rising to his feet. "It's about time to go down to the cruise terminal. Tell your mom to text me when they dock so we can coordinate."

"Okay, I'll do that now." She stretches up to receive his kiss.

"We'll be back in an hour, hour and a half." He sees that Jasmine is still asleep and leaves.

Felicia sits in the quiet and watches her daughter's shallow, raspy, breathing. She vaguely shakes her head, fingers resting over her lips in thought. The phone vibrates on her lap, startling her. It is a text from Bryce: OSCAR WANTED TO COME, SO HE'S WITH ME. JAKE STILL HANGING OUT.

She replies: OK.

About 15 minutes later, Jacob sulks in, iPad in hand, and reclaims his position on the couch.

"Where are your friends?"

He sets the iPad on the seat between them, and glances at the sleeping Jasmine. "Their mom came and took them out to lunch." He pulls his phone out of his pocket.

"Oh. I'm sorry."

Jacob freezes for a moment at the sound of Jasmine's breathing. Then he swipes across his phone and turns it sideways.

"No Big." He pulls his earbuds from his pocket, puts them in his ears, and concentrates on his screen.

About a half hour later, Felicia shakes Jacob's knee lightly.

"Jake."

He looks up and pulls one earbud out of his ear.

"Jake. Jasmine wants a hot tea. Will you go get it for her?" He sees his sister sitting up in the deep pillow, watching him.

He pulls out the other earbud, "Oh, yeah, sure," and hops to his feet.

"No, Mommy," Jasmine protests with breathless, even words. "I want *you* to go."

Jacob glances sharply at her, surprised.

"I want Jake to stay."

Felicia evaluates them both. “Oh. Okay.” She lifts her purse from the floor and shoulders it awkwardly. “Well, I might as well get myself a tea. Jake? Would you like something?”

Still wary, he scans the room for time. “Uh, I don’t know. I’m hungry. Maybe I should come with you.”

Felicia goes to the door, “No. Dad texted that they’re picking up lunch for all of us and bringing it here. You just stay. I’ll be right back,” and she slips out before he can respond.

Jacob watches after Felicia until Jasmine rouses him with her stern whisper.

“Why are you over there?” she challenges him.

He obeys and comes to her bedside. She gazes firmly at Oscar’s vacant chair. Jacob turns it and pulls it near, then sits with trepidation.

She looks at him until he reluctantly meets her eyes.

She studies him, taking smooth, even breaths.

“I know you’re mad at God,” she harshly whispers.

Startled, his eyes break from hers and immediately well up with tears. Head bowed, he swallows and fights to control the sounds. Her quiet wheezing fills the silence as she waits for him. Small drops fall from his eyes onto his jeans. He begins to tremble.

“Jacob. Do you love me?”

His head snaps up with fire in his eyes, cheeks damp and red with strain.

“Yes!” he vows vehemently, lips parting with strands of saliva webbing his mouth. He wipes his tears away violently with the palms of his hands, then draws his sleeve beneath his nose, snorting in the profuse mucus.

“Yes!” he repeats angrily. “God, Jasmine! I love you!” His fists rest on the arms of the chair, then open again to vanquish more tears.

After a pause, she calmly resumes, in even, winded words.

“Listen, Jacob.” She waits until he looks at her again.

“Listen. When I die—”

His arms fly up in the air, “No!”

“Jacob. Listen.” She waits again, chest rasping with shallow breaths. His broken spirit relents, but he does not lift his eyes to hers.

“When I die,” she measures carefully, “I will go to heaven.

You know that, right?"

He nods his hanging head.

"If you are mad at God," she whispers, "you'll *never* see me again." She slowly inhales another, raspy breath. "Do you *want* that?"

He shakes his head emphatically.

She breathes carefully in the quiet pause. Jacob is tiredly, silently, sobbing.

"Do you want me to be," catching her breath, ". . . *so* sad?"

He shakes his head again, swallowing and fighting the sounds in his throat. He wipes his tears with his palms.

She waits a long time, now, patiently drawing breath for these last words.

"Then tell Jesus you love him."

He runs his hands firmly through his hair. He grips and pulls it.

"I know," he mumbles, restlessly. "I know, but—Ahhh!" he expels.

Felicia appears in the doorway. She reads the scene and attempts to extract herself. But for Jacob, it is his moment to escape. He jumps up, slips past her, and plods down the corridor, bursting with one loud sob as he retreats.

~

When Bryce returns with Felicia's parents, they try to suppress their elation upon entering the peaceful room. However, their exuberance overflows, much as they endeavor to restrain it.

In the turbulent reunion of greetings and hugs, Felicia sends a text after Jacob.

Bryce and Oscar set out the little white bags and drink trays.

"In-N-Out Burger, huh? Smells good," evaluates Felicia.

"Yeah," Papa explains, "We got sick of Mexican food. We wanted burgers and fries and shakes, right Alicia?"

"Ha! Not me, Old Man," she smiles teasingly, "I am never sick of it."

They boisterously distribute the food and shakes, with conversation continuing to escalate in volume. When Jacob slides into the room, Papa sets down his burger and grabs the lad for a hearty embrace.

"There's my grandson." He holds out Jacob and grins, "Look at him! So big!" He hugs him again with crushing force. Jacob, once released from the rigorous affection, stumbles back a step, and smiles sheepishly.

"Hi Papa. Happy New Year," he offers.

Alicia holds his cheeks admiringly in both hands, "My sweet boy." Jacob hugs his Nana, lingering in her kind, comforting embrace, which always smells of soap and freesias.

Jasmine works sporadically on a wedge of cheeseburger, a small stack of fries, and a few spoonfuls of strawberry shake as she watches the family engage in clamorous cross-discussions that amount to a third-floor hullabaloo. She is gleefully enthralled in the din, engaging in stories and judiciously communicating in various ways as videos, photos and messages are produced and handed around with greasy fingers.

Hardly noticed by the crowd, Dr. Moreno comes to the door and signals for Bryce and Felicia to come into the corridor.

"I need to do a thorough assessment of Jasmine soon. But I can wait until you're done visiting," she somberly suggests.

Bryce and Felicia look at each other.

"Well," Bryce broaches, "We still need to get your parents settled at the hotel. Then after a rest, they'll want to go out to dinner, probably."

Felicia turns to Dr. Moreno. "They just got here. Can we have maybe another hour, and then we'll take them and the boys to their hotel? Would that be okay?"

Dr. Moreno considers the plan. "Yes, that should be fine. I'll want to examine her thoroughly without all the distractions. Perhaps she can rest after that."

"Okay, doctor," Bryce acknowledges.

She takes an iPad from beneath her arm. "In the meantime, we continue to see a decline in Jasmine's oxygen levels, her fever is steadily rising, and her blood pressure is dropping as well. These can be serious warning signs of CRS, the toxic syndrome I talked with you about earlier."

The parents grimace solemnly at each other.

"Okay. Okay. So, what's the plan?" worries Bryce.

"For now, we are addressing her symptoms. We've given her low doses of vasopressors for her blood pressure and antibiotics for her fever. She's on oxygen, but we'll watch her levels. The next stage is to put her on positive pressure ventilation—like a

BiPAP—but we're not there yet. When I assess her, we'll be checking her cytokine levels, which are the proteins that react to the CAR T-cell infusion and create the toxicity. It should confirm where we are, and we'll likely administer a therapy to suppress this reaction."

"Will this therapy stop her symptoms?" Felicia hopes.

"Yeah," Bryce adds, "ultimately, can this syndrome be managed?"

"As I said before, some type of toxicity reaction is common. There is a protocol laid out to manage CRS, so we will address each stage as it comes."

"Oh my," Felicia sighs.

Dr. Moreno rests her hand on Felicia's, "We're taking this one step at a time. Let's see how her body responds to these treatments, okay?"

"Yes, of course. And we can pray," Felicia adds soberly.

Dr. Moreno smiles. "Yes, above all, pray."

Bryce pushes up his glasses and runs his hand through his hair, "Okay, thank you Doctor."

"Yes, thank you," Felicia reiterates.

"But," the doctor adds, "she is going to need a lot of rest. And while I think that having family around her is absolutely curative, the next few days need to be tranquil, so her body can recover."

"Okay, good to know," Bryce chimes.

"Yes, of course, Doctor," Felicia nods. "Thank you."

"Okay," Dr. Moreno looks at her watch, "I'll come back in about an hour. If anyone is still here, I'll be the bad guy and give them the boot."

"Yes," Bryce agrees, "Sounds good.

~

At the end of an hour, the family obediently rises, gathers their things, and one by one pours love over the waning, yet delighted Jasmine, and all depart. Felicia takes her parents back to the hotel to check in, unpack, and get refreshed for a few hours. Then they come down to the family's suite to visit. After a few minutes of greetings and receiving a tour from Oscar, Alicia and Felicia settle down with cups of tea on the couch, while Papa spends time with the boys.

It is unanimously decided that Jasmine would want Papa to

shoot her pistol, and he becomes enthralled with firing the little pink ammunition, first at targets, and then relentlessly at the boys. They spend most of their time in the boys' room, checking out Jacob's favorite game on his phone, sharing stories, and after a while, they settle down and talk some about Jasmine.

Finally, they wander out and offer Papa the last of Aunt Tiana's Christmas cookies. Jacob finds the container and ceremonially removes the lid, revealing a lone Christmas tree, covered in white frosting, and green sprinkles, though its top point had broken off. Papa accepts the gift with reverence, and then chomps into it.

Oscar giggles.

Papa interrupts the ladies with an announcement, "Alicia, I'm hungry!"

She smiles and waives him off, "What's new Old Man?"

"No, I'm serious. Let's go out to dinner. A *nice* dinner."

Everyone eagerly agrees, and they decide on Italian food, so Felicia locates a good restaurant on her phone. As they assemble themselves to leave, Oscar notices the little Christmas tree which had been moved aside to the end table.

"Hey," he suggests, "should we take the Christmas tree back to Jasmine's room for her tomorrow?"

Alicia thoughtfully considers the little tree, now dry and pale. Then she diplomatically concludes, "You know Mijo, it's losing its needles. See?"

Oscar looks at the scattered gray strands on the end table. "Oh."

She strokes his back as he evaluates the fading relic.

"It's not as vibrant now," she consoles him, "but we can *always* remember the joy it brought, can't we?" She jostles his shoulder encouragingly. "Huh, Mijo? Can't we?"

He turns back to meet his grandmother's loving eyes, and nods.

Jacob shakes his head and turns his face away.

Felicia slips her hand behind his head and cradles him to her shoulder.

After a moment, CLAP!

"Okay familia," urges Papa, rubbing his hands together hungrily. "Let's go eat!"

At dinner, Felicia and her mother discuss giving Jasmine a rest the next day. Papa suggests that he and Alicia pick up a rental car in the morning and take the boys to the zoo to spend some time together, which seems like an attractive solution for everyone. They call Bryce from the restaurant and offer to bring him some food, but he and Jasmine have already eaten. Felicia's expression turns serious a moment, but when she hangs up, she doesn't mention why.

The family returns to the hotel—grandparents fatigued from the long day, boys tired from rising so early, and Felicia encumbered with many things. All so weary, yet each wrestles that night to rest.

Chapter 22: Rejoice, and Do Good (Ecclesiastes 3:12)

When Felicia arrives at the hospital room, Bryce exits the bathroom rubbing his hair with a towel.

"Morning." He lays the towel across his shoulders and greets her with a somber kiss. "Did you bring my razor?" He returns to the bathroom to comb his hair.

"Yes, I have it." Felicia sets down the coffee carrier and breakfast burritos to retrieve Oscar's Christmas gift from her purse.

"Here you go." She hands it to him, soon followed by the grazzly sound of shaving. She observes her daughter, still sleeping, now wearing a BiPAP oxygen mask. Her blue Christmas sweatshirt is draped next to her over the bed rail.

Felicia sits on the couch and sips her coffee, watching. The razor shuts off and exposes the electric hum of Jasmine's BiPAP machine now intruding the silence. Her lungs fill and deflate with raspy breaths. The bathroom water runs as Bryce brushes his teeth, and again masks the distressing sound. After a moment deep in thought, Felicia blinks, and reaches down into her purse. She pulls out her Bible, opens it to the marker, and begins to read. Bryce walks out and searches through his duffle bag, finds a fresh shirt, and returns to the bathroom. A moment later, he pops his head out to say something, applying deodorant under his arms, then sees Felicia occupied, and withdraws.

Moments later he comes out, puts his things back into the duffle, pulls out a fresh pair of socks, grabs his new shoes, and sits in the chair to put them on. He takes a sip of coffee before proceeding. After he ties his shoes, he sits up and sips his coffee a moment, observing Jasmine. Then he unwraps one of the burritos, peeling down the paper, and takes a bite out of the top before pouring hot sauce on it, the way Jasmine taught him.

He goes to share this story with his wife, but she is peacefully reading. He pulls out his phone and to check his messages and finds instead the videos he took in Big Bear. He finds his earbud on the table and inserts it, watching them over and over. Watching his daughter feed the birds with such joy. He spies the little pinecone still sitting on Jasmine's table in a place of prominence. He indulges in the bright images of the day once more. Then he shares the unsent videos with Felicia for later, and resumes checking his messages.

After several minutes, Felicia closes her Bible and puts it away, then opens her own burrito. Bryce looks up from his phone.

"Thanks for picking these up."

Felicia smiles, "You're welcome, Amore. They are actually pretty good."

"Yeah, they're not bad," he chuckles.

Felicia pulls out her phone. Jasmine's breathing grows harsh and crescendos, until she moves her head slightly, and it diminishes. She seems to smile within a dream.

"Bryce, I updated Jasmine's condition last night online so people would pray for her symptoms to clear. There's a lot of people responding so far."

"I know!" Bryce lifts his phone and scrolls through messages. "I got a nice text from Keisha saying that they're praying for us. They released her and her son from the hospital yesterday and transported her back to San Diego." Bryce scrolls some more. "And her husband, Travis, and I have been texting all week. He says that Justin prays for Jasmine every morning and every night." He looks up at Felicia with a hopeful expression. "Isn't that a great kid?"

Felicia laughs and then reaches over to poke him teasingly, "Yes, Bryce. You did good."

Bryce turns up his palms, chuckling, "What?"

Felicia laughs more and then waives him off, "Oh, you know what."

"What? Did I say anything?" Bryce blushes, trying to contain his grin. "He's a good kid, that's all I'm saying."

Felicia smiles, eyes twinkling. "I know, Amore." She rests her hand on his and softly squeezes it. "You did *good.*"

~

The two parents pass the gloomy day in quiet vigil, sometimes sharing messages from family and friends, while busy hospital staff surge through the room in waves.

At about 1:00, Bryce leaves to make work phone calls, and to get some sandwiches. Felicia is texting with Christiana, when Jasmine stirs. She opens her eyes with a sleepy twinkle.

"Hi, beautiful." Felicia croons, setting aside her phone. Jasmine replies with a dopey smile beneath the mask, and stretches out her legs, then curls them up again.

Felicia brings the chair closer to her bedside and bends to kiss her warm, clammy, forehead. "Sleep good?"

Jasmine nods goofily.

"What? Did you have a good dream?" she prods, caressing Jasmine's hair.

Jasmine nods again, eyes glinting, and draws a deeper breath to answer. Her body convulses with coughing, and the congestion audibly dislodges into the dense cavern of her lungs. Her face reddens with the fit until she can pace her breathing and regain control. Felicia's eyes narrow, patiently watching her daughter manage the spell until Jasmine's breathing evens out again, her oxygen mask fogging and clearing steadily.

Jasmine takes a slow, even, breath, then lifts her mask and whispers in delight.

"Yes. I was with Jesus."

Felicia's face shadows.

"He's so wonderful," she softly continues, her face full of light.

She sprouts a smile, "Jasmine, that's amazing."

Her breaths are tight and shallow, and she replaces the mask. After a few moments, she lifts it again.

"Mamma?" she whispers carefully. Why did you name me Jasmine?"

"Put your mask back on, Mija, and I'll tell you."

Jasmine complies.

Felicia lays her hand on Jasmine's and leans back. "Well . . . we thought it was a beautiful name."

Jasmine looks puzzled and lifts her mask again. "But Oscar . . ."

"I understand. Keep that on." Felicia nods and pats Jasmine's hand. "You know that Oscar was named after Papa, and Jake is named after Daddy's Grandpa. So, you want to know who *you* are named after."

Jasmine nods with a curious expression.

"Hmm—" Felicia smiles, bemused. "Okay. Now, I never told your dad this. Actually, I haven't told anyone, okay?"

Jasmine nods excitedly.

"Ha. Okay." Felicia fidgets with Jasmine's fingers. "Well . . . You know the Disney movie, Aladdin?"

Jasmine's eyes grow wide with surprise.

"Yeah. I know. It's crazy," Felicia laughs embarrassedly. "I first saw that movie when I was maybe, 9 or 10? And I thought that Jasmine was *so* strong, and brave, and smart, and beautiful . . . and good. And I wanted to be *just* like her." She smiles proudly at her daughter. "And so when *you* were born, I just knew." She leans close.

"You *are* Jasmine."

Jasmine beams and wriggles a little at this revelation.

Felicia takes Jasmine's hand in both of hers and looks steadily into her eyes. "And I was right. You are *all* those things, Mija." Then she smooths away the thin hair from her daughter's forehead, grinning with adoration.

"You are her, and *more*."

~

Jacob picks up a snowglobe and shakes it disinterestedly, then watches the glitter swirl around the colorful Los Angeles Zoo icon. "That's dumb," he mutters. "It doesn't even snow here." He sets it down and wanders through the store.

Alicia walks over to where Papa is standing at a mirror, evaluating an Indiana Jones safari hat pulled over his eyes like an adventurer. "Hey, Old Man, you look kind of sexy," she admires, viewing his reflection.

"I think so too," he concurs decisively.

"You should buy it," Alicia goads him.

He scrutinizes himself from another angle with obvious approbation. "I think so too."

Alicia swiftly pulls out a colorful, silky scarf and slings it around her neck with gusto. "And you should buy this for *me*."

He evaluates the reflection of his wife's determined expression, framed by the beautiful scarf.

"I think so too," he concedes.

"Good." Alicia turns and floats away, with the scarf trailing, "I'm getting one for Felicia and Tiana too," she calls over her shoulder.

Papa watches her go, and shrugs. Then he returns to his own reflection again with satisfaction. "I think I'll get one of these for Bryce."

Jacob watches this interesting scene between his Grandparents as he drifts past and finds himself at a display of gadget toys.

"Hey Oscar, come here!" He calls in no particular direction.

Oscar's small head swivels around trying to locate his brother.

"Over here."

Oscar trots through the crowded aisles and arrives with rosy-cheeks and nose from the day outside.

"Oscar, check this out." Jacob points at a bin of items. By now Alicia and Papa are curious and make their way toward the boys.

"What did you find, Mijo?" Alicia asks.

"Isn't that the ball you gave to that kid?" Jacob teases.

Oscar picks up one of the balls and examines it. "It looks like the same one."

"What ball? What are you talking about?" Alicia presses.

"Ha! He got this ball as a present from Aunt Tiana," Jacob gestures flippantly, "and then he *gave it away* to some little boy in the airport just like, *three* hours later."

"Well, Oscar," Papa announces proudly, grabbing his shoulder, "That was a very generous thing to do!"

"I think that calls for a reward, Mijo," Alicia proclaims with fanfare. "You will receive *this* ball, and *another* item of your choice," she smirks with glee.

"Thank you, Nana!" Oscar gushes, and squeezes her tightly around the waist, then runs off to select another item.

The three of them watch him dash away, and then Papa turns to Jacob.

"Jake, what are you getting?"

Jacob shrugs. "I didn't see anything."

Papa holds out his hat, waiving it jauntily. "I'm getting this for me and your dad." He elbows Jacob in the ribs. "Come on, let's get one for you too."

Jacob looks at the hat, then shrugs again. "Sure."

"That's my boy," Papa winks, and leads the sedate teen back to the hats.

When everyone is finished exploring the souvenirs, they head toward the cash register with their finds. Along the way, they notice a large, circular tower in the center of the store, stacked with a vast display of plush zoo animals. The family stops, of one mind, and begins to scan the array of creatures. After a few minutes, Alicia points at the peak of the circular mountain.

"There. That one," she proclaims resolutely.

Their eyes scale the display and see the lone figure at the top—a plush, golden lion, with a kind expression, and a fiery mane. He is wearing a glistening fabric crown of shiny gold threads and colorful jewels.

They all agree with awe, "Yes, that's the one."

That evening, the family arrives at the hospital to deliver the gift and their love to Jasmine before returning to the hotel for dinner. Jasmine is languidly awake, propped up as Jacqui finishes her assessment and pulls down the Christmas sweater, which Jasmine had requested to wear again. Jasmine turns brightly toward Jacob, and Oscar, and Nana, and Papa upon seeing them enter the room.

Papa comes through the door, and is drawn to Jasmine, "Chiquita!" he exclaims, trying to subdue his enthusiasm. "You're awake!" his hands are outstretched to cup her masked face.

"Papa, you need to wash your hands," Felicia reminds him.

"Oh, yeah, yeah, yeah," he realizes, walking back to the sink where the others are.

Oscar is the first to Jasmine's bedside, and she watches with twinkling anticipation as he approaches, hastily drying his hands on a paper towel, and setting it on the end table before he reaches her.

"Hi." He grins with satisfaction.

Jasmine returns his smile, as the mask fogs and then clears as pressure assists her congested breaths.

Oscar turns to Bryce, "Daddy, can I touch her?"

Bryce is standing beside Felicia, and at some point in watching the scene, has put his arm around her waist. He assesses the request, then nods solemnly. “Sure, Buddy.”

Oscar carefully reaches for her hand and cradles it in his.

“We missed you today at the zoo.”

Jasmine smiles again, mask fogging and clearing. She squeezes his hand.

Papa is now standing behind Oscar and suffices to reach around him and gently squeeze Jasmine’s upper arm through her royal blue sweatshirt. He remains standing behind the boy, hands resting on his shoulders.

“Te amo, Chiquita,” he smiles admiringly.

The quiet hum from Jasmine’s BiPAP machine fills the gaps in conversation. Occasionally, beeps emit from the monitoring unit, or the rush of air fills the blood pressure cuff as it mechanically inflates.

Alicia is busy at the sink counter, and Felicia walks over to see what she is doing.

“This is the lion I told you about,” Alicia whispers. “It comes in a box, so no one has ever touched it.”

“Oh,” Felicia admires, watching her mother free it from the packaging. “It’s perfect.”

Oscar and Papa comically describe and imitate for Jasmine some of the funny animals they saw, as Jasmine tiredly resists laughing.

Alicia is ready to present the majestic, plush lion, and hides it behind her back as she turns and walks toward Jasmine’s bed. She notices Jacob leaning with his back against the wall near the door, looking at his feet.

“Come on, Mijo,” Alicia whispers excitedly. Let’s give it to her.”

Jacob shakes his head.

She leans close to him. “Jacob, what are you doing?” she scolds worriedly. “Come on.”

He shakes head again, eyes downward.

Alicia resets her smile. “Mija , look what we found!” She cheerily reveals the cuddly, regal lion, and extends it to her granddaughter.

Jasmine’s eyes widen with joy as she accepts the gift and envelops it in her thin arms. Then she holds it out on her lap, and studies the soft, golden fur and fiery mane, the shiny threading of the cloth crown, and the lion's benevolent expression. She hugs him again and tucks him into the crook of her arm. She attempts to whisper through her mask.

"Don't try to talk, Mija," Alicia assures her. "Do you want to write something?"

Jasmine nods, eyes still bright with delight. Felicia hands her the pen and notebook they have used throughout the day. Jasmine writes slowly in squiggly letters, then offers it back to her expectant Grandmother to read.

Alicia studies the words. Her eyebrows furrow, then relax.

"Are you going to read it to us?" urges Bryce.

Alicia looks down at Jasmine, meeting her eyes with a tender knowing, and smiles. Then she reads the message:

"Jasmine says, 'I love him because I'm going to see the King.'"

Everyone looks at Jasmine's illuminated face, nodding peacefully on her white pillow, the Lion cloaked in the blue fabric of her arms.

Everyone except for Jacob. Upon hearing these words, he pivots quietly out the door and leans in the corridor on the other side of the wall, his hands stuffed deep into his pockets.

~

The boys and grandparents enter the darkened hotel room, fast food bags in hand, and quietly unload from the long day. Jacob walks into his room, flicks on the light, kicks off his shoes, and closes the door behind him. Alicia sets down her purse and the shopping bags, and shares a glance with Papa, as Oscar unpacks the chicken sandwiches onto the table.

She goes to the boys' room and taps lightly on the door before opening it a crack, then pops her head in.

"Jacob, why don't you come and eat first?"

Jacob is laying face-down, spread out on his bed, his feet and one arm hanging over the edges.

"I'm not hungry," he mumbles into the pillow.

Alicia pauses at the door. Then she quietly closes it behind her, sits on the bed, and begins to gently rub Jacob's back. After a moment, she pats him, and urges, "Come on Mijo. Sit up a minute." He doesn't move initially, and she continues to nudge him.

"Come on. Sit up."

Jacob reluctantly lifts himself from the mattress with some effort and sits with his back against the headboard to face his grandmother. She smooths the shaggy hair away from his eyes.

"Mijo, I know you are sad, and afraid."

He looks away.

"It's okay to be sad, and afraid, and even a little mad," she reassures him. "And we can talk about all those things, you know?"

His eyes remain downward.

"Look at me, Jacob," she admonishes, and finally his eyes meet hers, red and wet.

"But what we *can't* do, Mijo," she warns "is *waste time* being selfish, and stubborn."

Jacob turns his eyes away sharply, and Alicia gently directs his chin back to face her.

"You may only have a *little time* with Jasmine," she cautions him. "How do you want to spend it, Jacob?"

He shakily runs a hand through his hair, then lets if fall again onto his lap.

"Huh, Mijo?" she persists. "How will you give her *your love*, before it's too late?"

Jacob looks down at his hands. His grandmother studies him, then pats him on the leg before rising.

"I hope you come join us for dinner, Mijo." She stands and kisses him loudly on the forehead, swiping back his hair to do it. "Te amo." Then, she recedes from the room, and closes the door behind her with a quiet click.

Jacob lifts his knees and rests his forehead against them. Wrapping his arms around his legs, he rocks.

~

The next morning, Alicia wakes the boys early with the smell of bacon. When they come out, Papa is sitting at the table with an empty plate in front of him, sipping coffee.

"Come over and eat, boys," he directs somberly as they come to the table. "We're going to the hospital."

Alicia scrapes some scrambled eggs onto plates with bacon and sets one before each of the troubled boys.

Oscar looks at his plate and then studies both of his

grandparents' faces. His brows pinch as he wonders, "Is Jasmine sicker?"

Alicia wipes her hands on a towel with seriousness before answering. "Yes, Mijo. She's very sick."

The boys pick at their food in silence, and then dress in yesterday's clothes before all filing out the hotel room door.

When they arrive at the hospital, there are thirty or so people standing on the sidewalk near the driveway with signs that say, "We Love You Jasmine," or "We're Praying for you Jasmine." Oscar waives bewilderedly at them.

"Why are they here?" he asks, but no one in the car answers.

At the room, they find Jasmine lying sedate, now wearing a full mask on a ventilator, forcing air into her lungs every several seconds. Jacqui is standing alone in the room by the bed, assessing her patient, and talking quietly to her as she works. She turns when she hears the family enter, and a sad smile crosses her face.

"Hi." She greets sympathetically taking a few steps toward them. "Bryce and Felicia needed a little break from the room, so they went down to the chapel while I do a work-up on Jasmine."

"Oh, okay," Alicia considers.

"I can tell you where it is, if you want to go down there. I think that the Chaplain might be praying with them."

Oscar looks somberly at Jasmine, then tells Jacqui, "I want to go and pray."

Jacqui smiles, "You do, Honey?"

Oscar nods.

Papa looks around at his family, "Yes, can you tell us how to get there. I think we all want to go."

Jacqui gives them directions, and the three of them turn to leave. Jacob is standing inside the door, eyes fastened on his dormant sister, his mouth parted some.

"Don't you want to come pray?" prods Oscar, a little wounded.

Jacob wills himself a few steps inside the door toward Jasmine, mechanical sounds of ventilation and monitoring equipment pervading the atmosphere of the room.

"I want to stay here," he faintly answers, as he sits in the chair nearest her.

Alicia and Papa exchange looks.

"Okay, Mijo," Alicia replies. "We'll be back in a little while." The three burdened faces turn and leave the room.

Jacqui assesses Jacob. "Honey, I have some charting to go do, if you're okay alone with her. Otherwise I can wait here with you."

Jacob shakes his head vaguely. "No. I'm fine."

"Okay, then." Jacqui goes to the door, "I'll be right out here, so let me know if you need me."

Jacob watches the air pressure rise and fall in his sister's body. One arm is wrapped devotedly around her loyal Lion. He gets up and goes to the sink to wash and dry his hands. Then he returns, scooting the chair closer toward her head as he sits. He studies her face, flaccid except for her mouth, which is forced wide open beneath the oxygen mask with the air. He reaches hesitantly, lifts her limp hand, and holds it. Then he squeezes it, takes a deep breath, and leans toward her ear.

"Jasmine. You were right." He licks his lips. "I *have* been mad at God." Jacob finds more room and scoots the chair closer to his sister.

"But I love you. I don't want you to be sad." He looks up to find the words somewhere in the room, then squeezes her hand again when he discovers them.

"So, I'm going to ask God right now to help me. And I want you to hear it."

Jake bows his head, gathers his thoughts, and then speaks just loud enough to be heard over the ventilator.

"Dear God. I don't understand what you're doing, but I don't want to be mad at you anymore." He pauses, waiting for the next words.

"My sister loves you, and she is good, and she loves me, which is crazy. She says *you* are good, and even though I'm so sad, I know she's right."

Her ventilator seems to time with his breaths. "I really do believe in you. Help me to trust you." Breathe.

"Forgive me Jesus. And take *good* care of my sister."

Jake takes a last big breath, wipes his eyes, and sighs.

"No matter what happens, I *know* you will."

He rubs his sleeve over his eyes and nose again and looks up at his peaceful sister. Her eyes are narrowly open, adoring him. He is surprised, and laughs suddenly, forming a little saliva bubble over his mouth. Her eyes wrinkle tiredly in response, and she faintly squeezes his hand. Then her eyes close again, the large breaths rising and falling in her limp body.

"I love you, Sis," Jake repeats.

He sits thoughtfully in the waves of rhythmic sound, and warmth fills him with peace.

When the family returns, they each take note of Jake's demeanor, still sitting with his sister's hand in his. Oscar stands next to him and holds onto Jake's arm as he studies her.

"We were praying," he whispers.

Jake nods with a tranquil grin. "I know. I have been too."

"You have?" Oscar smiles. "Jasmine, did you hear that?"

Jake nods again. "She knows."

Doctor Moreno comes to the door, and Bryce and Felicia go out into the hall to speak with her. After a few minutes they return somberly.

"Hey, listen everyone," Bryce quietly announces. Everyone turns to hear.

"Dr. Moreno and the staff have been vigilant these past few days," he begins "but here's what's going on with Jasmine at this point. You know that after she got the CAR T-cell infusion, her body showed symptoms of a toxic reaction."

"Is it like the GVH disease she had with Mommy's bone marrow?" Oscar wonders.

"Ah, good question, buddy. It's along the same lines. Her immune system over-reacted to the CAR-T cells and is now attacking her own body and creating a kind of storm. It's been a tricky balancing act, and they've tried to manage the symptoms and to counter the reaction, but so far, it's not working as they'd hoped. Dr. Moreno explained that this sever reaction can happen sometimes with kids that have had their cancer come back aggressively. They administered the medication, and now we can just wait and hope that her body can ride this out. It's just that we need to prepare for the reality that she's getting worse quickly."

Jake interjects, "So did the treatment actually. . ." but then he trails off.

Bryce shakes his head. "Look, we all knew that this was Jasmine's last medical hope. She knew it too. It was very promising, but it seems this treatment won't be able to save her.

Her body has battled for so long, and we knew that without a cure, she would have to suffer through her cancer until the end. This treatment hasn't turned out as we hoped, but it was her best opportunity. There just aren't any more options for a cure at this stage."

Everyone is quietly absorbing the grave information.

"But we can keep praying, right?" Oscar offers. "God can still heal her . . ."

"Of course, we can." Felicia encourages. "Of course, He can."

Inspired, Jake erupts, "Mom, let's ask everyone to pray more!" He points to the window, "We saw all those people outside. They'll pray. Can you tell them?"

"Outside?" Felicia wonders, walking to the window. "Oh my. What are they all doing here?"

The family joins her to behold the crowd, still growing as new people approach from wherever they find parking, carrying balloons and signs.

"That's even more people than when we came up," Papa notes.

Oscar takes Felicia's hand, as they survey the array of people on the sidewalks and walkways surrounding the hospital, with some of the signs of support written big enough for them to read.

"Can you ask them, Mamma?" he appeals. "They'll pray for Jasmine."

Everyone shakes their heads in wonder at the display of love and good will.

"Yes, of course Oscar." Felicia takes out her phone and sits down to post an update.

Alicia takes Jake's seat beside Jasmine and holds her hand. "My beautiful granddaughter. . . see how many people you have inspired."

"Oh, good," Felicia reports, looking at her phone, "Tiana is flying in at 4:30."

Bryce clears his throat, "Okay, I'll get her."

"No, no, Bryce. I'll get her," insists Papa.

Bryce nods, "Okay. Thanks."

Jacqui comes in again and smiles sadly at the family. The room holds its breath as she assesses Jasmine and the machines monitoring her vitals, then enters notes on her tablet. When she retreats, they exhale. She returns with a vial and syringe and proceeds to inject medication into Jasmine's IV line.

Inaudible prayers fill the room as the family watches Jasmine. Eyes redden in the silence.

Felicia stirs, and chuckles a little, "You know, I don't think that Jasmine appreciates us sitting around the room crying while she's still here with us. She's fought very hard, and we just want to enjoy her, and tell her we love her."

Some smile and wipe their eyes.

Papa nods resolutely, swiping a single finger across each eye, "Agreed. No more sad faces."

"That's right," Alicia sniffs, and touches a tissue to her nose, and then bends to kiss Jasmine's forehead. "After all, one way or another, she's going to see the King. Isn't that right, Mija?" She wipes away a few more tears and squeezes Jasmine's hand, her thin arm still wrapped around the noble Lion. Jasmine's eyes flutter beneath her lids.

Oscar nears the foot of her bed. "Jasmine, there's so many people outside who are praying for you." He lightly holds her foot through the covers. "You've helped all these people to think about God."

"That's good Oscar," Felicia encourages. "The Dr. said that Jasmine can hear us, and even though we need to let her rest, maybe each of us can take a few minutes to sit with her."

Over the next few hours, the family members each take turns in the seat nearest to Jasmine, sitting quietly for the most part, but sometimes talking to her and sharing memories. The others give them privacy by sitting a ways off, where voices are obscured by the sounds of the ventilator, and the blood pressure cuff inflating. But periodically sounds of muted laughter, or singing, or a change in the pitch of the visitor's voice rises above the constant *huuush-click* and vibration of machines.

At some point, Felicia suggests that Papa should go to the airport and pick up Christiana. He offers to bring back food, but no one responds.

Later, Papa arrives with Christiana. She slips in unnoticed, removes her coat and drapes it across the counter, then sets a small paper bag and her purse on the coat. She washes her hands, then takes them all up again and stands near the door, purse and coat looped over her arm.

After a moment, Felicia looks up from her Bible and their eyes meet. They exchange comforting embraces and quiet greetings as each family member comes to welcome Aunt Tiana, urging her to settle in. Jake hugs her and goes out to find another chair.

She steps reverently to the end of Jasmine's bed and watches with sadness the mechanical cycle of air forcing into her body.

"Hi, Jasmine. I see you have a new friend, there sweetie." She touches her foot. "Uncle Tyrell and Alex want you to know they love you very much, and they're praying for you." She turns to Felicia. "Can she hear us? Has she opened her eyes today?"

"She opened them for a moment this morning, but not since then. But she can hear us." Jake returns with a chair and sets it in an open space. Felicia signals for her to empty her arms. "She's fluttered her eyes few times responding to things we say, and has even squeezed our hand, but we're trying to let her rest. We just want her to know we're here, we love her, and we're praying for her."

Christiana thanks Jake and sets her things on the chair. She holds the handled paper bag a moment longer, glancing back at Jasmine, and then sets it down as well. "Well, you're not the only ones praying. I saw all the people gathered outside supporting her."

"Are they still here?" Alicia asks, glancing toward the dark window. "It is hard for us to see them now."

"Oh yes, Mamacita," injects Papa. There's even more now, I think because of Felicia's post. Even the news is here. I think they are having a candlelight vigil for her."

"Ah, Dios mio. That is so amazing."

"Yes, Mama. And not only here," adds Christiana. "They are having them in Phoenix and Peoria, and some churches across the nation are also having gatherings, praying for Jasmine to get better."

Jake goes to the window and tries to block out the reflection with his hands to see the supporters. "Oh yeah. . ." he reports, "I see people with candles down there."

"We should go see them, and thank them for praying," Oscar urges.

Jake turns from the window to see his sister. "I'm not leaving. Besides, it's my turn." He walks to the vacant chair and sits down, leans gently toward Jasmin's ear, and whispers to her. He puts his hand on hers and toys with her fingers as he talks.

"I'll go down with you, Mijo, if you want," Alicia offers.

Oscar considers a moment, then takes Felicia's hand beside him. "No, that's okay Nana. I want to stay too." Felicia sits back down in her chair. Oscar slides onto her lap and leans back into her arms. The family settles in again to their vigil, sometimes sharing memories or quiet conversation.

~

After a while, Felicia goes and sits by her daughter's side for an hour or so. She croons encouraging words for a time, her face alight with love. Then she sits quietly humming as she strokes Jasmine's face. At first, it was "You are my Sunshine," and then "What a Friend we have in Jesus."

A peaceful atmosphere fills the room, comforting and lulling the family into their own drifting thoughts for a long while.

But at some point, they become aware that Felicia's voice has changed tone, now calm, but distinct, and they listen again.

"Jasmine, what is it?"

A sense of alarm charges the atmosphere, and the family draws near.

Jasmine appears awake as she strains to peer through narrow eyelids, her face and eyebrows pinched with discomfort.

"What is it, Mija?" Felicia soothes with her words. "Do you need something?"

Jasmine's face sours as she faintly shakes her head, eyes now closed again.

Felicia leans closer to her daughter's face.

"Jasmine." Her voice is certain, and soft. "Baby, what is it?"

Jasmin faintly shakes her head again.

"What are you trying to tell us?" Felicia smooths the hair from her daughter's warm forehead. A moment passes, as Felicia appears to be reading her little girl's face.

After some suspense, the mother then takes a deep, deliberate, breath and slowly releases it.

"Are you tired, Baby? Is that it?"

Jasmine's legs stir. She forces her eyes wide to look into Felicia's. Her brows scrunch with strain. A tear trickles down the side of Jasmine's face.

She nods twice.

Felicia strokes the smooth skin on her daughter's forehead, holding her eyes a moment. Then she begins nodding before the words will come. She lifts the tips of her fingers to her lips, guarding them from escape. Then she scoops up Jasmine's hand and looks into her face resolutely.

"It's okay, Mija." Felicia wipes a silent tear from her smiling cheek. "It's okay, Baby."

Bryce pulls a chair to the other side of the bed and leans in. He envelopes Jasmine's other hand, still encircling the Lion.

"We love you, Pumpkin."

Voices around the bed warmly echo, "We love you Jasmine," or "Mija," or "Sis," or "Chiquita."

"It's okay." Felicia wipes another tear. Her timbre is tense and staccato. "It's okay." She sniffs, and swallows hard.

"You can let go, Baby."

After another moment, her voice drops to a forced whisper.

"It's okay. We'll see you soon."

With this, Jasmine's expression relaxes. Her body releases and recedes into the bed. Her face smooths with peace.

A moment later, a tone emits from the machine, and Jacqui quickly strides in to shut off the warning.

Soon, Dr. Moreno enters with a sad glimpse around the encircled faces. Everyone makes room while she examines Jasmin. When she resettles her stethoscope on her shoulders, she looks at Bryce and Felicia with empathy. Then, she places her finger on the ventilator switch, awaiting consent. They both nod. She switches off the machine, and it winds down into sudden silence.

Jacqui removes the oxygen mask from Jasmine's face, her body limply complying.

"We'll give you some time," Dr. Moreno quietly confides as the two step back to exit. At the door, the doctor turns and adds. "You are probably aware of the people and the press gathered here at the hospital offering their support. Would you like me to make an announcement of her passing?"

Bryce and Felicia look at each other and agree. "Yes, that would be nice," Felicia confirms.

The family envelops Jasmine's bed once more, laying tender hands on her. The sounds of quiet crying do not fill the void left by the ventilator, still concussing in their ears.

"She looks so beautiful," Alicia marvels. "So peaceful."

Their eyes are fastened on the vision of Jasmine's gracious demeanor. Oscar takes a few steps to his mother, who is seated again, and slides onto her lap. Felicia wraps her arm around him, and gently begins to rock, humming, "What a Friend we have in Jesus."

When she finishes, there is silence.

~

Oscar is studying the face of his sister.

"Did you see her?" he quietly wonders. He looks to the others for confirmation. "Did you see how happy she was when the angel came and took her?"

He turns in his mother's lap to tell her. "She was so happy!"

Oscar's words effervesce in the room.

Jake, standing at Jasmine's feet, is the first to relent to full sobs. His hands cover his face, as he hunches weakly over his sister's body. His grandmother wraps her arm around him, and he buries his face in her neck.

Chapter 23: Whatever God Does, it Shall be Forever

Nothing can be added to it, And nothing taken from it. (Ecclesiastes 3:14)

Jacqui steps into the room about 30 minutes later.

"I thought I'd let you know that the café is closing soon, if you needed something. We can send for it."

Papa looks at the thoughtful faces. "Thank you. We will probably get something on the way back to the hotel."

"Okay, just let me know if you change your mind." She goes to the bed and tenderly removes Jasmin's IV, her monitor leads, pulse oximeter, and blood pressure cuff. "Let's just get our girl all comfortable here."

"Thank you, Jacqui." Felicia offers. "You've been terrific. I know Jasmine really loved having you on her team."

Jacqui winds the leads around her hand and holds them. She looks thoughtfully at Felicia, eyes welling now. "Well thank you. That means a lot." She turns away, places her foot on the ventilator stand, and rolls it aside. She swipes the back of her finger under her eyes before turning around.

"You know, I loved her too." She nods, looking down at the leads in her hands, composing herself. "You probably don't know this, but because of her, I believe in Jesus now."

Felicia smiles softly, "You do?"

"Ha ha. Yeah. I think that's the first time I've actually said it to someone."

"That's wonderful," Alicia adds."

The family all agrees.

Jacqui's voice quavers, as she nods and takes a tissue from her pocket to dab her nose. "It was actually . . . ah, Christmas Eve." She finds Bryce's face. "When you were gone, looking for Lily."

"No Kidding," Bryce wonders. "That's great. Glad all that was good for something."

"For TWO things," Felicia reminds him.

Everyone joins in "Ah, yes. That's right."

"Well, I don't mean to intrude at this time. I just thought you would want to know how much of an impact your daughter has had, at least on my life." She lays her hand shyly on herself.

"Oh, that's great to hear," they all agree.

"That is very uplifting, at this time," Felicia adds. "To hear that about our little girl."

Jacqui smiles. Then she gestures toward the window, "Clearly, I am not the only one whose life she has changed."

"That is true," Alicia observes.

"Yes," Bryce adds, "thank you for that reminder, Jacqui."

"Well, I'll leave you now." Jacqui walks to the door, but then hesitates, and turns around.

"I have to tell you something, because I promised, but honestly I don't know how to do it."

"What is it?" Felicia urges.

"Well, that night—when I was with Jasmine… She confided something to me and made me promise to tell you."

The room unsettles.

"Well, go ahead," Papa pushes.

"Okay. She told me that when she got GVH disease, and became very ill . . . Well, she said she actually died."

The room stirs with whispers.

"She said that when she did, she met Jesus. He told her that it wasn't her time *yet*, but that she would come home very soon. That he had something important for her to do. She told me that after she came back, an Angel would come and stay with her sometimes and comfort her. She said he would reveal heavenly things to her because it was so hard for her to stay here. She described how *wonderful* heaven is and full of love." Jacqui scans the startled faces before continuing.

"She wanted you to know that she always knew she was going to die, and that you shouldn't be sad for her because she is *so happy* in heaven." Jacqui laugh-cries a little and adds, "With Jesus."

All eyes turn now to observe Jasmine's peaceful face, bright and fresh with joy.

"The King," Oscar whispers, reverently.

Jacqui turns brightly to him and nods, "Yes. The King."

After the family reflects on this revelation for a time, the vacuum of emotions sets in, and it is determined to bring their vigil to an end. One by one, they gather their things, kiss Jasmine a final time, and pull themselves away, leaving her parents to finish things.

The last to leave is Jake. Standing with head drooped by her bedside, he wipes tear after tear frustratedly from his eyes. Finally, he composes himself and dips to kiss her cheek.

"See ya later, Sis," he manages to blurt before retreating out the door in sobs.

Bryce kisses Felicia, "I'll walk down with them. Do you want me to go sign the paperwork?"

"Yes Amore, would you? I'll get her things together. And please, find out what you can from them about arranging her flight home."

"I will. Will you be okay?"

Felicia shrugs and shakes her head some. "I mean . . ."

"I know. I love you."

He steps to the door, then remembers. He returns to Jasmine's bedside and reverently takes the little pinecone. He pauses looking at his little girl, "I'll take care of this, Pumpkin." His voice falters to a whisper as he kisses her forehead.

When Bryce arrives downstairs, he finds the family just inside the automatic glass doors, careful not to encroach close enough to open them.

"What's going on?"

"They're still here."

"Who?"

"Everyone."

Bryce steps forward and the door opens revealing hundreds of people holding candles and singing.

"But I thought. . ."

Papa steps up, "They just want us to know they care. That she really touched their lives. Do you think you can say something to them?"

Bryce runs his fingers through his hair, eyes wide with exhaustion. "Ahh. . . I guess."

"Come on Dad. Let's do it for Jasmine," Oscar brightens.

Bryce considers the task. "Okay, buddy." Then he looks at Jake.

"Not me. I'll watch." He stuffs his hands in his pockets.

~

Bryce steels himself and steps through the doors. Several camera lights turn on and approach, along with reporters and their microphones. He sees Maizie, and she steps forward, mic down.

"Hi Bryce," she privately offers. "I'm so sorry. I was really praying for a miracle."

"Yeah. So were we. Thank you."

"I mean, she has been so inspiring to us. We've all been praying."

"We know. That means a lot to us."

"I know it's a tough time, but did you want to say something? Everyone who's here and following this story really cares a great deal for Jasmine. They would love to hear from you and your family."

Bryce looks again at his family, and they all nod.

"Sure."

"Okay." She lifts the mic and signals her camera man. The other news organizations apparently are already rolling. "Go ahead, Bryce," She encourages. "Whatever you want to share with Jasmine's supporters would mean a lot to them."

Bryce, fatigued-looking in the bright lights, sighs involuntarily. "Huh." He looks past the cameras to all the people, who have gathered closer.

"It's been a crazy couple of weeks, huh?"

"Yeah," the crowd encourages.

"We're sorry Bryce," Breaks out from somewhere in the crowd. Bryce is overcome and lowers his head into his hands.

The crowd continues declaring their support.

"We love you!"

"God bless you, Bryce!"

"It's okay."

"We're so sorry!"

"We love you guys!"

"We love Jasmine!"

"God bless your family!"

Bryce sobs. The encouragement keeps coming.

"It's okay. We know!"

Papa puts his hand on Bryce's back, and pats it. Finally, he leans in and talks in his ear.

Bryce shakes his head. "No, it's okay." Oscar wraps his hand around Bryce's arm.

Bryce looks up. He wipes his face. The encouragement continues.

"Okay." He puts his hand on Oscars head, and looks around for Jake, who has receded to the back. "Okay. Listen. I can't tell you how much it means to us to have your tremendous support and prayers. I mean. . . Who are *we*?"

"You inspire us!" comes the answer.

"Well, you've inspired us. You've helped us see that ordinary people can have a tremendous impact on each other."

"God bless you!"

"Thank you. God bless you, too. I mean, really. God bless you. Most people will never get this kind of support in their time of heartache. But this is a reminder that we need each other. This means a lot. It means a lot. We don't know how to thank you."

Oscar raises his hand.

Maizie notices. "Hi little fellow." She redirects the mic to him. "Did you have something to say?"

"Yes. If that's okay." He looks at his dad for affirmation.

"Absolutely," Maizie urges. "You're Jasmine's brother, aren't you? Can you tell us your name?"

"Yes. I'm Oscar, and I just wanted to remind everybody about why we're all here. That's what my sister would want."

"We love you Oscar!" Other encouragement breaks forth.

"Well, she would say that God has a plan for everything, and I think we can all see that's true." He looks around, and then his voice begins to crack.

"I mean, I am really sad about my sister." He stops and wipes his eyes with his palms, then swipes his nose with his sleeve. He tries to compose himself, but when he can't, he fights through his breaking voice and tears.

Support calling from the crowd buoys him.

"I am SO SAD. But she's with Jesus now. And SHE'S happy. She is so happy to be with Him. So, I am going to try and remember that. Right?"

He has a crying outburst that briefly disrupts his speech. "But, I'll see her again someday, okay?" He busily wipes his tears and his nose.

"But you HAVE to remember what she told us, Okay? Remember?" He looks around the crowd and connects with so many of their faces. "Remember?"

"We remember!" comes their rousing response.

Oscar wipes his whole face with his hands and sets it. "Okay, so say it with me. Come on, remember?" He gestures for them to join him.

"She said that we need to 'Trust God—"

"AND BE A HERO!" the crowd thunderously replies.

~

Felicia sets the small duffle bag of Jasmine's belongings on the floor and sits again in the chair nearest her daughter. She studies the resting face, enveloped in white. After a moment, she tentatively reaches with her fingertips to stroke the soft, thin hair from Jasmine's forehead. The smooth skin, though still warm, feels foreign. Felicia withdraws her hand and settles back into the chair. Her eyes uneasily scan the room for a purpose, and they wander to the plush Lion, set aside on the table. She picks it up and rests it on her lap to examine it. It is soft, and amiable, and she lifts it to her nose to smell if Jasmine is there. She detects only the sick Jasmine of hospital scents, and returns the Lion to her lap, holding him around his middle with both hands.

She looks at her daughter again for a long moment, then back at the benevolent, gold-crowned monarch. She searches his shiny button-eyes sown into his fuzzy golden face.

"You'll take care of her, won't you?"

Her throat constricts. Tears well and spill down her cheeks. She pulls the Lion tightly to her and rocks, crying quietly, clutching the little plush King. Her whole body contracts with the strain.

After several minutes, her breathing relaxes, slowing and

calming with fatigue. Still rocking imperceptibly, she whispers her prayer, eyes closed.

"You take care of my Baby. . . I know she's safe now. . . I know she's free . . . she has peace. . . Thank you for the gift of my little girl, Jesus. . . She was worth *all* of it."

~

Jake sits on the edge of his hotel bed, staring unfocussed at the ground. His palms rest on the mattress beside him, as if he just sat down, or were about to get up. He blinks but doesn't move.

Oscar is seated in his place at the kitchenette table. Jasmine's Christmas stocking is on the table with him, and he is sucking on the end of a candy cane. The scrapbook album is open before him. He thoughtfully flips another page and reads the notes and the little words stickered around the photographic memories. After a moment, his mind drifts, and his eyes wander upward to the little dry tree, gray like tinder on the end table. There, he props his chin in his hands, and becomes lost in Oscar thoughts.

The door opens and Alicia comes in with Christiana after dropping off her things in their hotel room. Christiana sets her purse and the little handled paper bag on the end table by the Christmas tree. Alicia stands behind Oscar, and kisses his head, observing over his shoulder.

"What are you doing there, Mijo?" Oscar looks up at her, candy cane in his mouth, and simply points to the album. "Oh, isn't that nice. Can I see?"

He nods and she sits in the chair beside him. They begin looking through the pages together.

Christiana stops at the boys' room and peeks in, finding Jake staring at his feet. She sits next to him on the bed and hugs him around his shoulders. He appears too tired to cry.

Why don't you come out with us? Papa is coming with the food. Hmm?" He sits another moment, and with a final nudge, breaks his inertia and lifts from the bed to follow her out.

An hour or so later, the boys are sitting drowsily, waiting up for their parents. Papa is at the table drinking coffee, surrounded by half-excavated fast-food bags. Nana and Aunt Tiana are on the couch sipping tea, and Oscar is seated between them leaning on Nana. Jake is sitting in one of the big chairs, leg slung over the arm, with his phone out and his earbuds in.

"What are you watching there, Jake?" Papa asks.

Jake pulls out an earbud. "That news station did a story about Jasmine and the things Dad and Oscar said."

"Oh yeah? Can I see it, or is it too late?"

"Yeah, it's on their website so we can watch it any time," he stirs as if he might get up, when the door opens and Felicia and Bryce somberly walk in carrying a bag of Jasmine's things. Upon seeing the family, the two try on smiles. Oscar goes and hugs Felicia before she can unload, and she bends to kiss him.

"Daddy told me what you said, Mijo." She takes his eyes into hers. "I am so proud of you."

"Chia, Jake says it's on video, so you can see it," Papa lets her know.

"Oh, that's good," she pushes Oscar's hair off his forehead, against the grain, and smiles.

Bryce walks behind Jake and lays his hand on is head. "How are you doing, Buddy?"

Jake looks up, "Aw, you know. . . not great."

"I know. I love you."

"I love you too, Dad.

Bryce goes to Papa and holds out his hand. "Glad you're here, Oscar." Papa rises and shakes it, then pulls him in for a hug. Bryce sits at the table and kicks off his shoes, and Papa gets him a mug of coffee.

"You two hungry?"

Bryce takes the cup, "I don't know. Maybe. It's pretty late." He remembers the pinecone in his shirt pocket and takes it out. He considers it for a moment, then sets it before him on the table, and touches the top.

Felicia goes into the bedroom to take her coat off and set her things down.

Jake is still watching the coverage, and he reports to everyone about the vigils. "Hey, they're saying that about 3,000 people came to the hospital."

"That's amazing," Nana and the others respond.

"Yeah, and Aunt Tiana was right, they're having vigils back home, and even a bunch of churches were holding them around the country! Like thousands of people!"

"No Kidding?" Papa reflects.

"Yeah, you can see the footage of some of them."

"I can't believe it! Our Jasmine!" Nana wonders. "I want to see that tomorrow, Mijo."

Felicia comes out of the room with something hiding behind her back. She walks up to Oscar, who has returned to his seat between Nana and Aunt Tiana.

She pauses. "There's something that I think Jasmine would want you to have."

He sits up, "For me? What is it?"

She squats down and then holds out the Lion toward him, watching his reaction. "Would you like this?"

He studies the noble King, and then accepts it reverently. He looks at his Mom, "Yes, thank you." As he studies it again, his eyes water. Then he hugs it close, tucks up his legs, and curls closer to his Nana.

Jake watches this exchange, then returns to his screen. Felicia goes into the kitchenette and makes herself a tea.

After a few moments, Jake reports again, "You guys need to see all the things people are saying about Jasmine. I mean, they're even giving speeches on her, and talking about the things she said. They are posting things like 'She changed my life,' and 'We'll never forget her,' and all kinds of things."

Felicia comes out with her tea and sits tiredly in the other big chair with a sigh. She perches her bare feet on the edge of the coffee table and attends to the warm cup between her hands.

Jake continues to watch for a few minutes, then drops the phone into his lap and pulls out the other earbud. "You know, I don't get it."

"I know, it's amazing," Nana repeats."

"It's really hard to take it all in," Felicia adds. "It's astonishing how much people have been inspired by her. By her words, and her whole story." She looks over at Bryce. "By you too, Amore, and what you did."

"But that's what I don't get, ALL THOSE PEOPLE!" Jake rebuffs, sounding a little misunderstood.

Christiana stirs, "Jake, we can't really understand it all right now. But I think we agree that God is doing something special with Jasmine's life. It's like what her nurse said, 'she had something important to do.' Even Jasmine sensed that." She looks around the room. "You see it if you think about all that has happened . . . Right?"

The others agree, almost in disbelief, reflecting on all the extraordinary things that have occurred.

"That's not it!" Jake sits up and plants his feet on the floor. "I mean, it's not about all the things people are saying—that's all good. It's about *all those people*—THOUSANDS OF PEOPLE!"

His voice breaks again and he starts sobbing in an instant. Everyone is startled by Jake's explosion, watching him flood with their own pain.

"I mean, come on!" He runs his sleeves over his eyes, then gestures with firm hands in frustration. "All those people praying! You know? I mean . . ." He drops his head into his fingers, like he's pressing away a migraine.

The room fills with dread again, everyone sniffing and wiping their eyes as Jake disintegrates.

His hands lash out from him again. "I mean, what more does God want? Huh? I mean . . ." He searches the shocked faces for some answer, some understanding.

"Right?" He pleads. "After all that! Why did we still have to lose her?" He slumps forward and buries his face into his hands, choking now on sobs.

Felicia, moves behind him, leans over, and wraps her arms around him. "I know baby. I know . . ."

Christiana gets up and lifts the little paper gift bag from the end table, then sits on the coffee table in front of the melting Jake.

When his sobs subside some, she jiggles his knee.

"Hey. Do you believe that you'll see her again?"

He doesn't respond.

"Jake. Do you?"

After a moment, he lifts his head and rubs his palm across his eyes. He nods.

"You do?" Christiana smiles warmly. "I believe that too!"

She sets the little paper bag on her lap.

"You can't ever forget that. Okay? Because God really *is good.* Jake, do you believe that?"

Jake reflects for a moment and sees the Lion in Oscar's arms—the Lion that inspired his confession to Jasmine.

He surrenders the tension from his body. "Yes. I believe God is good."

"That's right. Because you see, Jake. . ." Aunt Tiana peeks into the bag and parts the tissue.

" . . . with God, *nothing* is ever lost."

Then she slides her hand into the bag and lifts out, to everyone's amazement, Jasmine's lamb, as white and flawless and gangly and cheerful as the day it was last in her arms.

"Lily!" Oscar exclaims with awe.

Felicia and Bryce watch Jacob's face fill with uncertain relief.

Christiana holds the lamb toward him, until he takes it in his hands. His eyes, wide and damp, drift over to the tiny, dry, Christmas tree on the end table. Then they return slowly to the restored little lamb, fluffy white with her bright pink bow, now safely in his hands.

He looks at Tiana again, astonished, and she repeats.

"*Nothing* is ever lost."

About the Author: Wendy S. Scott

Wendy is a part-time college lecturer of Rhetoric & Writing Studies in San Diego. She has traveled on outreach missions to Russia, China, and within the United States, in addition to her personal travels to Europe, Israel, and Jordan.

In her weekly outreach, she shares the love, truth, and hope of God with others. She writes her stories to reflect God's goodness in ordinary life and encourage believers to let their lives shine each day. Her website contains articles and short stories for tools to help believers share their faith, and to guide non-believers into salvation: mywordsforHIM.com

Made in the USA
Middletown, DE
17 November 2021